Into The Hard Hills

<<<<<<<<<<<<<<<<<<<<<< • >>>>>>>>>>>>>>>>>>>>>

A novel

by

Anthony Whitt

Anthony Whitt, Austin, Texas at www.anthonywhitt.com

ISBN-13: 978-0-9898868-4-0 (softcover)
ISBN-13: 978-0-9898868-5-7 (ebook)

Into The Hard Hills is a work of fiction. Although actual locations are mentioned, they are used in a fictitious manner, and any resemblance to persons, living or dead, or to places, events or locales is purely coincidental. The characters are the products of the author's imagination.

Cover design by Philip Whitt, www.philipwhitt.com
Cover image copyright @ iStock/23037763
Editing by Steve Statham at www.stevestatham.com

**FT
Pbk**

This book is dedicated to my son, Philip. Thanks for helping tame the raging technology beast.

Acknowledgments

I owe a special thanks to a couple of great friends that provided feedback during the story development. Tim Keane, an avid reader full of a wealth of literary knowledge and Greg McCroskery, a talented photographer, graciously accepted the challenge of reading the manuscript and their suggestions proved to be vital contributions. I am deeply indebted for their generous assistance.

Just when a writer thinks they have the story nailed is the time to take a step back and hand it off to a skilled editor. Regardless of the best writing efforts, a good editor can always find improvements that need to be made. My hearty thanks goes out to Steve Statham for the critical eye and professional help in making this story the best it could be.

As always I cannot thank my wife, Cathy, enough for her steadfast support through all the trials and tribulations of developing this tale over six years in the making. Words are inadequate to describe her calming influence as the storms and doubts about the project raged. She knows how much I appreciate her assistance and without her support it's safe to say there would not be a *Hard Land to Rule Trilogy.*

And finally I would like to express my deepest gratitude to the readers for allowing this story to be a part of your life. It has been an honor to be included in the ride that binds us all together and I sincerely hope you found the trilogy enjoyable. Be assured your kind comments and reviews kept me encouraged through many a long day behind the keyboard.

Lastly, if you find *Into the Hard Hills* a good read, please post a review and help me spread the word to your family and friends. You can also find me through a variety of social media sites at www.anthonywhitt.com. I blog and post my photos about a broad array of subjects you may find interesting. Many thanks to all of you for your support and I look forward to seeing you on the sites.

ONE

His work was never done.

Ames shoved his chair back from the desk covered in paperwork. He began massaging his ink stained fingers against his temples. The dull ache had grown into a throbbing pain he could no longer ignore. Beads of sweat collected on his forehead. The room burned with an oppressive heat. Seeking a reprieve from the mind-numbing drudgery, he leaned his chair back until it clunked against the wall.

Eying the disheveled legal documents spread before him, he cringed at the difficulties they represented. A lot of money, and the future of many interested parties hung in the balance of his decisions. But that was a minor consideration, and not the real problem that stuck in his craw. What troubled him was the unreliability of those he depended upon.

Kern didn't get the job done. Obviously, the highly paid gunman didn't measure up to all he claimed to be. Kern had assured him that Matt and Bull would be dead. Not only dead, but also mutilated beyond recognition. Scalped, gutted, and sliced Comanche style. His creative handiwork would get the blame placed on Indians and shift the focus away from the true reason for their murder. After all, the Indians were marauding at will all across the hills. Nobody would suspect a thing. A piece of cake he had said. The perfect plan.

Turned out Kern couldn't deliver. His promises dissipated like smoke in the wind.

Ames resented the bad break. Matt was still alive and continued to be a pain in the ass. He hated the fact that the cocky Ranger had eluded Kern's trap. A bead of sweat rolled down the sharp point of his nose. He brushed it away in annoyance. The parlor stove crackled with heat. The warmth of the room was stifling.

Cussing, he plopped his chair to the floor with a *thunk*. Breathing deep, he shot up from the seat and stalked to the door. The sweltering air in the room sucked the life out of his lungs. Gripping the doorknob, he was surprised at the fiery touch of the metal. He twisted the handle in a hurry and threw the door open. A rush of red light from the blazing sunset lit up the interior walls.

Glancing up and down the avenue, he saw nothing of interest. The streets were empty. Disgusted at his remaining workload, he turned in submission to the chains of labor binding him to his desk. The transformation of the room caused him to pause. A muted red hue filled him with a sense of evil inhabiting his office. A strange awareness crawled through his thoughts. He felt uneasy at being alone. Looking over his shoulder, there was only a vacant street. Where was everybody? There should be people out and about completing their last chores of the day, but nobody stirred. What the hell? Things didn't feel right.

He mumbled, "Room's too damn hot. Can't think straight."

Leaving the door open to cool the office, he returned to his chair and bellied up to the desk, deciding to ignore the peculiar feeling of isolation. The tasks facing him never ended. It was one important obligation after another. Endless details that required his supervision. His father had warned him, "The devil is in the details." The old man had been right. And how he had grown tired of the incessant fortitude the details demanded.

What he craved was a woman. Bad. It had been way too long. Mary had been ready to give it up. If only that bastard Matt hadn't shown up at the worst possible moment. The accusations of attempted murder hurled by the Ranger had ruined his meticulously planned seduction of Mary. All of his carefully orchestrated efforts to bed her had been doused in one unexpected outburst from Matt.

Damn! Kern had really let him down. He could use the release. She was so beautiful. She would have been his finest conquest ever. Instead of relishing her soft feminine charms, he sat here working late and baking in frustration.

Mindlessly preparing the papers, his thoughts drifted to Carmin. Her slim waist and rounded hips. Her pouting lips. She was the answer. She would be easy. He had seen the look in her eye. He knew what she wanted. Hell, she wanted it as bad as he did. He figured it wouldn't take much exertion on his part. These simple Southern gals were as easy as picking peaches. He made up his mind. She would be his. And soon. His excitement began to rise while reflecting on her sensual appeal. The red glow of sunset radiated off the walls of his office as his carnal fantasy grew wings and took flight.

Distracted with images of Carmin floating in his head, he gazed absently at the stack of papers needing his attention. The tax foreclosures were mounting. The Ellis papers required one more signature. The documents on the Johnston ranch were spread over the paperwork of several other properties lined up for seizure due to delinquent back taxes. It irked him that Matt's place was not on the list.

Matt's homestead was the largest in the district and a key to the tactics of the syndicate he worked for as manager and partner in direct command of the Texas division. The prime cattle land and fertile river bottoms of Matt's ranch were a perfect complement to the other properties already acquired and under the company's control. Enormous wealth would be made consolidating the holdings and placing them back on the market after the new roads were built. Additional tax revenue from the legislation Senator Archer was pushing through would fund the expansion and improvement of roads connecting the far-flung ranches out in the hills. Once connected to the Austin market, the values would skyrocket.

He rubbed his hands together in anticipation of the profit. Combined with his other business interests, it would be more than enough to fund an early retirement. A life of luxury in New York was waiting on him. Finish the details here in Austin, and the big payoff was his. He deserved it all. Fine food. Entertainment. Willing women at his beck and call. It all waited for him back East. He could almost taste the decadence.

Absorbed in his daydream, he didn't notice the glow in the room had dimmed.

An ominous presence standing in the doorway blocked the light. Dawson leaned against the doorjamb, enjoying the sight of Ames shuffling papers, ignorant of his arrival. Ames was the man with all the answers. Never did anything wrong. Always worked the angles for the best deal. He sneered in repugnance of the arrogant Colonel Ames.

After a moment, Dawson cleared his throat to announce his entrance.

Startled, Ames looked up, fright momentarily filling his eyes.

The man was a beast. Broad nosed and weather hardened, his face pocked with scars from chickenpox and a life of conflict. His ice-blue eyes were as remote and hollow as the glare of a wolf, deeply set, and indifferent to the fate of others. His wide bearlike shoulders contained an inert strength ready to explode at the slightest provocation. Arms and legs of seasoned hickory, he hulked like a grizzly, daring anybody to make the wrong move. Intimidation was a natural result of his forceful appearance and matching demeanor.

Upon recognizing his employee, Ames recovered, and threw his pen to the desk. This animal was bought and paid for. He did as he was told. There was nothing to fear.

A snarl on his lips, Ames said, "Where have you been?"

Spitting on the floor, Dawson growled back, "Taking care of business."

"You're long overdue."

Dawson didn't respond to the bait.

"Did you get the job done?"

"I always do. That's what I'm paid for."

"What took so long?"

"Them boys in Fredericksburg didn't fancy giving up their freighting routes. Took a little convincing."

Ames waved his hand. He didn't want to know the details.

"Could have used you here. I'm disappointed it took you so long to handle amateurs."

"Don't worry, didn't waste any of your time or money. You've got their routes now. They agreed to get in another line of business."

"Wise men."

"The ones that are still walking are. Others, not so much."

Ames calculated the numbers in his head. A nice bottom-line was shaping up with less competition. Only a couple of small outfits left, and they would crumble once word got out they were in the way. Things were looking up. His queasy feelings were fading.

"Well, I may have another job for you."

Dawson appraised the colonel. The man was relentless in his pursuit.

Leaning back in his chair, smug in his authority, Ames said, "Matt's a problem."

"Figured the Ranger wouldn't go easy."

"He's proving to be stubborn."

"Thought Kern was taking care of him."

Nodding in agreement, Ames said, "Kern's days are done."

"You fired him?"

"Buried him is more like it."

"Buried 'em?"

"Courtesy of Matt."

Dawson chuckled. "Sounds like Kern wasn't as smart as he thought." His chuckle developed into a full-blown cackle.

Ames waited until the poor taste in humor tapered down.

"No he wasn't. He underestimated his foe. My advice to you is to not make the same mistake."

Dawson's posture stiffened.

"I don't have his problem. You tell me what to do. It gets taken care of. End of conversation." Kern had made a mistake. Underestimating a man was a dumb thing to do. That meant this Ranger named Matt warranted a close study. He made a mental note to get to know the man better.

Ames watched the reaction of Dawson to the news and considered the decisions he had made managing Kern. He had been too confident in the man's abilities. He should never have paid the bonus to him in advance. Dawson was a different sort of employee. One that required a different tack. He wouldn't make the same mistake twice.

.

TWO

Matt plunked into the chair, lethargic, resting his elbows on the table and pressing his eyes into the palms of his hands. Ignoring the surroundings of the café, he tried to rub out the fatigue. It was useless, he felt like a bear ready for hibernation.

Mary approached his table unobserved from the kitchen with a pot of coffee in her hands. She stood to the side in awe of the man and his ability to persevere. He had been through hell the last couple of days and staying up with Bull all night surely tested his endurance. She had wanted to tend Bull, but Matt had insisted she go home and take care of her kids. He assured her that he would see to it that Bull was not lacking for anything. Reluctantly, she had agreed to his suggestion.

Now he sat in the café a few hours after daybreak.

She plopped a cup in front of him and filled it with the steaming black brew.

He lowered his hands and gazed at her through bloodshot eyes.

"Mornin', Mary."

His detachment was obvious.

She slid into a chair next to him and lightly rested her fingers atop his bandaged hand.

"How's the hand?"

He held it up and contemplated it like he had forgotten the injury suffered in the fracas with Kern.

"It's doing fine, I guess."

"I can put on another bandage if need be."

"It'll do for now."

Afraid to ask, but desperate to know, she inquired, "How's Bull?"

Matt eased the cup to his lips. After sampling the brew he said, "He seems to be weatherin' the wound pretty good."

"What's the Doc say?"

"Hell, he ain't gonna go out on a limb. He says it could go either way."

"What do you think?"

Matt looked into an expanse seen only by him.

"Bull's a tough old goat. He'll pull through."

"You mean that?"

"He's gotta. I known him too long."

"I hope you're right. He's been good to me."

"Bull's rough around the edges, but you won't find a better friend in these hills."

"I don't know how I would have gotten by without him . . . after losing Frank."

"Good friends are hard to come by. And harder to keep."

"Speaking of which, I'm glad Robert happened along to help Travis get your wagon back home to Cora."

"Yeah, me too. We were fortunate he heard about our scrape with Kern. He's in the same class of friend as Bull."

"You're a lucky man."

Matt laughed. "Don't feel lucky this mornin'."

Looking away, Mary hid the want in her expression from Matt. Nothing would change between them. It had been all she could do to resist giving her love to him the night out on the trail rescuing Bull. The evening had been crisp. He had been bedded down within sight and she needed his reassurance that all would be okay. The nearness of the others is all that kept her from making him an offer he would be powerless to refuse. His allure was like a strong magnet that kept pulling her back. She was too damned old to be reeling like a lovestruck teenager.

Matt was watching her when she turned back to face his questioning assessment. The ordeal with Bull had an enigmatic influence on her that night. Death could call on them at any time. Nobody was immune from the unforeseen ending of things as they had always been. It was this realization that made her want to reach out and grab what little pleasure there was to be had in this hard life they all lived on the frontier.

With Matt, he seemed to want more than some temporary indulgence. He too searched for some type of satisfaction, but his yearnings ran deeper than most men who took what they wanted and quickly forgot the consequences. That quality about him was one of the attractions that exerted such a strong pull on her heart. He was different than the other men she had known. He could be trusted to do what was right. That was rare. She had no right tempting him. It wasn't fair to either of them.

Reading her thoughts, he said, "Mary, we can't go there again."

Her focus fell to the pot sitting at the edge of the table.

"I'm doing the best I can."

He said nothing. The silence lengthened. She sighed.

"I'm getting off after the breakfast shift. I'll look in on Bull the rest of the day if you have other business that needs tending."

"Actually, that would be a load off my mind. I intend to stay long enough for Granny to show up and take care of Bull. I'm in a big hurry to git home and check on the family. Somethin' is botherin' me. I've been gone far too long and I'm worried about 'em."

She shoved her chair back and said, "I'll keep a watch on Bull all I can."

"Thanks, Mary. It'd be a big help."

"I'll go fetch your chow."

Biscuits smothered in cream gravy and heavily sprinkled with chunks of sausage provided Matt the first satisfying meal in days. He emptied the pot of coffee and began to feel human again. During the meal, he noticed that Carmin was working the other side of the café. She kept casting glances his way that made it impossible to overlook her intrigue. His presence was distracting her from her waitress duties. She grinned at him a couple of times. Being courteous, he returned her grin with a cautious smile.

Slapping the cash down to cover the tab and leave a little extra for Mary, Matt stood up to leave. Out of the corner of his eye, he saw Carmin fall in behind him. Ignoring her intentions, he started to the door. Getting back to Bull was the most important thing on his mind.

Just outside the door and out of view of the café dining room, he felt a tug on his sleeve. A little surprised, he turned to find Carmin looking up at him. She was a short, petite, but well figured woman with an abundant head of brunette hair. Her lips were full and she had the most seductive brown bedroom eyes Matt had ever had the pleasure to behold. The most memorable thing about their last encounter was her direct manner. She said what she thought without hesitation, no matter the implications. And her insinuations were of the sort not talked about in mixed company. She was unlike any woman he had ever had the satisfaction to know.

"Hello, Carmin."

"Matt. I just wanted to have a few words with you."

"What's on your mind?"

"First, I wanted to let you know I'm sorry about Bull, and I hope he heals up real soon."

"Thanks. We all do."

"I also wanted to let you know I'm glad you took care of Kern."

"He didn't leave me no choice."

"He gave me an uneasy feeling. He wasn't right, watching me when he thought I didn't see him. There was something going on behind those eyes that was creepy. He had a problem with women. I've got intuition enough to spot his type."

"I reckon you're right."

"No doubt. He's also the one who murdered that poor gal that worked at Madam's Palace. You've done the whole town a favor. I was afraid to walk home alone with him around."

"Ain't ever easy to take a man's life, but he had it comin'."

"If the sheriff had been doing his job, Kern would've been behind bars and Bull wouldn't be shot. Would he?"

"Right again."

"I've got no respect left for Sheriff Cole. He's missing some backbone."

Matt glanced over her shoulder and saw the sheriff marching their way. The man wore a stern grimace when he recognized Matt talking with Carmin.

Matt said, "You've got a chance to tell him how you feel. Here he comes."

She whirled and put her hands on her hips when she saw Cole closing the distance. Her body language was stiff with defiance. Matt harbored little doubt she would tear into the sheriff given half a chance.

Instead, she faced Matt and purred, "It's you I worry about. This town's full of forces out to destroy good men like you."

She caressed his arm. He felt a genuine concern in her tender affection. Sensing his appreciation, she wrapped her arms around him in a hug that flattened her breasts against his chest. The soft womanly touch of her embrace inflamed the desires always simmering just beneath the cool outward appearance he tried to maintain.

Knowing what she was doing, she tightened her squeeze and whispered in his ear, "You take care of yourself. The woman in me needs a man like you."

The clomp of Cole's boots grew louder as she released Matt and stood at his side returning the sheriff's judgmental inspection.

Cole rested his hand on his revolver as he neared them.

Matt couldn't resist the jibe. "Expecting trouble, Cole?"

Cole gave Carmin a lookover. She spotted an unusual flicker in his scrutiny. There were some unresolved issues brewing within the man. She wasn't sure if it was sexual, or some other form of torment, but the man had unintentionally exposed a weakness of some sort. The eyes of a man provided a window into his soul, and she was an expert at peering through the shroud of deceit most men hid behind. She marked him as a man to be handled with care.

Puffing out his chest in false bravado, Cole said, "That's up to you, Matt."

"I ain't one to cause trouble. Seems like I took care of one of your problems. You don't have to hunt for the whore's killer any more."

"There ain't no proof Kern killed her."

Matt shook his head as if he couldn't believe what he just heard. "Have it your way, sheriff."

Cole caught Carmin's attention in the suggestive way he said, "I believe I will."

Her eyebrows arched in revulsion, but she held her tongue. She needed a better understanding of the man before she responded to his goading.

"Some things you can't have, Cole. Don't matter what you think," Matt said.

"I'll be the judge of that. You'd best remember you're in my town."

Matt's expression hardened.

"Got your attention now," Cole taunted.

"What do you want?"

"Just doing my job."

Nobody said a word. From the tone in his voice, it was obvious his job would be disagreeable. He fumbled for some papers stuffed in his vest. He handed them to Matt with a smile exposing the joy he got out of exercising his authority.

Matt smoothed them out until he could read the words summoning him to appear in court that afternoon. He felt the fine-edge of a knife held to his throat. They had him again.

Speechless, he had a vacant stare when Cole repeated, "Just doing my job."

"What is it?" Carmin asked.

Swallowing hard, Matt replied with a tone of disbelief, "Says I'm being sued for slander."

"Slander? Of whom?"

Cole answered Carmin, "He said some mighty inaccurate things about Colonel Ames. The Colonel doesn't play games with those that oppose him. I'm sorry, but you crossed the wrong man."

"You know what I said about Kern operating under his instructions is true."

Cole shook his head no.

"Come on, Cole. I showed you the money he paid Kern."

Cole remained impassive to Matt's plea.

"It was two thousand dollars hard cash. That was murder money. The murder of me and Bull. Come on. You said it. Ames don't play games with those that oppose him."

Cole scrunched up his nose like he smelled a skunk, but he wasn't giving in to Matt's argument.

Matt saw the future. This was how it was going to be. He was on his own in a den of snakes. Each one spewing its own particular venom. He was to be the sacrificial lamb.

"You're in a dirty business, Cole. You don't have to hunt for the whore's killer any more, but you do need to hunt for a compass."

"Compass?"

"Yeah, to help to find your way."

THREE

The hours crawled by as if mired in thick axle grease. Matt visited a lawyer feeling like a child tossed into the alley to wage a battle he couldn't win. The slick-dressed attorney granted him ten minutes to explain his case, but offered no constructive advice. His services were far beyond Matt's ability to pay and therefore there was no way he or any other lawyer in town would take the case. And that wasn't even taking in the fact that Colonel Ames was the offended plaintiff. It was explained to Matt that no attorney in town would take on one of the most influential businessmen in the capital city. You didn't get to practice law successfully by taking unwinnable cases against men that enjoyed ruining the lives of others as if it were sport. That was the logical explanation given to Matt by one of Austin's finest defenders of the innocent.

With only an hour left before he was due in court, Matt decided to check on Bull one more time. The smell of medications assaulted his senses when he entered the doctor's office. The doctor was out on a call, so Matt walked directly to the back room where Bull was trying to recover.

He was awake and grinning like he didn't have a care in the world. Pain treatments took the edge off his dilemma and the most beautiful woman in town sat at the foot of his bed. All things considered, he was a contented man.

"Looks like you're well cared for."

"About the size of it." Bull's yellowed teeth shone in a drug-induced grin.

"Can I git you anything?" Matt asked.

"Could use some of my brew. Doc won't allow it. Said it gits in the way of proper healin'."

"What does he know?"

"Exactly!"

His excitement caused him to cringe at the pull of newly healing flesh.

Mary shot Bull a look of disapproval.

"Sorry. I just miss strong drink."

"Later, Bull. I'm sure your stock won't spoil before you get better," Mary said.

Matt walked over and examined the bandage on Bull's shoulder.

"They got you fixed up good. The Doc knows his stuff. I've heard he can heal the dead."

Bull gave Matt a hard stare.

"I aim to git home long before death comes knockin'."

"I'm sure you will. You're too damn mean to let a little gunshot put you under."

"Got that right. Plus this here pretty lady is the best reason to hang on a little longer. Ain't she sweet to look at?"

Mary blushed and said, "Bull, I'm gonna keep your medicine away from you if you start acting up. Understood?"

Bull looked sheepish. "Don't mean no harm. It's just that an old man like me remembers the good old days when I could prowl the streets and howl at the moon with a lady under my arm. Don't mean no harm."

He let a long yawn escape.

Mary tucked the blankets in tight around his neck. She gave Matt a glance that exposed her concern about Bull.

Matt nodded toward the door. He wanted to speak in private.

Bull observed the sly communication and shut his eyes as if to nap. They needed time alone. He felt sympathy for their plight even in his own current state of peril.

Matt said, "Bull, you git all the rest you can. And do what you're told. I'm sure Granny and one of your boys will be here soon."

Bull wiggled his nose and waved adios.

Taking a long look at Bull, Matt shook his head in apprehension before he turned to leave. Mary followed him to the front parlor that served as the doctor's office. They had a seat on a plush couch and faced each other not two feet apart.

Matt got right to the point, "Mary, I've got trouble. I've gotta ask for your help."

Already aware of the problem, she nodded yes.

"I've been charged with slander by Ames. He wasn't bluffin' about seeing me in court when I accused him of payin' Kern to ambush me and Bull."

Her gaze fell to the floral rug at her feet.

"I hate to git to this point, but I need you to go with me to court. Not sure how it'll go, but you can bet the deck will be stacked against me."

Things had changed. She could not believe Ames had her so fooled. He was a despicable man, and Matt had tried to warn her all along. She felt like a fool for ignoring his advice to be leery of the Colonel's intentions.

She said, "They sure were quick to bring this to court. Cole served me a subpoena to appear right after you left the café. I'll do anything I can. I feel responsible in some way."

"Not your doin's. Don't worry."

Doctor Hays burst through the door and came up short at the sight of Mary talking to Matt on his couch.

Obstinacy in his voice he asked, "What's the meaning of this?"

Matt stood at full height, looking down on the doctor, and took command of the room when he said, "The meaning is we're leavin' to attend business. Can you watch over Bull while we're gone?"

Huffing at his abrupt loss of control in front of the lady, he stammered, "Well, yes, I can. I . . . don't see why not."

"Good then. We'll be on our way and check back later."

It was a short walk to the courthouse and they discussed their dismal options along the way. They were in agreement that the chance of a fair trial was negligible, but the summons had to be answered and rebuffed in the best possible manner. Neither of them spoke optimistically about the chances for success. For Mary the whole ordeal since the death of Frank had been an education on the wily ways of men. She had had enough. Her will to make a positive change in her life and the lives of her children hardened in the face of continual adversity. It was time to make a change for good.

Judge Parker sat behind his desk as they timidly entered the courtroom. Matt once again found himself out of his element in Austin. Here in the courtroom, the rule of law prevailed. Not what was right or wrong, but what the judge perceived as right or wrong. That could be two very different conclusions. The silver-haired old judge had a renowned temper that he often used to punish those who aroused his ire. Mary took a seat next to Matt and Judge Parker never once looked up or acknowledged their presence.

He wore a scowl while he concentrated on a mound of cluttered papers spread across the top of his large oak desk. A clerk came and went a few times, whispering in the ear of the judge. Parker scoffed aloud after one of the communications. He shook his head in disgust and papers rustled under the shuffle of his swiftly moving hands. Anger about some drawn-out issue in the legal documents bubbled to the surface that he couldn't hide any longer. His narrow eyes, red with whiskey, peered in condescension across the courtroom. Scorn filled his face when he spotted Matt waiting for the proceedings to commence. He obviously found the upcoming trial distasteful. He had more important matters to rule over than this trivial dispute.

It was at that time that Ames and his cohorts made their entry. Senator Archer, Captain Harris, and Sheriff Cole accompanied Ames with his attorney Bob Payne leading the way. They casually strolled to their seats on the opposite side of the aisle from Matt and Mary, smiles and jokes flowing as if they were on a picnic.

The stranger that followed them was a sight Matt would never forget. His matted coal black hair hung to his shoulders above an intimidating and muscular build. His broad chest reminded Matt of an anvil with arms as thick as an oak trunk attached. Dawson left an impression. He stood separate and behind the others with his hard gaze sweeping the room for any signs of trouble. He made a formidable replacement for Kern.

Matt looked away when he heard the judge clear his throat.

Parker delivered his first broadside to the Ames delegation. "I'm glad you gentlemen finally decided to join us."

Dumbfounded at the rebuke, they all took the nearest chair they could find. Matt glanced at Mary and grinned.

Pulling his watch out to verify the time, Judge Parker said, "You men are two minutes late. What do you have to say for yourself, Mr. Payne?"

Straightening his jacket as he stood, Payne said, "No excuse. We beg the court's forgiveness."

"I'll remind you this proceeding is on borrowed time. We have a full docket and you gentlemen are here at my largesse. I will not delay the start of the next case if this runs too long." His voice boomed, "Are we clear?"

Ames shot the judge a piercing glare before he pivoted in his chair to mumble a complaint in the ear of his high-priced attorney. Payne nodded his head as he listened to Ames and answered the judge at the same time in a passive, "Yes, sir."

Matt didn't miss any of the nuances and began to feel more at ease.

"Good. Payne, I'm acquainted with the charges. In the interest of time, I shall dispense with most formalities and seek as rapid a hearing as possible. If I was to miss time for a lunch, I'd be mighty hard to deal with. Understood?"

The judge didn't mince words. Payne had been on the receiving end of severe reprimands from Parker before. He got right to the point. "Sir, I'd like to have Colonel Ames take the stand."

"One second," Parker said. "I have a question for the defendant. Where is your legal counsel?"

Matt stood to answer. "Your Honor, I don't have a lawyer."

"Can't afford one?"

"None were interested in taking the case."

"Humph. Well . . . we can have a trial without one. I run a fair court. You'll be given every opportunity to defend yourself. It won't be a problem."

After swearing in Colonel Ames, Judge Parker instructed him to summarize the complaint as quickly as possible just to have it on record. He was satisfied he already understood the particulars and didn't have time to waste.

"It's a pretty simple complaint I have," Ames began.

Parker cut him short. "I'll decide what's simple and what's not. Now, get to the point."

Ames nodded his head in submission. It was an unfamiliar feeling for him to stomach, but he sucked it up and continued, "A few days ago Matt approached me as I escorted Mrs. Mary Ellis down the street. He had some wild accusations that he hurled at me. He claimed I paid a former employee to ambush him and the revered frontiersman, Bull Johnston. He called me a "thieving bastard" when I denied knowledge of this despicable act. I had already dismissed this deranged man from my employment because of his erratic behavior."

Payne assumed his role and asked, "And who is this former employee?"

"Kern Daniels. He was in charge of security and had begun to show signs of mental disease. I had to release him." He pointed at Matt and said, "He witnessed my dismissal of Mr. Daniels, and knew the man was no longer employed by me, but made the wild accusations anyway."

"Go on," Payne said.

"Matt assaulted me while I was minding my own business. He became aggressive and attempted to provoke a fight. He was extremely unreasonable and physically pushed me, making the lady very frightened at what he might do next."

"And what did you do?"

"Tried to reason with him. But he became even more animated. He claimed I had orchestrated the entire affair. Claimed I paid the man a ridiculous amount of money to kill him and Mr. Johnston. It was absurd. Mr. Johnston had previously insulted Mr. Daniels at my office and vowed to get even with him somewhere down the road. Bull brought the assault on himself. Mary eventually left me in tears because of Matt's belligerence."

"How much money?"

Ames laughed. "Two thousand dollars. He claims he saw me personally pay the money. Absurd. I'm a respectable businessman."

Judge Parker interrupted, "We don't need to hear your high opinions of yourself. That's not relevant."

Ames dropped his head in deference.

"So Mrs. Ellis left you in tears. Did she return?" Payne

inquired.

"No, sir. The confrontation ruined a promising relationship. I was offering her moral support during her hard times as she adjusted to life as a widow. She has innocent children depending on her. I felt I could be of assistance to them all."

Payne summarized, "The defendant accosted you, provoked you, slandered your good name with false statements, and ruined a proper and upright relationship with a widow in need of faithful companionship. Does that sum it up accurately?"

"Yes."

Parker said, "Thank you, Mr. Payne for a brilliant summary of the obvious." Turning his attention to Matt, the judge said, "Now you may question the Colonel if you like."

Matt stood, his skepticism clouding his thoughts.

"Not sure it'll do any good, Your Honor."

"It's your call, but be quick about it."

Matt glared at the colonel, doing his best to hide the hatred.

Ames returned the sentiment as cool as ice.

"I do have one question."

"Proceed," Parker said in boredom.

"Did you pay Kern a bonus when you let him go?"

"Absolutely not."

"Where did he git the two thousand dollars I found on his body?"

"Object!" Payne shouted.

Judge Parker explained, "Colonel Ames doesn't have to answer or speculate about things he doesn't know."

Matt's premature enthusiasm sunk like a rock. The cash he saw Ames give Kern was his only hope to tie him to the attempted murder. Cole had been right. His most valuable evidence was not admissible in court.

"Judge, this is my only evidence. I saw him pay Kern the money."

"Objection! He can't make incriminating statements as part of his questioning."

Payne gave Ames a smug look of superiority. This was like shooting fish in a barrel.

"Calm down, Mr. Payne. In the interest of fairness, we're gonna disregard these small matters." He then addressed Matt and said,

"The issue of money has been settled. Do you have any other questions for the Colonel?"

Matt gazed at his boots, his mind churning to come up with an inquiry that would expose Ames for the charlatan he was. Drawing a blank, he said, "No. No, sir I guess I don't."

"You can step down, Colonel."

Ames took a seat while Payne shuffled some papers and glanced toward Mary.

"Your Honor, we would like to ask Mrs. Ellis to take the stand."

She meekly made her way to the seat and was sworn to the truth.

Payne approached her in an aggressive posture. He intended to make her pay for turning her back on his client.

He opened abruptly, "You have heard the testimony. Do you have anything to counter the truth of the statements of Colonel Ames?"

Gathering her courage, she stared straight into the eyes of Ames.

"It's all a pack of lies."

Rattled by her venom, Payne took a moment to recover.

"All a pack of lies? Let me remind you that you are under oath."

She said nothing, but turned to face Payne with a look of contempt.

"Did the defendant approach Colonel Ames?"

She said nothing.

Parker spoke in a respectful voice, "Mrs. Ellis, you have to answer him to the most truthful of your abilities."

Hesitating, she said, "Yes, he approached us."

"So it is a fact the defendant approached both of you. Did he not accuse Colonel Ames of paying for the attempted murder of him and Mr. Johnston?"

"Yes he did, but . . ."

"No elucidation needed. We are focusing on the facts. Simple and concise facts. If I need more information, I'll ask." He clasped his hands behind his back and his chest expanded as he probed, "He then physically assaulted the Colonel, did he not?"

"There was no assault."

"The defendant bumped into the Colonel, did he not?"

"That's not assault!"

"Did he bump into the Colonel? Yes or no."

"Yes, but he didn't mean it as an assault."

Payne let the statement hang in the air. The judge frowned behind his salt-and-pepper beard.

"Okay. Now that the mood of the encounter is established, let me ask you. Did you take leave of Colonel Ames after the assault ended?"

"I had to."

"Had to?"

"Bull needed my help. Mr. Ames would not assist."

"Strike that last statement if you please, Your Honor. I didn't ask if my client offered assistance. That's not the issue here."

"It's struck. Just answer the question please."

"So you left the Colonel alone and disregarded the plans already made for the day?"

"They weren't important plans."

"Matt approaches without invitation, assaults and insults the Colonel with false statements. You take a leave of absence. That is a fair summation of the events. Is it not?"

"No."

"Your testimony says otherwise. No further questions. I would like to put the defendant on the stand."

Parker looked down his nose at the attorney with disdain.

"I'm sure you would."

"We have a right to query him about his actions."

"Yes you do, but like I said, time is an issue. The next case is complicated and will start on time regardless of this trivial matter."

Weighing his options, Parker assessed Matt's position.

"Seeing as how you do not have legal counsel, let me offer some free advice. I wouldn't take the stand if I were you. The evidence does not favor being subjected to any further examination. I have sufficient information to make a fair verdict. What say you?"

"It sounds worse than it is. The truth is being buried."

The judge jerked back at the accusation. His famous temper was riled.

"Let me straighten you out. The law is all about truth and its discovery during the trial process. Your claims of innocence are baseless in fact as proven by testimony and evidence presented.

Conjecture on your part does not create truth, as you would prefer. And any more statements like that will find you in contempt. Keep that in mind before making inflammatory comments about *my* court."

Concentrating on the papers before him, the judge sipped on a glass of water spiked with a shot of whiskey. His stomach grumbled with hunger. He scribbled on the papers and stuffed them in a folder.

"On the charge of assault, I find you not guilty. A slight chest bump in the heat of the moment is something Colonel Ames is man enough to bear. My decision on the charge of slander is that you're guilty. Guilty of slandering the good name of one of our leading citizens. Your false statements in front of the lady were defamatory and caused harm to the carefully nurtured and honorable intentions of Colonel Ames. This type of conduct cannot be tolerated."

A lump of dread formed in Matt's stomach. Mary reached for his arm and gave him a squeeze. Their ordeal was not over and they both feared the final outcome.

It didn't take long for Judge Parker to verify their worst suspicions.

"The law is clear on the punishment of slander. I have a wide leeway in applying whatever restitution I deem is appropriate. So far the damage done to reputation is minimal. Let's keep it that way. I'm issuing a gag order. No talking about this case in any form or fashion. Those caught talking will be dealt with severely."

The clerk produced more papers and the judge signed them in a hurry.

"This is what I propose. Damage is minimal to the public reputation, but harsh in the personal. A cash award of two hundred dollars to the Colonel should be adequate for his grievance."

Matt sucked in a deep breath. The times he had two hundred dollars in his life had been very rare and well before he had children to support.

Gauging Matt's reaction, Parker inquired, "Do you have the means to pay?"

"No, sir. Not hardly."

Taking the answer without losing his momentum, the judge asked Ames, "Would you be willing to swap jail time for his inability to pay?"

Consternation darkened the chiseled face of Ames while he contemplated his response. Disgruntled, he said, "No, I suppose not."

"Fine then. My judgment is ten dollars credit for every day. That's twenty days in jail with today credited for a whole day. Sheriff, you may take him at this time."

The exuberant slamming of the gavel echoed in mockery of everything Matt stood for in his life.

FOUR

Cole seized Matt by his arm to lead him out of the courtroom. Jerking free, Matt said, "I know where the jail is."

"Just doing . . ."

The go-to-hell expression halted Cole's explanation cold.

"Mary, I'm gonna have to git word to my family. And you'll need to keep an eye on Bull until one of his sons show up."

"Don't fret about Bull. I'll do what's needed to care for him."

"Thanks, Mary. Do me one more favor if you will. Come check on me when you git a chance."

Impatient, Cole barked, "Come on, Matt."

Matt detected Dawson's black derision as he observed his humiliating exit from the courtroom. There was no way a decent man could miss the ugly contempt for others that the brute proudly displayed for all to see. His chuckle as Matt was escorted out the door accompanied the robust congratulations passing back and forth between Ames and his cronies. They exulted in victory while Matt slumped away defeated and suffering yet another major setback. He doubted whether he would ever escape the clutches of the town where injustice flourished like weeds and positive encounters were rare.

Cole marched beside Matt on the way to the jail as if he was parading a prized catch. It wasn't long before the good citizens of Austin started a fast-moving buzz about the respected Ranger marching off to jail. It was an embarrassing scene that confirmed their own beliefs that the scales of justice were tilted in favor of the

Yankee powerbrokers infecting their town. They knew it was best to keep a low profile if someone as invaluable as Matt could be humbled and led away in disgrace.

Mary lingered at the door, watching as Matt disappeared around the corner.

Off to the side, Ames made a point of ignoring her. She had made her decision and it didn't include him. He had no further use for her, although her beauty would continue to haunt him in the lonely hours late at night. His chance at capturing her had been shattered, but he had the satisfaction of seeing the guilty culprit marching off to confinement. It would be punishment a man of Matt's character would find very difficult to weather. The thought of Matt's torment brightened his day. He felt like celebrating.

"Gentleman," he said, "lets head to the café. I'm in the mood for a thick steak. My treat!"

Hearty approval rang out and they all bounded across the rutted street, delighted to fill their bellies at the Colonel's expense.

Mary watched them as they tramped off in the same direction that Matt took on his way to jail. Same direction, but different destinies, she thought. Both of the men she looked to for rescue had faded from her life as if they never existed. The reality came crashing down like a rockslide. She was truly alone in a world that showed no concern. An icy lump formed in her chest. She drew her shawl tight, but it did no good. There was no enjoyment left in life. With no one to turn to for solace, the tears began to flow.

Dabbing at her cheek, the thought of Bull trying to recover from his wound while being left alone materialized as a force expelling her self-pity. That was the motivation she needed. Her duty was to care for him. Get the old neighbor healthy and on his feet. She owed him that much. Pulling herself together, she turned her back to the lost possibilities and made her way to the doctor's office.

The scene in the café had grown boisterous. Ames was in a celebratory mood and copious amounts of whiskey arrived alongside the mounds of hot food delivered by Carmin. Toasts to their continued success passed back and forth amongst the men whose future appeared as bright as the morning star. The power they had as a group was intoxicating and the liquor added fuel to a euphoric confidence that all they dreamed and schemed about would soon be theirs. The world was in their grasp with all the dominos falling in place as plotted in their late night meetings held behind closed doors. The residents of Austin were just pawns to be manipulated in their plans for financial dominance.

Archer dug into the pile of mashed potatoes doing more listening than talking while Ames held court on his grandiose strategies. Dawson sat quietly devouring his steak. The conversation of these highly esteemed men was of little concern to him. They made the money through their conspiracies and crooked deals and that was all that mattered. He just wanted his pay. The details only interested him when his services were called upon. Until something happened he just tagged along for the security Ames was always nervous about. And he had good reason to be concerned. The Colonel had cheated many men over the years and they both knew trouble could pop up at any time.

Captain Harris was an interesting case in Dawson's mind. The man engaged in a lively dialogue with the Colonel, but something about Harris didn't fit. He seemed to lack the heart for the dirty deals that always swirled around Ames. Senator Archer fit right in. The fat bastard couldn't be trusted. His beady eyes sized up all circumstances for his benefit. He would sell his mother out to the devil for a dollar profit.

But this Captain Harris appeared tense at times. Observing him at the trial, there was no doubt the guilty verdict troubled him. Ames was too caught up in his glee at the judgment to notice the look of consternation on Harris. He seemed outright disappointed. There still lived a trace of honor in the man. Dawson chuckled at the irony of the situation. Honor was a trait Harris would have to forfeit if he intended to keep company with this bunch. Ames broke his contemplation with a loud boast.

"I tell you men that our time has come. I'm completing the last details to acquire all the property needed for our long-range goals. The bottom-line of the freighting business is growing by the week. Thanks goes to Dawson for his recent efforts making this possible."

Ames raised his glass in salute to the brawny hired hand.

Dawson refrained from displaying emotion. All he had done

was rough up men trying to make an honest living. He had learned a long time ago that emotions got in the way of effective performance in his line of work.

"Our other interests are starting to churn up a wad of profits. I'm happy to report the long hours I've been putting in may soon be on the decline."

They all held their glasses high in a celebratory toast and downed their potent amber brew with gusto.

Ames caught the attention of Carmin with a flick of his hand.

She warily approached the table.

Draping his arm around her waist, he pulled her in with a request.

"Sweetheart, how about another round for my friends here?"

"Coming right up," she replied as she backed out of his grasp, his hand slipping down to her hip in a lingering touch.

Dawson flinched at the boldness of the Colonel.

Ames slipped into a trance watching her shapely figure sway as she made her way to the bar at the back of the dining room.

"Now that is a dessert I intend to taste someday soon," he mumbled.

Archer spoke up in agreement. "She does possess an undeniable charm."

Ames ran his tongue over his lips watching her load up the drinks.

Leering, he said, "She certainly does."

She returned with the whiskey-filled glasses.

"Can I get you gentlemen anything else?"

Ames motioned her closer and whispered in her ear, "I'd like a chance to meet with you later."

Carmin knew it was coming. The more he drank, the more his wishes became evident. She wavered with a reply. Ames wasn't somebody she should get involved with. She had observed him with Mary. He was too manipulative and domineering. But he did have money and could show her a good time. He also moved in the upper crust of society and that could lead who knew where.

"I get off after the supper shift. Drop by and walk me home."

Ames narrowed his eyes as his prey tested the bait.

"I'll see you then," he said.

Another table hailed her, and she hurried to their needs while the lustful assessment of Ames intensified.

"Well, I must say, things are shaping up."

He surveyed his partners and they were all smiling except for Dawson. His dark manner was something Ames disregarded. He paid the man well and supposed his profession sapped him of any agreeable characteristics.

Dawson threw his fork to the plate and said, "I've got to go. Chores to take care of."

The Senator tossed back the rest of his drink and thanked Ames for the tasty meal. He explained that he had to hurry back to the Capitol where the legislature was still in session. A little wobbly on his feet, he trailed Dawson out the door.

"Two good men to have under your control," Ames said to Harris.

"Takes a team."

"Yes it does. And it takes a good eye to assemble the right men."

"You've done a fine job."

"You're not troubled by the misfortunes of Matt?"

Harris thought a moment before replying.

"I'm sorry to see his hardship. He's a good man. Did an outstanding job on the mission to rescue the Havens children."

"Answer the question."

Harris knew it was a test. He also knew Ames did not take failure kindly.

"I figure he brought it all down on himself."

Lighting a cigar, Ames puffed on it until the tip glowed a bright orange. He let out a sigh of gratification as he released a billowing cloud of smoke from his first draw.

"Indeed. He is responsible for his own actions. He can't deal with white men as if they are Comanche."

He drug a cherished cigar from his vest and offered it to Harris.

Harris took the reddish-brown Cuban and admired the fine quality of the wrapper leaf. Ames spared no expense. He dressed impeccably and lived the highlife. The very life Harris craved. "No he can't. Austin isn't the hills," he agreed.

Harris squinted his eyes as the aromatic smoke curled into his face. Impressed, he took a deep pull of the finest cigar flavor he had ever experienced.

Ames said, "Austin has changed. The time for men like Matt has passed. His kind is best suited to remain on the leading edge of civilization. His talents are best used where the red man and outlaws roam."

Harris nodded in approval of the analysis.

Glowing from the fine food, liquor, and smoke, Ames continued in confidence of his superiority, "Let me tell you a secret. I could have requested that the judge order a judgment against Matt to pay me monetary damages for his slander."

He let the assertion hang in the air.

"But I didn't. Judgments are just a piece of paper. Not worth a damn thing. If a man doesn't have money, I'd never be paid. Doesn't accomplish what I'm after."

He had the attention of Harris.

"No. I wanted something else. I wanted the bastard's pride. Putting him in jail puts him in his rightful place. He'll have time to think on his errors. He'll sink into depression. Right where I want him. Out of my hair and unable to cause me trouble."

Harris didn't say a word.

"While he's in jail, it'll buy me some time. We still need his land. His ranch is the key to our overall strategy. We'll eventually get his place. Just have to develop another plan."

Harris thought about Kern and Matt's claims in the courtroom. If they were true, Ames was a cold-blooded killer. Paying to have it done was as bad as pulling the trigger yourself. It was beyond his means to even consider the actual planning of murder. Thinking, he took a long pull on the cigar. He had to get over his sense of right and wrong. Ames was showing him the way. He would benefit if he learned from a master at achieving his goals. This was his new career. Archer and Ames were the most notorious movers and shakers in town and he had to adapt or be left behind. That was a nasty possibility, and he never wanted to follow. The air was much sweeter at the front of the pack.

Judge Parker entered the café and caught the eye of Ames while he made his way to a nearby table. Several renowned politicians followed in his wake. He winked at Ames and they both cut a winning smile. Harris caught the message in their discreet communication. No, he thought, it really wasn't that hard of a decision.

FIVE

The slamming of the cell door rattled Matt like a volley of Union cannon fire. It was a clanking sound foreign to his experiences. He had seen to the lockdown of hardened criminals in the past. The outlaw gang that pillaged and roamed in the San Saba River valley back in the late fifties had been a tough bunch to bring to justice. Despite the challenges, the Rangers he served with spent many hard months tracking them down and depositing them to their day in court back here in Austin. The clatter of bars represented a job well done to him at that time. Now the isolation of jail sent a chill through his soul. He better understood what those criminals must have felt when the bars banged shut.

Now there was nothing to do except dwell on the things he was powerless to change. Lying on the cot and staring at the ceiling, a melancholy mood settled over him. This wasn't fair. Problems needed addressing. He had a family waiting on his return. Something wasn't right on his homestead. He could feel it in his bones.

Cole didn't care about his concerns. He had repeated, "Just doing my job," as he rotated the key in the lock. Matt got up and began to pace like a caged lion. He pounded his fist against his palm. A build-up of relentless energy yearned to be unleashed and he had been locked up for only a few hours.

"Twenty days! I'll go crazy before then."

He heard Cole greeting somebody at the front of the jail. Then he heard the mention of his name. His suspicion rose as keys jiggled in the door and Cole stepped through.

"Matt, you got company."

Dawson filled the small corridor outside the cellblocks with a commanding presence. Matt could not recall a more intimidating specimen in all his years dealing with every sort of hard man possible.

They locked in a staring contest.

Cole slithered back to his office out of sight, but he left the door open behind him. Matt was sure he was listening.

Dawson relaxed and spoke first, "Sorry way to meet a man."

Matt didn't have anything to say to the brute.

"You don't have to say a word. I just come to see the famous Ranger behind bars." He gave Matt a haughty sneer and nodded his head in amusement. "Don't feel good, does it?"

"I would imagine it's a feeling you know well."

He spit in the corner, "I knowed the feeling a time or two."

"This ain't no social call. State your business."

"Ain't got no business. Just taking the measure of a man on the wrong side of right."

"Mister, you've got perception problems."

"I ain't the one in jail." Dawson laughed at Matt's expense and needled him; "You seem to be the one who's got it wrong."

"Kangaroo court," Matt explained.

"Watch yourself, Matt. Judge might not think highly of you disparaging his authority."

"Judge can go to hell."

"That's what got you in trouble. No respect for them above you."

"Git to your point."

"Got no point to make, although I'd like to compliment you on your nice place on the river."

The recognition in Matt's eyes burned with loathing.

"That's right. I was with Ames when we stopped by to pay you a visit. Shame you weren't home that day. Out chasing Comanche I hear."

He played with Matt like he was a mouse.

"We saw your wife that day instead of you. I must say she didn't show us much hospitality. In fact one of your boys damn near got shot."

"You talk brave on the other side of these bars."

"No reason to take offense. I admire the boy's spunk. He handled the scattergun with confidence. David is his name from what I gather. And you can call me Dawson now that we've met." He pulled out a cigar and lit up in front of Matt, exhaling a curling cloud of blue-gray smoke directed at the ceiling. "But I have to say, this David boy of yours ought to be instructed in restraint and proper time to use a weapon. Else he could end up on the short end of a stick someday."

There was nothing to say to a man tied up with the likes of Ames. Matt crossed his arms and burned a hole into the cold blue eyes of his nemesis.

Unfazed, Dawson filled the room with smoke from his cigar. The silence lengthened until they heard Cole greet another visitor. His salutation was less than friendly to the newcomer.

Matt was surprised when Nate barged into the room, nearly colliding with Dawson. Nate gave the large man a wary glance as he detoured around him to Matt's cell.

"Matt, I'm damn glad to see you, but this beats all."

"Yes, it does."

"Twenty days!"

"It was that or give up money I don't have."

"Crooked bastards."

Matt looked Dawson's way. Nate shrugged, indifferent to Dawson's allegiance.

"How's Bull?" Matt asked.

"Holdin' his own, thank God. Mary's with him. Granny came in with me and she's here 'til he gits good 'nough to come home. Which needs to be soon. The doc is already makin' noise about needin' pay."

"Figures. It's all about the dollar with him."

Nate gazed at his boots. Matt could tell something was on his mind.

"Let's have it, Nate."

Nate chewed on his lip before he spoke.

"Comanche been by your place."

Matt's eyebrows arched. His suspicions were valid. His stomach tightened in a knot. He noticed Dawson perk up at the news.

"Now, don't worry none. Everybody's okay."

Worry was all Matt could do behind bars. He had been neutered.

"They snuck in early one mornin'." He hesitated before continuing, "Made off with Becky."

"Son of a bitch!"

"It's okay. Me and Lee got her back."

"She alright?"

"A little scratched up is all."

"Did they?"

"No. We got to her too quick for 'em to have their way."

A sigh of relief escaped Matt. Dawson now had a keen interest in the direction of the conversation. He stepped closer to listen.

"She's shook up about 'em sneakin' close 'nough to make off with her. Won't wander away from the cabin unless Lee's at her side."

"How many of 'em?"

"Hard to say. Ten or so, but there's one less."

Matt smiled. "Good job, Nate."

Nate beamed at the compliment.

"Yes it was. One shot dropped the devil while he was makin' off with Becky. We even rounded up his pony. Lee said you'd be tickled pink seein' how you want to raise horseflesh for cash."

"Good. Good. Any other news?"

"They arrowed one of the cows. We butchered her up. Got a nice supply of meat now."

"What else happened?"

"Not much. Them devils lit out. Ain't been back since. Then Travis showed up in the supply wagon without you and Pa. Robert said he'd stay around to watch the cabin 'til you git back. So I loaded up Ma and come to town quick as I could. Brothers got an eye on our place 'til we git back."

"Robert's a good man."

Nate shifted his stance. Something was bothering him. He glanced at Dawson and said, "We could use a little privacy."

"That right?"

"It won't trouble you none."

Dawson crammed the stogie into the corner of his mouth. Pulling hard, he relished the flavor before a thick cloud of smoke curled out of his lips. He said, "You got five minutes."

Nate gave Matt a wink after Dawson ducked under the doorway. Cole immediately struck up a conversation with Dawson when he entered the front office. They talked as if they were old buddies from years ago.

All Nate could mutter was, "Damn!"

"Big fella ain't he?"

"Falls harder," Nate said.

"Humph. Don't try it."

Nate didn't show any sign of hearing Matt's warning. He had other things on his mind, and got right to it when he asked, "Now, Matt. I gotta know. Did them thievin' bastards make good on my pay?"

"Not much chance of that ever happenin', Nate."

"That's how I figured. Cheated me on my pay and then try and kill my Pa."

"That's the size of it. Don't do no good to fight 'em. Look where I wound up."

A string of profanity bounced off the brick walls. Nate slapped his hat against his leg and ran his hand through his crumpled hair.

"This is such . . . I can't stand by and do nothin' while that Ames gits away with everythin'."

"Gotta be smart."

Nate eased closer to Matt where he couldn't be overheard.

"I'm gonna kill Ames and the Cap first chance I git."

"Slow down, Nate."

"Oh, I'll slow down long 'nough to figure it out."

"There ain't no perfect murder. They'll string you up."

"So, I'm supposed to turn my back?"

"Didn't say that. Let time help correct the course."

"No offense, Matt, but that don't seem to be workin' for you. Your family's worried sick about why you ain't home and look at how you're gittin' treated."

"Cora's used to me being gone."

Nate chuckled like he'd heard a joke.

"Ain't nothin' right in this town. They're stealin' from us. Tryin' to kill us. Hell, they want everythin' we got includin' our pride."

"No argument here. You got it summed up pretty accurate."

"What's a man to do?"

Matt shook his head and said, "I'll let you know when I got that figured out. Meanwhile, you leave them boys alone. They play for keeps. It's a different set of rules they live by."

"Can't say I'll do that. Sorry, Matt. I only got so much give."

Nate began fidgeting and Matt knew he was itching to leave. Digging in his pocket, he fished out his last few dollars.

"Here, Nate. Take this to Doc."

"I can't accept that."

"You got no choice. Give it to him for Bull's care."

Nate considered the crumpled money in Matt's hand.

"Sorry. I certainly appreciate the offer, but I can't."

"Look, Nate, I know it ain't enough, but it'll keep the doc off your back for a while. You can pay me back when you git the chance."

Matt thrust the cash through the bars, leaving Nate with no chance to refuse.

"Okay. We'll pay you back soon as possible."

"No problem. Git on back to Bull and tell him I'm fine."

Nate nodded his approval and disappeared out the door to the front office.

He meant to pass through with nothing to say to the lawman talking to Dawson, but a huge paw reached out and snagged his arm. He turned to see the callous gaze of a killer staring him down. A momentary flush of fear burned in his chest. This man had a grip like a vise.

He had no option but to stand fast. Angry words tumbled out, "Unhand me you bastard."

A startled expression came over Sheriff Cole. He was sure he was getting ready to witness a murder. Instead, Dawson released Nate and calmly said, "Just wanted to pass on some advice. No need to turn angry friend."

"Ain't no friend of you or your gang of back shooters."

"I understand. But let me clue you in. I work for those . . . how did you put it? Crooked bastards wasn't it?"

"Callin' it the way I see it."

"Sheriff, take note of his foul mouth. Nate, your partner in there made similar comments. Look where he'll sleep the next twenty nights."

"Don't threaten me. I won't back down."

"You're wrong on several points, but I try to overlook ignorance until folks have a chance to understand. So understand this. I work for them crooked bastards. It's simple. Mind your manners around them or you'll pay a high price."

Nate bristled. He squared off to deliver his reply. "Ignorance works both ways. I ain't Matt. I don't much care what you," motioning at Cole, "or the law says."

Cole just grinned. He knew the Johnston family well enough not to let their independent streak be a worry to him.

Dawson's face drained of emotion. His eyelids drooped in contemplation of the combative attitude spilling from the lanky Texan. It was a guise that wilted most men, but didn't register any influence on Nate.

"We have an understanding then. Sheriff Cole is our witness. You've been warned to watch your step around my employer or his associates."

Nate backed out of the room never trying to mask his hatred.

From the cell, Matt heard it all. He plopped down on his bed, sick at his helplessness after hearing the exchange.

Speaking to the emptiness, he said, "Let sleeping dogs lie Nate. Let 'em lie."

SIX

Doctor Hays slid his chair a little to the side for a better view of the room where one of his patients rested. He wanted to get a clear angle to observe the activity surrounding the bed. The wounded old coot in the bed wasn't his reason for spying. Bull occupied the space and was on the edge in his treatment. His health could fall to either side. The gunshot to his shoulder had splintered some bone and the old man wasn't out of the woods yet. But that was secondary to the real object of his vigilance. Other, more urgent matters dominated his thoughts at this moment.

Pretending to be engaged in bookkeeping, he constantly surveyed the room for the source of his stimulation. She occasionally stood at the side of the bed tending to Bull, her blond hair long and flowing like silk down her back. She floated with grace across the room carrying out her nursing duties. Just the sight of her voluptuous figure drove him mad with lust. She had always been at the top of his list, but she rarely got to town when her husband was alive. Now that the Indians had murdered him and she had lost the ranch, things were different.

She was a woman in need. That was his specialty. Women in need were an easy score. It was a situation he had capitalized on often. He could faintly hear her voice down the hall. She was talking to Bull.

"Come on, Bull, wake up," Mary said.

Bull was having trouble escaping his medicated slumber. She gently tapped on his good arm. He raised it up to rub his sweaty forehead. The fever was low, but upsetting to Granny and her. Fevers could mean bad times ahead.

"That's better. I brought you some soup."

"Good to see you," he mumbled.

"Try this. It'll give you some strength."

She fixed him up with a bed rest for the soup and a spoon to eat with. He wouldn't tolerate spoon-feeding by a nurse even if it had been Granny. Too much Johnston pride. He let it be known he wasn't an invalid and fed himself with his good arm. She and Granny had to be content watching while he slurped on the chicken soup and munched a slice of cornbread smothered with butter from the café.

"Damn good," he said when he tossed the spoon in the empty bowl.

"They have good chow at the café," Mary said.

He noticed Nate was missing and asked, "Where's Nate?"

Sitting in the corner, Granny spoke up, "He's out hunting for work."

"Work? Nate?"

Laughing, Granny said, "He won't know what to do if he finds it."

"The question is—why is he huntin' work?"

Granny got up to move to his side. She patted on his leg.

"We need some cash to pay the doctor."

Bull tucked his bearded chin to his chest.

"Sorry to be so much bother. Why don't we load up and head back to the cabin?"

"We will, but you gotta beat the fever first. Doctor Hays says if you travel them rough roads home too soon, you'll pay a high price."

"Higher than his?"

Granny gave him a concerned nod of her head.

He knew the meaning of her facial expression. He looked out the window at the dusky gray clouds hanging ominously over the rooftops. His mood sunk.

Mary approached the other side of the bed and caressed his hand.

"Mary, the sight of you is the best medication a man can have."

From the front room, Hays glanced up from his desk in an

admiring appraisal of her pleasingly curved figure. His distraction was complete. His decision made. He had to have her. And he knew just the ploy.

She saw Hays leering her way, but ignored him as she rummaged for the words to handle Bull's comment.

"Thank you, Bull," was all she could manage to say. Men never lost sight of their main attraction in life; even in the face of death they remained fixated on feminine charms.

Granny spoke up with her keen perception that cut like a knife, "Don't think you can fake your way. You ain't gonna milk more care from her. She's got kids to raise and a livin' to earn you lecherous old goat."

"Ain't lecherous! Ain't an old goat neither."

"I'll tell you what you are. I known you too long for you to hide your intentions from me." She turned away from Bull and winked at Mary where he couldn't see the sly message.

"Mary, don't listen to her, she's just contrary."

"It's okay, Bull. If having me around gets you home sooner, I'm okay with it all."

"You're an angel. Are you listenin', Granny?"

A scolding glower was all Bull got in return.

Mary envied the comfortable rapport the longtime married couple had established. It was a relationship she coveted and would never acquire. It was good to be near them both, although the circumstances were dire.

Bull tugged on Mary's dress and whispered as low as possible, "Can you git me some of my hooch?"

She hissed, "Are you crazy?"

"No, Doc won't let me have none."

Granny spoke up with vehemence, "Because you don't need it! Don't be pullin' any stunts."

"Stay out of this," he said. "I swear she's got bat ears!"

"She's right, Bull. You're on medicine. Drink might get in the way," Mary said.

"He's so ornery," Granny complained. "It'll do him good to be off the stuff for awhile."

Bull cringed like a whipped pup. He didn't stand a chance against a united front. The thought of getting out of bed occurred to him, but the soreness was an effective deterrent. He would have to tough it out.

Mary said, "I'm sorry, Bull. When the doctor clears you, I'll have a celebratory drink with you. How's that?"

His possum-like grin flashed.

"It's a deal," he said.

"Good. I look forward to that day."

He tried to suppress a yawn. The fatigue glazed over his eyes.

"I'm sorry, Mary. Fightin' with you two has plumb worn me out."

"No problem, Bull. I needed to leave anyway. I'll be back as soon as I can."

Bull squeezed her hand in gratitude as she eased away from the bed.

Granny said, "Thanks, Mary," as she closed the door so that she could nap in peace with Bull.

Mary noticed the doctor move out from his desk as she headed for the exit at the front door. He met her as she got to the door and stood in her way.

"Mary, can I have a word with you?"

"Well, certainly. What can I do for you?"

His heart fluttered at the possibilities of what she could do. Her clear blue eyes hid a smoldering passion. He could sense it in her every movement. Her every word. She was a cauldron of bubbling frustration. A widow in her position had to be searching for relief. And he had the solution.

"How do you think Bull is progressing?" he inquired.

"He seems to be doing better. Why do you ask?"

"I'm just curious if you thought his treatment was satisfactory."

"I've no complaints."

"Good. And may I ask how are you faring?"

"All things considered, I'm kept warm, safe, and dry. I shouldn't complain."

"Good. I extend my condolences for the situation you find yourself in. It must be hard. I can't imagine your difficulties."

"Thank you, Doctor."

"I too have difficulties of my own."

"We all do."

"So true. It's a pity we have to bear them alone."

Mary's intuition took hold. She hid her suspicion from the

doctor's view.

"Yes it is."

"Perhaps we can talk about it over supper this evening."

Too quickly, she replied, "I'm busy tonight."

"Perhaps tomorrow?"

She knew where this was leading and sought an easy way out.

"Doctor Hays, I'm not sure it's a good idea."

His anger flared. He had to keep it under control in order to possess what he so desperately wanted. He had to find the right words to bend her to his will. *No* wasn't an answer he accepted when he had set his sights on something he craved.

"Now, Mary. Two adults sharing good food and drink isn't a thing to be afraid of. Is it?"

Feeling cornered, she said, "No, I suppose not."

"Good then. We can have dinner tomorrow evening."

This was not what she envisioned. She just wanted to leave. The edge in her voice was apparent.

"No. I'm sorry."

Alarmed, he realized his quest might be failing.

"Mary, please reconsider."

She fought down the anxiety. Granny and Bull could hear her if she required help. The man's leer was chilling. His insistence telegraphed bad news.

"Doctor Hays, I appreciate the offer. I really do, but I can't."

Stymied, he had one last card to play that had worked for him in the past.

"Mary. You say you're happy with Bull's care. Correct?"

"Yes."

"Well, one of my concerns is the cost of his treatment. Nate brought in a pitiful attempt at paying down the bill today. Plumb pitiful. These hill country frontiersmen don't have money. They barter for their needs. Do you follow what I'm saying?"

"No," she lied.

"Bull will never have the money for my services. We use money here in the city. Bull's successful treatment will be expensive. *Very* expensive. Do you catch my drift now?"

"No."

He sighed. She was either being stubborn or she was more naïve than he expected. It didn't matter. He believed he held the key to success.

"Rethink my offer. A pleasant dinner and fine drink to set the mood for a meaningful conversation. Two consenting adults discussing their experiences. No strings attached."

She didn't know what to say. His boldness startled her. He was no different than most men, but crass in his confidence. Not smooth like Ames.

"Doctor Hays, you astonish me."

She reached for the doorknob to make her escape. His strong grip on her hand froze her efforts to leave. Caught in a trap, a cold chill flowed in her veins.

"Mary, this is your last chance to reconsider. Please think about it. Your decision could have a profound consequence on the level of care Bull receives."

Angry now, she said the first thing that popped into her head.

"Go buy yourself a whore!"

She had unwittingly hit a sore spot. Kern killed the blond whore he had groomed for his personal satisfaction. And she had been an excellent student who took extra care of his incessant needs. That was why he was here playing this unsuccessful hand with a woman driving him crazy.

"You've got it all wrong. Call it bartering. It could be good for all of us."

Fire shot from her eyes as she yanked her hand from his grasp and bolted out the door.

Left standing alone, he came to the conclusion she was right. He would visit Madam's Palace for a quick fix. The whores that were now employed were not high class, but he had arrived at the point where that small detail no longer mattered.

SEVEN

Nate trudged along the boardwalk on his way to the cafe. It had been a long night while he slept on the floor at the doctor's office, but the hard floor was the only alternative considering his lack of cash to pay for better accommodations. And now that poor option for overnight bedding had also been removed.

Hays had been in a dour frame of mind proudly put on display when he entered the room for his morning examination of Bull. His bedside manners were curt, and his temperament boorish when he demanded that Nate locate another place to sleep as he "practiced medicine and wasn't running a hotel."

Bull put up a meek protest at the doctor's rude behavior that went ignored. Doctor Hays gladly reminded him that he controlled his own business and was showing remarkable understanding by allowing Granny the privilege to stay overnight. He was under no compulsion to offer hospitality to every family member that showed up in want of lodging. And furthermore, there was the matter of finances with no assurance he would ever be paid for his services. Unable to counter the doctor's charges, Bull had quieted down submissive as a lamb.

It was a side of his father that Nate had never witnessed. The father he knew cowered to no man. The painful wound had drained him of his spirit.

Lost in his depressing thoughts, Nate plodded in a collision course with Mary carrying a basket covered with red gingham and loaded with biscuits and eggs.

She called his name, "Nate!"

Shocked, he deftly stepped to the side and avoided contact.

"Sorry, Mary. Not payin' attention."

The strained appearance told her all she needed to know.

"What's on your mind this morning?"

Shaking his head he said, "Pa's not doing well 'nough to go home yet."

"It's a bit soon. What did you expect?"

"He's always been the strong one. I didn't expect him to be tied down to a bed here in town."

"He needs good care."

"Humph. If that's what you call it. Doc is an irritable son of a bitch. He run me off this mornin'. Said he ain't runnin' a hotel for folks that cain't pay."

Mary knew what this meant. The doctor wasn't bluffing. It was already starting.

She said, "I'm sorry to hear that, Nate. Doctor Hays may be a grump, but he's the best hope for Bull at this time. How is your Dad?"

"'Bout the same."

"I'll stop by and see him later today."

"Thanks, Mary. It means a lot to Mom and me."

"I wouldn't have it any other way. He's always been there for me."

Nate's posture sagged. She couldn't remember seeing him so sad.

"How are you doing, Nate?'

"Been better. I've been cheated out of my Ranger pay. Matt's in jail. Cain't even find temporary work."

She nodded in sympathy. He was out of his element here in Austin.

"Hang in there, Nate. It's bound to improve."

"It's the only choice we have. Maybe a cup of coffee and a biscuit will help."

"So you're headed to the café?"

"It'll 'bout break me, but yeah."

She felt compelled. The mother in her spoke out.

"You stay out of trouble. You hear? This town's full of meanness."

He perked up. She was warning him.

"No problem," he said as he tipped his hat goodbye.

His blood started to boil. Meanness was a trait that meant something to him. It was exactly the emotion he felt churning in his gut. He had a deep pool of anger to draw upon. Breaking something or *somebody* sounded appealing.

Reaching the café door, he swung it open a little harder than he intended. The cowbell clattered overhead like the ringing of a church bell. The room hushed as heads turned his direction. He surveyed the dining area and located one table in particular that attracted his attention. His footsteps echoed in the silenced room as he stomped across the wooden floor.

There was an empty table beside the one that caught his eye where two snappy dressed businessmen were seated next to a giant of a man. Nate slid out a chair and took a seat that provided a clear view of his antagonists.

In moments, Carmin sidled over to set a hot cup of coffee in front of him.

"Hello, Nate. What can I get you?"

"Coffee is fine for now."

She spoke in a low voice heard only by him, "How about a table over by the window? The view is better there."

He gazed up at her. There was wisdom in those brown eyes. But he wasn't in the mood for good judgment.

"No. I like this view just fine."

"You should rethink that," she whispered.

He shook his head no, as his uncompromising stare bored in on Captain Harris.

The captain met Nate's unmistakable defiance without a sign of backing down. He mumbled something to the hulk of a bodyguard sitting next to him with his back turned to Nate. The beast of a man nodded without bothering to turn around.

The air between the tables hummed with voltage.

Colonel Ames cast a surreptitious glance at Nate. He hated conducting business during breakfast, but one look told him all he needed to know. This was the scout that stirred up so much difficulty with Harris over his withheld pay, and he had just telegraphed his hostile tendencies.

Carmin sat down with Nate, hoping to talk sense into him.

A few minutes of small talk did no good with the high-strung Johnston. He was from the hills and lived by a code of conduct foreign to most folks in town. There was no convincing him of the overwhelming odds against him. She got up and left with reluctance to attend to the men waiting on her at other tables.

Nate sipped his coffee, feeling the caffeine do its trick. He never lowered his icy glare from the man withholding what was rightfully his. He needed that money. It was his. He earned it. The more he pondered the injustice, the more his anger grew.

Captain Harris tried to avoid the intense scrutiny Nate put him under. The proximity of the scout applied a steady pressure he was unaccustomed to bearing. It was hard to enjoy the juicy fried ham on his plate. A burning acidic sensation rose from his stomach drowning his desire for the strong black coffee he normally relished. His breakfast was ruined.

Colonel Ames continued to scarf down his pile of scrambled eggs covered with a hot chili sauce, melted cheese, and sautéed onions. Breakfast was his favorite meal by far. He smiled as he put his fork down and guzzled his coffee, determined to finish breakfast before any disturbance ruined the fine meal.

Dawson sat impassively picking at his plate while he maintained focus on the reactions of Harris. The source of the anxiety was behind his back, but that was okay. He could tell what was happening from the apprehensive expression on the face of the captain. It was all under control. Actually it was a thing he looked forward to dealing with. He couldn't wait to move into action.

Responding to a strong buzz between his ears, Nate stood. He couldn't deny his impulse. All of his basic instincts required him to confront those that did him wrong. Muscles coiled like a spring yearned to explode in righteous vengeance against deceptive men abusing their power. It was an inequity as old as time. There was nothing he could do about any of his compulsions. Now was the time to act regardless of the outcome. He couldn't live with the injustice any longer.

His steps carried him around the monster of a man he watched out of his peripheral vision. That was a brute he would have to shoot. There was no way he could handle a man of his size and muscle. His voice dripped with contempt when he addressed Harris, "We need to step outside."

"We don't have anything to discuss."

"You're right about that. The time for talk has passed. You've got two choices this mornin'."

Harris never backed down. Now that he was engaged, the nervousness dissipated and he spoke with irritation, "I'm the judge of my options. Not some half-ass scout."

Out of patience, he bounded from his seat and poked Nate in the chest as an added emphasis.

Striking as quick as a rattler, Nate's fist connected in a blur against the cheekbone of Harris with a loud *smack*.

Harris tumbled backwards, tripping over his chair.

Nate leapt on him like a wildcat with fists landing hard cracking blows.

Harris thrashed wildly trying to block the surprising effectiveness of a man he had always considered his inferior. The taste of warm blood trickled down his throat. He tried to seize Nate's arm, but Nate fended off his counter moves with ease.

Snatching Harris by the hair, Nate secured a tight grip and held him stationary for a particularly violent punch.

The captain's head snapped backwards like a rag doll, blood gushing from his nose. His vision narrowed. Breathing was becoming difficult. A second and third blow followed. A curtain of darkness overcame Harris.

Harris was out, but blinded by rage, Nate connected with several more jaw breaking punches. Unseen by Nate, Dawson had crept up behind him after getting the signal from Ames.

Dawson sucked in a breath and reached for the surly backwoods hick.

Nate felt himself jerked off the prostrate Harris. Somebody had him by the collar, manhandling him as if he were a toy. He saw the emotionless black void of a killer. A hammering fist drove deep into his belly. Doubling over, he gasped to regain his breath.

The next strike landed on the top of his head and he received an elbow to his right eye that toppled him to the floor. That wasn't enough to end the vicious attack. Plucked from the floor as if he weighed nothing, another blow to the stomach left him helpless. He stumbled backwards toward the door.

Dawson pounced on him with a series of punches to his head. He fell out the door into a crumpled heap on the boardwalk.

Unconscious, he didn't hear the pleas of Carmin imploring Dawson to stop.

Hovering over Nate, ready to deliver another punishing blow, Dawson twisted to face the panicked cries of Carmin.

"Stop! You're gonna kill him!"

His pummeling ceased. Once engaged very little could sidetrack him, but he found the terror in a female voice distracting. He felt he had to calm her and said, "Sorry you feel that way, ma'am, but it was him that started it all."

Her fury building, she blurted, "No it wasn't. I saw it all. Captain Harris made the first move!"

Dawson considered her assertion. She was right.

Ames appeared at the door casually picking at his teeth with a toothpick.

He said, "You may be right Carmin, but Dawson couldn't let Nate beat a man already defeated. Now could he?"

Carmin ignored Ames and elbowed between Dawson and Nate. Kneeling next to Nate, she went to work trying to revive him.

Ames said, "Dawson, please disarm Nate and report the incident to the sheriff. Confiscate any weapons he may have and turn them in to Cole for safekeeping."

Dawson pulled the Remington revolver from Nate's holster and patted Carmin on the shoulder.

"He'll be alright, ma'am. He'll come to and be his old self by tomorrow."

Carmin shoved his hand away with fire in her voice, "What's wrong with you men? Beating each other like animals!"

"Just doing what I'm told," was the reply of Dawson as he stepped away from her malice, hands in the air.

Ames reiterated, "Go on Dawson, take the gun, and make a report to the sheriff."

Carmin gave Ames a bitter look.

Unfazed by her brazen behavior, he asked, "How about I go fetch you a wet towel for Nate?"

She nodded in approval as she tenderly stroked Nate's face.

Ames took a moment to admire her caring instincts, thinking of his ultimate goals. The crowd parted as he pushed his way back into the café where he saw Harris struggling back into his chair. He had a handkerchief pressed against his nose, blood curling into his mouth.

Stopping beside Harris, he patted his partner on the back.

"Hell of a licking he gave you."

Harris spat a wad of gooey blood on the floor, unresponsive to the taunt.

"Embarrassing to see you put up so little fight."

"He got . . . lucky is all."

Ames glanced around the room, aware that all eyes were on them. He bent close to avoid anyone overhearing, "He whipped your ass outright. Do me a favor and don't let this happen in public again."

Harris removed the handkerchief and inspected the blood soaked garment. Flexing his jaw back and forth, he determined nothing was broke and he still had all his teeth. The swelling in his nose created an ugly red bump hampering his ability to breathe. A gargled "Uh-huh," was all he could mutter.

"We have a reputation to maintain. No more setbacks like this. Your election is at risk when citizens see you beat like a puppy. Understand?"

Harris grabbed his hat off the floor. Heading to the door on wobbly legs, he pulled it together long enough to whisper, "Go to hell, Ames."

"That's more like it. Keep your chin up."

Harris was out the door and down the street by the time Ames returned to Carmin with some wet towels. He knelt next to her and placed the cool cloth on Nate's forehead.

She softly dabbed the towel across his face until he began to groan.

Ames couldn't help but relish the dexterity of her delicate fingers massaging Nate back to life. She was blessed with that special feminine quality of tenderness. Applying a light touch, she managed to wipe off the blood, and at the same time caressed Nate with care along his cheeks. Her fragrance was heavenly and Ames breathed it greedily. Unable to resist the opening, he lightly brushed against her breasts as he stood. She worked on getting Nate to sit up, too busy to notice the colonel's sly maneuver.

It wasn't long before she had Nate able to stagger away on his own. He didn't have much to say when Ames told him his guns were being held in safekeeping at the sheriff's office. The beating did a good job of removing the starch from his attitude. His head swirling, Nate thought better of any smart comments he would like to deliver. Vulnerable and naked without his Remington, he just wanted to retreat somewhere secluded until he recovered from both the humiliation and the cloud of pain he felt himself floating inside. He knew where he could crawl into a hole and hide. Jed's stable had a soft mound of hay in the loft calling him. It would be a good place to rest and recuperate out of everybody's sight.

Ames stayed at Carmin's side until Nate rounded the corner.

"He'll get over it," Ames said in a soothing voice.

With her hands on her hips, Carmin turned and said, "It didn't have to happen!"

"Right you are. Men like him make bad decisions all the time."

"Men like him?"

Ames chuckled as if entertained by the naïve comment.

"Yes, Carmin. Temperamental and hotheaded men like Nate should think before acting. He verbally assaulted Captain Harris. That's something a man can't do in public, or private for that matter."

"You didn't need to have him beat up."

"I didn't. He made his own decisions."

She didn't look convinced.

"Would you rather have him continue to beat Harris senseless?"

"Well, no, but Harris poked him in the chest first."

"Nate left him no choice. He wasn't going to stop the verbal assault. By the rule of law, he was out of line. As unpleasant as it seems, my man Dawson had to intervene when Nate became violent. Believe me when I say conflict is always disagreeable in my book. Unfortunately, men like Nate feel different." He shrugged his shoulders as if he shared her view and said in a tone of regret, "That's the world we live in."

She relaxed in the face of his logic. He saw the change transform her. His suave way with words had worked their magic again. The time was right.

"I have an idea."

"What's that?" she asked.

"Why don't we get together over some fine food and wine? We can get to know each other better."

The look on her face gave him the answer he sought. She

softened at the proposal. It was the perfect ploy. Women were always more susceptible to suggestions after an emotionally charged encounter. The timing was perfect. He imagined her soft embrace as she melted in his arms and submitted to his charm. She would be easy. Easy as pie. It wouldn't take long.

EIGHT

The night dragged on forever in the frigid dark cell. There was no kerosene lantern. No source of heat. The mattress was stuffed with cotton rolled up into uneven lumps, and reeked of sweat and urine. For comfort Cole supplied one threadbare wool blanket riddled with holes. Coziness was the last thing the county planned for their guests. If it cost money, the prisoners did without. The food they supplied did not qualify as slop fit for a pig. After a pointed complaint from Matt, Cole did manage to scrounge up a second blanket to toss in the cell before he retired to his warm and comfortable bed at home for the evening.

Matt tucked the blankets in tight to fend off the early morning chill seeping through the gaps in the bar-covered windows. His breath frosted over as he exhaled toward the cracked plaster hanging loose from the ceiling. Sleep eluded him as he contemplated the tortuous path that put him behind bars. It didn't matter what he did, he continued to run headlong into obstacles. Bull's saying "No good deed goes unpunished" kept running through his head all night long. He certainly couldn't argue with the truth of that belief. It had proven to be accurate too many times in his life. The problem was that he kept testing it, and circumstances kept on verifying the reality that good men rarely got a break. Hell, he was in jail. That was proof enough.

The mouse dawdled on top of his chest, whiskers twitching as he sniffed the air. Matt didn't move. The vermin had been rustling on the floor all night long. It was the only companionship he had in the lonely confining space of the "bucket." The tiny feet left light impressions on Matt's skin as he scurried off in search of food. Matt heard him scratch along the floor and squeak in annoyance at the unwelcome competition he encountered.

Fed up with the insomnia, he crawled out of the lumpy bed, wrapped the blankets across his shoulders and began to pace. The cramped cell didn't allow much room for exercise, but he kept it up thinking of all the men he had escorted to this very cell. He had dealt with many a bad hombre before the War of Northern Aggression had called him away. The outlaws from San Saba County had been a tough bunch of cold-hearted murderers. It was hard to believe he was occupying the same cell he had deposited them in so many years ago.

His humiliation haunted him all night long until the sun finally made a weak appearance indicating another cold and discouraging day lay ahead. He thought of Cora and the kids vulnerable to Indian attack. He couldn't do anything to run the Comanche to the ground while he was stuck in jail. His time away from home was stretching far beyond what he had anticipated. Travis would bring his family news of the ambush with Bull, but the boy had no idea he was locked up. Twenty days before he could return home! Twenty days before he could return to the hard hills where death stalked the unsuspecting. These were going to be some long boring days. He wasn't sure he could make the distance. This was torturing to him on so many levels and he had plenty of time to think on it.

Later in the morning, Cole ambled into the cell room. He appeared rested and well fed as he sauntered up to the bars.

"How'd you sleep, Matt?"

"Like a baby."

Cole gave him a knowing look.

"Hungry?"

"Tasteless oatmeal with weak coffee? I'll pass."

"Have it your way. Change your mind, let me know."

The click of the door closing behind Cole echoed off the red bricks. Matt slumped to the bed, lost in isolation. The hum of conversation outside the cell did nothing to alleviate his sagging spirits. Cole and his deputy existed in a separate world as far as he was concerned. Their carefree banter and laughter only worsened the blue mood growing out of his sense of impotence. With nothing to do, he puffed up the flat pillow under his head, kicked his legs straight out, and gazed at the cracks running across the ceiling. Twenty days seemed like an eternity to spend in this dump.

Several hours passed with Sheriff Cole and the deputy attending to the busy affairs of law enforcement. Citizens came and went about their business in the front office ignorant of Matt's occupation of the back cell. He preferred to keep it that way. He was in no mood for visitors. Or at least that was what he thought.

He heard her voice address Cole. She sounded as delightful to his ears as the morning song of a dove. What business did she have in this dank hellhole?

It didn't take long to find out. She stuck her head through the door to take a peek.

"Need some company?" she asked.

"If you can stand the cold."

Mary stepped in carrying the basket of food.

His stomach rumbling with hunger, he eyed the basket.

She observed his interest and folded the red cloth back to reveal the mound of warm biscuits sitting on a big pile of hot fried eggs.

"Thought you might like something good to eat."

"Mighty kind of you."

"I'll get some coffee."

She returned with the brew put on by Cole.

"Looks pretty weak, but I didn't think to bring coffee too. Figured anybody could make decent coffee. Should've known better."

"No complaints. The eggs and biscuits are plenty."

They made small talk while Matt munched on the hot chow. She brought him up to speed on Bull's health condition and purposely left out the objectionable behavior of the doctor. Finishing the last biscuit, Matt sipped at the coffee while admiring his unexpected guest.

"Sure is good to see you, Mary."

Her blue eyes clouded over with sadness.

"And you too."

"Helluva mess."

Reaching through the bars, she grasped his hand and pulled him close. Their breath intermingled as she gazed deep into his eyes.

Nothing needed to be said. They both knew what was happening. Lingering in the moment brought a temporary hope for things that would never be. She held his hands in a gentle caress while dreaming of a different life. A life that included him without any of their responsibilities tying them down.

For that fleeting moment, she thought it might be true. He was a man she was attracted to, and he was available. All her problems dissipated as he swept her away from reality. They rode off into a fairytale world where there were no murdering Indians, no crooked men, and no dependent children acting as a ball and chain around their necks. It was a trick of her mind making it seem real.

Sensing her flight of fantasy, Matt eased back. Not far, but enough that she snapped out of her trance. A slight giggle of embarrassment broke her spell.

"We keep doing this," she said.

"Maybe it's best I not see you," he whispered.

"That's not what I want."

"All we have together is regret."

"I'm beyond that. I've had enough of hard times. I know what I want. I'm tired of doing without."

"It's not been fair," he said.

"That's the irony of it. Frank is gone. But I'm still alive and have all the needs and wants that come with living. I can't help it. It's the hardest thing I've ever done. His trials are over, but mine have just begun. What I'm trying to say is Frank's gone, but I'm still here. This is my last chance. You could give me all I'd ever need. I could love you."

She was near tears. Part of him wanted her to leave. The subject was old hat and not likely to change. But he held back on stating the obvious out of consideration for her feelings. He searched for the right words to say. There were no right words. She had the situation pegged.

"Fair don't seem to be in play. Does it?" he asked.

She started to reply when the door flew open. Dawson barged in like a charging bull. His intimidating presence stopped Mary cold.

He held up upon finding her in an intimate conversation with the prisoner. He hadn't expected her to be so familiar with Matt considering the Ranger was a married man. His surprise quickly passed.

"Didn't mean to intrude," he said.

Matt said, "Try knocking next time."

"What? It's not a hotel."

"Just plain old good manners when I have a visitor."

"My apologies to you, ma'am." He tipped his hat to her in a courteous gesture. Turning to Matt, he said, "As for you, you'll have to deal with it. Price you pay when you break the law."

Dawson gave Mary a motion towards the door.

"Sorry, ma'am, but I need a word alone."

Mary grabbed the empty basket and made a hasty exit. Dawson was polite to her, but his demand left little room for doubt. She departed without a backwards glance.

"I don't think much of your manners," Matt said.

Dawson pushed his hat back on his head when he said, "Don't care much what you think, Mr. Ranger Man. Also don't care much what your scout thinks. The one that goes by the name of Nate."

Matt cringed at the mention of Nate.

Not one to miss much, Dawson knew he had Matt's attention.

"Yeah, you got it. Nate stepped over the line. I understand he's good at that. Lacking common sense, he's prone to being corrected. Well, you might say he ran into an education this morning."

Dreading the answer, Matt asked, "Where's he at?"

Shrugging, Dawson said, "Who knows? I dropped his guns off with Cole for safekeeping."

Breathing a sigh of relief, Matt was glad Nate wasn't dead.

"That's why I'm here," Dawson said. "You're getting a warning to deliver to Nate." He paused to let the request sink in. "He used up his one chance with me. Won't be called off next time."

There was nothing to say. Matt stared into the face as blank as a wall. He meant what he said and would kill Nate with as little remorse as if he killed a skunk.

They faced off with no words passing between them. Matt had experience dealing with Dawson's type although he topped the list as the most intimidating hulk of a man Matt had ever seen. It wasn't just the size that made him somebody to fear. It was his incredibly dark disposition. He towered over everybody like a black cloud yearning to rain down on the unsuspecting and innocent. His movements were supple for a man of his size. Like surging floodwaters, he presented an ominous threat to those foolish enough to resist him.

Fully aware of his impact on people, Dawson stared back into the cool gray eyes of the famed Ranger. He had heard a few tales about the man's exploits, but decided then and there to make it his mission to learn more. Behind bars, Matt was harmless, but in a little under twenty days, he would become a force to be reckoned with. And more importantly, a source of potential income. A lucrative source at that. It would pay to learn more about the man in order to make his task easier. He would not repeat the mistakes of Kern.

"Got the message?" Dawson asked.

Matt's reply spilled out covered in resentment, "Got it."

"Good."

Dawson stepped up to the bars and taunted Matt, "One more thing for you to think on. This David boy of yours. It'd be a shame if he didn't have a dad. It's gonna be up to you."

Dawson tapped on the bars before he turned to leave. Matt's tremendous self-control impressed him. The Ranger remained stoic despite his best attempt to antagonize him into a reaction. This critical information was filed away for future reference.

Pausing at the door, Dawson repeated, "Think on it, Ranger Man."

NINE

Nate stumbled into the sheriff's office late that afternoon. From his bed in back, Matt heard him enter and listened intently to the awkward start with Cole. Nate got off on the wrong foot when he asked for his guns. He neglected to lay down the necessary conversational groundwork. Etiquette wasn't a part of Nate's social skills.

Matt shook his head when he heard Nate say, "What do you mean I cain't have my guns? They're mine!"

Cole said, "They may be yours, but you've caused trouble."

"The hell you say. Harris cheated me outta my pay! I got a right to call him out. *He's* the one that shoved me. I just defended myself!"

"You and me both know that's a stretch. You went up to them while they were minding their own business eating breakfast. And then *you* started it."

"Bull! I'm after what's rightfully mine."

"That's not for me to judge. All I know is you're lucky Harris hasn't filed assault charges against you."

"Hell, I may file against his ass."

Cole shook his head in frustration. He always liked the Johnston boys even if they were a little backwards from too many days doing whatever they fancied out in the hills with nobody to answer to. The whole damn family could be stubborn as a mule.

"Look, Nate, you're not getting the guns back. Not until you ride out of town a ways and promise not to come back and make my job hard. You've gotta leave Ames and Harris alone. Don't make no difference what you or Matt think about what they may or may not have done. Law sees things different and that's all that matters."

"It's all a load of bull crap."

"Did you hear me? Or am I going to have to arrest you?"

"Bull," Nate said under his breath.

"When you're calmed down and ready to leave town, let me know. Me, or one of the deputies will ride out of town with you. At that point you can have your guns back with your vow not to cause more trouble."

Nate stood stoic in front of Cole.

Cole softened his tone when he asked, "How's your dad?"

"'Bout the same."

"Give him my regards when you see him next. If there's anything I can do, let me know."

Perked up, Nate said, "Arrest the bastard that paid to have Pa shot."

"Get out of here Nate before I arrest *you*."

Cole meant what he said. Nate realized he had pushed as far as he could. That fact satisfied him and he made his way to the cell room in a better mood. He entered the lockups all grins beneath an eye as swollen and purple as a ripe plum.

Matt said, "Damn it, Nate. I told you to stay away from 'em."

"Some things I just ain't good at."

"Nothing good will come from tanglin' with 'em."

"Do I look worried?"

"No, you look like you been dropped off a roof."

"Landed like a cat."

"Yeah, on your face."

Nate pressed his lips together and shrugged.

"Nate, the big fella came by and warned me he wouldn't hold back next time."

"Okay. I'll use my brains next time. But let me tell you it was worth it to put one on Harris. I'd still be beatin' him if that gorilla hadn't pulled me off."

"He laid a whippin' on you, didn't he?"

Nate rubbed his sore chin. A half-closed eye peered out of a puffy fold of flesh.

"Ain't nothin' to be ashamed of. Nobody in town could whip that monster."

"Aha! Now you git the point. Leave him be or you'll wake up dead."

"Okay, I hear what you're sayin'. I'll try to keep it in mind."

Concerned, Matt asked, "What's the latest on Bull?"

"He's holdin' his own. Too stubborn to let a hole in his shoulder take him under."

Matt didn't say anything about the clear and present danger of infection. He had seen many men survive the wound only to succumb to a rapid spread of fever and what he called the "red burn."

"Good. Glad to hear it. Wish I could git out of this," he waved his arms at the cramped cell, "and be of some help."

"Pa's burned up at the way you been railroaded. You shoulda heard him go off."

Matt laughed. He could hear Bull, if only in his head. God, how he missed being free.

"Give me some other news, Nate."

Nate didn't hesitate. There were few subjects closer to his heart than the constant difficulties confronted in the hills. His cheeks puffed up before he let the news spill out in a rush.

"Well, there's the Comanche trouble. They're still comnin' close to town. Latest is they slaughtered a man and his wife travelin' Hairy Man Road. Scalped 'em and tied 'em up alive to their wagon." His voice sizzled when he added, "Then they set it afire."

"Son of a bitch. The Feds cavalry even trying to catch 'em?"

"They've been in the field, but they cain't do nothin' right. 'Bout like a blind dog that cain't smell. They're useless at trailin' the Comanch."

"You know, I never liked that bastard Custer occupying Austin, but he had what it takes to fight in the big war. Shame he's gone. Maybe he could've put a whippin' on the Comanche."

"He had what it takes, no doubt. But he ain't here and there ain't much interest from the other commanders to do much 'bout the problem. I think they figure us Southerners got it comin' to us. Ain't no skin off their back. We're left with Hobbs out with a small detail patrollin' the hills. He's been ordered to act as a buffer by the gov'nor."

Matt gave Nate that notorious glare and said, "Hobbs is about as useless as tits on a boar hog."

TEN

Hobbs tossed the dregs of the cold coffee on the smoldering ashes of the campfire. A sizzling hiss floated across the camp where the men lounged in an early morning stupor brought on by a night of heavy drinking. Hobbs stumbled back from the rising cloud of steam, mesmerized by the dying embers. Sluggish and in a hung-over state of mind, he was having a hard time getting motivated for a day in the saddle. The damn Indians were giving him and his men an education on elusiveness. He was ready to call it a done deal. Another long day of fruitless trailing and an uncomfortable camp with pathetic food was almost more than he could bear. Stepping up to edge of the fire, he used his boot to shovel dirt over the glowing cinders.

He wanted to be back in a bar in Austin at this very moment. He wanted a saloon gal draped across his lap. He wanted to lose himself in the smell of cheap perfume and cheaper companionship. Sally would do the trick. She was a whore he could afford. The thought of her plump legs wrapped around him as he rode her for all she was worth helped him make up his mind. They would follow the faint Indian trail up to the Pedernales and Colorado River junction and no farther. Either they found Indians today, or they called it quits and returned to Austin. Sally was always ready for him. He grinned at the thought. He couldn't wait to get back in her saddle.

Positive they wouldn't run into Indians, he pivoted to face the men and bark orders. That was the one thing he enjoyed about being in charge. The men did as they were told. He didn't tolerate a difference in opinion out here in the folds of wilderness.

"Mossberg! Get the men mounted. We're heading out."

Charles Mossberg was an accomplished and capable hand, and it burned him up that he was desperate enough for money to serve under a washed up Rebel like Hobbs. The man was far past his prime. He had seen some notoriety as a captain during the Civil War, but that was before the bottle sucked him dry. Hobbs preferred to camp early and start late. That allowed more time for drinking and spinning the elaborate yarns he was known to weave. Under his leadership, there was no way they would ever overtake any of the bands raiding in the hills near Austin.

Throwing his saddle over his sorrel, Mossberg shouted at the men, "You heard him. Mount up!"

A general moan leached out of the lazy men. They mirrored the lead of their captain and felt an overall apathy about their assignment. Slowly, and one by one they struggled to rise and get their gear organized. Charles was mounted and ready to ride well before any of his fellow Rangers. Sitting tall in the saddle he asked Hobbs what the orders of the day were.

Hobbs gave him a smirk of disgust.

"Orders of the day?" he asked. "Mount up and put miles behind us. What do you think? We ain't finding any Indians today. Hell, they know where we are and have long skedaddled."

Charles held his tongue. Hobbs was fast to cut a man down. He had learned it was best not to question what the boozy captain said. He had also learned it would be wise to be on the watch for trouble because whatever his former successes against the Yankees were, Hobbs had little appreciation for Indian fighting. In fact, as far as Charles knew, the man had never encountered an Indian while out on patrol.

Careful not to offend the captain, Mossberg inquired, "Do you have a general idea of our destination?"

Hobbs reached for a nip of whiskey. Sloshing the bottle to his lips, he focused a bloodshot and skeptical eye on Mossberg. Taking a healthy draw on the bottle, he smacked his lips together savoring the fiery jolt.

"Nothing like the warm burn of a fine whiskey to get a man ready for a day's ride. What do you think?" he asked Mossberg.

The loaded question piqued his caution. He responded with a calculated reply. "Anything warm on a chilly morning is appreciated."

"Hear-hear," Hobbs saluted before he took another swipe at the bottle.

After tucking the bottle away between the folds of his blanket, Hobbs awkwardly swung his leg over the saddle. Mossberg grimaced at the poor dexterity of his overweight leader.

"Our destination, my good friend, is the junction of the Pedernales and Colorado. There aren't any Indians there. I'm sure they know of our existence by now and have made their exit from the region out of fear. That, my good man will fulfill my orders to rid the hills of their threat." Hobbs wore a big grin as he explained what he considered the brilliance of his plan. "At that point we can label the mission a success without a shot fired. Not too bad in my opinion. Take a jaunt through the countryside and in the process pick up a little coin to put in our pockets."

Charles turned away to hide the disdain he felt.

Noticing the scorn, Hobbs gladly exercised his authority and gave him a command, "You can ride sweep today. I need a good man to bring up the rear. Them Comanch like to hit the last in line, so I need you back there to keep watch. It'd be humiliating to be taken by surprise right before we head home."

It took another twenty minutes before Hobbs led the men away from the camp. He rode at the head of the column acting as both scout and leader of the half dozen inexperienced Rangers. Charles brought up the rear of the column leading two packhorses burdened with extra food and ammunition. Taking charge of trailing the pack animals had been a change Hobbs dumped on him as a form of punishment. The captain's vanity didn't allow any criticism and Charles had been unable to hide his disapproval one too may times in the judgment of the only one that mattered.

They broke out of the creekside camp in a clatter of hooves tromping on loose white limestone. The creaking of leather mixed in with the hollow *thunk* of the rocks flipping under the step of the horses. The men swayed in their saddles as they inched up the steep trail climbing out of Hawk's Nest Hollow.

Hobbs led the men along a broad and open ridgeline that provided a sweeping view of the endless folds of hills and deep valleys bathed in a violet haze. Burnt orange swaths of Indian grass rippled under the bellies of their mounts as they cut a fresh path through the undisturbed grasslands. An occasional island of green live oaks created a deviation in the route favored by Hobbs. He had just enough frontier savvy to recognize the threat of ambush and rode away from the thick growth of oaks that could conceal Indians known to be equipped with rifles.

High overhead, Charles heard the shriek of a red-tailed hawk. Shielding his eyes with the brim of his hat, he combed the sky until he spied the rust-colored belly of the bird standing out in contrast against the slate-gray clouds. Soaring free in a rising thermal, the hawk circled above the Ranger column in a ceaseless quest for sustenance. His keen eyesight made him an outstanding hunter. Charles watched as the hawk, unseen by his prey, plunged in a sudden attack that proved deadly to a cottontail.

It was obvious to any thinking man. The trail favored by Hobbs led over the uplands in a direct passage to his stated destination. It was true they could make better time on the ridgeline compared to following the meandering course of the shallow streams common to the hill country, but in the mind of Charles the tradeoff could be costly. They were also visible to unfriendly eyes for miles in any direction. Their column of men on horseback would stand out like a herd of buffalo to the perceptive eyes of the Comanche that made their living from stealth much like the hawk now feeding on a rabbit that didn't use ample caution.

Another high-pitched screech from above sent a tingling shiver down his spine. The companion of the hawk was trying to flush out its own quarry. Grave danger was in the air for the unsuspecting. The woods had a way of communicating if a man was to listen closely. Charles was hearing the message, but at a loss on how to get the point across to Hobbs.

Lagging in the rear, all he could see of the captain was his hat bobbing up and down with the uneven gait of his long-legged bay. Hell, the captain even wore a white hat that stuck out like a sore thumb. It was like a sign declaring their presence. Hobbs was right about one thing. The Indians surely knew they were in the hills. The question became; would the Comanche worry enough to leave? Charles had his doubts.

It was a long all-day pounding ride that brought the men to a cliff overlooking the confluence of the two rivers. Across the Colorado from their location stood a charcoal-gray bluff running the length of the valley as far as the eye could see. The fifty foot high precipice jutted straight up from the timbered bottomland. A narrow gash split the rim apart like a hatchet had been driven into the rocks. Winding up from the river a game trail passed through this opening between huge boulders that had tumbled from the limestone ledges overgrown with cactus.

Hobbs stuck his fist up at arm's length in the space below the sun. He determined the sun hung the width of one fist above the horizon. They had a little over one hour of daylight left before dark forced them to make camp. Hobbs grumbled under his breath about the lateness of the hour and said, "We got here a little later than I thought we would."

He stretched upward on his stubby legs to get a better look at their options to cross. To their right he located what appeared to be an easy descent over an open and gentle slope leading down to the banks of the Colorado. It seemed perfect to him as the drop was covered with short buffalo grass and provided direct access to the riffles where the trail crossed.

Charles worked his way through the waiting men to come even with Hobbs. He immediately saw the potential hazards. Any river crossing in Indian territory was perilous. A proper reconnaissance was the best course of action before committing all the men to the water in an area conducive to attack.

Charles asked Hobbs, "Are we camping on this side?"

"We could. I'm ready to call it a day."

Responding to Charles is when Hobbs spotted the lost pack on one of the horses. "Where's the ammo bag?" he asked Charles in an alarmed voice.

Looking back at the packhorse Charles was sickened at the absence.

"Son of a bitch! I never heard it fall."

Behind them Rodgers ducked his head to stare at his pommel. It didn't do any good. The ire of Charles rained down on him.

"Damn you, Rodgers! You were supposed to check the knots at our last stop."

He didn't look up. The packhorses were normally his responsibility and he had been enjoying a day off from tending them. He was caught and knew better than meet the challenge when he had done wrong.

Charles couldn't believe the lack of professionalism. He roared, "That's half our reserve ammo!"

Hobbs spoke up with indignation; "Rodgers, you just earned you some extra camp duty tonight."

"Yes, sir," came his meek reply.

Turning to Mossberg he blurted, "You should've kept a better lookout on the supplies. You can go back to fetch it."

Charles flipped the lead rope to Rodgers and said, "Here you go. They're all yours now."

Hobbs watched until Charles disappeared down the back-trail. Addressing the men, he said, "No point in waiting for him to return. We'll cross over and camp in those oaks above the bluffs. Should be plenty of wood for a fire and it's early enough to have a drink or two before the sun sets."

He was met with unanimous approval after dropping the hint of another early start at the bottle. Hesitating for a moment, he thought of Charles heading off alone and not aware of his decision. Puckering his lips, he said, "He'll figure it out."

Clicking his tongue, he eased the bay toward the slope where the cliffs tapered to an end on their side of the river. The men fell into a line behind him with Rodgers bringing up the rear in control of the packhorses. Hobbs had figured the route correctly and the gradual slope made for an easy ride to the river. Reaching the bank of the Colorado he held his hand up for the men to halt.

His bay wasn't going to be denied water and lunged off the low bank and buried her muzzle in the gently flowing current. The other horses followed suit and soon all the mounts were getting their fill of water. Taking the time to give their steeds all the refreshment they needed, a few of the men lit up smokes. The temperature was cool, but agreeable for the time of year. A relaxing evening around a cheery blaze was ahead. They were headed for home the next morning, their mission a success. Although it would be small, they had a little spending money waiting for them once they got back to Austin. It could definitely be worse was the general conclusion amongst them all.

Hobbs eyed the trail across the river. The shadows were deepening in the cleft splitting the bluff apart. He was ready to get out of the saddle. The thirst of his mount quenched, he tapped her in the flanks and she responded in a slow splashing walk through the riffles. The men were strung out with Rodgers bringing up the rear when Hobbs spurred his bay out of the water and onto the game trail snaking between room-sized boulders.

Halfway to the top he thought he saw movement inside a screen of cat's claw and bee brush. He reined to a stop, holding his hand up as a signal to the men. They pulled up behind him. Rodgers at the rear, halted in the middle of the ford. One of the packhorses neighed in annoyance at the delay that left him standing in the water.

Eying the brush and boulders, nothing moved that Hobbs could see. He breathed a sigh of relief. For a moment he regretted not sending a couple of men to check that the trail was clear. He nudged his mount forward. There was nothing to fear. No Comanche in his right mind wanted to face armed and dangerous Texas Rangers. Any Indian near the crossing was miles away and riding hard to avoid his men.

He paused again when he got to the point where he could see over the last lip of the trail and into the woods beyond. It was better to err on the side of caution. He gave the clearing in the trees a good onceover. He knew it. His instinct was impeccable. Clear again. He saw the large trunk of a downed oak that would make a great place to sit next to a campfire and have some stiff drinks. Grinning at the thought of a pleasant evening, he prodded his bay forward. He saw exactly where he would dismount next to the trunk.

The boom of the rifle never registered in his ears. His hat flew off his head when the round tore through his chest and exploded like a geyser spewing a fountain of bloody tissue on the surrounding brush. Blown backwards from the impact, he tumbled to the ground when his horse bolted in fright. He hit the dirt hard, limp, and lifeless.

Concealed behind a boulder, the Comanche warrior that shot him roared a bloodcurdling whoop that was the signal to attack.

Down the trail from Hobbs the men realized too late that they were now trapped in a narrow defile facing completely hidden enemies. The explosion of numerous rifles echoed off the bluffs. Each booming report spelled the end of another Ranger. Only a couple of the men cleared leather with their revolvers, but they never had a chance to acquire a target. They fell dead from their horses in a sea of raging confusion.

The Ranger directly in front of Rodgers had a chance. He had not exited the water when the shooting started. He stood his mount on her rear legs with a violent yank of the reins. Eyes rolling in fear, the dun reared high with her front legs pawing the air for balance. She couldn't turn in time and floundered to her side in a full panic. The Texan reached for leather, but missed, and fell to the water with the reins still in his left hand. It did no good; he couldn't hold his grip, his mount broke free to race across the river in a flood of terror to escape.

Seeing Rodgers in the middle of the crossing with the packhorses, the Ranger's eyes widened in recognition of his exposure without a ride. He stumbled to his knees, his first steps mired in the resistance of thigh deep water. His arms flayed in the air in a terrified attempt to regain his footing.

Stunned at the sudden turn of fate, Rodgers tarried long enough to see a Comanche step out from behind a boulder with his bow already notched. It happened in the blink of an eye. The arrow flew in a lethal blur. The Ranger froze in mid-step as the iron tipped arrow severed his spine. The sight of the arrow quivering from the belly of his companion broke Rodgers' hesitation. The last thing he saw was the Ranger toppling face first into the riffles of the Colorado.

Releasing the lead rope on the packhorses, Rodgers made a deft turnabout. He spurred his pinto hard and they escaped back the way they had come. His saddlebags bounced wildly as they made a hasty retreat across the gravelly bed of the river. Cold water splashed in his face. His hat flew away and was swept downstream. He was sure he had it made when the slug burrowed into the muscle at the top of his right arm. The white-hot burn was searing. He couldn't help slumping in shock, the reins slipping away from his fingers. Left with no choice, unsure how long he could remain in the saddle, he doubled over and leaned into the neck of his horse while his right arm flopped useless at his side. All he knew was that falling meant a horrible death at the hands of savages.

Another round zipped by his head. And then a second and third whizzed by in narrow misses. He was putting distance behind him. Regaining the reins and spurring hard, his mount responded with a jump, clearing the low bank.

Now on land they launched forward. He could hear the war whoops of the Comanche as more rounds buzzed by his ears. Fountains of topsoil erupted on the slope around him. The whine of ricochets split through the air.

Gaining ground, he started to rise in the stirrups when he heard the dull thump of a bullet slam into the flank of his horse. Dropping her head in pain, confused, his mount slowed, unsure of what her rider wanted.

"No you don't! Keep goin' you bitch!"

Fiercely spurring her haunch, his pinto recovered just as another slug blew a branch out of a sycamore between him and the Comanche. The splintered bark pelted his back. He lowered himself along the neck of his horse and struggled to maintain his balance as they accelerated up the hill.

Luckily, the cover of a thick stand of oaks soon sheltered him from the rapid fire of the Indians. He snuck one final glimpse their way before he disappeared into the timber. He saw four Indians standing on the opposite bank with their rifles trained on him. What he didn't see were their ponies. He figured they must have secreted them away from the ambush. That could give him time to make a getaway before they mounted up.

He could feel the warm blood dribbling down his ribs. A blazing sensation traveled through his arm. The bone-jarring gait of his ride produced a fresh surge of blinding heat with every stride. He felt lightheaded, unsure if he could continue. He had to find Mossberg.

It didn't take long. They almost collided with each other careening around a blind corner. Mossberg immediately saw the telltale slump of a wounded man. It was a sight he had become more than familiar with over the course of many battles.

He captured the reins of the wounded pinto and halted both of them in place.

"You gotta let us go!" Rodgers implored. "They'll be after us sure 'nough!"

"Ambushed?"

"Hell yeah! They got all of 'em!"

It was bad. Worse than Charles supposed.

"How's your arm?"

"Hurts like hell! We gotta git!"

Mossberg held the reins tight while he calmed the pinto caressing her neck. He saw the wound behind the shoulder. It wasn't in a bad location and was barely bleeding. The horse would be fine. But the rider was a different story.

"We ain't leavin' them men unaccounted for."

Rodgers turned to look down his back-trail. He faced Charles like a deranged man.

Charles realized it was no use with Rodgers. "You head back. I'm gonna go check on the men,"

"You're crazy as hell!"

Those were the last words Charles heard as he released the reins and Rodgers raced away without a backwards glance.

Dismounting, he said, "You're probably right." He found an oak limb drooping to the ground and tied his mount up tight. The next steps were some of the hardest to take in his life. He was alone with no chance of assistance. All of his gut instincts told him to flee, but he sucked in a deep breath and grabbed an extra box of ammo before he headed into the teeth of danger.

If the Comanche were hot on their trail he figured he could move into the woods and waylay a few of them before they discovered his whereabouts. After that, he would have to improvise. The odds against survival were long, but he would never abandon men that it might be possible to save.

He cautiously eased down the trail until he located a gap in a thick growth of cedar trees. Crawling under them to the outer edge, he could see the river crossing. Repulsed by what he observed, he would never forget the sight. All the men were clearly beyond help. There was nothing he could do except catch up to Rodgers and pray they could make it back to Austin before the Comanche decided to pursue.

<<<<< • >>>>>

Black Owl peered across the valley. One Texan had slipped out of their trap. The coward had run like the mangy dog he was. But that was okay, they had his dead brothers scattered inside the gully to celebrate. They had special plans for the remains of these white braves that fought like women. His Comanche brothers were busy dragging their bloodstained bodies down to the river.

His responsibility at the top of the bluff was to keep an eye out for the return of any Texans they had missed. He wasn't concerned. Only two Texans they knew of had survived their attack, and they would not return to face a war party as large and powerful as this band. It had been an exceptionally well-laid trap. The Texans had ridden like fools straight into their teeth and made their destruction easy. Buffalo Hump had discovered them several days ago and then shadowed their every move while remaining undetected. He planned and gathered all the brothers together for this ambush. It was their best success as yet on this long lasting raid among the palefaces.

Looking down on the exultant warriors working on the white men, Black Owl noticed the frenzy that possessed Buffalo Hump. His thirst for blood, plunder, and revenge was unquenchable. Several new scalps dripping with gore dangled from his belt. He directed the braves to prop the dead men up against tree trunks and secure them facing the river with rope wrapped around their chest to hold them upright. Stepping back to observe their efforts, he still wasn't satisfied.

More rope was produced and they set about running the ropes across the open mouths of the Rangers to bind their heads to the trunks. With their heads fastened to the trees, Buffalo Hump now instructed his warriors to pluck the eyes from their foes and toss them into the brush. They whooped and hollered as they completed what they considered an amusing task. Now the white men faced the river absent their eyes and it was as it should be. These white braves couldn't see the injustice of their actions against the Comanche when they were living, and now Buffalo Hump had made a mockery of their shortcomings as men. He paced back and forth admiring his work. Howls of excitement echoed in the river bottoms when Buffalo Hump declared the visual effect satisfactory. Black Owl saw that Buffalo Hump had an idea when he ceased pacing and jerked his knife from the scabbard on his waist.

What happened next didn't surprise Black Owl. Buffalo Hump took a knee next to the carcass of the plump Texan that had led his men up the trail. He was a difficult specimen to behold. Stripped of his clothes, his pallid and soft body was an appalling sight in the opinion of young and vigorous Comanche braves. They had laughed at his rotund corpse tumbling over rocks as they used their ponies to drag it down to the banks of the river. Now Buffalo Hump applied the razor-edge of his blade to the protruding belly of the Texan that dared to ride against the People. With a quick slash, the entrails spilled to the dirt in a slimy pile.

Up and down the line of dead Texans the other Comanche warriors followed his example of mutilation. It was an old trick that would provide a feast for their four legged friends of the night and send the defeated white men to the spirit world missing their dignity. Buffalo Hump could not contain his exultation any longer. The sight of his dishonored enemies caused his excitement to bubble over. He broke out in a celebratory dance insulting them in their downfall. He shook his fresh scalps in front of their empty eye sockets. Prancing back and forth became contagious and before long all the Comanche brothers dipped and strutted in a joyous celebration of victory over their despised foes.

Black Owl observed the scene from his placement high on the bluff above the dancing and singing. He understood the frustrations of his tribesmen. They deserved this moment of victory after all the hardship forced upon their people by the hairy-faced invaders. For years his tribe had been pushed farther and farther from their beloved homelands here beside the clear flowing streams and game laden hills. He gazed across the canyon to the opposite side where the other Texans had disappeared in flight.

They were still out there.

He could sense the presence of one of them now. Sharpening his focus on some overgrown cedar trees, he couldn't see the man, but he knew he was there. Under the trees watching. He certainly wouldn't like the treatment of his mutilated brothers. It was no matter to Black Owl. The white men deserved a taste of defeat and the bitter sorrow that came with the experience.

He let out a long quavering howl that carried throughout the river basin. He too had felt much sorrow. This paleface that got away needed to feel the agony of what the Comanche had suffered for far too long.

ELEVEN

Outside his cell Matt could hear the racket of a normal day beginning. Men cussed as their teams strained to pull wagons heavily laden with supplies. He could hear the hustle and bustle of freight being distributed at one of the warehouses owned by the syndicate from the North that Ames represented. A buckboard flew by at a high rate of speed heedless of the warehouse crew tasked with unloading bulky sacks of flour. Harsh criticism was flung in the direction of the buckboard operator as he swiftly put a gap between him and the foul-mouthed laborers. A quick flash of the middle finger let them know how he felt.

The reeking scent of horse manure seeped into the cell room. Wagons churned the fresh droppings into the perpetually muddy street and the odor mixed with the other obnoxious smells Matt had to endure in his cramped cell. There was always a slight tinge of ammonia in the city air he found particularly offensive. The prevailing breeze swirled against his window delivering a steady dose of pungent aromas. Accustomed to the clean air of the country, the stench of the soiled town gnawed on Matt's nerves.

Reclining on his back with his hands clasped behind his head, he gazed at the ceiling. He knew every crack and defect in his cell intimately after days of boredom. The monotony caused him the most grief. There was no way for him to adapt to inactivity. A few books provided some diversion, but they were no substitute for a brisk ride on Whiskey. No substitute for the modest pleasure of rounding up the stock. Or just sitting on the porch with Cora watching the early morning wildlife feeding on the hill.

Thinking of Cora, he knew they needed to talk. Bad. Things had to be ironed out. Their alienation had gone on far too long. The discussion would be unpleasant due to her natural tendency to avoid the subject at all costs, but the damage in their relationship had to be dealt with once and for all. If the distance between them wasn't bridged, they didn't have a future together. It was that simple. It wouldn't be easy to overcome, but it really was that simple. Either she moved on with him or they continued to live in misery, and the time in the cell was providing enough misery to last him a lifetime. He couldn't take any more. His decision made, he intended to change things with her once he was released. He wasn't sure how or when, but something between them had to give. The yearning to feel the wind among the leaves in his heart had grown too strong to ignore any longer.

Idling away the time, his thoughts were wandering when a fleeting image of Mary crossed his mind. She had not been back to visit him since Dawson disturbed their last meeting. It was for the best. But that didn't mean he wasn't disappointed. She was a nice distraction to help chip away at the long hours spent in isolation. Hell, anything helped. Even the occasional game of checkers with Cole broke up the mind-numbing boredom.

At least she was kind enough to make sure one of the other girls delivered hot meals to him from the café. They always said she was too busy to make the trip, but Matt knew better. Mary was making it easier on both of them. Close daily contact would only feed the fire of temptation neither one had the strength to resist.

Cole envied the consistent delivery of food and began to complain that Matt was eating better than he was. The sheriff could not afford café-cooked meals three times a day and it started to get under his skin that Matt got his meals hand delivered for free. The owner of the café was the only citizen in Austin that risked supporting Matt. The old man had roots in Kentucky just like Matt's family and he took personal offense at the way Matt had been treated. One of the waitresses told Matt that when he was released he could drop by the café for a free meal of whatever he desired. The owner would be proud to celebrate with the Ranger that risked everything to bring back the Havens girl. He thought it was a damn disgrace the city folks didn't speak up for a man that protected all their interests at the risk of his own life and limb.

A memorable feminine voice from Cole's office brought Matt up to a sitting position.

Cole greeted the lady with an obvious tone of acute interest. They engaged in small talk for a few minutes that Cole craftily diverted into an invitation for her company to share an evening meal. She politely declined with an explanation that she would like to have permission to see Matt instead. Cole didn't respond, but threw the cell room door open with a *thud*.

Ignoring the sheriff's display of emotion, Carmin was all smiles as she entered the cell with thanks to Cole for his kindness. Her eyes widened when she saw Matt. Out of Cole's sight, she shook her head in disbelief.

In a whisper she said, "He saw the basket of food and knew why I was here. Had to make a play anyway. What is it with some men?"

"Don't have a good response."

"Just being facetious. You men are not hard to understand."

"No. I suppose not."

Here she was again. Just being Carmin.

She uncovered the bowl of roast beef drowning in rich brown gravy. Chunks of potatoes and carrots crowded the beef for space almost overflowing the bowl. Two large slices of toasted bread rested in the basket. Saving the best for last, she let him have a peek at a thick slice of dark chocolate cake bundled separately in a napkin.

"Mighty fine of you, Carmin," was all he could mutter in surprise of her visit.

Looking up from the succulent meal, he noticed her eyes dancing with mischief.

She handed the food through the slot and he sat down to dig into some fine cooking that compared to Cora's skills in the kitchen. While he was distracted with an excellent meal she returned to the front office and briefly conversed with Cole to sooth his wounded pride. Shortly after Matt emptied the bowl she pulled up a chair and had a seat next to the bars of the cell. Close enough that he caught a strong whiff of perfumed honeysuckle surrounding her. Setting the bowl to the side he asked, "To what do I owe this pleasure?"

"I finished my shift and figured it was my turn to see you."

"Well thank you. The food was mighty good."

She leaned forward, her voice sultry. "I'm glad you enjoyed it. Means a lot to me to be appreciated."

"You've been that. The days are long in here."

"You belong in the saddle, don't you?"

"That's my preference. I like to be on the move."

"Me too."

She laughed at the thought.

Matt said, "Tell me what you've been up to. Not much goin' on where I'm at."

"I stay busy. Here lately I've been to a couple of parties."

"Parties? I've forgotten what those are like."

"You're not missing much. Men that are full of themselves mostly. Women parading around in expensive clothes. Boring conversation most of the time."

"Why do you go?"

"Keeps me busy. You never know who you might meet."

A troubled shadow crossed Matt's face. Power and money had a strange appeal to women. They all seemed partial to a well-padded nest.

Her intuition always perceptive, she said, "It ain't that."

His bottom lip puckered up and he nodded in doubt of her answer.

"No, it's not what you think."

"Okay then. Do you mind me askin' who brings you to the dance?"

She hesitated knowing he wouldn't like her motives.

"Now don't go off on me. Remember it's not what you think."

The intensity of his gaze was intimidating. She didn't want him to think badly of her.

"I know you won't like it none." She gathered her courage. "But Colonel Ames has been my escort."

She was right. He felt a stabbing sensation of disappointment.

"There's nothing there. He's been a gentleman and I'll not let him get any ideas."

"Wrong. He already has them. Didn't you learn from watching him with Mary?"

"I saw what happened. That's why I keep him at arms length.

He respects my desire to keep it friendly."

Matt shook his head and lectured, "It don't work that way with men like him."

"I can handle him."

"Why chance it?"

"It should be obvious. I work in a café. Don't you think I want a better life? He could be the right man to introduce me to the right man."

She was spot-on. Who was he to judge? She deserved the right to search for a better way. He didn't know anything about her and it would be wrong to look down his nose at a gal just trying to get by.

"Listen, Matt. I appreciate your concern. I've been around more than Mary. She was desperate and desperate people do desperate things. I'm patient. It'll work out for me when the time is right, but I know nothing positive will happen sitting on my hands at home."

"Convince me you're right. I don't know anything about you."

Her voice purred with passion, "I like it that way."

"Why's that?"

"That way, I can be anything you want me to be."

Intrigued, he said, "Anything?"

She reached through the bars and folded his hand into hers. Her soft warm touch was stimulating. Her sensual brown eyes melted in thoughts of rapture a man like Matt could deliver. Leaning in, he could feel the light caress of her breath when she whispered, "Anything at all. I know what you like, and I wouldn't disappoint."

Her full pouting pink lips mesmerized him. He would give in right now if he were free. A man could only take so much.

"Anything at all. Anytime," she cooed.

"You make an offer that's hard to refuse."

"Don't refuse. Drop by my place when you get out. We can talk."

"If I came by, we'd do more than talk."

"That's okay too. I ain't looking for what Mary is."

She let his hand drop, moving away slowly.

"Anything. Anytime," were her last words as she peered over her shoulder watching him watch her glide out the door.

TWELVE

Cole whistled a catcall when he stepped into the cell room.

"Anything? Anytime? Now that's an offer I'd take her up on."

His tone brusque, Matt asserted, "You've got no right to listen."

"Wrong there, Matt. This is my jail. I've got every right to know what's going on."

"You're a son of a bitch, Cole."

Chuckling, he said, "No argument here. Hell, Matt. It ain't your fault. Two of the most attractive ladies in town have been visiting while you rot behind bars. No, sir. It ain't your fault. Everybody knows that ladies love outlaws."

He almost doubled over in laughter at his own joke.

Matt turned his back on Cole and stalked to the window. He clutched the bars with both hands and stared at the dreary cloud cover hanging low and cheerless over the town like a wet blanket. The impulse to be lost on horseback was eating him alive, but he didn't want to give Cole the satisfaction of seeing the frustration on his face. He thought of a way to turn the tables.

"Sorry about the loss of your favorite whore."

Cole wasn't smiling when Matt turned back to face him.

"Seems to me you owe me one," Matt chided.

The sheriff didn't like the sudden turn in the conversation.

Matt said, "I took care of your job for you by gittin' rid of Kern." He burrowed his eyes and scorched the sheriff with his menacing glare. "You may find I have something valuable you need to know."

"Humph! I know everything I need to know and I don't owe you squat."

"Yeah, well, let me ask you. Where's the cash I found on Kern?"

Not sure where Matt was headed, Cole paused to think before he answered, "It's locked up as evidence."

It was Matt's turn to laugh. He chuckled a bit before saying, "Evidence? That ain't considered evidence by the judge. What's your plan for it?"

"Ain't thought that far."

"Well, you better. Ames will be by for it soon."

Cole's face blanched at the suggestion. He began pacing, his attention riveted on the floor. He stopped and said, "I haven't thought that far out."

"Time to consider the likelihood. That's two thousand dollars we're talking about."

"I ain't forgot the amount. It's sure enough a wad."

"Yes it 'tis. And let me tell you a secret. I wish now I'd kept the damn stuff. I tried to do right and look where it got me." He waved his arm across the dank cell. "That cash would've bailed me and Bull outta back taxes we owe. Kern was dead, and nobody needed to know about the money."

Cole rubbed his chin in appreciation of what Matt said. He couldn't argue with the logic. Matt had always been a smart man in his opinion. Honesty was his main shortcoming.

"I've regretted a lot of my decisions that day. I should've known there would be a good chance of Kern laying in wait. He'd already confronted us once in the same neck of the woods on our way into town. My fault Bull got shot is how I see it. I should've been more careful."

"You had to get home. That crappy road is the only reasonable way to take a wagon back to your place."

Matt shrugged as if he wasn't convinced. He sat down on the bed and broke out in a devilish smirk when he said, "Ames will be back for the cash. Mark my words."

Apprehension tapped a root into Cole. He was responsible for the evidence and the judge had offered no guidance. This could get delicate.

They were both lost in reflection. The noise of wagons rattling down the street filled the room. Several barking dogs passed under the cell window. A teamster hollered obscenities when the mongrels cut in front of his heavily loaded freight wagon. Matt got up and tried to catch a glimpse of the commotion. Cole took a seat in the chair after shoving it against the wall.

Neither one said anything for a few minutes. Cole broke the silence with a question. "How can you be sure he'll come for the money?"

There was no hesitation when Matt replied, "It's his. A man like him will never let that much cash go without a fight. It ain't in his nature to lose."

The answer produced a visible sag in Coles posture.

"Sorry to say it, Cole, but when you sleep in a lion's den you might end up gittin' bit."

Standing slowly from the chair, Cole faced Matt. Looking at the Ranger, his bearing straightened. He had made his decision and would live with the results just as Matt was doing now. Innocent and locked up in jail, but not giving in. Confidence returned, he said to Matt, "Guess I'll handle it the best I can when the time comes."

"It's all any of us can do."

"Yes it is. But now let me give you a piece of advice." He bid his time to let Matt concentrate on what he had to say. In his opinion it was nothing but common sense that Matt needed to hear. "Why don't you sell out and move on? Make a smart play and get out of the way of Ames."

Matt didn't get a chance to reply. The front door banged open and a deep voice boomed, "Cole! You here?"

Cole rolled his eyes before he trudged out the cell room door to greet the new arrival. Matt could hear the boisterous conversation in Cole's front office and that's where he preferred it remain. After a few bits of lie swapping between the sheriff and his visitor, Matt was disappointed to see familiar blue eyes peek around the corner of the doorframe. Dawson stepped in with an enthusiastic, "Hello, Mr. Ranger Man!"

Matt gave him the look that melted soldiers under his command.

"What's the matter? Figured you might want some company." Dawson sized up the cramped cell. "Don't it get boring in there?"

"No, I like it just fine."

Dawson snickered, "Yeah, I'll bet you do."

Impatient, Matt said, "What do you want?"

Dawson picked the chair up and flipped it to face the wall. Sliding into the seat, he rested his arms on the top rail and returned the hard stare of Matt. Neither man spoke. The silence lengthened. Tiring of the charade, Dawson said, "We can have an intelligent discussion. Or not. It's up to you."

"I don't imagine we've got much to talk about."

"You might be surprised. I've learned some things about you since we last met."

"Not sure I want you knowing anything about me."

"Ain't no harm in getting to know a man. Helps avoid mistakes if you get to know the folks around you."

"Mister, I don't think much of your employer. The company you keep tells me all I need to know about ya."

"Well, that don't surprise me none. Fits what I've learned about you."

"It don't matter what you think you know. I ain't interested in your opinion."

"Suit yourself. But it ain't all bad." Dawson stuck the stub of an unlit cigar in the corner of his mouth. Chewing on the stogie, he said, "I know you walk a straight line. Try to do things by the good book. That's all fine and dandy. I don't put much faith in them notions, but that's me."

This conversation didn't make sense to Matt. He couldn't see where anything was to be gained from small talk with a man that crushed Nate like a bug. Any employee of Ames was naturally on the wrong side. But here the man sat. He appeared ready to stay regardless of Matt's preferences.

Figuring he might be able to move him on his way, Matt said, "Like I asked. What do you want?"

"Oh, just a little talk. I'm curious. You've got quite a reputation."

"Don't believe all you hear."

"None of what you hear and only half of what you see is what I abide by."

"Sounds about right to me."

"Well, there you go. We agree on something."

Matt sat down. He might as well be comfortable talking to this intimidating character.

"We can agree on things, but that don't make us compadres," Matt said.

"Ain't looking for that. My employer wouldn't like it much if we was to be sharing drinks at the bar. Man's gotta keep up appearances for the ones that pay the way. No, sir. I just got a curious streak about some of what I heard."

"You don't believe what you're hearin'?"

"That's already been established. Only half of what you see."

Matt grunted.

"No, what I want to hear from the horse's mouth is about the girl you rescued."

Nodding, Matt said, "Wasn't only me. I had lots of help."

"Ain't the way I heard it. Heard you snatched her outta the middle of that Injun camp. Heard there was plenty of lead flying. You took a round. That right?"

"Close 'nough. But you left out the parts about the fine scoutin' that put us on the camp before sunup. Left out the part about the coverin' fire that gave me the chance to git her to safety. Hell, I ended up half dead and unable to ride. Harris is the one that brought her back to her mother's arms. I barely made it home." He paused in recollection of the heartrending loss of Mark. "And a boy much too young took a Comanche bullet while I rested. Seems to me you missed a lot of the important details."

"No I didn't. I heard all them facts." He rolled the cheap cigar between his fingers, his expression drifting to a different place and time, a dark shadow coloring his face. Cramming it back in his mouth, he said, "Now I got a personal question for you."

Matt had exposed all the personal information he cared to for one day. He crossed his arms in defiance.

Sensing the wall separating them, Dawson demanded, "Where were you back in sixty-one when my sister took an arrow in her chest? Where were you when I watched her take her last breath crying for mom?"

Matt sat poker-faced. Dawson eyed him like a hawk, his penetrating stare probing his caged quarry.

"Thing is, you see. It didn't do her much good to cry for mom. Seeing as how the Sioux had already gutted her like a pig." He removed the cigar, looked at it smugly, and shoved it between his lips. "Indians got some mighty cruel ways. 'Course you know about that."

Dawson drifted back in time. Matt could see him reliving the tumultuous events behind his vacant blue eyes. Snapping back to the present, Dawson's expression clouded with a suppressed fury. "Tell you what. Her folks should be damned glad you got at least one of their kids back. Me, I lost my mom and sis at the same time. Might as well lost my dad too. He wasn't ever worth a penny after that day. Not that he ever was. After that, he drank himself senseless most the time. No point in me hanging around the house no more. I joined up with the Yankees. Met Ames, and been rambling with him ever since."

Surprised at the raw emotion the story elicited, Matt stood, his arms hanging loose at his sides. "Indians got the devil in 'em," was all he could say.

His voice subdued, Dawson said, "I don't have any use for 'em,"

"Ain't nobody in this county that'll argue with you on that point."

Dawson stood. Matt stepped back in awe of the physical dominance the man exuded as he moved towards the door. He stopped at the doorway and turned to address Matt. "Well, I'm sure we'll be seeing each other again. Might not be on friendly terms. That's up to you. You know what to do to stay on the good side of my boss." He adjusted his hat and tightened his belt up a notch. Before leaving he made a final comment. "You've done a fine job against them murdering Indians. That's something I've never had the chance at, but I keep hoping. Keep up the good work when you get out."

Matt watched him disappear out the door. It was like a vacuum sucked the air out of the cell. Matt had an acute understanding that an indomitable aura was gone. Chuckling inside, he remembered others had said the same thing about his own authoritative temperament. He also remembered that Robert once told him that the very things a man didn't like about others was more than likely the same characteristics he possessed. Matt sat on the bed fully aware that he still had a lot in life that he could learn. It was hard for him to swallow that a man like Dawson could be an instructor.

THIRTEEN

Hell broke loose outside the jail just before sundown. Matt heard agitated voices drifting up the street right before Nate came busting through the door. Cole held Nate up in the front office demanding to know what all the excitement was about. Nate rattled off a quick description about a Ranger defeat that sent Cole into the streets to investigate the distressing news.

Nate was breathless when he charged into the cell room. His eyes met Matt's, a mixture of anger and hurt at the same time. For a moment words failed him. Gulping, he started with an explanation no Texan wanted to deliver.

"It's bad, Matt. Them boys with Hobbs never stood no chance."

Matt ground his teeth in frustration. Stuck in this cell, he was compelled to endure what he found the hardest thing to do—listen to bad news and do nothing. He stood motionless with his anger simmering as Nate explained why only two Rangers from the latest mission returned. Matt screwed a lid down on his emotions. His face became an expressionless void. It was the only way he could handle the news.

He finally asked, "How many lost?"

"Six dead," came the grim reply of Nate.

"How the hell did it come to this?"

"Hobbs led 'em into an ambush at the Pedernales and Colorado junction."

Matt shook his head in disbelief. Nate fumbled with his hat in his hands.

"Hobbs one of the dead?"

Nate looked at the floor and nodded.

"Who else?"

"The Jones brothers and a couple of men from Bastrop. Ain't none of 'em had much experience fightin' Injuns. Carlson was also caught in the crossfire. From what I hear Hobbs led 'em straight into the Comanche at the crossin' below the Pedernales."

Appalled, Matt continued to shake his head in abhorrence of the facts he couldn't change. Carlson was a good man. The fact that he was green when it came to fighting Comanche didn't mean he deserved to die. He said, "That's a good spot to set up an ambush."

"Hobbs led 'em straight into it accordin' to Mossberg. Hobbs must've felt safe for some reason to ride first in the column."

"Stupidity or ignorance. Either one will git you kilt every time."

"The good news is Mossberg made it back unscratched. Rodgers is wounded, but he should be okay. He's at the doc's right now."

"What the hell was Mossberg doing with such a sorry bunch?"

"You'll have to ask him yourself. I ain't seen him. He went to report the loss to the gov'nor."

"It's a helluva note to lose men like that."

"Matt, them Comanch worked the men over bad. Cut 'em up for wolf bait and left 'em on the banks of the river."

Matt pounded on the bars, his face now a fountain of anger at the mention of mutilation. "Don't surprise me none. I heard all I want. Can't do nothin' locked up in here."

Nate pulled up a chair as the harsh reality dampened their spirits. They both stewed at the thought of what the Comanche were capable of doing to a defeated foe. Neither one of them felt like discussing the subject any further. Both of them were more suited to taking bold actions to correct a wrong than sitting around brooding about events they had no control over. They knew what needed to be done.

Nate broke the silence, "Jake came in earlier this afternoon. He's with Ma and Pa right now. Doc Hays is raisin' hell. Says nobody else is roomin' for free at his place. Jake will be beddin' down with me at the stables."

"He's an ornery old bastard. He does good doctorin', but I got little use for the man."

"You'll have even less use after what I got to tell you."

"You're just full of good news tonight, aren't you?"

"Hey. We're in Austin. What'd you 'xpect?"

"Go on then. Git it over."

Nate hesitated. "I probably shouldn't tell you this." He thought on it a moment longer before he finished, "But what the hell, it needs to be said."

Matt's attention focused on Nate like a cat eying a mouse.

Nate said, "Don't mean to bother you with it, but I think you should know."

He searched for the right words, but came up empty.

"Git to the point Nate."

Nate took a step, spit in the corner like he tasted something foul, and said, "Doc Hays has a little too much starch. He made an offer to Mary that's made her uncomfortable."

"An offer?"

"Yeah, an offer. He suggested she had the means to pay off Pa's bill."

"The means? That so?"

"Mary spilled the story to Ma the other night. Hays had been actin' crabby. Seems like he didn't care for it none when Mary declined his suggestion. He's been makin' us feel unwelcome since then. Mary broke down and told Ma what Doc said. Pa don't know nothin' 'bout it though."

"That's best for now. No need to rile him up. How's he doing?"

"He's better. Not ready to travel yet. But least ways we got Jake here to help bring him home. Just gotta git him over the hump."

"Hays is still givin' him medicine?"

"Yeah he is. But his manners are short. I cain't say nothin' or he'll quit treatin' Pa and run us all off."

"Best git Bull outta there soon as you can."

"Agreed. We'll be left with a helluva bill at that point."

Matt's eyes narrowed. His thoughts were simmering. His hands wrapped the bars in a vein-popping grip. Nate noticed the change come over his friend. This was the man that had earned his never-ending confidence. It was a shame he was still locked up in a town that exhibited no mercy.

Reading Nate's mind, Matt said, "I'll git out. When I do, it'll be my pleasure to deal with Hays. Meanwhile, make the most of a bad situation and make sure Bull gits the treatment he needs."

They shook hands and Nate left to get Jake settled in before dark. Matt walked to the window for a look at the deepening gloom of twilight. Men in the street were still engaged in loud conversations that he couldn't understand. They all tried to talk at once. The creeping sense of impotence sprung up again. It wormed its way into his thoughts and took up residence. What else could he do? Nothing. Men that were on the outside held all the cards. He couldn't make a play. Clenching the iron bars on the window he was reduced to nothing more than a spectator.

FOURTEEN

The cell walls were smothering him.

He felt their claustrophobic presence surrounding him, pinching out his breath. Pitch black obscured the details of the red brick wall, but he was suffocating inside the enclosure of the small cell. He could hear mice scurrying across the grimy floor. At least they could come and go as they wished. Trapped in a dark hell, Matt was forced to wrestle with thoughts of escape. He *had* to get out.

He couldn't sleep and it was three in the morning. There was no reason to sleep. He had done nothing for days and it was driving him crazy. He desperately needed to break free. The woods were calling him. He wanted to get lost in the hills. He wanted to be camped out next to clear running water. He wanted to be on a hunting expedition with good friends gathered around a roaring fire. If he listened close he could hear the water bubbling over a rocky ledge. The smell of roasting venison permeated the air. Owls called to one another with their hoots echoing through the silent landscape. Woodlands bathed in the glow of a full moon. It was heavenly.

But not as divine as the feel of a woman. He imagined the perfumed scent of a lady beside him on a bedroll under the milky-blue haze of a star-studded night. Gazing at the wondrous panorama of the expansive night sky, they would fall under a spell. The moment would become magical. Full of passionate stimulation and adrift in ecstasy, all their travails would be forgotten. Joined together as one, they would collapse on the blanket exhausted and gratified in each other's arms. It would be a heated moment experienced for all its worth and a memory to last a lifetime.

It dawned on him that this was not a fantasy. It was a blissful night he had spent with Cora years ago before children entered their lives. She had been a willing and eager partner on their spontaneous camping trips. They picked up and left whenever the mood struck. And it struck often in the early years of their marriage. After completing the long hard days building their cabin, they often treated themselves to a few nights alone in some secluded canyon enjoying the freshness of their vows. She had been enthusiastic and excited to please his desires. And he the same.

A wave of remorse crushed his ardor.

Things were changed now. They had drifted apart. Josh had passed on as well as her love for him. They no longer shared much together except the responsibility of nurturing their four remaining children. Good kids, they deserved a stable family, and he was determined to provide for them to the best of his abilities. Sitting in jail was a waste of time. He needed to be out working and raising cash to feed the ravenous appetite of the government. He needed to be home taking care of business.

Taking care of business was something the incompetent Hobbs had botched. Now the bodies of Rangers were littering the banks of the Colorado far upstream from his ranch. It was an unimaginable error to lead the men straight into an ambush. There had been no plan! He tossed to his other side trying to remove the disturbing image of mutilated men from his overactive imagination. It didn't do any good.

The rest of the night passed in a slow torturous ticking of individual seconds. After what seemed like an eternity, a lethargic sun crept above the horizon still hidden behind more of the same steel-gray clouds. The dreariness of the day's start only served to deepen his sense of emptiness. He felt as if he could climb the walls like a spider and hang from the ceiling. His mental stability began to seem doubtful.

Cole didn't help Matt's mood when he peeked in with his usual cheery greeting as if the jail couldn't be a more charming place to call home. He only laughed when he got a good look at Matt's scruffy hair and swollen eyes.

"Long night, heh?" he mocked.

"Every night's long."

"Least you still got your hair."

Matt ran his hands through his black hair. The sheriff had a good point. He wasn't sprawled out dead and left to feed a pack of wolves beside the river. Despite the long hours in jail, he would get out eventually. Or would he? The idea suddenly jumped out from nowhere. Would he get out? He hadn't thought of that possibility. What if Ames came up with some other trumped-up charge? What if the crooked judge saw fit to find him guilty?

Seeing the worsening expression, Cole asked, "You okay? Look like you lost your best friend."

"Hell no. I ain't okay. Don't be askin' stupid questions so damn early in the mornin'"

"Have it your way."

Cole stepped out of the cell room and went back to his duties behind his desk. His incessant whistling as he flipped through correspondence got on Matt's nerves to no end, but he bit his lip and suffered in silence as the long hours passed. He considered silence the best option with the weight of injustice bearing down on him until he couldn't trust his next response to provocation.

One of the girls from the café brought him a late breakfast that helped steady his nerves somewhat. He was actually relieved that Carmin couldn't make the delivery. He wasn't in the mood to face her tantalizing candor. Her tempting offer had played over and over in his mind during the lengthy night. A sense of culpability accompanied the realization that he would take her up on it if the right chance presented itself. Cora had deprived him far longer than he could stand. Enough was enough! He threw the plate on the bed in disgust when he finished the meal.

He spent the next thirty minutes pacing from one side of the cell to the other. It wasn't much exercise, but it was as good as he could expect. Irrepressible urges to hurt somebody began forming. This confinement was filling him with a dangerous mixture of resentment and hatred. He realized that he was changing. After twenty days in jail he was going to come out a different man. He could feel the transformation occurring as he paced. His skin prickled with an electric energy. Muscles twitched in irritable anticipation. He wanted to cause harm to those that set him up to endure the humiliation of confinement.

Stepping to the window, he took stock of the predicament. *He was changing.* He didn't like it, but it was inevitable. Now he understood the hardness of the men that had done time. It robbed them of their humanity. They became predators when released from jail for a reason. And he was only doing twenty days. He would never make it through a lengthy sentence. He wasn't sure he could make it through the rest of *this* time. At the least he wasn't sure he would emerge from jail happy with the man he was becoming.

Across the street he caught sight of a man and his wife strolling arm in arm. It was a somewhat unusual thing to see in Austin. Most couples maintained a specific decorum. Public displays of affection weren't unheard of, but were rare on the streets. In this case they seemed full of life and oblivious of what anybody thought. The picture of contentment struck a chord in his heart. He envied the couple. He yearned to be as they were rather than a bitter man locked away like an animal. He seized the cell bars in a grip that whitened his knuckles while he watched the two of them disappear into the mercantile.

Boisterous voices from the front office broke his contemplation. He recognized one of the booming salutations bombarding Cole. The new arrival spoke with the bass tone of a man used to being in command. Cole's response seemed tepid in comparison.

Surprised at the appearance of one so esteemed, Matt turned to see Governor Throckmorton enter his cell room. Several imposing men accompanied him and took up positions outside the door with their backs to Matt and facing Cole in his office. Crossing their arms in a defiant posture, it was evident nobody was to interrupt the Governor's conference with Matt.

Throckmorton was an imposing figure in his own right. He had served in the Confederate Cavalry Regiment as a captain in the Civil War and spent time as a Texas Ranger. His bearing still retained the military influence. He stood tall, proud and confident. His eyes reflected the clarity of a superior intellect without condescension. What he saw profoundly disturbed him. He ran his hand through his hair in disbelief.

"How are they treating you, Matt?"

"About as good as the Federals treat you."

"That's a damn shame. They're always a pain in the ass."

"I've never much liked the attitude of Yankees."

"And now we've got a whole pack of 'em breathing down our necks."

Matt frowned and said, "What's a man to do. They whipped us."

Throckmorton reached into his vest and produced two premium cigars. Passing one to Matt, he said, "I try not to think about that. What's done is done, but if I remember right, you like a good smoke."

They both took a moment to fire up the fine Cubans. Nothing was said until a cloud of smoke circulated in the drafty room. Matt held his smoke out at arms length to admire the quality he was rarely able to sample. He puffed in enjoyment of the rich tobacco flavor.

"Thanks gov'nor. This Cuban smoke could spoil me." He gave Throckmorton an appreciative nod and asked, "Now what can I do for you?"

Chuckling, the governor said, "Not much from where you're at, but I think we can come to an agreement that will remedy that dilemma."

"I'm all ears."

Growing solemn, Throckmorton said, "I'm sure you heard about the Hobbs tragedy."

"Shouldn't of happened."

"No argument here, but I'm obligated to deal with the reality. Which is that the Comanche are running wild across the hills. The Feds are slow learners and incompetent. Can't rely on them."

"Nothing new there."

Throckmorton eyed Matt, searching for insight. He wasn't sure of the Ranger's depth of knowledge. There was only one way to find out. He asked Matt, "Have you heard about the attacks on the freight wagons run by our friend Ames?"

"That one has escaped me. All I've heard is that some of their raids are mighty close to Austin."

"Too damn close. And too damn many. They've killed some freighters working for Ames. Destroyed or made off with all kinds of valuable goods carried on his wagons. Cash too."

"Sorry, but I can't sympathize."

"Those are commodities badly needed by the community. Our feelings about Ames don't enter the equation."

"I understand."

The governor let the comment sink in. Matt needed a moment to realize the sales pitch was coming. Matt's countenance changed. He was ready.

"I'm organizing another mission for a handpicked group of Rangers. No more drunks like Hobbs. I got bad counsel on the man's capabilities. This ones going to be my baby all the way." He paused for effect, and said, "I want you to lead."

Matt waved his arms across his enclosure. "Hard to do much while I'm in here."

"That's where I can be of assistance. I've got pardon papers with me. All you've got to do is agree."

Matt stepped up to the bars and took a long drag on the cigar while he appraised Throckmorton. Raising his head, he blew a gray cloud of smoke to the ceiling.

"I had a helluva time gittin' paid as a Ranger last time."

"Payroll will be handled directly out of my office. Harris and Ames are cut out of this deal."

Matt nodded in approval. "You've got my attention." Staring the governor in the eyes, Matt asked, "I pick the men?"

"You pick the men. You lead as captain with my full support."

"How about spare mounts?"

"Funny you should ask. Those mounts you sold the government that Harris said were scattered all over the state? Well, I've put my men on it and most have been located. They'll be yours to use."

"You're makin' a temptin' offer."

Throckmorton remained silent. Sometimes a man required a quiet minute to reach his own conclusions. It was a good sales technique he learned from a relative in the merchandising business.

After thinking on the proposal, Matt said, "I pick the men. I pick Nate for my scout. Is that a problem?"

"Nate's the scout that didn't receive his pay?"

"That's right."

"I'll go you one better. You pick him to scout. He does his job to your satisfaction. I'll make sure he receives his back pay."

Matt thrust his hand through the bars and vigorously pumped the governor's hand. Both men grinned at the satisfaction of a mutually beneficial arrangement.

Throckmorton laughed in relief. He said, "You want the icing?"

"What do you mean?"

"I've done a little digging since we last met."

Throckmorton's face brightened as he dawdled. Matt appeared perplexed while he was left hanging. The governor enjoyed the suspense before he said, "I have an associate working on the appeal Ames supposedly filed on your behalf."

"The appeal asking for my back pay before you stepped in and paid me?"

"That's the one Ames threatened you with. If you lost the appeal you'd have to pay back your money."

It was the axe hanging over Matt's head. If Ames controlled the appeals board, and Matt was sure he did, he would be compelled by court order to return all the money and that would put him back to facing bankruptcy. Selling his place would be the only option left to feed his kids. Then Ames could swoop in and scoop up his homestead for pennies on the dollar.

Throckmorton reassured him, "Don't worry about that threat no more. My man on the inside says he'll get you a favorable ruling."

Matt literally sensed a weight sliding off his back. This was too good to be true.

"I'm pulling out all the stops, Matt. I'm on the way out. It's just a matter of time. There's no way I can keep the Yankees in this town happy. Ames no longer matters to me. I'm going to create a stir. Run things the way I see fit until I'm removed from office. I'll leave a legacy talked about for years."

Throckmorton broke out in a big grin. He resembled a boy hiding a big secret. He was giddy when he said, "Won't this be something? I've got you heading up the Rangers out to prevent the Indians from robbing Ames. He raised hell about the Comanche raids that are costing him so much money. He'll drop dead at the idea of you earning cash to fix a situation he cried about."

Matt was taken aback by the rolling fit of laughter that overtook the governor. He couldn't help but join Throckmorton and smile at the irony of the proposed solution. They shared a moment of bonding in pure enjoyment at the turning of the tables.

Composing his wits, Throckmorton said, "I never cared for that damned Yankee one bit. He was always strutting around like he was the only rooster in town. This'll take him down a notch." Lowering his voice, he said to Matt, "Now watch the reaction of Cole. He ain't gonna like the news I'm fixin' to deliver."

Matt was amazed at the transformation of the governor. The man was in his full glory. He sprang to the door and poked his head between his bodyguards to demand, "Cole! Get me your keys. We've got a prisoner to release!"

The lack of a quick response spoke volumes. Matt couldn't see him, but knew Cole was stunned at the request.

Throckmorton elevated his voice a notch, "Let's have the keys. Now!"

Cole fumbled for the right words and finally blurted, "On what authority?"

The fierce scowl of the governor burned a hole in Cole. Pulling papers from his vest, Throckmorton slapped them on Cole's desk with a *thwack.*

"There you are sheriff. That's a pardon for the trumped up charges against an unfairly prosecuted citizen. A citizen that I might add is now a captain in the Rangers. I'd suggest you treat him with respect."

Cole picked up the papers and thumbed through them. He checked the governor's signature and stamp. He had never seen pardon papers before, but these looked authentic. Throckmorton was staring down at him like an eagle sizing up a rabbit. Standing to meet the challenge, he pitched the papers back on his desk.

"I'll have to see the judge about this," Cole said.

"I don't think so. Those papers are a decree issued by my office. The judge doesn't have a say in this matter."

Cole scratched his head. He wasn't sure.

"Sir. I won't ask again. Unlock the cell and let this man free."

The two bodyguards moved forward. There was no possibility to resist. His deputies were out patrolling the streets and he wasn't going to get into a scuffle with a governor and two men built like bulls. He opened the drawer and grabbed the keys. Throckmorton shadowed him as he entered the cell room. The keys jingled as he turned them in the lock and swung the door open.

Matt had never heard a sweeter sound. He quickly gathered his hat and belongings and barged out the door. He faced Cole and said, "Just doing your job, Cole. Don't mean Ames has to like it."

They made it to the front door when it dawned on Matt they had unfinished business. He tapped Throckmorton on the shoulder and said, "One last thing gov'nor. I may need your backing on this."

Throckmorton nodded okay and stood at the door.

Matt addressed Cole, "When I send Nate back for his guns, there won't be a problem, will there?"

Trying to preserve his dignity, Cole said, "That's a different issue altogether."

"I'm a captain in the Rangers. I'm using my authority granted by the governor of Texas to assemble a group of Rangers to protect the interests of businessmen like Ames. Do you really want to stand in my way?"

The governor's men crossed their arms in a show of contempt. The governor himself wore the air of a man who had run out of patience. Matt just looked like Matt. He always appeared like he was ready to lower the hammer.

In a flat voice Cole said, "He'll get his guns."

Matt tipped the brim of his hat and turned to leave with Throckmorton. He never wanted to see the inside of a jail again as long as he lived.

Behind them Cole took a heavy seat in his chair. He knew there was going to be hell to pay with Ames. Muttering to the walls, he said, "I might be out of a job."

FIFTEEN

Matt and the governor discussed the details of the upcoming assignment on the stroll back to his office. With the immediate problems solved, a bond grew between them as they swapped stories about their participation in the seemingly endless violence that raged across the Texas frontier. Throckmorton told Matt that he had originally joined the First Texas Volunteers as a private at the outbreak of the Mexican-American War in February 1847. His health did not hold up and he found himself assigned as an assistant surgeon to the Texas Rangers. During the Civil War he served in the cavalry as a captain until poor health once again compelled an early resignation. Throckmorton did most of the talking. He was a practiced orator, and like most politicians loved to hear himself pontificate. Matt wasn't complaining. The man spun an interesting tale and was a saint compared to most of the snakes denned up in Austin.

Taking leave of the governor after he received half of his pay, Matt felt a strange elation. He had spendable cash in his pocket and he was a free man! True, there were plenty of details to take care of with men and supplies to be rounded up, and rightfully so, the governor expected him to be out on the tail of the Comanche as soon as possible. But in the meantime he was a free man! The chains were lifted. He felt light as a feather as he made his way through town to the doctor's office. First he had to stop off at the hotel for a hot bath before checking up on his old friend, Bull. Then he could locate Mossberg and learn more about the Hobbs disaster. He hoped the Kentuckian would be interested in another mission. It might be too soon for him considering his recent experience, but Matt held out hope. Charles Mossberg was a good man to have, especially without the influence of Harris to color his opinions like he tried to do on the rescue mission of the Havens children.

Feeling like a new man after the bath, Matt stalked with confidence to the doctor's office. Arriving at the door, Matt composed himself before he heaved it open and stepped inside, a force to be reckoned with. Looking up from his desk, Hays instantly sensed the hostility of his visitor with his chest puffed out ready for a confrontation. Matt's notorious scowl was gloomier than usual. Hays considered the man a menace to those that adhered to the honorable code of gentlemen residing in the city. Disturbed by the unanticipated arrival, he wondered what the hell Matt was doing out of jail. It was much too soon. And he damn sure didn't like putting up with an attitude in *his* office.

In a condescending tone, Hays asked, "What can I do for you, Matt?"

Matt bored a hole through the doctor with a look that withered most men. Hays was no different. He immediately regretted falling into the trap of overconfidence in the face of the rugged frontiersman. Everybody knew to treat Matt with respect. He knew it too, but after all it was his office, and that should count for something.

Matt continued to stare at him. He didn't say anything. He just stood there glaring.

"Can I be of help?" Hays asked in a more conciliatory manner.

Snapping out of his trance, Matt said, "Here to see Bull."

Without explanation he stalked past the doctor and found Bull alone in his room. He was dozing. Matt placed his hat crown down on the bedside table. The ragged hat with a bullet hole in it didn't need to be cared for, but it was an old habit for him when in a public setting.

Bull heard Matt shuffling around and cracked open an eye. Approval registered in the gleam of Bull's surprised expression. Matt was always welcome.

"Well, I'll be damned! Didn't 'xpect you for some time yet," Bull said.

Matt took a seat next to the bed pleased to see his neighbor improved in health.

"I flew the coop."

Bull wrinkled his nose. He smelled a skunk in Matt's excuse.

"It ain't what you think," Matt said.

"Good." Puzzled, he asked, "What is it then?"

"Throckmorton saw fit to pardon me."

Matt finished his clarification and emphasized the details of the imminent Ranger mission. Bull received the full story in amazement. He was particularly delighted to hear the role of Nate as a scout.

"That'll make him a happy man. He hasn't been able to find work and we need the money in a bad way. I cain't wait 'til they git back from eatin' to share the news with 'em. Damn glad of your help, Matt."

"Proud to do what I can. Speakin' of which, have you considered my offer to move over to my place and help out with the work?"

Bull nodded yes, but Matt noted the pall of defeat come over Bull's normal demeanor. His entire face sagged in resignation. He visibly aged ten years. Matt knew it would hurt to fall back on the assistance of neighbors after losing his place to Ames, but he had a plan to alleviate Bull's wounded pride.

Matt said, "I've been thinkin' on the idea. Here's what I propose. You and your boys farm the black lands beside the river. It's more than my boys and Lee can handle. Help with the mustang roundup and horse rearing we plan on. Y'all are old hands at that kind of work."

"Ain't nothin' we cain't do," Bull agreed.

Now Matt could lay in the salve to sooth Bull's sense of independence.

"This is a business deal. The first five years you pay me twenty-five percent of your annual take on the crops and mustangs we corral. Whatever that figures out to be will be the price for the thousand acres between the river flats and Panther Hollow, and then on up to Four Points."

"That's a lot of land. You ain't askin' much for it," Bull said.

"I'm gittin' strong backs to help me build a dependable stream of income. Not to mention a good neighbor which may be hard to come by after Ames cuts up the land to sell to who knows who. It's a helluva deal for both of us."

Bull thought a moment and nodded in agreement. A spark lit his eyes. Matt could tell Bull was pleased.

"I think it's a good plan, Matt. Yeah, I like the idea of a fresh start. We need to toast to the partnership."

"What does the doc say about drinkin'?"

A frown replaced Bull's enthusiasm. He complained, "I ain't had a pull since I got here. Doc cut me off. Says it gits in the way of healin'."

"That right?"

"Sure 'nuff."

Matt looked around the room and didn't see any of the whiskey jugs that always accompanied Bull. He held a finger up to Bull and said, "I'll be right back."

Hays had his nose buried in his ledger adding up the numbers for the treatments of the past week. It was a fine tally. The residents of Austin were in dire need of his overpriced services and he was more than happy to accommodate them. His concentration when it came to counting his money was so intense that he didn't acknowledge Matt's existence.

Matt cleared his throat.

Hays said, "I'll be right with you." Penciling in the closing amount, he looked up at Matt and pompously asked, "Can I help you?"

The doctor involuntarily flinched when Matt moved toward him. It was the piercing scrutiny driven home with a tone of voice that Hays would never forget. He heard Matt say, "I'll start with that jug behind you."

Pushing his chair back to stand, he made room for Matt to grab the jug on the shelf above his desk. Not sure where the courage to speak came from, Hays protested, "That's my liquor."

Matt held the jug up to inspect the contents.

"Looks like a gallon of Bull's finest to me."

"Well, yes. Yes it is, but it's part of his payment for my treatment."

Tightening his focus on Hays, Matt stepped up chest to chest as he said, "Gittin' paid is important to you. Ain't it?"

Heming and hawing, Hays finally uttered, "It's important to any professional."

Standing six inches taller than the doc, Matt closed the remaining gap to Hays and stared directly into his eyes taking his measure as a man. Unnerved, Hays took a step back.

"Important enough to make an improper offer to a lady?"

Hays couldn't be sure what Matt knew, but he definitely knew enough to make waves. The roar of a waterfall commenced in his ears. Not sure how to counter, he said, "I . . . I don't know what you're talking about."

Instantly, Matt closed the distance again. This time he pressed up against the chest of the doctor. Hays froze in his steps. He was out of room. Matt was out of patience.

"I won't listen to nonsense. I'm here to put an end to your behavior. I won't tolerate inappropriate suggestions to Mary or harassment of Bull and his family. You'll git paid when he's got the cash or barter goods to make it even."

Tongue-tied, Hays couldn't form a response.

"Are we clear?"

Hays didn't have a choice, he nodded yes.

"Good then. You'll also find the courtesy to offer an apology to Mary for your unsolicited advances."

Matt got a blank look in return.

"I'll check with her to make sure she's treated like the lady she is." Pointing at the doctor's ledger, he said, "Make an entry in there for the debt owed her. You can never tell when I'll be back to audit your books." His tone hardened when he said, "There'll be hell to pay if she's not satisfied with your apology."

Matt turned his back on the humbled doctor and winked at Bull when he entered the room. Bull grinned and gave Matt a thumbs up. He had heard the entire exchange. Matt poured a generous shot of moonshine for both of them to enjoy without the ladies or doc around to badger them.

Bull raised his glass to Matt's in a toast. Their glasses clinked as Matt said, "Here's to a successful partnership."

SIXTEEN

Stepping out of the doctor's office, Matt gazed up and down the busy streets. He needed to find Mossberg. Several places stood out as the most likely spots to locate him. He could be occupied with filing the papers detailing their costly defeat on the Colorado, but Matt assumed that requirement had already been completed. Charles would most likely be at the saloon or at the cafe. Matt decided the saloon was the best bet and he strode down the boardwalk with a purpose.

Arriving at the saloon, he pushed through the door and surveyed the sparse crowd. It was early yet and Mossberg was nowhere to be seen. Several hard-edged drinkers twisted to catch a glimpse of the new arrival, but Matt didn't see anyone he would be interested in putting to Ranger work. It was off to the café with doubt building about the difficulty of securing the most qualified Rangers that he knew in the Austin area.

When he came to the café door, he balked before entering. There was the possibility of running into Ames and he had to gather himself for the encounter. It was sure to be an ugly scene. He had to exercise restraint. Taking a composing breath, he grabbed the knob and shoved the door open.

The aroma of food frying and bread baking swept over him. Jail time had deprived him of these sensory delights and he lingered at the door to relish the intoxicating scent of freedom. The hum of normal conversation in a pleasant surrounding was music to his ears. He had begun to wonder if he would make it out of the jail with his sanity intact. It was good to be back in action where he belonged.

Sweeping his eyes across the crowded room, he was glad to see Charles sitting at a table near the kitchen. To make it even better, he saw that Tom, the cook and horse holder at the Enchanted Rock battle, was with Charles at the table along with JB. That made three men he wanted with him on this operation. It was a great stroke of luck to run into them all at once.

Mossberg saw Matt standing at the door and his expression signaled a genuine happiness at the surprise meeting. He pointed at the empty chair and waved Matt over to take a seat. Eager to share the good news about the company of Rangers he was forming, Matt suffered from tunnel vision on his way to the table.

Halfway to the table, a familiar voice held him back like a river crossing flooded with spring rain.

"Matt?"

He turned to find Harris at a table next to him. There was no avoiding the man. It was like finding a scorpion in your boots. The sting would hurt like hell if you ignored the threat.

"Harris."

His surprise obvious, it took Harris a moment to ask, "How are you doing?"

Matt knew Harris didn't give a damn how he was faring. It felt good to see the shock on his face. Senator Archer sat across from Harris and looked even more stunned than the former captain of the Rangers. Matt saw his opportunity to pile on the awkwardness, pulled out an empty chair, and took a seat. Harris gave Archer a muddled look as their uninvited guest sat between them. Matt waved over at Mossberg in a gesture letting them know he wouldn't be long.

Grinning, Matt said, "Go ahead gentlemen. Don't let me interrupt your meal."

Archer's jaw hung loose. Matt's appearance stood between him and a pork chop covered in thick cream gravy. He grabbed a slice of toasted bread and dipped it into the gravy. Cramming the bread in his mouth, he gave Harris a disturbed glare. This hick from the hills got under his skin and besides Ames had promised he would be out of the way for a long time. Yet here he sat. Something had gone wrong and he intended to get to the bottom of the fracture in their carefully laid plans.

Harris forgot his half-finished meal while Archer never missed a beat attacking his plate with a renewed vengeance. The presence of Matt perturbed him to no end, but he would not give the Ranger the satisfaction of disrupting his feeding time. His beady eyes burrowed in on Matt who seemed oblivious of his inspection.

In fact, Matt wasn't ignorant of details surrounding him. He had already surveyed the entire room and knew where any potential problem makers were located. Archer was in his peripheral vision, but the loud smacking as he devoured his food let him know that the Senator was going to let Harris do the talking.

"So, Matt, I'm glad to see you're out of jail," Harris began timidly.

"Is that a fact?" Matt retorted with a chilly tone.

"I never wished you any harm." Harris resented the inflection in Matt's question. He added, "You'd show more intelligence if you'd just get out of the way of Ames."

"Insult isn't going to git you anywhere Harris." He waved his hand across the room. "Dawson's not here to pull you out of the fire if you should cross the line."

"Okay. We know where we stand with each other. You're free to leave."

Archer sawed away at his pork. Cream gravy dripped from his lip when he said, "Before you depart, I'd like to know why you haven't completed your sentence."

Matt leaned back in his chair to get a good look at both of the scoundrels at the same time. He wanted to see their faces when he told them the specifics of his early parole. Lingering a moment for suspense, he finally lowered the boom on them. "I'm working for the gov'nor again. He delivered a pardon straight to the hands of Cole. It seems like Ames has tired of Comanche disrupting his freight business."

He wasn't disappointed in the response. Both men looked like they had just witnessed the death of a favorite dog. Archer rested his knife and fork. Their jaws dangled speechless while each one waited for the other to offer a snappy comeback.

Neither man had anything to say, so Matt offered a parting bit of wisdom. "I took his offer to serve as a captain. Seems like you suggested that to me one time, Harris. The difference is that you two have been dealt out of this hand. There won't be any of your dirty accounting tricks this time. Pay's guaranteed. I'm empowered to do my job to the best of my abilities. Indian raids are first on my list, but arresting anybody breaking the law is included in my duties."

Matt stood to peer down his nose at the politicians. There wasn't a group of men he despised more than the slick dressed and double-talking lawmakers making the capital city their home. Their main purpose in life was to see to their own reelection and fattening their own wallets. In his opinion these two were members of the worst group of offenders in Austin.

Tipping his hat in a display of manners, Matt said, "Good day to you men. Enjoy your meal."

Harris sat back in his chair, glad that Matt had left without any violence erupting. That's when it dawned on him. Matt had insinuated he was out to arrest them if he got the chance. Archer chewed his food in ignorance of the threat.

Harris said, "He's a man to be reckoned with."

Archer became contemplative. He patted at his mouth with a napkin. Nodding, he said, "I think you're one hundred percent correct. He is convicted of conduct unbecoming a gentleman. He's not fit to lead men." Thinking on the threat Matt posed, he remarked, "It's a shame we can't toll the new roads. We could hammer him every time he came to market. Instead we'll have to raise the taxes as high as possible. We'll pluck his wallet, along with the others, as much as we can get away with. And in as many ways as possible."

"Count on my help when I'm elected."

A wry grin lit up Archer's face. He looked around the café with mischief on his mind. In a low voice he confided to Harris, "We'll have plenty of time to work him over. Once you're in office we can dream up all kinds of ways to pick the pockets of the unworthy citizens in this county. We'll also have the time and means to get rid of Throckmorton. The tide is rising against that egotistical bastard. His time is running out."

"Can we count on that?"

Cramming a slice of fat pork in his mouth, Archer said, "Take it to the bank. He'll soon be gone. Then making law gets easier." Beaming with anticipation, he gloated, "And our wallets get fatter."

Matt was unaware of the plots being discussed behind his back as he ambled to the table where Mossberg sat with men that he considered the salt of the earth. He received a vigorous handshake and a friendly welcome to have a seat at their table. Glad to share good camaraderie, he pulled up a chair and began explaining his plans for the upcoming assignment. He had a captivated audience hanging on every word. By the end of his presentation he had enlisted three men eager to make a difference in the Texas Hill Country.

Mossberg signed on to be his second in command as a sergeant while Tom would once again serve as cook and anywhere else Matt deemed necessary. He put all three of them in charge of rounding up more Rangers that had a good reputation. He didn't want inexperienced men on this hazardous undertaking. It was in all of their best interests to have men riding beside them that could handle the heat.

There was only one exception Matt asked the men to ponder. He requested that the dad of the Havens girl be allowed to accompany them into the hills. After a brief discussion, nobody objected and Mossberg volunteered to ride out to the Havens place and bring him in by the next morning. Charles felt a sense of loyalty to the despondent father who also happened to be his friend. Vouching for Cliff Havens, Mossberg said he was a good hand and he felt no reluctance at having him serve at his side. He knew him to be a good shot and cool under pressure.

Thrilled at the lucky turn of events, Matt didn't think it could get any better, but he was wrong. The owner of the café peeked out the kitchen door and saw Matt sitting at the table. Without hesitation he rushed up to the table in good cheer and happy to see Matt out of jail. He apologized for the unjust treatment at the hands of a biased court. True to his word, he personally grilled a thick juicy steak for Matt and slopped on a heaping pile of creamy mashed potatoes alongside a sea of black-eyed peas spiced with chopped onions and slabs of fat bacon. Chunks of bread hot from the oven and dripping with butter helped Matt forget the long and lonely days locked up in jail like a common criminal.

Finished with eating, the men headed for the door to get started on the business of organizing a dangerous Ranger operation. Matt was detained while thanking the café owner for the generous food arrangements during his time in jail. His social obligations complete, Matt broke loose, his attention now dedicated to final preparations. There were a dozen details that needed completion. He strode past the table vacated by the two shysters, glad they were gone.

Stopping outside the café door, he ran the errands through his head trying to put them in order. First he had to get Nate rounded up and on the right path. The volatile scout required a little handholding at times to keep him pointed the right direction. Then he had to make sure the stock Throckmorton promised had been delivered to Jed's livery stable. The list grew the more he contemplated just the basic necessities, and he wanted out of Austin by tomorrow if at all possible.

That's when he heard her beckoning him. There was no mistaking the sensuous quality of her speaking his name. His arousal was instant. He reasoned that he wouldn't be normal to resist such a temptation. No man in his right mind could.

Her sweet fragrance floated to him on the gentle breeze. He was seduced before he even laid eyes on her. Breathing deep, he let the enchanting scent of her perfume carry him away. The time had come. He turned to face one of the women of his fantasies.

Touching him lightly on the arm, Carmin said "Matt? How'd you get out so soon?"

She was just arriving for her shift and a sight for sore eyes. He marveled at the allure that enveloped her. She was all curves and fully conscious of what that meant to a man. He felt fortunate that she was attracted to him, and uneasy at the same time.

"The gov'nor saw fit to release me. I'm on Ranger duty now."

"Ranger duty? So you're heading out to take care of the Indian problem?"

"That's the idea."

Her reaction was familiar. Her shoulders sagged and she seemed disturbed. It was an all too familiar scene. And one he had seen too many times in the past. She looked just like Cora when he delivered news of his Ranger duties. A pang of guilt stabbed his heart.

"When do you leave?"

"Soon as we git organized. Maybe tomorrow."

"So you get out of jail one day and leave the next?"

"That's 'bout the size of it."

A change came over her. She was thinking. Sorting things out.

"Doesn't give us much time to share."

Not believing the words coming out of his mouth, he said, "We've got tonight."

Frowning, she said, "I've already made plans for this evening."

"Change 'em."

"I can't."

The brooding expression on her face told the truth. She meant what she said. She couldn't change her mind. Matt had no way of knowing the importance of her plans and it wasn't in his nature to push a woman to get what he craved. Either it flushed out the way he wanted or it didn't. He had made it a habit to go with the flow when it came to women in his roaming days. That saved everybody involved a bundle of frustration.

She read his response and saw his disappointment. He had no way to understand her plight, but she had to attend the party tonight with Ames. It was to be a big gala and a lot of influential people would be there. Maybe somebody that could rescue her from the life of a waitress. It was her only hope to escape the never-ending drudgery of working for tips and fending off the unsolicited advances of men with no future. She saw no other way out of the trap her life had become. When she moved to Austin it was supposed to be the best option to supply the answer to her dreams. For heaven's sake, it was the capital of Texas. She had presumed the men would be different, but she had been wrong. Dead wrong.

Matt was the only man she felt a genuine attraction for, and he was married. It was rotten luck. Her patience had about run its course. Tonight's party might be her best chance yet to meet the right man. She couldn't miss this opportunity. But there stood Matt. She couldn't miss this opportunity either. It had been too long for her just as she was sure it had been too long for him.

She wanted to reach out and hold him, but refrained. They were in a public setting and it wouldn't be right to put him in an awkward position. Instead, she turned on the charm, purring, "Stop by the café for breakfast. Then drop by my place after I get off the early shift." Her bedroom eyes spoke volumes. She meant what she said. "It's that easy. Wait one more night."

Matt's pulse quickened at the thought. Carmin was definitely not like other women he had known. Cora's comment, "You can buy a cure for what ails you," echoed through the vacant cavity of his conscience.

SEVENTEEN

Colonel Ames was having a productive day. The backlog of paperwork on his desk had been completed. Several large tracts of land west of Austin were now officially under his control. The bill to fund the road expansion with higher taxes was progressing through the legislative process to his satisfaction. Once the new roads connected his freshly attained properties the value on them would rise steeply. Everything appeared ready to fall into place like clockwork. He had one final chore to take care of before he could call it a day and get ready for the ball.

Thoughts of the upcoming dance brought a quickening sense of euphoria. It would be a grand occasion. Numerous high-powered politicians, dignitaries and businessmen would be in attendance. Fine food would be in abundance and potent drinks would flow like honey. The stimulation of such opulence would be enthralling. All the attendees would be under the seductive influence of their shared wealth and privilege on public display. It was a club of which he had toiled long and hard to become an accepted member.

He drifted down the boardwalk lost in dreamy meditation of his success. He was on the brink of phenomenal riches. Already wealthy, it was never enough. All that he had acquired only fed the desire for more. His insatiable appetite continued to grow with every new conquest. He enjoyed the craving. It made him feel alive. He received never-ending satisfaction in the envious glances of those beneath him in social status. He had earned his prestige and high community standing from hard work and perseverance.

Superior intelligence, strong work ethic, and diligence in taking care of the details made up his strong attributes. He didn't waste time on the concerns of those who didn't measure up to his standards. Those poor saps were put on the earth to provide for men like him that possessed the aptitude to manage the big picture.

He was the man. He had a grasp on the big picture. The only thing missing was the company of a woman. And he had that drawback figured out. Carmin. Her presence at his side would make the perfect accessory to complement his superiority at the ball. He absolutely loved to lord it over his competition. And of course there was the undeniable sensuous charm she had been blessed with. He couldn't wait to taste her skin and hold her supple body next to his. Tonight would be the night. He could sense the inevitability in the air.

Pausing at the door, he brushed a stray piece of lint off his glossy black coat. Silently pushing the door open, he caught Cole with his feet propped up on his desk, a newspaper in his hand. Cole gave him a quick study out of the corner of his eye and dropped his boots to the floor. Plopping the paper to his desk, he casually stood to greet Ames.

"Hello, Colonel. To what do I owe this unexpected visit?"

Ames surveyed the room. There was nobody else present.

"Where are your deputies?"

"Out making their rounds."

"Good. We've got business to take care of."

Cole nodded and sat down, waving for Ames to pull up his own chair. Instead, he strolled over to the cell room entrance and peered around the corner. He froze in place. A grim scowl scorched Cole when the colonel faced the sheriff and growled, "Where's the prisoner?"

Cole shrugged as he replied, "It ain't my doings."

"What the hell do you mean? It's your jail! Where's he at?"

"Had to release him."

Astonished, Ames struggled to find the right words.

"Had to release him?"

"Was ordered."

It hit Ames like a mule kick to his gut.

"Throckmorton?"

Cole dug the pardon papers out of his desk and tossed them to

Ames. They landed on the edge of the desk with a plop. Ames gawked at the documents like they were a rattler, not willing to pick them up. Disappointed, he tramped to the window lost in thought. Cole waited patiently while the man that controlled his future gathered his wits.

Speaking to the window, Ames calmly asked, "Do you have more information?"

"You're not gonna like it."

"No surprise there. Let's have it."

"He's leading the Rangers out to end the Indian raids."

"Humph! Careful what you ask for Matt. It's mighty dangerous out there in the hills."

An awkward silence hung like a weight in the office while Ames gave the new situation thorough consideration. After a few minutes, he tore himself away from the window and took a seat across from Cole. The hawk-like glare of the Yankee bored in on the sheriff. Cole felt his stomach tighten.

"Okay," Ames said. "Throckmorton pulled a quick one. Not much you could do about it. That's understood. Don't like it none, but what's done is done. What's imperative is that we retain control from here on out. Understand?"

Cole realized Ames was letting him off lightly. There had to be a catch. He nodded yes, happy not to get a tongue-lashing.

"Good then. I've got another question for you."

"Shoot."

Ames leaned forward to ask in a sly voice, "Where's the two thousand?"

The colonel was asking about the dirty money he had paid Kern to murder Matt. Cole had been anxious about the ultimate distribution of the cash after the conversation with Matt. He had a hunch he was getting ready to find out more than he wanted to know. With a false bluster, he answered, "Locked up as evidence."

Ames snickered. "Evidence? *Hell*, that's my money."

"What would the judge say?"

"That's already taken care of."

"Guaranteed?"

"I run this town don't I?"

Motioning to the empty cell, Cole replied, "Ain't everybody under your control."

Doubting the allegiance of Cole, Ames said, "You've got no worries."

"My job's on the line."

The glower of the hawk intensified.

"I want the money back. Don't make trouble over this."

Cole rebutted, "If I'm fired, I can't do you no good. Folks know about the money. Matt made sure of that."

"Put it in my hands. I'll handle the details."

Cole knew he was vulnerable in this situation. Somebody could start snooping at any time. He could lose either way, but he didn't stand a chance if he rejected the demand of Ames.

Sensing the uneasiness of the sheriff, Ames said, "Report it as stolen if the wrong person asks."

"Stolen?" Cole chuckled at the absurd suggestion. "Yeah. They'll think I stole it."

"You're not very creative. Are you?"

Cole bit his tongue and shut up. Sometimes that was the best course to take when dealing with master manipulators like Ames.

"Look, Cole, I have techniques to deal with this sort of thing. It won't be an issue. The judge will see to that. He's bought and paid for. On the same side as we are."

Ames started to tense up, but hid the signs from Cole. The two thousand dollars was to become his personal play money. The syndicate ledgers itemized the funds as already spent. They would never suspect that he had reacquired the cash. There would be no audit trail. It was the perfect solution to pad his pay. The only hitch was Cole. By rights he shouldn't have to explain anything to the sheriff. Cole owed his livelihood to the influence he wielded in Austin, but his control of the sheriff was slipping away. It was time for a replacement. And the to-do-list just got longer.

Tapping the desk, Ames assured him, "Leave the cover-up to me. Nothing will be said."

His stomach in knots, Cole rose from his chair. In too far to back out, he snatched the keys and unlocked the cabinet. The cash sat in a corner next to Nate's revolver. He fished out the hefty bundle and fondled the currency dreaming that it was his. It was a hopeless dream. He would never have that much money unless he aggressively worked the other side of the law, and he didn't have that kind of courage. Reluctantly, he handed the cash to Ames.

The feel of the paper brought a great satisfaction to Ames. He squeezed the wad as he shoved it to the bottom of his pocket. It felt so soothing in his hands. It was a nice sensation to be rich. He wondered what Carmin would think when he flashed the green. It was almost time to find out. Distracted with thoughts of the evening to come, he strode out the door without a word of consideration for a sheriff bought and paid for with the proceeds of a heartless syndicate.

Matt had some vital tasks completed. He had the extra ammo stored securely at Jed's stable. A few of the horses promised by the governor were now in the corral behind the barn. More were on the way. It was all coming together nicely. He needed to pick up some poultice and bandage materials from the general store down the main avenue from the livery yard. He was making good headway and on his way to complete the errands when he saw him.

There was no mistaking the long strides of a man going somewhere. His erect posture reminded Matt of a strutting rooster. He considered himself the cock of the yard. Master of all that he could see. The arrogance of the man turned Matt's stomach with revulsion. There was nobody he least wanted to encounter. There was also nobody he wanted more to confront.

Patiently, he waited behind a post to avoid giving away his location. Like a spider's web, he spun a trap to ensnare his quarry with no chance for escape. At the last moment he stepped out from the post and blocked Ames with his arms folded in defiance. The colonel stopped without a show of emotion. Like two rutting deer, they faced each other with growing determination before the inevitable clash.

Never patient, Ames spoke first. "You're a lucky man."

"I would say you're the one ridin' a streak of good luck."

"Luck has nothing to do with my fate."

"Seems like the Comanche have turned the tables on you."

"Nothing that can't be handled."

"That's where I come in. Looks like they're a problem grown bigger than you can manage."

"Don't kid yourself, Matt," he said. "What you think is of little consequence. Go on and tackle the Comanche. They cause minor inconveniences. The events happening here in Austin are where the real profit is made. So go on. Do whatever tickles your fancy against a tribe of barbarians. And good luck. Remember, it's your scalp that could end up hanging from their lodge poles."

"Let's git this straight. What is it Kern called me? Oh yeah. Backwoods hick. How'd that turn out for him?"

Ames fell silent. Kern wasn't a subject he liked to discuss. Matt gauged the difference in the expression of Ames. He knew he struck a nerve that tingled. It was time to drive the knife home.

"Speaking of Kern. Where's the cash you paid him?"

Ames was capable of maintaining a straight poker face. But Matt had him on the ropes and he felt the warmth of anger flush across his face. Management of the conversation had slipped from his grasp. He had to turn the tide as a matter of pride.

"Careful, Matt. Your tongue is what got you behind bars last time."

"Careful, Ames. Your ignorance is causing you to misread the change in circumstances this time around."

Ames narrowed his eyes on Matt. His sharp nose jutted forward in a challenge. Chest swelling, he said, "Ignorance? There's very little I don't understand about our peculiar connection. You're free for the moment, but don't think you've escaped from the noose that's slowly tightening around your neck. No, sir. It's just a matter of time. And I'll be there to watch you dangling with your feet kicking in the air. Nobody is going to rescue you. And I mean *nobody*."

Matt stepped up eye-to-eye, chest-to-chest.

"Let me help you, *Colonel*. You've been outranked. I'm free to enforce the laws. Against *you* or the Comanche."

Neither one spoke. Time crawled while they each took the measure of the other. Sensing the futility of the Mexican standoff, Matt repeated his question, "Where's the money, Ames?"

Ames flinched. A split second of uncertainty flashed in his eyes. Matt knew he had found a weak spot.

"I'm a busy man. This conversation is over," Ames said.

Matt stood his ground. Ames hesitated, waiting for Matt to stand aside. That was the deferential thing to do. It was the norm for him. People showed him respect. The longer he waited, the more he grew frustrated with the insolence. Patience at the end, he stepped half around Matt making sure he pushed him to the side with an aggressive shoulder brush.

A chuckle leaked from Matt as he taunted Ames, "Careful there. That's considered assault by your loose definition."

Ames heard the comment, but chose to ignore the implications. Matt was a pain in the ass that needed dealing with. He had some hard decisions to make. Dawson's expertise was going to be required. And fast. The two thousand dollars grew heavy in his vest as he put space between himself and Matt. He could feel the Ranger watching him depart. This problem had a different component to it. Matt had the determination to make trouble. Returning the money to Cole was out of the question. There was a better solution. But first he had to get ready for the celebratory evening. The mood for a party eluded him, but he knew how to fix that momentary lapse. There was a bottle of Kentucky's smoothest bourbon tucked away for an occasion such as this. A few drinks of the smooth and rich flavored spirits would take the edge off a rough day. And there was Carmin. Tonight was going to be the night. Tomorrow would take care of itself.

EIGHTEEN

Ames stepped back from the mirror to take in the full view. He had on his finest black three-piece suit and starched shirt. Fashionable broad lapels spread outward on the coat draped over a matching three-button vest. A wide black bowtie contrasted with the brilliance of the white collar on the new shirt he had purchased for this special occasion. He ran a comb through his hair slicked back with a light application of oil. Pivoting to view both sides of his apparel in the mirror, he was satisfied he looked debonair. He had to be at the top of his form. His goals for the evening depended on presenting an undeniable temptation to his lady friend. Reaching for his crystal glass, he guzzled another round of the warm amber whiskey. The flavor of his favorite brand was tinted with just a bit of oak and brought a gratifying release from the stressful day. He smacked his lips in pleasure and refilled the glass.

Tossing his head back for yet another stiff drink on top of the many he had consumed caused a temporary loss of balance. He staggered a bit, but it was nothing he couldn't handle. He had always had a firm grip on the amount of liquor he could hold. The complications of the day could not get in the way of his plans for the evening. He needed the liquid reinforcement. The absence of intimate female companionship in his life had been going on too long and it would end tonight. He couldn't, and wouldn't take no for an answer.

He weaved slightly on his way to the door. Gathering the flowers on the table, he also grabbed a small bottle of whiskey to take to Carmin's where they could share a drink before the short stroll to the Walker Hotel. The recently constructed hotel boasted superior accommodations and had a ballroom large enough to handle all the dignitaries and prominent men in attendance. He imagined the notes of the band as they played a slow waltz. Slow waltzing was his specialty. Women swooned in his arms as he glided them across the floor in unison with the beat. His confidence soared as he strode into the night and felt the cool invigorating air wash over him.

Knocking on Carmin's door gave him a moment to contemplate what he had in mind for the night's entertainment. He really didn't know much about her. She was unusually tightlipped about her past, but he considered her a simple girl when you got down to what mattered. She didn't appear to come from an affluent background. She slogged through her days as a waitress. Women of a higher pedigree would never stoop that low to support themselves. That was fine with him. Simple women were easier to manipulate. The level of the society she would be exposed to while in his company should do the trick for what he expected. He pictured her overcome with gratitude to be included in the higher levels of society where he mingled. After a night of high-class diversion, her natural instinct to resist his overtures should melt away like wax in proximity to a hot flame. He still had the charm he was known for and his reputation as a ladies' man was well deserved in his opinion.

Carmin cracked the door open just enough to confirm it was the guest she expected. Finding Ames at the door, she waved him inside. A strong odor of whiskey assaulted her nose when he passed. Caution warnings started flashing at the back of her mind. Excessive drinking before the evening got underway usually signaled trouble ahead. This was a scenario she had experienced too many times before. She had learned it was smart to head that kind of problem off at the pass. In this case, the pass was her front door, but the conveyer of trouble had already penetrated her boundaries. She sighed in exasperation and wondered why men had to be so hard to deal with. The thought crossed her mind that she should have spent the night with Matt rather than put up with this latest uncertainty.

"How're you doing?" Ames said as he handed her the flowers.

She smiled and took the flowers over to her dresser where she had an empty vase. The flowers were a nice gesture on his part, but the leer in his eyes made her wary. "I'm doing fine," she replied, glad that her back was to him while she fiddled with arranging the bouquet. Adding water to the vase she could feel her clothes falling to the floor under the intensity of his lustful trance. Turning to face him only verified her worst fears. He was drunk and barely in control of his passions. She regretted her faulty decision-making. Being in the company of a drunken and lecherous companion would be a high price to pay for a night among the movers and shakers of Austin.

"You're looking grand this evening," he said to Carmin, powerless to take his eyes off her bosom.

My God she thought. He had always been a gentleman before. It was amazing how drink made the true beast inside a man blossom. They couldn't hide their lechery when their inhibitions were drowned with alcohol. She was in trouble. This situation would take a delicate touch.

"Thank you, Colonel." He liked to be addressed using his military rank. It was an idiosyncrasy she should have considered a warning. His narcissistic ways were common among successful men, but he carried it to extremes she had never seen before.

Pulling out the bottle of whiskey, he said, "Let's have a drink 'fore we go."

"Are you sure that's a good idea?"

"Certainly! It'll set the right mood."

Caught in a trap, she produced two glasses and he poured them a drink. More than she wanted in her glass and much more than he needed in his. Raising his glass, he offered a toast. Their glasses *clinked* as they met, and he said, "Here's to us. May we enjoy each other's company tonight."

She took a small sip. He tossed his back in one gulp. Any semblance of restraint vanished with the downing of one too many drinks. He stumbled toward her with his arms extended for a hug. Backing away, she tried to avoid him, but he wrapped his arms around her shoulders in a tight grasp.

Breathing heavy in her ear, he said, "I've waited for this a long time."

"We still have the ball to attend," she said in a tone that hid her alarm.

"There's time for that later."

She squirmed in his staunch grip. He was drunk, but still physically dominating.

"There's time for *everything* later," she reasoned.

"*Everything?*"

"The night's young. Why rush?"

Even in his foggy state of mind she made sense. Why rush things? If the lady wanted to take her time, let her. He eased his hold on her, but as his hands slithered across her arms, he resumed control. He wanted to look at her up close. She smelled heavenly. Strange, he thought, her brown eyes looked different. There was an unusual message in them that he didn't recognize. Perhaps she wanted what he did. Encouraged, he leaned forward to kiss her.

She turned her cheek to him and that's all he got. His lips tasted her skin, but he craved more. Coming around to her mouth, she averted her lips again. Puzzled, he backed away with his fingers unintentionally digging into her arms.

"What's wrong, Carmin?"

She was in dangerous territory with a man that had never acted aggressively before. The whiskey had done its damage. She had to think fast. "Can we talk?" she pleaded.

Her question seemed to register. He released his grip. She was free. Immediately, she moved to the side and out of his reach. His drunken gaze followed her. He displayed no emotion. Just the devious assessment of a man searching for a way to obtain what is always close to the center of his thoughts.

"Carmin? Why're you acting this way? We both want it."

Now a safer distance from him, she relaxed a little. He was a man and couldn't help his behavior. The whiskey made him this way. He didn't mean anything by his overt actions. It was a breach of etiquette he wouldn't repeat. He just needed a reminder of their former discussions. She felt her confidence return as she achieved control over the issue. He had always seemed reasonable, although he, like every other man, was a hostage to his wanton appetite.

"Can we slow down a bit?" she asked.

Ames flared his eyes. Stupefied by the request, he struggled to heed her words. She sounded different. Distant.

"Slow down a bit?"

The reality slowly dawned through the fog. He was losing his opportunity.

"Think back," she said. "We've had this conversation before. Remember?"

"'Member what?"

"Remember when I said our time together was just as friends that needed company. And I wasn't looking for love."

Yep. He was losing his chance. The drink had dulled his comprehension, but she was spelling it out in black and white.

"So, what is it, Carmin? What're you looking for?"

The question was too loaded for a response. If she said what she truly thought, there would be hell to pay. The Colonel had proven to be an incredibly superficial man. He wasn't capable of understanding or caring about the feelings of others. Family meant next to nothing to him in his bankrupt value system. He was the polar opposite of a true man. True men were a rare breed, and hard to find on the Texas frontier. She had searched far and wide without success. There was currently only one man that fit the bill. What she wanted, she couldn't have. She whispered, "Matt."

Ames straightened like he had been shocked. He wasn't sure he heard right.

"Say what?" he demanded.

Caught, she didn't reply.

He made an aggressive move toward her.

"Did I hear you right?"

"I was just mumbling. You asked the big question. We're all looking for something in life we'll never find."

She backed up to her bed. He had her cornered again. A strange look came over his face. He had hardened. His resolution was like steel. The hawk eyes peered down his narrow nose at his cornered prey. There was nowhere to escape. He clasped her by the back of her head. His hands dug in like talons forcing her to submit. She smelled the pungent odor of whiskey on his breath. His lips found hers and forced her to accept his offerings. He kissed her long and deep.

Coming up for air, he warned her to be quiet. His stare glazed over in passion as he pulled her firm against him, leering into her eyes. He liked what he saw and was going to enjoy what was rightfully his. Inches from her face, he never heard her say, "No."

The time had finally come. With one hand he held her tight and forcibly kissed her again. Using his free hand he popped the buttons open on her dress and pressed her down onto the bed. Distracted by the exposure of her smooth rounded breasts, and the uncontainable rising of his voracious hungers, he let up on his kiss to take in the pleasing view.

She struggled under him and cried out, "No!"

Looming over her, he never heard her pleading to stop as he stripped her clothes off and ravaged her like an animal.

NINETEEN

A thin red line traced the eastern horizon an hour after Matt got off to an early start on his busy day. He had a lot of loose ends to take care of and motivation was no obstacle as he set out on his errands well before the lazy sunrise was greeted by the crowing of roosters. Satisfied with his predawn progress, he was optimistic things would come together for a midafternoon departure. Enlisting the aid of competent men made the formation of the small company of Rangers a much easier task to accomplish. Confident in the assistance of men impatient to get the job done, he wandered over to the café for a quick bite to eat, the euphoria of freedom still burning strong in his chest.

He lingered near the door to take a quick survey of the dining room. There was always the possibility of another hostile encounter that he wanted to avoid. It was too early to deal with Yankees or political swindlers. Fortunately, there was no sign of Ames and his hangers-on. There was also no sign of Carmin. He hadn't imagined her offer. It was real and she had meant what she said. But she was nowhere in sight. He saw an empty table in the far corner and decided to make his way to the seat thinking that Carmin could be tied up with her duties back in the kitchen. On the way to the table he made temporary eye contact with Mary hustling to top off several cups waved in the air for refills by groggy patrons.

She took care of her customers and made her way to Matt's table lifeless and robbed of spirit. Matt thought it was a shame and looked out of place for a woman of her appeal. Life had a way of doing that to good people regardless of their best efforts. Once again the rumblings of discord started on their tortuous paths through his thinking process. He wondered if the dissonance would ever cease. Women and their charms could be an unequaled blessing and a wicked curse at the same time. His musing ended when she said in a flat voice, "Good morning, Matt."

"Yes it is, Mary. I'm glad to see you."

A flush of recognition lit up her face. She seemed pleased to hear his genuine compliment. She asked, "How's that?"

"Despite all that can't be, there's still what could've been."

"That's all we're left with?"

"That's it. It wasn't meant to be. So we'll always remember what could've been. Cherish the thought, and move on."

"You make it sound simple."

"Sounding is one thing. Reality is another. You and I both know the truth. It's not easy by no means. So, we have to learn to live with it, like it or not."

She chuckled at the way Matt summed things up. He was right. It had all been discussed and analyzed. There was no way the two of them could ever make it happen. It was time to move on with life. Her internal battle ceased with the plans she had been making. It was time to tell Matt.

"Matt, I've made some decisions."

She gazed into his eyes to determine if he cared. She wasn't let down. Those cold gray eyes registered a warm concern. He was a good man. Behind the rough exterior lived a considerate gentleman that sincerely cared about others and tried to do right by them. Cora was a lucky woman although she seemed to have forgotten that fact.

He was waiting. She said, "I'm leaving Austin. Headed to Galveston."

Matt nodded his head in agreement. "Sometimes a drastic change can be a good thing."

"It's a hard move to make, but staying here is harder." She turned inward; apprehension darkening her face as she considered the challenges she would have to face alone. Unwilling to succumb to her doubts, she sucked in a breath and went on, "The girls are excited. That is except for Sarah. She's fit to be tied moving away from Travis."

"She'll git over it."

"No. Not much chance of that. She's grown a lot since Frank passed. She says things I remember saying at her age. Won't be long before I'll have no say-so in her life at all."

"The hard part of mothering is letting go I suppose."

"Yes it is."

Both of them drifted away on their personal thoughts. They laughed at the awkwardness of the moment, but it became an overdue time of relief for Mary. She sighed. It felt like a weight had been lifted although something else soon replaced Matt's levity.

"What is it, Matt?"

He surveyed the room again. She was definitely not working this morning. It might make Mary suspicious, but he had to know.

"Where's you help?"

"You mean Carmin?"

"Yeah. Doesn't she work the breakfast hours?"

If Mary was curious why he was asking, she hid it well. That was fine with him.

"Funny you should ask. She was scheduled to work this morning, but came in and asked for all of her back pay. Said goodbye to me and said she was hopping the early stage to San Antone."

Matt hid his surprise, asking, "What brought that about?"

"Good question. She didn't seem like herself at all. Said it would be a cold day in hell before she came back to Austin."

"I can appreciate her feelings. It ain't my favorite place either."

"Count me in on that. We're leaving in a couple of days." She floated into a faraway trance. "I can almost smell the salt in the air. I used to love the sea. Maybe I'll get lucky and it'll work out alright."

Matt took her hand and gave it a gentle squeeze. She deserved a good life. Things had been hard for them all. It was time for a change. But he wondered about Carmin. Something drastic had to have occurred. Ames was involved. He was sure of that. The bastard spread heartache like a disease to those he encountered. If he found out Ames hurt Carmin he would see to it the Yankee paid a high price in retribution.

Mary's voice brought him back from his reverie. She was asking, "When do y'all leave?"

"Around three this afternoon."

"Mind if I see you off?"

Mind? Hell no, he'd be thrilled to have her present when he headed out on a mission he might not return from. A surge of relief washed over him with the other news. The sudden departure of Carmin saved him from what he knew would be a lifetime of regrets. He would have ended up paying a high price in guilt for such a temporary indulgence. He was glad to say, "I'd be more than happy to have you there. Meet us at Jed's livery. It'll be good to have one of my favorite ladies see us off."

"You got it then." She wore a grin that seemed a natural fit. It had been a long time since she felt optimistic. Maybe things were going to be fine after all.

TWENTY

Jed's corrals were bursting with a tangle of horses anxious to be out on the trail. They sensed the contagious excitement in the air created by citizens gathered to witness the departure of Rangers out to avenge their collective loss. The massacre of Hobbs had cast a pall over Austin making the townsfolk eager for men with the fortitude to ride down and punish the murderous Comanche.

Matt was surprised by the attention. Word had traveled fast around town that he was going to lead the Rangers out of Jed's stables. It was news that elated a lot of the old-timers that were sick and tired of the dirty dealings that defined the post Civil War reality of life in the capital city. Thirty or more men hung outside the fence gawking at the spectacle of serious minded Rangers exhibiting all kinds of lethal weaponry tucked in their scabbards and hanging on their hips. Matt glanced across the corral and was glad to see that the Rangers were just about ready to mount up. Hunter, from the Enchanted Rock battle, had joined them along with Tully, already mounted and wearing the steadfast mien of a warrior impatient to brawl. His reputation as a ferocious fighter made Matt thankful to count him on the same team. Any Comanche that got in Tully's sights would shortly be sent on a permanent visit to his spirit world.

Only one man was missing. Cliff was nowhere to be seen. Matt found Charles at the far side of the corral and weaved around several horses to have a word with his newly promoted sergeant.

"Charles."

Mossberg continued checking the tightness of his cinch straps without looking up. "Yep," was all he said. His concentration was legendary prior to mounting up for a chancy mission.

"'Bout ready to ride?"

"Yep."

"Don't see Cliff nowhere."

"He'll be here." He faced Matt and pledged, "Said he had to talk with his wife one more time. Say goodbye to his daughter. He'll be here."

Matt nodded in understanding. Cliff's relationship with his wife was in a bad way since the Comanche had killed their sons and ruined the harmony of his family. The little Havens girl had become severely withdrawn after her experience as a Comanche captive and Cliff's wife was being consumed by resentment according to the stories Matt had heard. He knew the feeling well. Cora shared the same emotions as Cliff's wife. The loss of their son, Josh, had forever altered their marriage. Death of a child was a heavy burden for any parent to bear.

"They still separated?"

Charles took his hat off and ran his fingers through his hair before he answered. "Cliff said this will do it for 'em. Said his wife told him not to count on her comin' back. Said their daughter takes all she's got and she ain't ever puttin' her little girl where the Comanch can git at her again."

"Damn shame the way it is."

"That ain't all, Matt. He told me his wife said she wouldn't have nothin' to do with him even if he agreed to move to town. He said he don't even know who she is anymore. Hell, she looks plumb crazy to me. I've seen her around town. Funny look in her eyes."

"Ain't good."

"No, sir. This is his chance to even the score." He spit a gob of tobacco to the dirt. "He'll be here on time."

Charles went back to checking his mount and Matt heard him barking orders to the other men, most of which he had handpicked for this outing. He would make an excellent sergeant. The men would follow his instructions without question and Matt knew he could count on him to do what was right without needing to be told.

The only detail left was signing receipts in Jed's office and the Rangers could be on their way. He entered the office and found the cranky proprietor with his nose buried in the newspaper. Barely acknowledging Matt, he tossed the paper to the side and threw the documents that needed signatures on the table. His role in assisting the Ranger's preparations for the mission was lucrative. Matt's signature was his ticket to a healthy payday courtesy of the government and he aimed to milk it for all it was worth. He clicked his tongue in greedy anticipation as Matt put his name to the bill.

"Pleasure doin' business with you, Matt."

Matt gave the little man a hard stare. Jed sank back into his chair wondering what he had done wrong. It didn't matter; Matt stalked out the front door without a farewell or backwards glance.

The front of the office was in the afternoon shade and Matt stalled just outside the door to inspect the streets. He couldn't hit the trail soon enough. Home was calling. It had been for a long while. Cora would be fit to be tied at his extended absence, but there had been nothing he could do about it. Now he could change things for the better. They would ride past his ranch on the trail out to intercept the raiding Indians, and he would have one evening with his family before he was gone yet again. He ran the risk of Cora reaching a breaking point like Cliff's wife, but riding as a Ranger was the only way to keep the taxman off his back. Those boys never slept when it came to scheming ways to fleece a man's pocket. He didn't like it any more than the other men he knew. They all had to cope with the strong-arming and oppression of ruthless bureaucrats.

Then she appeared. The sight of her always produced a rush of pleasurable sensations. He couldn't help it. The desire to have her ran deep. It welled up within him and burst free like a spring bubbling at the base of a cliff. It was something natural that occurred within a man. He could no more stop the yearning for her than he could stop the birds from singing. He enjoyed her sultry gait as she approached him, blue eyes blazing, his passion rising at her proximity.

"Hello, Mary."

"Matt." Her eyes fluttered. Battling her own cravings, she sighed, "It's good to see you."

Nobody was watching. Matt took her in his arms. He could feel her heart throbbing against his chest. Her breasts swelled against him as her breathing deepened. She was submissive. Glad to touch the hardness of his muscles. Glad to feel protected if only for a moment.

He took it all in. This would never happen again. He knew it. She knew it. He wanted to be able to forever remember her pressed against him. They held the embrace, each locking the mutual hunger away in a corner of their memory to be opened when the night was quiet and the hands of time ticked ever onward. It would be a special link known only to the two of them. Despite the barriers keeping them apart, they would share this bond. *Forever.*

Reluctantly letting her go, he held her at arm's length.

"Wasn't sure you'd make it," he said.

"Busier than usual. Getting ready to leave."

"I can imagine. It's a big move."

"Sarah's still not taking it too good."

"Travis?"

"That's it. She's got it in her head they're getting married."

"He's still just a pup. He's got to prove he's up to it first."

"That's what I told her. But you know how it is when you're young."

They both laughed at the irony.

"Or old," they said in unison.

They laughed again. But this time the laugh had a hollow ring. Matt saw the recognition in her somber gaze. This was it. It was time. One last haunting search of her crystal blue eyes was too much. He leaned in close, hesitating at her lips. They had been so near to surrender so many times. She closed her eyes in anticipation. It was time to end it once and for all. He gently kissed her cheek as he wrapped his arms around her in a final act to capture her memory. How soft and inviting she felt. Heavenly.

And then it was over. He released her from his embrace. He didn't trust himself to speak, but he stuttered, "Mary. I . . . I've got to . . . Got to . . ."

"Go Matt." Choking with disappointment she murmured, "Go now."

His eyes seized her beauty, held it in place to remember, and then he was gone.

She watched him stride away. The broad shoulders. The

purposeful walk of a confident man. A good man fading out of her life. He disappeared around the corner.

She spoke, but nobody heard. "Goodbye Matt. Take care. Come home safe."

It broke her heart, but she had to admit: What did it matter? She would be over two hundred miles away. They would never see each other again. *Forever.* And forever was a long time.

TWENTY-ONE

Matt was wrong. They had been discreet, but somebody was watching. Watching and seething. Plotting and planning. Ames ground his teeth in frustration at the offensive scene down the street. All he could do was wait for the answer to his problem to arrive. Dawson was late. He needed to be on hand for the departure of the Rangers. Damn the man. He was showing signs of being hard to control. Just like Kern had done before the end of their working relationship.

Ames had grown to despise Matt. It was personal. Watching him hug Mary was like suffering the thrust of a knife straight into his gut. A fatal plunge of hardened steel that penetrated where he lived. This sensation was a new experience. He wasn't used to losing. Mary was to be his. Carmin was to be his. He recoiled in regret. Carmin *was* his. He had seen to that. But she turned out to be a disappointment. Too independent. She was only good for the one time. Now he was confronted with finding a replacement and the options available to him were limited. There was the wife of Senator Knowles. She was attractive enough to meet his standards and had made eye contact in the past, but that would be a risky trick to pull off. Senator Knowles would be a formidable opponent should he discover them indulging in the carnal ecstasy he craved.

Damn Matt! *Mary* was to be his. She had all that he coveted. She would have been a trophy he could parade on his arm to the envy of every man in Austin. The Ranger from the hills had spoiled some of his most important goals. It was time to end that spell of bad luck.

He grumbled, "Where's Dawson?" His entreaty echoed in the empty room.

From a distance he could see the Rangers were close to completing their preparations before leaving. He also made out a wagon pulling up outside the corrals. It was hard to tell, but it looked like Bull's sons were accompanying the wagon. There was a gray-haired old woman sitting in the bench seat and she hopped into the back of the wagon once they came to a halt. One of the riders slipped off his mount and disappeared into the assembly of men and horses jostling for position inside the fenced corral. There was no mistaking the lanky stature of Nate. It was Bull's sons for sure, and most likely the old woman was Bull's wife. That meant the belligerent old man was probably in the back of the wagon. Healing up just fine or so he had heard. Too bad he thought. If Kern's aim had been accurate neither Matt nor Bull would complicate the picture any more. It didn't matter about Bull. He was a beat man incapable of slowing the changing times. Bull's homestead was now securely in the syndicate's possession. The sheriff would see to his removal if Bull chose to contest the issue.

Matt was a different story. He had plans for Matt. All he needed was for Dawson to show up.

And there he was turning the corner into view a block away. He marveled at the intimidating aura that surrounded Dawson. No man in his right mind wanted to be on the wrong side of the dark nature he projected. His weathered complexion resembled the belly of an approaching thunderhead, full of a latent power straining to be unleashed. All that was required was for the trigger to be tripped and nobody wanted to be around when that bolt of lightning struck.

Ames stepped to the side and waved Dawson into his office. He grinned when he took another look at the assembled Rangers. They had no idea what he had in store for their leader. Matt had no idea how short lived his promotion to captain would last. Ames pulled the door shut for privacy. It was time to put his solution into motion.

"How are you doing, Dawson?"

"Good as ever. What's on your mind?"

Dawson could be a man of few words, but that was fine in the opinion of Ames. It made the man easier to manage. Easier would be nice for a change.

"I want to work out the details we have been discussing."

Dawson nodded in agreement. He knew this occasion was coming. Ames had been perfecting his plans for the past week. Dawson only heard bits and pieces, but he realized the final decision would not bode well for Matt. That had been apparent in the stern tone Ames always assumed when the subject of the Ranger came up.

Ames took a seat behind his desk and propped his boots on the top, a self-righteous expression on his face. He removed a premium cigar from the box and offered a smoke to Dawson. He was surprised when Dawson waved him off on the offer. A good smoke helped him think when critical matters were under discussion. He had thought Dawson felt the same way. It didn't matter; he sucked in the first draft like a hungry calf on a teat.

"Are you ready for a little bonus money?" he asked Dawson.

Dawson couldn't hide his interest as he drew up a chair. He wasn't a poker player. His eyes betrayed his lust for money. He had plans like any man. They took cash and this might be his only chance to make a significant amount for some time.

"Don't ask questions you know the answer to. What do you have planned?"

"You saw the Rangers organizing. I want you to join them."

Dawson snickered. After regaining composure he said, "You've got to be joking. They won't let me near 'em."

The cigar glowed bright as Ames schemed and took a strong pull. He exhaled a cloud of blue-gray smoke directed at the ceiling. "Perhaps not. But you can trail them into the hills. Do what you do best. Shadow them. Find the right circumstance. Make it happen however you like. I trust your instincts."

"You must be kidding? He'll be surrounded by Rangers. How the hell am I going to make that work?"

"Join 'em or be near enough to make your play. When there's a fight, take a good aim on him during the action. Nobody will be able to tell who pulled the trigger."

"Humph."

"Happened all the time in the Great Rebellion. Men settled their differences with a shot in the back. Then they melted away in the confusion. Hard to pin it on any one person when there's bullets flying everywhere."

"That was against the Rebs. This is different."

"Not really. Those Comanche have stolen enough rifles that the shooting will be heavy on both sides. Most of the men with Hobbs were killed with bullets, not arrows. Things are changing out there."

"Gotta find the Indians first."

Ames shook his head. His subordinates just didn't have his intelligence. They could rarely fathom his brilliant strategies. They had to depend on him to explain the details. He actually liked it that way.

"Think about it, Dawson. You're going to join or tail the most respected Indian fighter in these parts. There's gonna be Comanche. The only question is, will you be able to handle the job?"

Bristling, Dawson said, "Don't insult me, Ames. I'm not Kern."

Ames forced himself to remain patient. He was a poker player. He knew when to bluff and when to play his hand. Dawson's sense of pride would keep him from backing down and prompt him to complete the task no matter how rotten or problematic it proved to be. The man had often stated that he could always be counted on to deliver when he was paid to do a job.

"No insult meant. It's just that I can't afford to have Matt make it back. Understand?"

There was no hesitation when Dawson responded, "I comprende." His right eye squinted when he narrowed his focus on Ames. He let the colonel sweat a moment before he asked, "Now, how much are we talking about?"

This is where it could get tricky. Ames had fifteen hundred dollars in the drawer next to him. The trick would be to convince Dawson to do the chore for the five hundred he had in his vest pocket. Two hundred fifty now, and the rest when he returned with verifiable news that Matt was dead. It seemed reasonable to his way of thinking. The other fifteen hundred he counted as his personal money since the syndicate books still recorded it as an expense already paid. It was a perfect setup. There was nothing wrong with cheating the company. He had earned it by dealing with the roughshod manners of the Southerners and agreeing to serve in such a deplorable location.

Ames said, "I'll give you two hundred fifty now as earnest money. You get another two fifty when you return with confirmable evidence you took care of my problem."

Dawson didn't flinch at the number. He didn't bat an eye. He stared into the cocky and self-assured smugness of his opponent. He worked for Ames, but despite what his boss thought, he never considered the man his master. This discussion of money was where you learned your true worth in the opinion of the top hoss. And Ames had just delivered an insult. He didn't comprehend he had just exposed how little he thought of his best hand as a valuable partner in their mutual success.

"Two fifty to start? Two fifty to finish the job?" Dawson asked.

"That's right. Very generous I know. But you're worth the extra expense."

"Generous?"

Ames felt the first wave of uncertainty.

"I consider it generous. The bosses up North will have a fit. They'll think me giving away the bank."

"Up North? Do we really care what they think?"

This was a puzzling development. Dawson's scrutiny was cold. Ames realized there was a penetrating and unexpected assessment taking place.

"I have to consider their opinions at all times. I have to answer to them. You don't."

Dawson had Ames right where he wanted the man. He saw the doubt flash in his expression. Dawson knew exactly what Ames paid Kern to do the dirty work. Kern could not keep from bragging that murder for hire was never less than two thousand cold hard cash. And he had confided that Ames had agreed to pay that much for the murder of Matt and Bull.

Dawson said, "You don't understand. Only you know how much this job is worth to you. I will not try to pretend to put value on my services. I'll only tell you that once I'm paid, you'll get your satisfaction. I get the job done. I'm not Kern."

Ames pulled the currency out of his vest and peeled off two hundred and fifty dollars. He threw it down on the desk. Dawson's attention never wavered from studying Ames. He ignored the money.

Ames pointed at the cash and said, "There's half." He waved

the remaining cash in the air. "The rest will be waiting for you when you get back."

A change came over Dawson. The storm behind his eyes grew intense. Ames recognized the hazard of pushing him too far. He stepped back when Dawson abruptly stood, his menacing bulk much too close for comfort. Ames realized his Colt revolver was in the desk drawer next to the extra cash if he needed the equalizer. He tapped the currency on the desk for emphasis. "There it is. That's real spending money. More than most of these hicks make in two years!"

Dawson took a deep breath. His already massive chest grew in size that dwarfed Ames. He placed his hands flat on the desk and gave the colonel a calculating glare that told Ames his bluff had been called.

Ames said, "Okay. You drive a hard bargain, but I can sweeten the deal by one hundred. It'll come out of my own pocket, but I want you happy with the offer."

"That's what I'm worth to you? *I* go out and kill a man. Maybe get myself dead. *You* stay here in the comfort of town. Do you really think I'll accept six hundred for such a risky proposition?"

Ames felt his indignation escalating. The other fifteen hundred was *his*. Who was this son of a bitch to bite into *his* money?

"Look here, Dawson. Money is hard to come by. That's a fair offer."

Dawson stomped around the corner of the desk. Ames was cornered. There was nowhere to retreat. Instead of fear, Ames felt his anger bubbling up.

"You work for me. Six hundred is my final offer. You can't make that kind of cash anywhere else. I suggest you take the deal."

Dawson eased closer to Ames.

"Here's what I suggest." Dawson said. "You come up with the money paid to Kern. Nothing less. Then I'll be happy."

Ames understood the negotiation now. There was the play. Dawson knew how much Kern had been paid. The mulatto had talked. The cat was out of the bag. There was nothing he could do about it now.

Standing firm, Ames said, "No way. I won't go down that path again."

"You don't have a choice. You want Matt dead. I want the

money. Now. All up front."

"*I* don't have a choice? Who the hell do you think *you* are?"

Dawson bumped into the chest of Ames. His hard gaze burned into his boss now converted into an adversary. Dawson growled, "I'm the man that'll take care of a problem that'll make you a mint."

"The hell you will."

Ames couldn't abide the intimidation; he stepped back and opened the desk drawer, nabbed the revolver and swung it toward Dawson. He was too slow. Dawson drove into him with the momentum of a charging buffalo. Ames straightened in pain as his back slammed against the wall. His grip on the Colt weakened, but he regained control. His life could depend on the revolver. He raised it up and hit Dawson against his temple with a *crack*.

It didn't faze the big man. Dawson pivoted at the waist, reared back, and brought a swift blow against the hand holding the gun. The revolver toppled to the floor between their feet.

Ames recovered swiftly and grabbed a wad of Dawson's hair. He twisted the locks in his grasp, forcing Dawson's head to the side, sending his hat flying to the table.

Dawson didn't resist the efforts of Ames, but used the twisting motion to heave him in the same direction. Ames tumbled head first against the table. The collision was violent, but he saw what he needed and lunged for the gun at Dawson's feet.

Surprised by the quick move, Dawson kicked Ames in the ribs as he dove for the revolver. It didn't slow Ames down. He rolled away with the gun in his hands pointed at Dawson.

Without a moment to spare, Dawson flung the chair into Ames knocking the gun loose. He then dove on top of Ames, but the chair got in the way. Ames squirmed to the side and avoided the maneuver Dawson was attempting.

Both men scrambled to their feet at once.

Dawson was astounded and impressed at the elusiveness of the Yankee.

Ames backed away in fear of his life. He had the big man riled. It was only a split second, but Ames detected Dawson telegraphing his next move. He had to avoid Dawson's powerful capabilities, and sidestepped the sudden rush of the raging bull his employee had become. He delivered a crushing blow to Dawson's head.

It was no use. The impact of his fist did nothing to counter Dawson's intent. He spun to seize Ames in an overpowering clench that lifted him off the floor. In command now, Dawson swung the colonel through the air and smashed him against the wall. Framed artwork crashed to the floor. Pinned against the wall, Ames clawed at Dawson's face.

This only enraged him further. He slipped his arm around the neck of Ames. Squeezing his head in a tenacious lock, Dawson took a few steps forward to gain momentum. With Ames in his control, the gap to the back wall closed in a hurry. A hollow *thump* filled the air as wood splintered against the crown of the colonel's head. He slumped to the floor in a loose heap, barely breathing.

Dawson gazed down at the results of his work. Ames didn't move or moan. It was regretful it had to come to this, but he had to admit it felt good to educate the arrogant Yankee. The bastard didn't consider the outcome of his selfish attitude. He would never understand men like Ames. It was just money and he had plenty. Why did men like him conspire to keep it all for themselves? After all, they were supposed to be on the same side. Working men had dreams too. But no, it always had to be doled out lopsided in the favor of the ones that controlled the purse strings. It had gotten old. He was tired of dealing with their kind.

He picked up the fifteen hundred dollars out of the drawer. Scooping up the two hundred fifty on the desk, he shoved the cash into his pocket. Dropping to a knee, he inspected Ames. The colonel was limp. He was out cold.

There was nothing left he could do. He rolled Ames over and dug in his vest pocket. He found another two hundred fifty in one pocket and fifty in the other. Combining the two hundred fifty with the other money made two thousand. Precisely what Kern had been paid. Now he had a fair deal. He put the spare fifty back in the vest pocket of Ames. He didn't want to be accused of robbery.

He lifted the eyelids of Ames. All he saw was the whites of his eyes. The man was in a deep state of unconsciousness. Dawson shook his head. It was so unnecessary. His mom had told him a man reaped what he sowed in life. Ames had instigated this situation. His fate was his own doing.

Dawson stood and took one more look at his former boss. There was no coming back. It didn't matter anymore. He had been paid to do a job. And that job had already departed for parts unknown. It was time to mount up and earn his pay.

TWENTY-TWO

Matt rode tall and erect in the saddle where he felt the most at home. He had finally escaped the shackles of Austin and led a handpicked group of battle-hardened men that would make a formidable fighting unit against the Comanche. This was what he was meant to do. Once Robert joined the men there would be thirteen well-armed Rangers at his command. Mossberg would serve as his sergeant and Nate would use his superior skills as a scout to ferret out the Comanche. From all the reports coming in on a daily basis it was simple to conclude that finding Indians wouldn't be a problem. The flipside was that finding more than they could handle was a distinct possibility.

Dealing with the plundering Comanche seemed preferable to him than being subjected to the greedy schemes of white men in Austin. The hills had been calling and now he was free to relish open country with fifty-mile vistas empty of civilization. They would have just enough daylight left to reach Mount Bonnell where he planned on camping. It was a favorite site of his and he knew Bull shared the opinion. His old neighbor would enjoy his first night out of town when he got the chance to see a sunset from the flank of the highest peak in the Austin vicinity.

Everything had come together at the last moment. Bull was up to traveling in a padded bed of hay in the back of the wagon and Cliff had arrived in the nick of time to accompany the Rangers on their mission. Bull had resorted to being his old talkative self while Cliff appeared preoccupied and silent. Riding at the front of the men, Matt wasn't sure if Bull's gregarious nature would pull Cliff from his pensive mood, but he did know if anybody could, it would be Bull. Cliff had agreed to Bull's request to ride beside the wagon so they could swap lies as they traveled the trail. Matt recognized Bull's intention. He knew Bull sympathized with the plight of Cliff and would do what he could to distract the man from his troubles.

A gusty wind from the south blew at their backs as the day wore into late afternoon. The temperature climbed to an agreeable warmth with the southerly flow of humid air from the Gulf of Mexico. It would make for a comfortable camp and a surge of excitement pulsed through Matt when he got his first glimpse of the trail starting its ascent of Mount Bonnell. The thrill of setting his eyes on the vastness of the hills after being cooped up in jail was too much to ignore. He turned to Mossberg and gave him instructions on where and how he wanted the camp organized. The rough wagon road they had been following did not reach the top, but it did gain elevation and there was a level area where Mossberg could pull over to make a pleasant camp to watch the sun dip below the western horizon.

Satisfied that Mossberg would see to it the men obeyed his orders and wouldn't be far behind, he spurred Whiskey, and they were off like a coyote hot on the heels of a jackrabbit. He found a faint game trail climbing over numerous ledges of crumbling limestone as he ascended the peak. Riding as far up the hillside as possible, he decided to dismount below the summit and finish the scramble on foot. The exercise and clean air was like a medication to his weary spirit.

Off to his left was an abrupt drop-off straight to the thickly wooded Colorado River bottoms. The stream flowed below him like a ribbon shimmering with the orange hues of the sun resting low on the horizon. He heard the raucous squawking of a green heron gliding across the river searching for a location to fish in the waning light. Stones rolled from under his boots and tumbled down the sharp incline. The pungent aroma of cedar filled up his senses. It felt good to be alive again.

Nearing the final ledge below the highpoint, he caught sight of a hawk silently floating right in front of him indifferent to his proximity. The bird of prey had his dark head tilted downward to detect the field mice that scurried through the grass right before dusk. At such a close distance, Matt immediately noticed the lethal appearance of the hooked beak. The hawk's gaze was concentrated on the wind-tickled grass, ready to swoop down for the kill at the first opportunity. He never veered off his intended route, his efficiency lethal, concentration unbreakable. He knew what he wanted.

Matt felt an unusual connection with the accipiter. They were both on the hunt. But that was where the similarities ended. What the hawk wanted was survival. He was not distracted with morals that clouded his actions. Soar low to the land and take what he wanted. It was that simple. Matt struggled with what he wanted. A big part of him yearned for the independence of his younger days when women were a conquest to be savored. Willing participants. No regrets and no ties to bind except for the fond memories they had made together. Those times were forever in the past. He had aged and held responsibilities now. His spirit was prepared to remain faithful to Cora, but his flesh was weak.

He thought back to the evening outside Austin when he wandered along the river and some mysterious essence permeated the air. There had been a haunting and urgent message conveyed in the solitude that he needed to return to his homestead upstream from Mount Bonnell. And now standing on the peak, if he stared hard enough he could make out the undulant ridgeline above his ranch. His heart ached to know that all was well. For all he knew the Comanche had returned to finish their vile deeds.

He clicked his tongue as the hawk glided over the edge and dropped out of sight below the rim of the bluff. My, how times have changed he thought. What should be wasn't and what shouldn't be was. What he wanted, he couldn't have. Willing women everywhere and he had to decline. He wasn't a young buck any more. Nothing seemed easy or as it should be. He watched as the hawk rose high in the ruddy sky, soaring on an unseen thermal deflected upward by the sheer precipice of Mount Bonnell. In some far corner of his mind he envied the bird. He longed to spread his wings and soar away to a distant land far removed from the complexity of human relationships.

He spent a short time lost in reflection about the turn of events. People came and went in life and that was the way it was. It had always been hard to comprehend the mystery of why things happened the way they did. There was little he could do about any of it now. Josh was gone. Dead at the hands of a marauding band of Indians. His memories of his son would forever be of the lost innocence. Josh would never grow up. Those memories of his young life were locked in place and would haunt him with guilt until he took his last breath.

Hanging his head in a heavy sense of remorse, he asked for forgiveness. He was fallible. Weak and susceptible to temptation at times. Always caught up in the rigid man he had become in order to survive. Too often obstinate and separated from those that loved him most. If Cora couldn't forgive him for the death of her youngest son, maybe the Good Lord above would. He whispered a prayer beseeching forgiveness and the strength to carry on. Minutes passed in contemplation while he gazed across the hills rolling away into a purple haze. He felt nothing in return to his invocation. That didn't surprise him. He knew it didn't work that way. Unanswered prayers were just a failure on his part to fathom the true nature of God's will. At times praying was all a man could do. That was all what mattered to him. A man always did all he could. It was one requirement in life he had come to fully understand.

The rattle of the wagon coming to a stop in the meadow carried up to Matt. He took one last lingering sweep of the hills near his cabin and trotted down the trail to Whiskey patiently munching on a clump of grass. When he got to the wagon, Mossberg already had the men engaged in making the camp a restful place for the night. It was a luxury they could enjoy before the pursuit of Indians became a life and death endeavor.

Sitting in the wagon, Bull greeted Matt in typical fashion, "Sure is a good spot for a sunset."

"It'll do."

"Yes it will."

"Beats jail," Matt grunted.

"Or the doc's office."

Matt nodded in agreement while gazing at the sun that hung suspended on the horizon as if reluctant to disappear. Spellbound by the moment, time seemed to stand still. Granny joined them and stood at Matt's side. She hugged Matt with an affectionate squeeze.

She said, "Mighty beautiful up here close to the sky."

Matt patted her hand. He said, "Can't find this kind of peace in town."

"Only in the hills," she concurred.

They shared the view of the sun sinking in silence until Cliff made his appearance. There was a disconcerting aura that surrounded the man. Matt had assumed that hitting the trail and listening to the gab of Bull would transform his disposition. He had been wrong. Cliff suffered from a palpable sense of depression.

Bull saw an opportunity to remedy the situation. He waved his jug to get Cliff's attention. "This here calls for a drink. We're free men again after gittin' delivered from a special kind of hell that makes Austin what it is."

Granny declined and made her way to start cooking over the fire Jake was preparing. It was going to be a night of celebrating with steaks and beans served up beside roasted corn. Nate was down the hill and distracted with caring for the horses on the picket line. The other men in camp were going about their duties in an efficient and orderly manner. Matt saw no harm in a quick celebratory drink.

Bull poured a generous round of whiskey with his good arm and he raised his cup to propose a toast. "Here's to good neighbors and good Injun huntin'."

They tossed their drinks back in unison.

Cliff smacked his lips and wiped his sleeve across his mouth. His eyes took on a peculiar glow. Matt wasn't sure if liquor could have that sudden of a result.

"I'm all about the hunt. That's what I'm after," Cliff said.

"You're hooked up with the best," Bull said as he motioned toward Matt. "He'll put you on Injuns. With Nate scoutin' for y'all, findin' Comanch won't be no problem."

Cliff arched his eyebrows. "Think so, Matt?"

"Most likely. Seems there's no shortage of 'em out in the hills."

"Gonna be a lively time. Sure 'nough." Bull said. He held his bandaged foot up and declared, "I'll have to miss another chance at the excitement. Foot's still tender as hell, and my shoulder'll never be the same again. I'm a changed man."

Cliff stiffened at Bull's comment. Crows feet radiated outward from the corners of his eyes. He puckered his lips up as if he had been gut shot. His gaze wandered to the horizon where the violet-crowned hills were gradually fading into obscurity.

Bull sloshed another drink in his cup and downed it in a deft motion for a one armed man. He discerned Cliff had turned inward again. Not one to stay silent, he said, "You're in good hands, Cliff. Matt here will make things as right as possible. Hell, me and him are gonna be partners. Gonna raise some crops for cash and try our luck at horse tradin'." He winked at Matt as the concept of the partnership had begun to sound appealing.

Cliff acted as if the words never registered. He scanned the slope leading to the top of the peak. His preoccupation blocked out Bull's attempt to remain optimistic. Waving a finger up the hill, he asked Matt, "Back to the top?"

Matt lobbed his cup to Bull and turned to lead Cliff to the summit. They got to the highpoint just as the full moon crawled above the flat eastern horizon beyond Austin. A peculiar spell existed on the peak. It was deathly quiet. Not even a murmur from camp rose to their lofty height. Miles and miles of wilderness unfolded at their feet, home to feral creatures and a few hardy frontiersmen attempting to carve a life out of an unforgiving land.

"I've never been up here before," Cliff said. "Always been too busy at my place to ride up here."

"Don't nothin' come easy from the hills," Matt stated as a matter of fact. "But you got good cropland. Level, and the soils deep enough to be easy on the plow."

"Don't matter none now." The bitterness in Cliff's voice was sharp.

Matt caught the implications. Just as he expected, the man carried a burden he needed to unload. Cliff took a couple of steps that left him precariously near the edge of the bluff. It was straight down to certain death on the rocks far below.

Cliff hung his head over the brink, peering at the crowns of pecan trees growing beside the river at the base of the mountain. He said, "It'd be easy to take a step off."

Matt felt a bloom of doubt in his decision. He didn't like this kind of talk. There were only inches between Cliff and a deadly tumble into open space. Cliff needed to face his difficulties with resolution and not talk like a fool. He started to question the wisdom of bringing the troubled man along.

"It'd be a swift end," Cliff said with a profound sense of

melancholy.

For a moment he seemed to waver at the edge. He leaned over as far as he could to get a good look at the path he would plummet down. Matt realized there was no stopping him. He wasn't close enough to reach him if he took one last step.

"Is that why you got me up here? Wanted a witness?"

Cliff kicked a fist-sized rock over the edge. It freefell for long seconds and then a muffled *thump* echoed as the stone exploded against a boulder at the bottom. Lost in his own world, he ignored the question. He teetered at the edge with his back to Matt.

While Cliff was distracted, Matt eased forward to keep him from committing a rash act. That's when he spotted a rider approaching on what barely passed as a road leading from the hills into Austin. The rider reined up when he saw the silhouette of Cliff and Matt against the darkening sky. It didn't take the stranger long to make up his mind. He spurred his horse off the rocky road and headed up the slope. Cliff showed no sign of recognizing the rider down the hill.

Matt took another step towards Cliff. He was almost near enough to snatch him from the brink of a grievous mistake. His breath began to come quicker. There was the possibility that Cliff could take both of them off the precipice at the same time. It would be a chance he would have to take. Cliff wasn't thinking straight and needed more time to overcome the tragic setbacks in his life making him talk nonsense.

Just as Matt was ready to grab Cliff, a defining moment transformed the troubled man. He turned to face Matt and said, "No, I don't want a witness. I'll not be taking the easy way out. Got better things to do." His gravelly voice rumbled with resentment, "My wife left me for good. She laid it all out to me. Said she's done with me. Them Indians ruined her. Our daughter ain't improving. Whatever them Comanch done to her—let's just say she ain't never gonna be the same. I've been robbed of my family. I figure getting even with them red devils is the best thing I can do with whatever time I got left."

Cliff stepped away from the edge of the drop-off. An intense fire burned in his eyes, his jaw clenched shut, square chin jutting forward in aggression. There was an unmistakable yearning for revenge that animated his stiff movement as he offered Matt a firm handshake to avow his goal. His fixed clasp was nothing like the first time Matt met the man. At that time, his handshake had been indecisive and weak like holding a dead fish. This was a different Cliff that looked Matt straight in the eyes and said, "Put me on some Comanche so I can balance the sheets."

Matt maintained eye contact when he replied, "Count on it. We both have a score to settle. That makes us partners."

A realization flashed in Matt's mind. Cora had been hard on him for the death of Josh. There was no doubting that fact. But there was also no doubt that she fought against her own despair as well as she could. As tough as it had been on both of them, they still managed to keep it together for the sake of the children. Cliff couldn't say the same. The thought ran through Matt's mind; what kind of woman was Cliff's wife?

The labored breathing of a tired horse broke the handshake sealing their mutual agreement. Matt was shocked to learn the identity of the unidentified rider when he heard his name shouted, "Uncle Matt!"

"Travis! What the hell are you doing here?"

Travis reined up and effortlessly slipped out of the saddle with the vigor and agility of his youth. He stuck his paw out to shake Cliff's hand first and than offered a manly grip to his uncle. Matt was surprised by the enthusiasm of Travis considering the situation. There was serious protocol he had taught the boy being flouted with him facing the dangers of traveling alone.

As he was prone to do, Matt got right to the point, "What the hell are you doing on the trail by yourself?"

The grin evaporated from his nephews face. His resolution hardened. There was no reluctance when he replied, "Similar question could be asked of you, Uncle Matt. The whole family's been worried sick. We've had no word on how you been. You're long overdue and I'm here to check on your whereabouts."

"That a fact, huh? We couldn't find anybody in town to bring you word of where I've been. Nobody wanted to make the trip due to the Indian danger. So, you just took it on yourself to ride through these outlaw and Indian infested hills to check on me when nobody else would?"

"Only option we had the way I figured it. Robert's been laid up with a sore back. Lee ain't gonna leave the women and kids by their selves." He poked at his chest. "That leaves me."

Matt scratched his head. The kid was right. He had known Cora would be worrying over his tardy return from Austin. He would have made the same ride to discover the truth when he was young and brash. He wouldn't let Travis know it, but he admired the pluck shown with undertaking such a perilous ride.

Cliff turned away to hide his grin. He had no business getting in the middle of a family discussion, but Matt was obviously in unchartered water with his nephew. It wouldn't do if either side detected the humor he saw in their predicament.

"So why're you so late gittin' home? And what're you up to out here on Mount Bonnell?"

Matt held his hand up to slow down the onslaught of questions. There was a lot of information Travis needed to get up to speed. Cliff saw his opportunity to leave and bid adieu when Matt started explaining the shady details of conducting business in Austin. Travis ate up the news in the typical wide-eyed fascination of a young man learning the ways of the adult world. He shook his head in disbelief several times. The sad fact that most people couldn't be trusted to do the right thing was starting to penetrate his natural tendency to think otherwise. Another layer of his innocence had been peeled away at the conclusion of Matt's tale.

"Now," Matt said, "tell me what else you had in mind."

"It ain't no secret. I was goin' to meet up with Sarah and make some plans."

"Hate to break it to you, but Sarah and her family are movin' to Galveston."

Travis studied the rocks at his feet. "Don't surprise me none. Mary's been makin' noise about movin'. Don't change my mind none though." He stared straight at Matt. "I know what I gotta do now."

"What's that?"

"First, I'd like to serve with you on this trip as a Ranger."

"Can't. You're still a might young."

Travis bristled with impatience, but held it in check to make his case, "I understand. That's why I'll do the camp chores to earn my way."

Travis had learned a few things in the short time he had been on his own working for Jed. Matt realized this negotiation was going to be tough.

"Earn your way huh? Think it's that simple?"

"It's a start."

Matt rubbed his beard while pondering his options to discourage the boy. The memory of Mark struck down by a Comanche bullet flashed through his mind. He recalled the sight of Mark's skull exposed after the Comanche sliced off his scalp, the crimson pool of blood, the buzzing of flies, and the poignant odor of death. The brutal reality of fighting Indians would crush the ambitions of young men like Travis. He had to make it seem boring.

"You'll be held back from the action you know? You'll be expected to tend the stock behind the lines if there's a fight."

Disappointment dripped from his response. "Really? I hadn't thought of that."

"There's a lot you ain't thought of. Trail life can be mighty hard."

"Missin' the fight ain't what I want. I want to make a name for myself."

"There you go. You're the kind that comes back draped across the saddle. Makin' a name for yourself is the last thing you want to do. Killin' Comanche is second to survivin'. If you're dead or wounded you don't do no one no good."

"But stuck in the back holdin' horses?"

"Listen up. That's one of the most important jobs there is. I knew some Rangers that lost their horses to the Comanch up near San Saba. Them boys had to walk over one hundred miles back to Austin. The point is that all the work out on the trail is important. Every man has to do his part. It ain't all you think it is." Looking down his nose he said, "You're not ready yet."

"I done my part when you and Bull got waylaid. I got the camp set up to weather some mighty poor conditions. Made sure Mary was comfortable. Fixed the wagon while you and the sheriff checked out Kern. Fire was made and grub served by the time you got back with Kern's horse. You didn't have to lift a finger."

"Uh huh," was all Matt could say to the rapid discharge of facts.

"Got your wagon load of supplies back to the ranch. Got everythin' unloaded and made sure Aunt Cora and the kids was taken care of while you've been gone. She'll tell you I did a fine job. I patrolled around the cabin huntin' for Indian sign. Didn't sit on my hands once. You'll see when you git back."

"Don't change nothin' though. You don't have trail experience."

"What do you call this ride? I'm out here alone and ain't backin' down from no challenge. Goin' in to see Sarah next."

"It'll be dark!"

"Don't matter to me. Full moon tonight. I'll see fine. I'm goin' to see Sarah before she leaves and that's all I got to say about that."

"You can't. It's too dicey in the hills at night."

"Can't never did nothin'. That's what you always said. I'm goin' to see Sarah before she leaves. We got lots to discuss before we git married. The only question is will I be workin' for the Rangers tomorrow or back to slavin' for Jed?"

Matt stalled for time. He didn't like being backed into a corner. Especially by family. But there it was. The problem was as plain as day and not that hard to decide when all the dust settled. It didn't do the family name any good to have Travis working at a stable for a cantankerous son of a bitch like Jed. The best way to keep an eye on his impulsive nephew would be to have him trail along with the Rangers.

Sucking it up to hide his pride in the man Travis was becoming, Matt said, "We leave before sunup. Be here on time if you want Ranger pay."

Travis clutched Matt's hand in a frank display of appreciation. He mounted his palomino in a blur of excitement. Looking down at Matt, he tipped his hat and spurred away in a clatter of loose rocks. Matt started to holler be careful, but thought better of the idea. Men knew to be careful. There was no need to state the obvious to a man.

TWENTY-THREE

A vivid pink glow set the high wispy clouds ablaze the next morning. Charles had the men roused and ready for the ride well before the sun broke free of the black horizon. Breakfast would be mesquite-smoked jerky and spring water from canteens while the men were mounted in the saddle. No time was allotted for coffee making. Matt made it clear they needed to get back to his ranch as soon as possible and the presence of the wagon carrying Bull would make the day's journey slow. He wouldn't tolerate a tardy start. In his opinion he was already days behind in the pursuit of those responsible for the massacre of the men serving under Hobbs. And even longer in delivering the mandatory retribution for the raid on his place. The fact that Indians had laid their grimy hands on a member of his family made it personal in his book. It required payback.

Matt looked the men over and verified their readiness before he waved his arm for them to follow. The men he had assembled for this task knew what to expect with him riding at the front. His disciplined approach to soldiering was renowned. As a group they wouldn't have it any other way and were happy to be on the trail, but Matt had to hide his own disappointment. Travis was nowhere to be seen.

The wagon carrying Bull rattled and creaked in protest accompanied by the scrape of horseshoe against rock as they crept around the flanks of Mount Bonnell. Dreary gray timber crowded the men as they slowly progressed on the road uncoiling like a snake off the high slopes. Eventually they bottomed out for a short interval and crossed a shallow creek above a waterfall where Matt let the stock drink before tackling the steep rocky climb out of the ravine. He gazed on the back-trail wondering if Travis had changed his mind. Women could have that kind of impact on a man's decision-making process and a youngster like his nephew was prone to distraction when confronting the temptation of a new relationship. The most he could hope for was that Travis wasn't making an error in judgment that would haunt him the rest of his life. Too many men he knew had done that very thing and lived the rest of their days regretting their decisions made under the influence of the fairer sex.

The morning wore on with a sluggish but steady grinding pace until the column approached the scene of Kern's ambush. Once again Matt remembered his actions of that day, dismayed by his failure to prevent the attack. He slowed his men to a halt while he waited for Charles to draw up alongside him. "This is where it happened," he said to his sergeant with a sweeping motion of his arm.

Charles stood in his stirrups to stretch out his muscles while he analyzed the woods. Spitting to the side he said, "It's a good place to bushwhack somebody. I'd pick the same spot if I was of a mind to set an ambush."

"I should've seen it."

"Probably not much you could've done." Mossberg gave the incident more consideration and said, "Could've walked it out. He'd of shot you dead sure 'nough if you was walkin'. Bull might've escaped, but I doubt it. Yep, it's a good setup. He knew his stuff."

"Damn glad that dog caught scent. It was enough warning to make Kern miss."

"Luck plays a role more than we'd like to admit," Charles said. "Take right now. There's nothin' says there can't be an ambush set for us today."

Nate rode up beside them. He said, "Pa says this is where you buried Bones."

Matt nodded at the thicket to the right of the road.

Charles said, "Come on, Nate. Let's earn our pay and go scout for trouble."

They slid off their mounts and cautiously looked the woods over as they made their way to the far side of the constricted area. Certain there was no danger, Charles waved the column forward. Matt led the men under the canopy of trees until he motioned for the wagon to pull over at the burial site of Bull's favorite hound. He knew Bull would like to pay his respects to the dog that saved their lives.

Nate assisted Bull out of the wagon and gave him a shoulder to lean on while they hobbled over to the grave. It took everything Bull had to cover the short distance through the thick brush and Matt had to hold back vines to clear the way to the flat stones marking the site. Bull grimaced in sorrow when he finally stood over his beloved dog. Granny stood at his side with her arm around her husband.

"You done a good job markin' it, Matt. I'll always be able to find this spot."

"Fine dog you had there," Matt said.

Bull nodded his head in agreement. He was unusually pensive. There was nothing to say that could heal the hurt. He simply said, "So long, Bones."

There was a visible slump to Bull when Nate got him settled in the back of the wagon. Granny sat next to him and they both peered into the woods lost in their respective thoughts. She cupped his hand into hers and gave him a gentle squeeze. Bull nodded in gratitude. He realized the most meaningful things in life didn't always require words and he was a lucky man. She had supported him through many long years and countless tests of their ability to adapt and survive. Most men only dreamed of a wife as dedicated and capable as his. They faced a heartbreaking challenge in giving up their homestead to Ames, but together they would endure. The two of them and their sons would build a new life on Matt's place. Their strength as a family could not be overcome.

Matt pushed the pace for the rest of the day until the column made a dusty entrance to Bull's yard in front of his dilapidated cabin. Hounds appeared from all corners with tails wagging in happiness to see him after such a long absence. He eased out of the wagon to kneel in an affectionate reunion with what he considered his best friends. The earlier mood of gloom disappeared under the onslaught of pushing and crowding to wiggle into his lap. A few slobbery licks to the face coerced Bull to stand with the assistance of Nate. The hounds circled and pawed at his boots unwilling to end their display of fondness for the alpha male of their pack.

Preoccupied with returning the love for his hounds, Bull didn't notice Jake sneak up with a blanket-covered box in his arms. Jake chuckled when Bull's eyes picked up on the suspicious squirming under the cloth.

Bull said, "What's this?"

Jake uncovered the box for Bull to get a good look.

"Damn!" Bull exclaimed. "I'll be damned! Don't that one look just like Bones?"

Granny said, "Yes it does. You've got Bones junior."

"Matt! Git over here. Bones has got a pup looks just like him."

Matt ambled over to take part in the excitement. Bull was all grins for the moment, but that didn't last long. He tired quickly after the long day and Nate assisted him up to the porch where Matt pulled up a creaky chair next to his good neighbor. Granny left them alone so she could scrounge up some fresh grub to feed the hungry Rangers.

Bull leaned back in his ancient rocker and closed his eyes to relish the moment. He said, "Wasn't sure I'd git back. Damn sure feels good to be home."

Choking down his overwhelming urge to hit the trail for his own cabin, Matt said, "I agree, it's good to be back in the hills."

Bull opened his eyes and surveyed the bustling activity spread out before him. Nate had the hounds off to the corner of the yard feeding them a meal of scraps from the latest hog slaughtering. Jake had returned the pups to their mom and was in the process of pulling the wagon into the barn that was teetering on the edge of collapse. The small barn was a chore they never seemed able to make the time to repair considering they were always too busy with serious things like hunting or fishing to be bothered with upkeep. Like their father the boys figured when the barn tumbled to the ground would be the time to build a new one. Bull let out a heavy sigh.

Matt took the bait and asked, "What's on your mind?"

Bull watched the men busy tending to their mounts and joshing with each other as if they didn't have a care in the world. He reached for the jug always kept handy next to his rocker. Using his good arm, he heaved the jug to his lips and partook of his first drink of the day.

"Here's to gittin' home," he said after he downed his first gulp.

Matt waved off the offer when Bull shoved the jug his direction.

"You gotta loosen up. This occasion calls for a celebratory drink."

Wound tight with eagerness to tackle his responsibilities, Matt felt a natural aversion to hard liquor before the day's chores had been completed. He declined Bull's second offer with a flippant wave of his hand. Bull grinned before he planted the mouth of the jug against his lips. His greedy gulps came in surges Matt could hear over the good-natured insults flying between the men out in the yard.

"Now that's good medicine! I don't care what the doc says. I'd of healed a lot sooner if I could've tapped my juice." Bull slammed the jug down on the porch. "But that's gonna do it 'til I git some food in my belly."

Bull's scrutiny of the Rangers in his yard grew intense. He said, "I'll tell you what I think. I think you're up against some Comanche that'll be confident. Hobbs' defeat will have 'em fired up. They'll be ready for you this time."

"Yeah, I been thinking the same thing."

"Gotta be careful on this one."

"You're right. This one's different."

"That feelin' in your gut is what you'd best pay mind to."

"The best guide a man's got."

Bull pulled out his tobacco pouch and awkwardly pinched off a big wad with one hand. Working it under his gums he said, "Men that don't listen to their instincts are the ones that git in more heat than they can handle."

Matt nodded his head in agreement. The problem was; *most* men *didn't* listen to their gut instinct. His obligation as captain on this mission was to do their thinking for them. Keep them out of trouble any way he could. This occasion was different. He was completely responsible. There would be no officer in charge above his rank. All the decisions would be his. And some of those decisions could lead to death. He didn't like thinking of one or more of his men dying at the hands of Comanche, but what he liked or didn't like was of no consequence anymore. He had a job to do, and it came with a feeling in his gut he couldn't ignore. Bull had affirmed what he knew to be a fact. Somebody was going to die on this operation. The question was which one? Or how many? He looked over the men he would soon lead into the hard hills that showed no mercy. Which one?

He stood abruptly and stalked to the end of the porch. The men needed to eat first, but he was ready to saddle up and ride away. Action was the best cure for the unsettling possibilities bubbling to the surface.

Bull took note of Matt's annoyance. He said, "You'll do fine, Matt."

Matt gazed on the trail they had just traveled from Austin, his back to Bull. He wasn't so sure he'd do fine. The hills had their own ways. He understood most of them, but the Comanche knew more than he did. They had called the hills their home long before he'd carved his niche out of the wilderness. If he underestimated them, it could end in the death of all the Rangers. Himself included.

A rapidly approaching rider in the distance caught his eye. He stepped off the porch to get a better view and whistled at Bull to take a look. His suspicion soon gave way to reality. Travis rode into the yard like a dust devil from West Texas.

He dismounted without a word and led his winded palomino to the watering trough, deliberately keeping his back to Matt while he tended his horse. The only sound in the yard came from chickens clucking and scratching in competition for what little food they could pluck out of the bare dirt. The men took notice of the late arrival and frowns of scorn greeted Travis when he cast a wary glimpse around the setting. The silent treatment was the surest way to get the attention of a neophyte. It worked. Travis finished tending to his ride and tentatively approached Matt sitting next to Bull on the porch. The gruff appearance of his two elders watching his every step made him long for a hole to crawl into and disappear. He had his hat in his hand when he stopped short of Matt like a cadet reporting to his sergeant for inspection. He had an ass-chewing coming, and he knew it.

Summoning all the nerve he could muster, he stared into the coldest gray eyes he had ever seen. Matt's stern appraisal melted many a better man than he had become, but he met the critical assessment head-on. Sucking in his gut, he said, "No excuse for bein' late. My errand took longer than I anticipated. Ain't slept a wink."

"That means you ain't fit for nothin'," Matt retorted.

"I'll do fine."

"That's doubtful on no sleep."

Travis had an edge to his rebuttal when he said, "The advantage of bein' seventeen is stamina."

"What are you implying?"

"Nothin', sir."

Matt turned an inquisitive scowl on Bull and asked him, "Is he saying I'm old?"

Bull spat a thick brown stream of tobacco juice off the edge of the porch. "That's what I heard."

"That makes two of us," Matt agreed. He focused his harsh glare on Travis. "You're not helpin' you're case by insultin' your captain. Remember you're supposed to be a Ranger now. Family don't mean squat when we're on the trail."

"No insult meant. I made up the time best I could."

"What took you so long?"

Both Matt and Bull noticed Travis choking down his exasperation. He collected his thoughts before he said, "I've been dealin' with women all mornin'."

"Women huh?" Matt seemed incredulous when he spoke.

"Yes, sir. I couldn't git loose."

"You let a couple of women work you over?"

He hesitated while thinking of the conversation with Sarah and her mom. "I didn't let 'em. It just happened."

Matt's voice raised a notch when he asked, "If you can't handle a couple of women, what you gonna do when the Comanche git ahold of you?"

Travis blew out a sigh. Tension exhaled with a whoosh as he explained, "I'd rather face a Comanch than the grillin' Mary gave me."

Bull spit another stream of juice off to the side. "Imagine that!" he said with emphasis. "Women can sure scorch a man."

Matt dipped his head and rubbed his knuckles across his eyebrows. Shaking his head in skepticism, he looked at the rotting slats above him. He avoided eye contact with Travis until he cracked the whip, "You'd rather face a Comanch out to lift your scalp than a couple of ladies in town?"

Travis spun the hat nervously in his hands. It didn't make sense to him either, but at this moment it was how he felt. He mustered the courage to explain, "That's right. I'd rather be out here with the Rangers than facin' all the questions them ladies posed. You weren't there so maybe you don't understand."

Bull cut loose with a guffaw that shook his rotund belly. He laughed hard enough that a shot of pain ripped through his tender shoulder. Grimacing, he clarified, "Don't git your hopes up you'll ever understand women."

"Despite being late, you still think I should let you serve?" Matt asked.

"Yes, sir."

Matt pursed his lips, thinking.

"Our actual jump-off time will be when we leave my cabin tomorrow. I'll overlook this failure on your part considering the circumstance." He bored in on Travis with an intensity seldom seen by his nephew. "It won't happen again. Right?"

"No Sir!"

"You're assigned to Tom. You'll help him with the packhorses and preparing chow."

"Yes Sir!"

"Git to it then."

Travis felt like he had dodged a bullet. He hustled away from Matt and posthaste made himself available to Tom. Matt was glad to see the men accept Travis without any qualms after they witnessed the jittery boy facing his scrutiny. It would have been hard on the youngster if the men held it against him for not joining them earlier at daybreak.

"He'll do fine," Bull commented.

"Where do you git your confidence?"

"Powerful amount of hill country schoolin'. I been watchin' peeps a mighty long time. I got a good idea on what folks are made of."

"Confidence never been a problem for you?"

"Nope. Can see things comin' before they arrive."

"What you see for our Ranger scout?"

Bull didn't hesitate. "Trouble." He was uncharacteristically somber when he said, "Those Comanch are gonna be ready."

"I believe you're right."

"I'm countin' on you to come back. I've been told to be off my place by the end of the week. They're comin' to take it whether I'm ready or not."

This news surprised Matt. He hadn't heard this disturbing detail yet. Ames was not wasting time. He was circling like a wolf eager to rip the belly open and feed while his victim was still breathing.

Bull said, "Sheriff come by the doc's office right before we loaded up to leave. Gave us the news. Said he's just doin' his job. Don't hold it against him."

"That's his favorite line."

"Told me he don't want no trouble. I'd better be gone when Ames sends his men out to take possession."

Bull grew quiet. Matt could see the memories prowling behind his usually mischievous eyes. Life drained from his demeanor as he gazed across the land he had fought hard to tame in order to provide for his family. There were the corrals needing repairs on the posts tilting toward the ground. The beat down and weathered barn with a decaying roof that provided some protection from the rain, but not for much longer. The field of oats that had grown a lush green stood out in contrast to his cabin of old logs infested with termites. Off to the side stood his smokehouse always kept well stocked with smoked pork, beef, and dried sausage of every variety.

The Johnston family may be dollar poor Matt thought, but they were rich in the important things. It was a crying shame men bent on capitalizing off the misfortune of others would soon run the ranch Bull had created with gallons of blood and sweat.

Bull read his mind and said, "It'll be alright. You and me got lots of work to do on your place. My boys are more'n ready. We'll have a good start on that new cabin by the time you git back from your Ranger duties."

Matt extended his hand to Bull and their firm grasp conveyed a solemn understanding of what was at stake. Bull was depending on him as much as his own family did. Life had a way of increasing the burdens the older a man became. It seemed backwards to Matt, but there it was. It did no good to wish for how things should be. All that mattered was how things actually were. No other concern held water. "I'm countin' on you to come back," echoed in Matt's head. Of course Bull was right. But that didn't matter. Despite a man's best intentions, life had a way of dealing bad hands. He gazed across Bull's foreclosed property and shook his head in disgust. Bull had lost it all. The same could happen to his family if he didn't return home alive and healthy from the assignment. Out in the hills, life hung by a fragile thread subject to breaking in a strong gust of wind. He wondered if the thread would survive a little bit longer. There were no guarantees.

TWENTY-FOUR

Peals of distant thunder rolled through the woods surrounding Matt's cabin. The advancing tempest lay hidden behind the cedar-covered hills and vertical limestone bluffs that plunged to the river's edge, but the low rumble was a preamble to violent rainstorms. Packed with energy, the churning black clouds fed off the abundant moisture funneling into the hills from the Gulf of Mexico in the unseasonably tepid weather. In advance of the deluge a blustery downdraft whipped the upper branches of the pecan trees against one another in hollow thumps of bark grinding against bark. Crows took wing in the swirling winds seeking shelter next to the heights across the river.

Cora sat unoccupied on the porch enjoying a moment of relaxation with her chores completed and the kids engaged in the happy games of children. It was a rare circumstance to have quiet time and she offered to share the luxury with Robert when he crept out of the cabin. He eased forward with a stiffness brought on by lower back muscles as taut as a fiddle string. Grimacing with the effort, he squatted beside her on the pecan trunk Matt had sawed in half to make a cheap stool.

Settling in, he said, "I love a good storm."

A sad smile pushed up the pockets of shadow under her eyes. Sleep had been hard to come by in her endless nights worrying about the fate of Matt and his late return from Austin. She also spent time brooding over the likelihood of Bull dying since Travis had delivered the news of his life-threatening wounds. The lack of definitive information was a load she carried that was as heavy as the moisture swelling the clouds bearing down on them.

"I do too," she finally replied. "I love the smell of a cleansing rain."

Robert pondered the weathered gray planks covering their sitting area. He said, "Of course it's easier to enjoy when you're dry. Out on the trail there ain't much I like about rain."

"I suppose not."

Robert recognized the anxiety in her tone. He felt old and worn out, unable to mount up and hunt down answers about the condition of Bull and the whereabouts of Matt. Concerned about Cora, he said, "Travis will be back soon. He'll bring us up to date."

Squealing erupted in the yard. Luke caught Catherine in a game of tag and she immediately launched in pursuit of Susan, the youngest and most vulnerable. The possibility of a dramatic squall energized the kids with a zest for play. Laughter filled the yard as they darted here and there like fawns cavorting on a cool fall morning.

"I miss those times," Robert said, watching the antics of the children.

"They grow up fast."

"Don't blink. It's gone before you know it."

Cora thought of Josh. His life cut short by bloodthirsty heathens.

"Josh should be here," she said in a voice as dry as an August afternoon.

Robert didn't have a response. He scrunched his lips, looked at his boots, and nodded in agreement.

Lost in a far-off gaze, Cora lifted herself from the rocker to wrap her arms around the porch post. She hugged her breast snug against the cedar as if it could replace the loss of her youngest child. Still mourning, she wondered if the hurt had an ending.

"Does it ever stop?" she said to the wind.

Reflecting on the harsh realities of losing a loved child, Robert took his time to form a reply. Carefully gauging the power of his words, he said, "Hurt will always be there. It's meant to be that way." Delving deeper, he measured his words as he said, "Remember this, Cora. There's no death as long as you're remembered. Josh has a home in your heart from here to the end. And when you meet again, heartache's gone."

She stared past her kids chasing each other, never seeing them in their innocence. Wistfully turning her attention to the darkening sky she said, "It's the waiting that's the hardest thing I do. Sometimes it feels like he's still here." She pointed at her chest. "And other times it seems like it's all been a dream."

Robert studied her clinging to the post as if it were an anchor mooring her in a flood that threatened to carry her away. She was oblivious to her healthy children at play. She was lost in days gone by. He forced himself to remain silent. Cora was working things out on her own terms. Her own timeline. He had no right to intrude any further.

He watched Lee and Becky pacing the new mares out in the corral. They were a happy couple with their entire lives ahead of them. Becky stuck to Lee like mud to a boot after her close call with the Comanche abducting her. She was slowly adjusting, but the woods surrounding the cabin now held unimaginable horror in her mind. She never wandered to the river alone any more and was determined to stay within sight of the cabin at all times unless accompanied by an armed defender. Change was the one constant in life and she had made her changes accordingly.

Robert thought Cora was a different situation. He'd never lost a child and could only imagine the depth of the grieving Cora endured. Standing at the post, she reminded him of a flower wilted with summer heat. He couldn't stay silent any longer.

"Look around, Cora. You're surrounded by blessings. Change what you can. Accept the rest. It's all any of us can do."

She faced him, a pleading look in her eyes filling with tears. "I'm trying," she sobbed.

Robert stood, his aching back momentarily forgotten. He squeezed Cora in a hug. "I know you are," he whispered.

He could feel the sobs budding from deep in her chest. She choked them down and hid her face from the children that had stopped playing and watched her with concern etched on their face. Robert stepped back as Catherine and Susan ran to her side and wrapped their arms around their mother. Instinctively they knew what she was going through. They missed their dad and Josh too. Words were not needed for communication between women.

"Matt's trying too," Robert said.

She draped her arms over her daughters where she could look Robert in the eye, recognition of what he said dawning in her expression. They stared at one another. He said, "You're not alone in this."

That's when the clomping of approaching riders drifted into the yard. It was faint, but there was no doubt that a group of horsemen was just out of sight. Robert whistled at Lee and the kids made a beeline for the cabin. The children carried out the rehearsed plans with no delay. They had no problem understanding their lives depended on a quick reaction. Lee raced to the porch with his Spencer at the ready. Becky scampered through the door shadowed by Cora who had to make room for David emerging with the scattergun.

Admiring the proficiency, Robert said, "Y'all done good."

David took his place at the end of the porch, surveying the side of the cabin leading down to the creek. He was eager to prove his worth. It was obvious to Robert that David shared his father's intensity. He was ready, willing, and able to shoot somebody.

Satisfied with their readiness, Robert turned his attention to the road running beside the creek upstream from the cabin. The first rider came into view. Robert was relieved to see it was a white man with a familiar posture in the saddle. There was no mistaking his distinctive riding style that was all his own. He sat tall and proud. A man at ease and in rhythm with his steed. In full command. It was Matt! And he wasn't alone. A company of rugged men rode behind him.

Robert heard Cora moan. The presence of the additional men could only mean trouble from her perspective. It was starting all over again. How much more did Matt expect her to bear? Living with the man was driving her crazy. She wanted to dive into bed and pull the covers over her head. She slipped past Becky standing at the door and ran to the bed where she collapsed in a mixture of relief that Matt was home and a strong feeling of dread at the same time. She knew what the extra men meant.

All of the children wanted to acknowledge the arrival of their long missed father and rushed outside to greet him. When he slid out of the saddle, a cluster of excited kids gathered around and mobbed him with affection, ecstatic that he had returned home. He knew his late return had caused them all grief and cherished this first reunion. The absence of Cora didn't surprise him. It was a reaction he had come to expect.

He didn't have to be concerned about his men. He heard Charles barking orders behind him. It wouldn't take the veteran long to have the men and horses squared away in time to avoid the onset of the impending storm.

Lee parted the kids and clasped his older brother's hand in a genuine show of admiration. He said, "Glad to have you back."

"Damn good to be back!"

Matt took stock of his place. It had never been so good to be home. He had a new found appreciation of the freedom he enjoyed in the hills after dealing with the shrews of Austin.

Lee asked, "What took you so long? We heard about Bull gittin' shot, but we expected you back sooner."

Matt's brow wrinkled as his right eye narrowed to a slit. There was a lot of information to cover and Lee took a seat to absorb the forthcoming explanation. He had seen that look plenty of times. He knew Matt was ready to unload.

Listening to Matt sum it all up left Lee dumbfounded.

"Hell, Matt. I don't know where to start."

"Don't worry about Austin. Those bastards are at bay for now. How's the place been since the Comanche paid a visit?"

"I've been busy. David and I went back for the Comanche that Nate shot. We were gonna bury him, but his brothers had plucked up his worthless ass. We trailed where a couple of 'em took him up into Panther Hollow. Found where they left him in a cave with his personal effects. Was kinda spooky. We let him be and got the hell outta there."

"You done right. Comanche got strong beliefs about their dead. It'd be best to leave him alone from here on out. His spirit can have the cave."

Becky was listening from the door. Her eyes widened at the mention of spirits. She dreaded the red man in flesh enough as it was without considering their ghosts paying the cabin a nocturnal visit.

Matt noted the insecurity in Becky's expression. Taking her measure created more than she could handle. She ducked back inside to work at her chores. That was the surest way to take her mind off the Comanche she perceived lurking behind every tree.

Watching Becky dart away, Matt asked, "Any other Indian sign since then?"

"None except for the pony we roped. It was the one the dead buck was riding."

"You caught his pony?"

Lee's face beamed with pride.

"Sure did. With the help of David on the way back from findin' the burial site. Was a stroke of luck them Comanche didn't git him before we did."

Matt glanced at the corral but didn't see the pony. He asked, "Where's he at?"

"That's the best part. I traded him and a cow to old man Overton for three mares. Breedin' mares."

"Helluva job, brother. That's a good start. We're gonna need the cash." Matt looked at Lee approvingly. Slapping him on the back he said, "So you're gonna be our horse trader."

Laughing, Lee said, "I reckon so. Gotta pull my weight anyway I can."

"Glad to hear good news, but let me ask you. How's Becky?"

Lee's grin faded. His focus settled on Robert talking to the men out in the yard.

"She's skittish. Sticks close to me all the time. What happened scared the hell out of both of us. Them Comanche puttin' their hands on her has been hard to forgit."

Matt studied the door that Becky had left open on purpose so she could watch the men from inside the cabin. He had also seen Cora duck inside after she saw him riding into the yard. He knew she was trying to compose herself. She understood what a gathering of Rangers in the yard meant and that meant he would have to deal with her quickly. There was little time left before his men headed out the next morning.

The image of the Comanche handling Becky upset him. She was family. She deserved the security of a safe home. He had let her down and intended to make it right. He responded to Lee's summary of her behavior, "I imagine it is. Had to scare a good girl like Becky half to death."

"Scared us all."

Matt's voice was hard as nails. "I intend to make amends for her trouble."

"We're behind you on that."

Motioning toward the door, Matt said, "Not necessarily all of you."

Robert came over to make his appearance with Travis at his side.

"Hello, Robert. How are you?" Matt asked.

"Been better. Damn old back is plumb give out."

"Sorry to hear that. Been there myself."

"Signed up for another go at 'em I've been told."

"You know how it is."

"Promoted to captain. I gotta say it's 'bout time."

"We'll see."

"You'll do fine. What's the objective?"

"You ain't heard 'bout Hobbs?"

"Hobbs? News travels slow out here at times. Hell, we didn't even know for sure 'bout you 'til today. What's the latest?"

"He fooled around and got his command ambushed at the Pedernales crossing on the Colorado. Only two men got back to town. Charles is one of 'em."

The news cast a shadow on Robert. He hung his head looking at the dirt mumbling, "Damn sorry to hear that."

Matt took a lingering look at his place. He was lucky the Comanche had not returned to wreak havoc. He was fortunate his family was still alive to meet him. Too many families had been devastated with all manners of loss. Cabins burned to the ground. Children butchered. Women raped. And in a few cases entire families wiped out. The animosity bubbled in his heart.

"Well, we aim to put an end to some of it starting tomorrow. We're ridin' out first thing in the mornin'. We'll find Hobbs and his men. Bury 'em. Then we'll track down any Comanche we can find and put an end to their murderin' ways."

"I wish you the best," Robert said. "Sorry I'll have to miss this one. My back's too stiff to ride home, much less hit the trail with your men. You know where I'd rather be."

"All things considered, I appreciate you helping out here at the ranch. I'll rest easier knowing you're here with all these Indians raising hell."

Matt's eyes fell on Travis now loafing with David out in the yard. His glare sharpened to a fine point, Matt barked, "Travis! What are you doing?"

Busted, Travis stumbled for an explanation. "I was just headed over to ask Charles if he needed any help." And he was gone before Matt could add any insults.

"Sorry to take Travis along. I'm kind of cornered on that one." Matt said.

"No problem. It'll be my pleasure to stick around until you return. My neighbors are looking after my place, so all's well," Robert said.

"Glad to hear that. It's mighty fine to have good neighbors. Speaking of which, you can expect to see Bull's sons start showing up any day to start on their cabin. They're moving in and we're gonna be partners. I'll explain more later, but that'll give you a few more guns to depend on while I'm gone."

Lee said, "Don't worry none 'bout the place. We'll git by fine and make Bull's family welcome."

Matt eyed the cabin, clasped his hands together and stretched his arms above his head. Twisting at the waist he loosened his muscles from the all day ride. Peering at the door he said, "Now excuse me, I've got to explain things to Cora."

.

TWENTY-FIVE

Matt lingered at the door to let his eyes adjust to the dim interior. Becky saw him leaning against the doorframe and crept by without a word. He watched her slide up beside Lee and snuggle against his arm. Lee was right about her. She reminded him of a lost puppy. Insecure, and in need of constant assurance, it was easy to read in her downcast gaze and drooping shoulders. It made him hate the fiendish ways of the Comanche. Becky was an innocent girl robbed of her happiness and security. He wondered if she would ever recover.

Cora had summoned the courage to get out of bed and was sitting at the table with a cup of coffee cradled between her hands. Forlorn, her cheeks were devoid of color and her face sagged like she alone bore the weight of the world. Her eyes looked past Matt, and rested on the men moving about the yard in their preparations for a rainy evening. She obviously didn't want to have a discussion.

A warm flush of resentment grew in Matt's heart. His chest tightened in a brewing anger he struggled to control. She was going to make this difficult. Again.

He couldn't touch her. She would freeze up as cold as ice at the touch of his hand. It was a response he had grown accustomed to since the loss of Josh. She made him feel like he was a beggar. Her rejections left him hollow, exposed, and alone.

"Hello, Cora."

Indifferent, she looked at him.

"Glad to see me?"

She knew what he meant. He was testing.

"I'm glad you're home."

He folded his arms across his chest and straightened up stiff as dried leather.

She sat silent, holding in her disapproval, not sure where the conversation would wander, but certain there would be a price to pay for how she felt about his disregard for her wishes.

Yep, as cold as ice he thought. He wasn't having it. He had been through too much.

"Let's go," he said.

"Go?"

"We're taking a walk."

"There's a storm brewing."

"You're damn right there is. Now git up. We're taking a walk."

Tentatively, and on wobbly legs, she stood. Matt was in one of his moods. She knew better than oppose him at this point. He waved her out the door where the excitement of seeing Rangers armed to the teeth kept the kids distracted. She dallied at the edge of the porch unsure of Matt's intentions. He stalked past her and she fell in behind his wake. He was headed to the river crossing.

The trail to the river was churned up in black clods of dirt by the frequent travel of cattle seeking water at the riffles. A canopy of huge pecan limbs spanned the path. Hundreds of years old, the trees grew enormously tall and bulky in the rich sediments of the wild Colorado River floodplain. Prolific vines of mustang grapes sprouted out of the creek bottoms and weaved into the branches above their heads as they trudged in silence down to the river.

Cora walked at a brisk pace in order to keep up with Matt and his determined stride. He never turned to check on her progress, assuming in his habitual way that she knew not to fall behind. When his mind was focused, there was little that could knock him off track. This was one of those times. She was delighted he had made it back, but the Rangers accompanying him had spoiled the homecoming she had envisioned.

She reasoned that she should be thrilled he wasn't shot up like Bull. She should be happy their homestead had dodged the forfeiture imposed on neighboring ranches that couldn't afford their back taxes. She knew these things, but all she could think of was that Matt was riding back in harm's way. She didn't know why, or where, or for how long, but Rangers in their yard only meant more heartache in her future.

Matt took a fork in the trail that meandered upstream. She knew where he was going. His thinking spot. He had arranged some logs for a comfortable place to sit where he liked to watch the ceaseless flow of water. He had told her the river was like him and she understood. It was restless, full of energy, and endless in its movement. He said the motion calmed his soul. He could drop his worries in the current to drift away and come back to the ranch a restored man ready to face life again.

He philosophized that the river characterized the existence people were destined to live. Long tranquil pools of peaceful times occurred where trouble seemed remote and insignificant—the place where most right thinking folks would prefer to spend all their days. But there was always the thunder of rapids if a person had the ears to listen. The rushing whitewater waited to snag the ill prepared, the ignorant or the lazy. If caught unaware it would overwhelm the weak and crush their hopes and dreams in a raging torrent. The key he said was to use the current of the rapids to your advantage. Let the tumult work to your benefit until a safe haven presented itself.

That was the method a smart man would use to deal with the inevitable rapids in life. And then he considered the floods. The Colorado could become a crazed brown monster foaming at the mouth as it ravaged anything within its reach. Trees were torn from their tenuous hold to fertile black soil and tumbled downstream bobbing like corks on the turbulent waters, small and stripped of significance. He said floods materialized from the hands of God and you had to pray for deliverance when you were caught in powers that ripped control from your grasp.

These thoughts and comparisons he had shared with her in their happier times. This was where he liked to let his mind roam if he had the spare time to indulge his reflective nature. She watched his broad back as he led them along the brushy bank thinking about his past ruminations and she realized if his comparisons of the river to life were true, she was in trouble. Her river was dry. She was suffering from a long lasting drought. There was little that stirred in her soul, but intuition told her Matt was floating on the crest of a flood. The torrential rain called life was carrying him away and she didn't have a clue how to pull him back to safety.

They arrived at his favorite spot where he pointed at a bleached-out trunk, bare of bark, and etched with the grooves of beetle trails. He said, "Have a seat."

With his back to her, he snatched a limb from the flotsam that littered the bank and flipped it into the water. It submerged with a splash and bobbed to the surface inside an expanding ring of ripples. Mesmerized by the branch drifting downstream, he kept his back to Cora. He watched the limb spin into an eddy, captured by the spiraling force of the current. It continued to swirl, caught by a force it couldn't escape. Much like his life.

He asked Cora, "Ever wish you could just float away?"

Surprised by his strange enquiry she replied, "No, I suppose not."

"Humph," he muttered. "Why not?"

"Don't see no sense in it."

"Why's it have to make sense?"

"We've got kids. Everything is for them. My wishes don't matter."

"*Everything?*" He picked up a rock and launched it across the water. "What *we* want doesn't matter?"

She glanced across the olive-green surface of the river where needle nose gars were rolling in their pursuit of minnows. Silver flashes darted in front of the gar as they breached the surface of the water in their attempt to capture a meal. Dimples from the fleeing minnows formed just beyond the razor-sharp teeth of the prehistoric and predatory needlefish. A kingfisher sprung from its perch with a clamorous rattle and his deep, irregular wing beats carried him to the pod where it dove into them and emerged with a minnow flopping in its beak.

Cora observed all of the late evening happenings on the river with jaded interest. These things were an occurrence as old as time, and held little appeal to her at the moment. Bigger concerns were on her mind, but she understood why Matt liked to sit beside the river to clear his thoughts. She had forgotten how relaxing it could be, and that was a pleasure she rarely experienced anymore.

"Well, does it?" he repeated.

She noticed his eyes. They were sad. Imploring. Not angry like she expected.

"Yes, it matters what we want. Just not as much as before."

His voice grew stern. He could change directions as quick as a cat. He said, "Consider this. The kids see what's going on. How do you think they feel?"

"Going on? What's going on?"

"You don't think they sense the chill in the air between us?"

"So, this is about you joining the Rangers again?"

"Hah! Don't play dumb with me Cora. I know you don't approve of my Ranger work. But you'll damn sure be happy to know that Ranger pay kept the wolves from our door one more time. Bull wasn't so lucky, now was he? No he wasn't and that's why he'll start building a cabin above the river pasture before I git back. We're gonna be partners in raising crops and horses."

She took a minute to let the news sink in. It would be nice to have close neighbors to keep her company and help work the property. They owned more land than they could manage. The news was good in her opinion. It was about time something transpired that could improve their living conditions. Having Granny nearby for the female companionship of an adult was a pleasant thought.

A distant flash of lightning raced across the black clouds above the hills. Downstream from them the river basin darkened under the building storm. A peal of thunder broke over their heads.

"I ain't playing dumb," she said. "You know I hate it when you're out patrolling. What if you don't come home? What's gonna save us then?"

"We're not here to discuss my choice of profession. I've been promoted to captain. Means there's more money. You should be proud. It's what I do. Serving as a Ranger is a dead subject between you and me."

"I've got nothing to say about it?"

Matt raised his foot to rest it on the trunk and leaned over to place his elbow on his knee. His scowl burned with intensity. Cora felt the heat. She knew the core of the matter was on the tip of his tongue.

He let her wait. She could simmer while his glare silenced her lips. He had wanted this conversation far too long. She had to listen. She had to know things needed to change. *Now*.

Another clap of thunder rumbled above the openness of the river. It echoed off the bluffs and shook the ground beneath their feet like boulders tumbling off a ridge. A raw energy sizzled in the air.

"Not anymore," he said. "We're done with that topic. You married a Ranger. End of story."

She sat stoic. It was futile to resist. And she no longer had the wherewithal. She felt the crushing manifestation of the truth inside her chest. He was right. They had dodged a financial bullet aimed at their head. Unpaid taxes would have been catastrophic. She had to accept the risk of his profession and deal with fears of his death in silence. She owed it to Matt. He was the one taking the chances with his life for the benefit of the family. Robert was right. Matt was doing all one man could.

"So, that's what you think, Matt?"

"That's the best you can say?"

"I don't know what you want."

"What I want?" His voice cut like a knife. "You're not being honest." He leaned in close. "You know what I want."

She averted her eyes. She knew what he meant. It was more than she could do to face him.

A brisk wind rose off the water and rustled the leaves at their feet. The wet scent of rain permeated the bottoms. Roiling black clouds now towered above them.

His tone softened when he said, "We haven't talked about it. Ever. Now's the time."

Tears welled up in her brown doe-like eyes. This was going to hurt. Bad.

"Now's the time. You know it. And I know it."

He let the idea settle. He couldn't bulldog her about this.

"I know it hurts, but not talking about it is smothering me." He hesitated before he added, "Josh is gone."

The tears fell. She gasped for breath at the mention of his name.

"Sorry to bring it up, Cora, but I've gotta git it off my chest. There's times I can't take another minute living with how I feel."

He handed her his handkerchief. She took it, daubing at her cheeks without looking at him. Memories of Josh playing at her side while she cooked in the kitchen broke her heart all over again. He liked to take a wooden spoon and bang on the metal pots she sat on the floor for his entertainment. She considered the racket he made to be soothing. All he wanted to do was be near her where he felt secure. He had been her youngest and such a joy to behold.

And Matt was talking about how he felt. *He* was responsible for the death of Josh. She had relived the misery of losing him every day since his death. She yearned to erase the hurt from her memory, but relived it over and over instead. What could Matt know about how she felt? The death of Josh and the brutal manner he had died had left her shattered.

He sat beside her careful not to touch her. She buried her face between her hands. He stared across the river where the kingfisher finished his meal perched on a sawyer wedged tight against the far bank.

"There's not a day I don't think of him," he said. Thoughts of Cliff's ruined family prowled through his mind. The man was living in hell. He began to falter, but summoned the nerve to add, "You're not the only one that misses Josh."

Her chest heaved with an expansive breath.

Matt bowed his head as he chose his next words carefully. "There's not a day that I don't beat myself up for not paying closer attention to his whereabouts."

He looked at her. She appeared to pay him no heed. Her mind was drifting down the river, distant and not comprehending although she heard every word.

"You gotta know that, don't you?"

She clutched the handkerchief in her lap and rolled it into a tight wad. "Do I?" she said vacantly.

His chin slumped against his chest. He should have seen the ants crawling on his boots, but his eyes were shut. All he saw was the laughing face of Josh the morning he was murdered by the Comanche. A thrust of pain stabbed his heart as if a Comanche arrow had penetrated his chest.

"You think I'm to blame for the death of Josh."

He looked up to see the emotions stirring in her eyes. This time she didn't avert her attention. She was peering deep. He had uncovered the truth. The wound was bared for them both to examine. It was time to confront the demon splitting them apart. She didn't utter a sound. She didn't need to say anything. The heat of her scrutiny said it all.

He said, "That must be hard to live with."

She puckered her lips unsure of where this was leading.

Continuing, he said, "I understand how you feel about me. And if I could change it, I would."

He tilted his head to inspect the sky. Ominous clouds were bulging overhead.

"The trouble is you're right." He kicked at the dirt. "What I live with is knowing you're right. I live with the guilt every day."

He turned to face her. Their eyes locked. He said, "Now, imagine living with that."

A bolt of lightning sliced a jagged path through the air and exploded against a peak down the river. A blinding white flash accompanied by a wave of thunder rippled through their bodies like a volley of cannon fire. A curtain of steel-blue rain obscured the hills as it advanced up the valley. In moments it would dump its load on the pecan bottoms where Matt sought refuge from the harsh realities of living on the Texas frontier. He knew there was no escaping the coming storm. The question in his mind was; would his marriage make it out of the tempest brought on by the death of Josh?

TWENTY-SIX

Yellow-orange sparks burst from the crackling embers of the bonfire, rising on the heated thermals into the cool night air. Black silhouettes of dancers bowed and dipped as they circled the flames to the to the steady beat of buffalo hide drums. Their knees nearly jammed into their chests as the rhythm pulsed through their veins driving them into a frenzy of convulsive dancing. Howling screeches occasionally erupted from the ring of observers caught up in the ecstasy of the moment. The dancing awoke their primitive longings to participate in the celebration of victory centered on the scalps hanging from lances stabbing into the night sky. Bells and high-pitched deer bone whistles complemented the pounding of drums that carried into the blackened timber surrounding the village tepees.

Blond, red, black and brown scalps flapped on the point of the spears in mute testimony to the savageness of the celebration. The blood of white men, their women and their children had been spilled to satisfy the lustful needs of the warriors seeking revenge for the theft of their homelands. It was how they proved their worth as men and as guardians of the People.

The tribe was happy. Most of their braves had returned from their perilous forays into lands now occupied by the whites. Scalps and stolen horses brought back to the People was a cause for a joyous festivity although not all took part. Several door flaps were closed while those that had lost relatives mourned inside their lodges. Instead of celebrating the return of their courageous young men some of the squaws had cut their hair off short and the mother of Weasel Dog cut her finger off at the first joint when confronted with the unthinkable death of her son. Their wails of grief were drowned out by the steadily growing clamor of the scalp dance.

Black Owl sat at the edge of the circling dancers while he munched on the fat chunks of bear meat served to honor his exploits among the hated white intruders. His fingers were covered in grease that he licked clean while he observed the lightning above the scalloped line of black knolls marking the southern horizon. Great billowing clouds were lit by an almost nonstop dance of electric-blue streaks of incredible power. Stripped naked of leaves, the nearby trees spread their web of limbs out in stark contrast to the clouds glowing purple with accumulated energy.

This storm was the most magnificent evidence of the spirits he had ever witnessed. It was good to know that the immortal ones were celebrating with the scalp dance as only they could. Returning to the tribal campsite with scalps and plunder and then witnessing the magnitude of the storms rejuvenated his desire to strike another blow against the white men. The hairy-faced men had spread throughout the hills like an out of control wildfire driving the Comanche farther and farther from their rightful lands. They deserved the death that would rain down on them like the bolts of fire he saw snapping across the heavens.

Buffalo Hump sat next to him on a plush buffalo robe of supreme quality and in the highest place of honor to witness the dance. They shared the same status in the tribe, but his revered companion was also celebrating a special occasion. The horses he took at the slaughter of the Texans on the Pedernales was enough to pay her father and insure the affections of his new bride, Little Fawn That Follows. She sat next to her new husband and from the look on her face the two of them would soon slip away to consummate their union in the privacy of his lodge. His other wife would have to make room for the addition of a new female to share the warrior chief endowed with insatiable needs. His taste for women was as strong as his dream to push the Texans from their wooden dwellings occupying the rightful hunting grounds of the Comanche. He had already organized the next foray into the hills where the dog-faced men polluted the streams and fields with their foul replacements for buffalo. His war party would leave before daylight in the morning.

The main goal of the incursion was to avenge the death of Weasel Dog. Buffalo Hump maintained a strong regret that he had left the scene of Weasel Dog's death without extracting revenge against the white men responsible for the shooting of his favorite cousin. He had wanted to return and ransack the home of the whites, but the counsel of his brothers convinced him to refrain. They all held the palefaces inside that cabin in awe of their medicine they considered supernatural. These whites were also the ones responsible for trailing Black Owl's raiding party into the Colorado River bottoms where they managed to kill Bear Claw even when he possessed the upper hand. To add further insult, they also found Walks Alone lying severely wounded and vulnerable beside the trail and finished him off as well.

The unexpected appearance of a skunk in the middle of their counsel on what to do about the death of Weasel Dog had sealed his decision. The skunk was a bad omen that none of the braves felt obliged to overlook. They also considered their numbers too small to engage an enemy that knew they were there and would be prepared to protect their families at any cost. At the time it had been the right thing to do. He ended up settling for retrieving the corpse of Weasel Dog for a proper burial in a secluded cave far up a rugged canyon.

Black Owl plucked a succulent piece of deer tenderloin from the bowl propped up at his feet by Whisper. She sat meekly next to him making an occasional comment in his ear to be heard above the wild rants and shouts of the warriors enjoying the extraordinary buzz in the air. She made him an offer that caught his undivided attention. Black Owl's tepee was at the edge of the camp and she suggested they retreat to a soft patch of grass behind his lodge. Her eyes glowed with devilment in the warmth of the flames. There was no way he would decline her offer knowing that he would be departing on a dangerous raid that not all would return from.

She stood and looked down at him with her sumptuous lips mouthing, "Follow me." He watched her hips swish under the tight buckskin dress as she drifted away, looking back provocatively to make sure he was relishing her flirtations. She knew that sending him off with a tantalizing memory was the best way to provide him with the extra motivation to return safely. She had said as much.

She wanted him to think of her often during his absence and assured him she knew tricks to ensure a place in his heart. As she disappeared into the celebration he knew she was right. It was time for him to make the commitment and she would share his lodge permanently upon his return. It was time for him to pass down his talents as a fighting man to a new generation of Comanche. The People required new blood if they were to stand a chance against the onslaught of the white race.

The thunderstorm on the horizon intensified. Brilliant veins of lightning flashed from cloud-to-cloud in their upper heights. Moisture bulged in the thunderheads like overripe plums. Too far away to hear the crack of lightning, Black Owl sensed the rumbling in his soul, and felt the might of the awesome forces being unleashed on the white warriors living alongside the river they called the Colorado.

Those pale enemies lived in sturdy built dwellings and grazed their prize horses inside wooden fences that Buffalo Hump had found impossible to overcome during his attempt to steal them. Both he and Buffalo Hump agreed this place on the river should be their main objective on this particular raid. These men had caused too much trouble to be ignored any longer. They had persuaded enough warriors to accompany them that he was confident in the bravery and Comanche skill to defeat the potent medicine of the white men. Buffalo Hump burned with an unquenchable thirst for the punishment of the white family. He intended to murder the men first, and afterward take his time to enjoy the rape of their defenseless women. And in particular he wanted to capture the young woman with skin the color of milk and taste of sweet honey. She had been the cause of Weasel Dog's ill-advised maneuver, but hearing of her charms, Buffalo Hump had special plans for her return to the village where she could supply amusement for all of the braves, young and old. She had earned this special treatment and he would extend her agony under Comanche dominance as long as possible.

Once the white men were dispatched, Buffalo Hump knew he could destroy the fenced horse enclosure and take possession of the particularly fine horseflesh that haunted him in his dreams. They had been so close in their last attempt. He was not accustomed to being deprived, and he often thought of the lost chance at the incredible wealth the horses represented. Their capture would make him one of the wealthiest men in their village. He *had* to have them. The best part of his plan was to strap any captured children to the horses for a speedy retreat back to the People. The young girls would be old enough to please many braves and work for the squaws as they saw fit until they either adopted the Comanche ways or perished. This gift to his brothers would guarantee the elevation of his warrior status he constantly strived to achieve.

Black Owl realized this raid was Buffalo Hump's to lead, but it didn't make a difference to him. They had worked out the details as equal partners unconcerned with the egos that other Comanche let get in the way of clear thinking. It was to be one last grand adventure before they retreated to the Caprock Canyons at the edge of the high grassy plains where they would hunt buffalo during the long days of summer. Those members of the village not accompanying them on this particular raid would depart for the safety of the game rich hinterlands after seeing the war party off in the morning.

The trembling screeches around the fire grew to a crescendo feeding the excitement of the village for the prospect of more victories. Black Owl finished his meal and stood to beat his chest with pride. His brothers belonged to a great nation that controlled vast territories from the edge of the green hills to the foot of snow capped mountains. They had ruled the land for as long as his grandfather could remember. His tribesmen danced with joy tonight. For the moment it seemed like the old times he had known as a young boy dreaming to participate in the glory of riding off to make war on those that opposed the People. He was proud to be Comanche and would defend their way of life to the death.

In the morning he would ride at the front of a formidable war party departing in a solemn parade before the rest of the tribe. They would leave to strike the white intruders hard and make them pay for their evil presence much as they had the Texans at the Pedernales crossing. Those men had been savagely mutilated and left tied up as a warning to any traveler that found them. The Comanche had made a statement meant to instill terror and respect for their traditions in the minds of the hairy-faced invaders.

All along the horizon the storm strengthened as if angry spirits possessed the heavens and sought destruction of the white men huddled below the fury raining down on them at this very moment. Numerous bolts of lightning streaked upward from the towering thunderheads as if seeking to strike the stars, their brilliant cobalt paths fragmented into a spiderweb against the ebony background of night sky.

Black Owl nodded in approval of the peculiar spectacle. It was a good omen for their intentions. The spirits had spoken. This raid would be successful. They had the number of warriors needed to accomplish their objective and they had the blessings of the war spirits. He beat his chest and cried out a vow to strike with a vengeance against the sworn enemies of the Comanche. The trill of those surrounding him increased in their approval of his threat. They were unified and of the same mind. The palefaces would soon have their scalps lifted and their women and children would suffer the wrath of the mighty Comanche.

TWENTY-SEVEN

Matt huddled outside the front door with Nate and Charles discussing the plans for the day's ride. It was a damp, miserable gray morning with angry clouds drifting ominously close to the land soaked by the ferocious overnight downpour. Water dripped from the oaks and a rivulet channeled across the bare yard on its way to the muddy Colorado. Inside the door Becky and Cora worked feverishly on the last home cooked breakfast the men would know for some time. She meant to give the Rangers a proper farewell taste of the home life they were duty-bound to protect.

Matt said, "Won't be any trail left for us to track after this deluge." He ambled into the yard to survey the leaden skies. "Helluva storm."

"I can still cut for sign out ahead of ya," Nate replied.

"You'll be earning your pay in these conditions."

"No problem. If we cross their trail, they'll be easy to follow in the mud."

Charles noted, "Creek crossin's will be tricky in high water."

Matt removed his hat and ran his hand through his hair. It was too early to be dealing with complications before they even left the comforts of his ranch. In his familiar blunt tone he said, "We'll do what we gotta do."

Cora poked her head out the door and announced breakfast was ready. With Becky's help she served up thick sizzling slabs of fried ham hanging over the edge of the plates. Piles of scrambled eggs that emptied her supply were heaped beside the juicy meat. Golden brown biscuits dripping with fresh churned butter rounded out the feast washed down with steaming black coffee thick enough to cut with a knife. Compliments on her cooking poured in from all the men. They knew that they faced scanty meals ahead with Tom's legendary beans providing the culinary highpoint while they pursued the elusive Comanche. The value of Cora's abilities in the kitchen was renowned and the men would not think of letting her go unappreciated.

After the hasty meal, Charles attended to organizing the men in the manner Matt preferred for the trail. Robert sat on the porch trying to ignore the unrelenting tightness of his lower back muscles. He hated to admit the truth, but his age had finally caught up to him. He had seen his last ride as a Ranger.

Matt appeared at his side and rested a hand on his shoulder. "Glad you'll be here to keep an eye out."

"It's the least I can do."

"I'm just glad you're here to help Lee."

"I think we have enough guns for *most* cases."

"*Most* is the problem. Never can tell what them bastards will do next."

"True enough."

Robert sensed Matt's uneasiness at the idea of leaving his family. It was a condition every Ranger living on the frontier grappled with when he was called to serve. Robert offered his assurances, "It's a risk that's gotta be taken. Clean the vermin from the hills one mission at a time and eventually it'll be safer for us all."

Cora peeked out the door and inadvertently distracted Matt's attention. She ducked back inside overcome with the conflicting emotions she always did her utmost to hide from detection. She preferred nobody know of the anguish she was suffering. It was a skill she had perfected over time and most people could never guess the deep-rooted turmoil she lived with every day. Nobody except Matt.

Matt contemplated Robert's observation and Cora's evasive behavior at the same time before he responded, "That's my intentions. Safer for everybody. Too many folks have suffered far too long." He thought of Cora in particular. The loss of loved ones left a raw scar that lasted a lifetime. "Ain't ever been easy out here. We still got a load of work to do before it's as it should be."

He gave Robert a pat on the back as he made his way to the door, his boots striking with a hollow thud against the damp planks of his porch. His broad chest filled the doorway as he peered into the dimly lit cabin and found his daughters assisting the women with cleaning up the breakfast dishes. It was a scene he would file away to recall when he needed a motive to justify what he was going to do. The violence he inflicted was not without cause. The vengeance he would perpetrate on the Comanche and the blood spilled because of his actions was just and unavoidable. The ways of life on the Texas frontier were harsh and unforgiving. He wasn't the one that made it that way. It was just the way it was. But he could live with that. Inside his cabin was the reason for his existence. He lived by a code that demanded he vanquish those that would do them harm. The time had arrived.

"I'm leaving," he said.

The room went deadly silent as they looked up from their chores all at once. Cora spun to grab a towel and nervously dried her hands without making eye contact with Matt. His daughters scampered to him with open arms and smothered him in a tight hug. He buried his nose in their fine hair and breathed openly of their youthful fragrance as if it would be his last chance. For all he knew, it would be. Disturbed with the thought, he gave each one a doting kiss on the forehead.

Becky stood mute at her post not willing to acknowledge Matt's departure, which left her more vulnerable. Her wilting posture wasn't difficult to read. Matt moved to her and dropped a strong arm over her shoulder and said, "You'll be fine, Becky. Plenty of men here to keep the place safe. Bull's family will drop by soon."

Her face wore an empty expression. She still relived the helplessness of the greasy muscular arm grasping her in a vise she couldn't escape. She could still smell his foul breath, and feel his tongue slippery and wet slide along her neck tasting her as if she was a chunk of meat. The memory of the strange Comanche dialect echoed in her head when she awoke at night dripping with sweat and lost in a nightmare where she was once again being drug through the mesquite that ripped at her clothes, the security she had always known fading in the distance. Matt's words rang hollow. His assurances were meaningless. He would be gone.

Matt could sense the isolation Becky had retreated to in her attempt to cope with the shock of being abducted by barbarians that appeared from out of nowhere. It was just like Lee had told him. Becky was a changed person. She looked beat.

Cora nodded toward the door. It was time for him to leave and his words to Becky were wasted on deaf ears although she did risk a glance at him before returning to her simple routine. She muttered a few words of garbled thanks as she furiously scrubbed the blackened frying pan held tight in her dainty hands. He realized he didn't have anything else to offer to his young sister-in-law. Her vacant eyes would haunt him in the future.

He repeated, "You'll be fine," as he backed out the door with Cora in tow.

Out of Becky's hearing, Matt told Cora, "I don't know what else to say."

"Nothing you can say. Time is what she needs. All of the men showing up has been too much for her. She'll do better when everything returns to normal."

Charles had the men mounted and in the formation they had agreed upon the night before. Things were about to get serious and the dour mood of the men reflected that realization. They sat grim-faced and ready to take care of business. Nate's high-strung dun pranced in a circle at the front of the column ready to be on the trail. Lee guided Whiskey up to Matt all geared up and trapped in the excitement of departure. Matt smiled his first smile of the day in appreciation of Whiskey's willing temperament.

Charles bellowed, "Ready to ride!"

Matt's boys took the cue and stepped up to their dad to take turns exchanging a manly handshake, leery of too much affection in front of the mounted Rangers. They both wanted to give their dad a hug, but settled for the handshake and grinned up at Matt with obvious veneration. He was a giant among men in their eyes.

This was it. The knot in Matt's stomach tightened the longer it took to utter the final goodbyes. The men were set, waiting on him.

He turned to face Cora. She was the most delicate to deal with at times like this and he preferred to slip away without the drama he felt bubbling beneath the surface of her outwardly calm appearance. He didn't like stirring up the turmoil between them with an extended departure that could turn awkward. This time was different. For the first time, *he* felt like this time could be the last time.

Her surprise was total when he grabbed her in an embrace and whispered in her ear, "I love you."

Stunned speechless—he had never said that before leaving on a Ranger mission—she stood by silent as he mounted Whiskey. He leapt into the saddle in a fluid movement full of the grace of a younger man. At home in his element, he was a poised commander leading men into conflict where the outcome was never guaranteed. Waving his arm forward, he bawled, "Move out!"

She didn't have time to gather her wits after his unanticipated words of tenderness. Things didn't feel right. Something was out of alignment. Something was wrong. She preferred the cold Matt. The hard Matt. The Matt she knew. Why was he behaving different? A distressing awareness of things changing beyond her control churned in her gut.

The last she saw of him he was saddled up on his favorite horse leading virtuous men out of the yard, determined to seek and destroy their enemies. They bounced in their saddles as they broke into a trot, throwing mud in the air behind them. There was no banter along the column as they found their pace and faded up the road that followed the creek running milky-brown from runoff.

A yellow-white glow illuminated the foggy air directly above the Rangers as they rode into the enveloping mist. It was this ethereal vapor floating above the men that captured their likeness. They were mirrored in the wisps of luminous moisture. In one brief glimmer they appeared to be ghosts riding in the hazy atmosphere. The phenomenon would have gone unnoticed if she hadn't been so keenly attuned to the departure of the husband she didn't expect to return from this mission to enforce what he called justice.

She wasn't sure if anyone else saw the reflection, but she certainly did. Immediately she perceived it as an omen. She had never witnessed anything like this before and decided to keep her disturbing conclusions to herself. But she knew this premonition was different. The semblance of the men momentarily reflected in the vapor above them could only mean one thing. She was a spiritual person and was humbled by the hand of God when she saw His work. It was an eerie apparition nobody else seemed to comprehend. She alone received the message. Tears welled up out of her control. Knowing the value of keeping up appearances, she wiped them away with a swipe of her apron before the children took notice.

She would deal with the unsettling portent alone just as she had dealt with innumerable heartaches in the past. The message was clear. Matt wasn't coming home. Not to this home on the Colorado. His destiny was tied into a higher calling. One that was beyond her capability to understand. It became obvious to her now that it was too late. She wanted to call after Matt. She wanted to hear his voice one more time. She wanted his assurance that she was mistaken.

There was only one thing for certain. She had been wasting too much time. There was no retrieving what should have been. The past was gone forever. It was shocking how it had blown by her like dust in the wind.

TWENTY-EIGHT

Nate assumed his role as scout and rode ahead of the men searching for fresh Indian sign while also keeping in mind Matt's instructions to make good time. Matt wanted to make it to the site of Hobbs' massacre as soon as possible. In Nate's opinion any sign he came across should be conspicuous in the soggy conditions that left pools of water standing in shallow depressions all along the muddy trail. In fact he thought it should make it fairly easy for him to scout a lot of miles and make good time too. The gap separating him and the other men suited him well while he took care of the scouting. He was at his best and most content riding alone where he was free to concentrate and let his thoughts roam where they wished. Free from social constraints he could scan the terrain for clues to any Indian activity without distractions. It was easy work. How could a man not be happy loping along on a good horse across the wild uplands where the green of the cedar and the burnt orange grasslands intensified in color from the saturation of a cleansing rain?

This was where he felt the most at home. It was where he belonged. He fit in the woods where a man answered to the natural laws of living. If he was hungry there was abundant wildlife for the taking. If he was thirsty there were plenty of streams winding through the hills and if a man knew where to look he could find sweet tasting spring water spouting at the base of cliffs. The land provided all that he needed. And the laws of nature made more sense than the laws dreamed up by the government serving its never ending hunger to rule every aspect of a man's existence. It would be fine with him if he never returned to the streets of Austin.

Matt spurred up next to him when he slowed to consider the options at a trail crossing that overlooked the meandering Colorado far below. They exchanged a knowing glance. Neither had to speak to recognize their shared appreciation of the wilderness despite the fact that death could descend upon them at any moment.

Whiskey snorted at the delay as Matt held his hand up to halt the column a distance back. He was united with Matt in his desire to make a move over new territory. Matt leaned over to pat him on his neck while he scrutinized the hills rolling to the horizon where they faded behind a grizzled curtain of clouds. The normal fifty-mile vista was impossible to see in the soupy conditions.

Matt's saddle creaked as he settled back asking, "No sign, huh?"

"Nope," Nate said, as he pulled out a plug of chew and crammed it in his cheek.

"Last reports put 'em out near Llano."

"Llano. Pedernales. Blanco. It's all the same to me." He waved his arm along the far horizon. "They could be prit near anywhere as fast as they ride."

Matt peered across the narrow valley at a flat-topped hill he remembered from a previous Ranger patrol. Below that distinctly shaped hill they had discovered a family scattered around a burned out wagon not far from their cabin. From all they could gather, the father met his doom first. He had been scalped, mutilated, and burned beyond recognition. The mother's body displayed signs of repeated molestation under a huge oak tree where she lay bloody and naked. The Rangers covered her up with a blanket before they went about searching for any survivors.

There was to be no such luck. Three older children were found back in the surrounding trees where they apparently fled what every frontier child knew would be the outcome if captured alive. Unfortunately for them, they were not fleet enough to escape. Too old and too much bother to carry off, the Comanche had made quick work of them except for the oldest girl. She made a valiant attempt to fight her assailants, but the evidence revealed her treatment was similar to her mother. Several younger daughters of the slain parents were missing from the scene and the Rangers deduced that they were carried away into captivity. Some of the Rangers had known the family and took a personal interest in the fate of the missing children, but to no avail.

Nate remembered the details of the savage butchery that had received a lot of press coverage in local papers. He said, "Them kids still ain't come home."

"Ain't gonna by now. Just as well. They wouldn't be worth two cents at this point."

Solemnly shaking his head, Nate said, "No. I reckon not."

They both fell silent thinking about the sad disappearance of the innocent children. Unaware of the subject being discussed, Charles rode up to Matt inquiring, "Time for a break?"

Matt took another look at the site below the hill. A tinge of bitterness was in his voice when he replied, "Lets make it a quick one. I'd like to git as close as possible to the Pedernales before callin' it a day."

Charles waved back at the men to dismount and added, "One other thing, Tom and Travis report a rider following us back a ways."

"That so?"

"They seen him a couple of times. Doesn't seem to be tryin' to catch up. Just kinda shadowin' us."

"Okay. Let me know if he gits too near. I don't need some yahoo causing us trouble."

The men dismounted and let their horses graze on the lush virgin grass. They kept a watchful eye on their mounts and a bit of good-natured ribbing broke out in their appreciation of a break. Matt spotted Cliff leading his horse to a particularly rich stand of grass away from the men where he took a seat on a downed hackberry, his focus on a grove of oaks, his thoughts drifting to God only knew where. Matt made a mental note to have a word with him at the first chance after camping for the night.

At the rear of the column Matt saw that Travis was making good use of the time and attending to the needs of the extra mounts. He saw him listen up when Tom made suggestions and his quick response told him that Travis meant to please his superiors. He never rested as he went about securing the supplies on the horses and kept them rounded up and in control. He had enough frontier knowledge to understand Indians would never miss an opportunity to steal poorly guarded horses and he was making sure trouble wasn't going to occur on his watch. Travis made a quick study and had matured into a good hand. Now the only reservation in Matt's mind was how would the young man respond to battle? Fighting against the Comanche had a way of unnerving even the most hardened frontiersman.

Fifteen minutes passed swiftly and the itch to be on the move got the best of Matt. He called for the men to mount up and they were in the saddle within moments, formed into a column, and ready to trail out. There wasn't a slacker in the bunch.

Matt pointed at the flat-topped hill and told Nate, "Head over to that hill. We'll check the area around the old cabin. Nothin' there, we'll strike a line straight to the Pedernales. I'd like to find Hobbs' men this afternoon. Or first thing in the mornin' if need be."

They dropped off the rocky lip of the ridge following a thin game trail and made their way into a valley with a small creek surging with runoff. Nate led them across the stream of knee-deep water gushing over a bed of flat limestone that offered good footing for the horses. After crossing the creek they entered a thicket of mature live oaks with massive limbs spreading wide and drooping to the ground. They had to track through the copse in a serpentine fashion until they arrived at the edge of a deserted field. The cabin sat at the other end of the fallow pasture slowly returning to the native grasses. The thriving weeds were a reminder of the shattered dreams of a man that paid the ultimate sacrifice to live where he was free to make his own decisions and chart his own course. His works were slowly returning to the soil as the cabin rotted from neglect and the wild vines and weeds grew unimpeded across his abandoned homestead.

Nate trailed a wide berth around the depressing site of the forlorn cabin. He felt a close kinship with the like-minded settlers that lost everything to a barbaric attack on all they treasured and held dear to their heart. He kept his focus riveted for sign and paid as little attention as possible to the sad remnants of the murderous behavior they hoped to one day eliminate. The men tracked behind him and an irritable murmur broke out amongst them as they spontaneously let their anger flow in the face of what they were up against.

After leaving the poignant scene, the day wore long without any fresh sign struck by Nate. The clouds began to thin and the sun broke out in an orange blaze as it sank into the horizon. Nate located a small brook that had cleared of the high runoff and ran clean enough to provide good drinking water. It also cut through a meadow to graze the horses and he suggested it would make a good spot for the night, as they were only a few miles from the Pedernales crossing, but too far to make it before dark fell. Matt agreed and gave the order to dismount and make camp. The men readily complied. It had been a long day in the saddle and their stiff backs and cramped muscles screamed for time on a bedroll.

Travis and Tom came in last and Travis rode straight up to Matt getting ready to slip out of the saddle. Tom had maneuvered the extra stock to the side with instructions for Travis to deliver an important message. His excitement hard to contain, Travis said, "That rider is still shadowin' us!"

Matt stopped dismounting with one leg halfway over the saddle. He eyed Travis, irritation in his hard gray eyes. Slowly he stretched his leg back over the saddle and into his stirrup. "How far back?" he grumbled out of the side of his mouth.

"'Bout the same as earlier. He's alone it appears. But there ain't no doubt he's on our ass. We been watchin' him. He's real careful not to git too close."

Matt sucked his bottom lip in, the consternation evident when he said, "That so?"

"Yes, sir. It don't seem right. Does it?"

"No it don't. Damn sure don't want to bed down with an unknown on our tail. You done good Travis. Glad you kept an eye on this stranger." He noticed Nate already dismounted and loosening the cinch straps on his saddle. "Hold on Nate. We got us an errand to take care of first."

Nate cast Matt a questioning glare.

"Mount up. We gotta ride back-trail to check out this stranger. I don't cotton to being followed."

Nate cinched his straps tight without another word. Whoever this stranger was, he deserved a severe reprimand for cutting into his time to relax. This extra task put him in the mood to deliver a rebuke or worse if need be.

They eased back to a motte of blackjack oaks growing dark and somber in the fading light. They secured their mounts out of sight of the trail where it cut across a meadow of grass belly high to a horse. Matt pulled out his Henry and took a stance resting it on a dead tree limb that made a good place of concealment. He could see through the branches, but his outline would be fragmented and hard for any rider across the pasture to detect. Nate settled into his ambush site on the opposite side of the trail from Matt, his Spencer ready for use, and him needing just half a reason to put his trusty weapon to work.

They didn't have to wait for long. The rider appeared as a shadow slinking first in sight and then out behind a screen of limbs on the far side of the meadow. Approaching the openness of the grassland, he reined to a halt while hidden by a thick cluster of brush.

It turned into a waiting contest, much like stalking a wild animal that moved on his own accord, never as fast as a hunter desired. Patience in the wilds kept a critter alive. This stranger sensed danger. Much like a deer he lingered inside the woodline until the time was right to make a move.

Minutes passed. Nothing changed. The stranger waited out of sight.

Matt glanced at Nate, absorbed in locating his quarry. This couldn't continue much longer. The sun had long set and the gloom of night was settling on the land. The far-off howl of a pack of coyotes floated through the thickets. Mice began to scurry in the detritus of the woodland floor at Matt's feet. Behind him he could hear the rustling of a larger critter of the night.

"I know you're there," abruptly broke the stillness as the stranger shouted a challenge.

Nate shot Matt a startled look. Matt shrugged, just as dumbfounded as Nate. They had been exceptionally discreet in taking up their emplacements. The stranger couldn't have seen them. It seemed impossible for him to know they laid in wait. Nate looked at Matt for a suggestion.

Their adversary sat still and patient lost in a mosaic of darkening shadows. The timber was becoming more treacherous as time slipped past. A pair of birds flitted into the sky above the stranger's last known position. Was he making a move Matt wondered?

"Show yourself! You know where I'm at," came a second

challenge.

Matt's eyes flared at the request. Nate shook his head and mumbled under his breath, "No damn way."

Matt leveled his gun in the direction he last saw the man. He appeared to be a large man from the little Matt saw of him. He put his fingers to his lips to shush Nate.

"Mosey on out where we can see your hands," Matt commanded.

No response.

A lone coyote yip from a grove of post oaks set off a wailing chorus for miles around the standoff. Another layer of darkness fell in a visible sheet across the woods. The coyotes ceased their yelping and the countryside returned to an eerie silence with the potential of death looming in the still, cool air of dusk.

Matt made out the slightest movement behind a tangle of limbs. He adjusted his sights on the location. It was no good. The man was within the Henry's outer limits but his .44 caliber bullet would be spent at that range and it would never penetrate the knot of brush.

He saw movement again. This time a hearty greeting followed the slight forward motion. "Hello, Ranger Man!" boomed across the open grasses.

Nate glared at Matt and mouthed, "What the hell?"

Matt shook his head as if to apologize. He lowered the Henry off his shoulder, but kept a sharp lookout on the grove of blackjack where the acknowledgment came from. Impatience in his reply, Matt ordered, "Come on out, Dawson. Hands visible, nice and slow."

A minute passed. Nobody moved. A screech owl warbled in the distance.

"Losing patience. Last time. Come out where I can see you."

"Not sure it's a good idea."

Matt saw that Nate was still holding his aim steady on the location of the voice. He saw Matt looking his way and asked, "Shoot the bastard?"

Matt waved his hand in the negative. He saw the disappointment on Nate's face.

"Come out. We'll hold our fire."

Dawson clicked his tongue and his mount stepped to the edge of the motte. Without exposing his body to the openness of the meadow he shouted, "Tell your companion to hold his fire too. I'm on a friendly ride."

Matt cautioned Nate to remove his finger from the trigger wondering how Dawson knew there were two of them hiding. He heard Dawson announce, "Coming out," as he emerged from the shadows like an apparition, his coal black horse beneath him near invisible in the deepening twilight. He seemed to float on the air, undoubtedly a huge man, but gliding with poise atop his splendid mount that started a prancing gait as they entered the openness of the prairie.

"Just like you wanted, Ranger Man. Hands in the air. I mean no harm. Coming over."

Matt held the sights of his Henry square on Dawson's chest until he approached close enough to stare straight down the business end of the muzzle. He reined up with one hand while he waved the other palm above his head. "You can lower that rifle. Like I said, I'm here friendly like."

Peering down the barrel, finger on the trigger, Matt asked, "Why are you tailing us?"

Checking his horse with just the hint of pressure on the rein, Dawson said, "Free country last I heard. Can do what I want."

"Sorry. Not true."

Dawson nodded his head like he understood. In fact he did. Freedom was a lie. Men had to live with shackles and chains whether they were so called free men or the former slaves countless men had fought and died over in disagreement about states rights. "Mind if I smoke?" he asked Matt.

"Help yourself. Careful though, my partner will blow your head off if you make the wrong move."

Dawson rolled a smoke and fired it up watching Matt keep his rifle pointed dead center. He couldn't see Matt's partner to the side, but perceived a very real sense of loathing directed his way. Taking a long drag, he inhaled the satisfying warmth that tasted of earth and wood. Smoke curled into the dusk as he exhaled saying, "Tell me how it is then. If it's not a free country, what is it?"

"You know how it is. You work for the other side."

The roll-up drooped from his lips, the tip glowing bright as he took a strong pull. Another cloud of smoke poured out as he hissed, "That don't make me a threat out here. Out here I'm my own man. Do as I want."

Nate was getting itchy. Matt glared at him with a look of disapproval. This was his call and Nate took the cue.

"All I want is to take care of a little unfinished personal business."

"Personal?" Matt asked.

"That's right."

"Like what?"

Dawson laughed. "Wouldn't be personal if I told you. It's my business. Nobody else's."

"Then it don't include me or my men. So why're trailin' us?"

"Got other business out here. I'm a busy man." He paused to take another drag like it was the finest tobacco he had ever smoked.

"I'm waiting," Matt said.

Dawson squashed the ember out between his fingers and flipped the stub into the brush.

"I've been tasked with making sure my employer's stolen property makes it back to its rightful owner."

"Well then, you're outta luck. We don't need you looking over our shoulder to do what's right. We return stolen goods whenever possible. Always have, always will."

"That may be, and I believe you when you say it. But you know my boss. He's got his own ideas."

Nate's impulse got the best of him and he blurted out, "Damn peculiar ideas!"

Dawson smiled. He recognized that voice too. "Can't argue that point, friend."

"I ain't your damn friend! You'd have a bullet between your eyes if it was up to me!"

Dawson didn't flinch. Nate's fiery words had little meaning when a man like Matt was in charge. He steadied his gaze on Matt and said, "Here it is. You can have it any way you want it. I'd thought I might join up and have a crack at them Comanche myself."

Matt corrected him. "Comanche had nothin' to do with your loss."

Dawson's face turned to stone. "I figure any Indian I meet owes me for my sister and Ma. It don't have to be a Sioux to help me even the score. Comanche will do just fine. It's your decision. I can bed down out here by myself if you don't want my help. I just figured you could always use an extra gun. One that don't cost the state any money I might add."

"We don't need no damn Yankee to take care of business!" Nate was riled and spit flew from his lips.

Matt motioned for his scout to take it down a notch. Nate shook his head like he couldn't believe Matt would even consider letting Dawson join up.

Dawson saw the opening. "What say you, Matt? I don't mean no harm to Nate here. I understand how he feels. Don't blame him at all. I was just doing what I was told. Nothing personal about it."

Matt cradled his Henry and stepped out to get a better take on the enigmatic beast of a man mounted on a ride he recognized. The glossy black horse possessed a distinctive spirit much like his former owner. His dead owner. Shot dead in a cowardly ambush on two unsuspecting travelers. It was Kern's horse.

Dawson noticed the recognition in Matt's appraisal of his ride. "He's a fine horse."

"Yes he is."

"You done a good turn bringing him out of the woods after what happened."

"Wasn't the fault of the horse that Kern was a crazy son of a bitch."

Dawson saw another opening. He said, "Crazier than hell. Never trusted him. You could never tell what he'd do next. Mean to women. Hard to tolerate on that accord alone."

"Yeah, well, he got what was comin' to him," Matt said.

"He was lucky to live as long as he did. He had a long dirty history all the way back to Louisiana."

Matt rested the Henry in the crook of his arm. Concentrating on the signals coming from Dawson he couldn't distinguish any deceit. Didn't mean much though. The large man moved like a phantom and had the sensory perceptions of an owl in the night. He knew things he had no right knowing. Something in his gut didn't trust the man. There was a secretive attribute to Dawson's perspective that didn't match up with the situation. Unfinished business. He was a busy man. Out here? In the middle of nowhere?

It didn't add up.

It didn't add up, but that didn't matter. He was here. He wasn't going anywhere he didn't want to go. Couldn't shoot him. Couldn't scare him away. He wasn't the kind of man to spook. The best thing to do was keep a close eye on him. He commanded a troop of thirteen Rangers that would be glad to do just that. If he got out of line just once his men wouldn't hesitate to put his lights out for good. It was wise to keep your friends close and your enemies even closer.

Matt said, "You won't last long out here riding by yourself."

Dawson rose out of the saddle and stretched his legs. "I've done this ride alone before. Got back from Fredericksburg on my own not too long ago."

"Comanche are mighty stirred up and confident after the Hobbs massacre."

"I can manage on my own. I'm not looking for no sympathy offer. I'll pull my weight and keep out of the way of your men. I understand I may not be welcomed by all."

The sound of Nate spitting resonated as a punctuation point.

"Follow me in. Nate will pull up the rear."

Dawson knew how to work a man. He was right where he wanted to be.

TWENTY-NINE

Black Owl insisted they had to close with stealth and absolute silence under the cover of night. Like a mountain lion stalking his prey, they had to allow their night vision to adjust before sneaking to within striking range. This kind of work had to be carried out with arrows. They couldn't risk the possibility of gunshots floating to unfriendly ears on some mysterious stream of wind. It was the method he preferred. Killing with the sacred tools of bow and arrow pleased the spirits always watching the exploits of Comanche braves.

He couldn't believe the good fortune delivered to their raiding party as if it were a gift from the spirits. It was only the first day out from the village and they had already discovered a couple of white men camped in the valley below. The Texans had chosen their camp wisely, but they remained completely oblivious they were being observed from the darkened ridge above them. The flames of their campfire burned hot and smokeless, but it silhouetted their movements from his angle on the ridge where he laid in wait.

Buffalo Hump and Little White Man lay sprawled out in the grass next to him. They peered down at the Texans, anticipation radiant on their face. None of his brothers craved the thrill of hunting the dog-faced men more than these two Comanche beside him. He had to convince them to use arrows to finish the Texans instead of knives. Little White Man favored a cautious approach in unison where they could catch the whites asleep. He wanted to sneak close enough to slash their throats. He had to agree with Little White Man that it would make a greater coup and a superior tale to brag about when they got back to the village, but that was beside the point. The risks were too high to make an attempt like that. What was important was success. Not boasting. The Texans had to be respected for their craftiness. A fact often ignored by Buffalo Hump and Little White Man in their blinding greed to spill the blood of the white intruders.

He watched as the slim paleface got up and moved over to his hobbled horse. He offered the pony a treat from his open palm. The horse lowered his muzzle and plucked the food gingerly from his hand and then held still while his neck was stroked. At this distance, Black Owl couldn't hear the words, but he could make out the bond between them as the white man slowly made his way around the horse talking and rubbing him all the while.

The other Texan sitting by the fire had a formidable build with shoulder length hair and a longer beard than his companion caring for the horses. He poked a stick into the fire to keep it going but knew better than build up a large blaze that could give their position away. The glow of the fire was low and didn't extend beyond the trees surrounding their camp they had wisely located well back from the trail used by passing travelers. He leaned over and rotated a slab of meat suspended across the flames. A pot sat steaming at the edge on a bed of coals. Their blankets lay on the ground yards apart and arranged against their saddles for views that covered the entire area around their camp. Camping deep in the timber and maintaining a low profile proved to Black Owl that these men deserved respect for their caution and skills in hostile country.

Black Owl could almost smell the coffee brewing. It was a wonderful concoction the white men possessed. The strong flavored drink buzzed in his head and made him invincibly energetic in the morning when his blood usually oozed as thick as honey. Pour in some of the white sand the whites called sugar and the coffee was the most incredible drink he had ever consumed. Despite their unwanted presence on the homelands of the People, Black Owl would like it if they retreated south to the great saltwater where they belonged and only ventured forth for trading purposes. That had been the way it once was according to other tribes he had spoken with. But those times had long passed. Now the white invaders spread across the hills like a stirred up anthill. They wanted it all. They had an insatiable appetite for land that was not theirs to own. How he hated them!

He heard the unmistakable sound of laughter from the camp drifting up to the ridge. Buffalo Hump grunted and whispered, "Their laughter will be short." Little White Man drew a slash across his throat. He still wanted to sneak close and see their blood drip from his blade. It was the only exploit to him that actually mattered. To touch a living enemy was the ultimate coup. But for now he watched the Texans recline against logs and enjoy their roasted meat and coffee ignorant of the impending attack.

Black Owl understood what the men below were feeling. There was little that compared to a contented camp, crackling fire, and fresh meat split with a like-minded brother. A small part of him felt remorse. As individuals it was possible he could like these men. It was possible they could share the same likes and dislikes. It was possible he could laugh at the same joke they had just experienced. It was an odd realization, an unchartered path for his thoughts to wander. It reminded him of something an elder chief had once told him. All men were the same. They all needed to see and hear and taste. To speak and to hunt. To lie down with a squaw. These white men weren't that much different. And then again they were completely different. It caused a burn in his head to think this way. It was coming to pass just as his elder had taught him. One day the chief had said that things would cease to make sense. The wrong would be right. The right would be wrong. Nothing would be the same. Everything changes. All that lasted was the rock, the water and the sky. Black Owl wondered if that day had come for him.

The three of them stayed on lookout until the Texans bedded down for the night. They watched them by the flickering glow of the flames as the men pulled their blankets over their shoulders. It was a relief to see that neither one would remain awake to serve as a guard. That oversight on their part would make the coup that much easier.

Scooting backwards off the ridge, a final council of war was held. The younger braves in the war party were selected to watch the ponies and maintain the position on the ridge as sentinels to warn of any unexpected arrivals. Black Owl held out that it was best for just three of them to approach the camp alone. His argument of fewer feet, fewer chances of awakening the sleeping Texans won the others over to his point of view. A backup party of ten Comanche would approach near enough to provide support if needed. Buffalo Hump, Little White Man and Black Owl would move in to count coup. Once in position Buffalo Hump would hoot like an owl as a signal to unleash a flurry of arrows. The Texans would never know what hit them.

Black Owl led them on a circuitous route around a small hill careful to keep plenty of distance separating them from the camp they intended to overwhelm. There couldn't be any chance taken on an inadvertent crack of a twig alerting the Texans of the death stalking their repose. Despite his excellent night vision the passage through the woods taxed Black Owl's skills. They had to move slow and easy, under and around thick growths of cedar peppered with cactus hidden beneath waist high grass.

Eventually they broke out of the tangled copse and their trailing was made easier when they found the faint tracks created earlier by the white men. The soft padding of grass muffled the sound of their moccasins as they slinked like snakes through the undergrowth. Hunched over while tracking, and kneeling during the pauses, they blended perfectly into the crosshatch of limbs, vines and brush. It would take the keen perceptions of a wolf to see their advancement and they had nothing to worry about. The Texans were lost in their sleep.

Black Owl made his final advance to within striking range with the patience of a cougar, the predator he most admired. He was the first to take cover behind a tree that gave him a full view of the slumbering men. The cinders of the dying fire pulsated and cast a subtle orange hue over the sleeping forms of the men nestled under their blankets. The longhaired and formidable appearing Texan was on the opposite side of the embers with his feet pointed at the tree Black Owl peered around. That meant the Texan would be looking his way if he awakened. The other paleface presented less of a personal threat facing the way he had chosen to sleep. The horses of the white men were hobbled just outside the camp and luckily had not shown any jumpiness at the stealthy approach of three warriors. The time was drawing near.

Buffalo Hump slithered beside Black Owl and explained with hand signals that he would slink around the camp along with Little White Man to locate a position where both of the white men would be within reach of their arrows. It was agreed that Black Owl would be responsible for the larger of the two men and Little White Man would arrow either one that made the best target. Even in the dark, Black Owl could see the eagerness in Buffalo Hump's eyes that absolutely burned with enthusiasm for this kind of work. Black Owl watched the pair move through the brush silently as an owl gliding in for the kill.

The woods were eerily quiet. It was as if the proximity of death had cast a spell. Not a creature stirred. Not even an insect. The only sound came from the snoring of the Texan he anticipated killing. The man slept unaware his time was fast running out. After they had finished with him he would no longer be able to return to his squaw. His children would weep with the pain of loss like the children of Comanche braves that went under because of his white brothers. From the depth of his snoring, Black Owl knew he had to be in the enchanted realm of dreams. He wondered if white men connected in their dreams with the spirits of their lost loved ones. Did they meet them in their visions and discuss past events in their lives? Did they make peace with the spirits while asleep like the Comanche did? How much wisdom did they acquire while in this magical state of being?

He watched while the paleface rolled to his side away from the glowing embers. His snoring ceased. A wave of concern swept over Black Owl. What if the man arose before Little White Man and Buffalo Hump were in position? What if they lost the advantage of surprise? How much longer before he heard the hoot of an owl letting him know it was time to release the arrows. Anxiety crept into his thoughts. Coordinated efforts required precise timing to be successful. Where was Buffalo Hump's call?

It didn't take long and the snoring resumed. Black Owl breathed a sigh of relief and fingered the smooth osage wood of his bow. He preferred the traditional weapon of bow and arrow to the loud shooting stick he had started using to meet the devastating firepower of the white warriors. The curve of his bow and the feathered fletching of his arrows were the result of the rigorous care he took in crafting them for sacred use. When he sent the arrow on its way it closed the circle on its intended purpose. All of his time spent in producing the finest weapons was rewarded when he struck down his quarry, be it man or beast. It was meant to be a revered event. Ordained by the spirits to ensure the survival of the People. He notched an arrow. The time was at hand.

An ember in the fire popped. One of the horses stomped the ground. An owl hooted.

Black Owl let fly the first arrow. He heard the hiss of multiple arrows slicing through the night. Their timing was perfect. Dull thuds told him the shafts had driven home against flesh.

A howl exploded from the longhaired Texan. He erupted from his bed waving his revolver across the woods. Belching fire, a shot cracked. The bullet hummed within inches of Black Owl causing his second arrow to fly wildly off target. He noticed the Texan had an arrow sticking out from his upper chest pinning the blanket to him. Yet he wielded his revolver with ease while leaping to and fro, snapping the arrow off with his free hand. The blanket fell to the dirt and freed him to counterattack.

Cursing at the top of his lungs, the Texan spun to see his partner struggling to rise from his bedroll with two arrows protruding from his torso. He rushed to his side, orange flashes from his gun lighting the camp as he fired in random directions. Kneeling to help him get up, a third arrow lodged in the base of his friend's skull. A pulsing fountain of blood ran down his back. His eyes immediately went blank. He wobbled a slight moment and fell unrestrained on his face. A fourth arrow missed when he toppled.

Black Owl let an arrow fly that struck the longhaired Texan in the thigh. He fell to the ground on his back; his eyes wide open in hysteria. Spit flew from his lips as he cursed his cowardly assailants with venomous insults. The arrow stuck out the backside of his thigh and splintered in half when he dug in his heels to scoot across the camp. He was desperate to escape to the illusionary refuge of darkness outside camp. A white-hot pain seared his senses. He was momentarily blinded, firing his last shot toward Black Owl, but hitting a tree instead.

Scrambling backwards, he came to a stop against his saddle. He knew where he was now, and made a move to grasp his carbine partially tucked under his blanket. Black Owl saw the effort and let loose a well-aimed arrow that penetrated his arm extended outward to recover the weapon. He rolled to the soil with the impact of the shaft driving straight through the meaty flesh of his bicep. Another arrow from Buffalo Hump sliced into his upper back when he rose to a kneeling posture, the iron tipped shaft quivering while buried three quarters of the way into his chest. The arrow broke off when he collapsed face first into the dirt groaning in unbearable agony.

Black Owl stepped out from behind the tree to take a steady aim. His arrow sighted on the heaving chest as the white man struggled to breathe. He took a couple of steps closer to give the shot more accuracy, surprised to see the Texan rise once again from the ground, not fast, but still game to fight back. He swayed, staring at Black Owl as if to ask why. Why had they been attacked? What had he done to warrant this brutality? Black Owl didn't see anger in his face. Just a look of bewilderment slowly replaced by an expression that confirmed he knew he was dead.

Teetering on his knees, he dropped his focus to the carbine that lay just out of reach. Black Owl saw his intentions. He was going to make a hopeless attempt to resist the inevitable. But the loss of blood had made him sluggish.

That's when Little White Man burst from the timber. He came rushing like a wolf that was first on the kill, determined to dominate the feed. The Texan made a dive for his gun, but Little White Man was faster. He captured the long hair in his hands just as the paleface brushed against the stock of the carbine. Little White Man gave a mighty jerk that snapped his victim back. Black Owl lowered his bow. The Texan was being dragged backwards by his hair like he was a defenseless pup being led to slaughter.

Buffalo Hump roared with a vicious laughter. The ambush had been a complete success. He threw his head back in the victorious wail of a wolf. His Comanche brothers secreted farther back in the thickets returned his cries and vaulted toward the kill site to share in the celebration. Buffalo Hump picked up a couple of logs to throw on the smoldering coals. It was about to get interesting. They had a live Texan.

Within minutes the entire war party had assembled around the now blazing fire. Black Owl felt a little trepidation since shots had been fired that might arouse the curiosity of any undetected Texans camped nearby. Buffalo Hump assured him that he had no reason to worry. This time was theirs to make the most of with the acquisition of several horses, not to mention additional weapons to later turn against the whites in the raid down the Colorado. This victory convinced them that their medicine was strong enough to defeat the white demons Black Owl held in such high regard.

Little White Man propped his prisoner against a tree and started his usual boasting about his prowess as a great warrior. He beat his chest as he danced around the fire hurling taunts at the longhaired white man who was turning as pale as a ghost. Working himself into a frenzy, he made a gyrating trip around the flames and darted toward his hostage with his knife. In one quick slice he opened arm muscle to the bone. A cry of anguish echoed throughout the woods.

Savoring his power, he grabbed the Texan's hat and thrust his hand into the crown, pushing it out in a round dome that he preferred. Next he tugged the brim down low, distorting it to the shape he said provided the most protection from sun and rain. Happy with his modifications, he slapped the hat against his prisoner, making a big show of his supremacy before he pulled the hat down snug over his oily black hair.

Declaring his coup as the deed of a true Comanche warrior he claimed the right to be celebrated for his bravery. He had touched a live opponent. It was the highest honor attainable for a Comanche to lay a hand on an enemy in combat. Little White Man went on to explain the hat represented his theft and possession of the medicine that resided in what he deemed to be a great white warrior. The Texan had put up a valiant fight and it took a Comanche with tremendous skills to capture such a man alive. He would be more than ready to accept the tributes of the tribe when they returned to the home village on the lush grasses of the prairies. He assured his brothers that they would return with even greater tales of their success against the white intruders on the Colorado.

The role of Black Owl in wounding the paleface was never mentioned and that suited Black Owl fine. The evidence was there for any of his brothers to see and soon enough the truth of the battle would be known. They all understood Little White Man had a lust for adoration that could never be satisfied. He always had to be the center of attraction. That was why he chose to wear the garb of white men. He had to stand out. Later he would remove red streamers from his pouch and wrap them around the hat in order to draw attention to his individuality. He wasn't content with dressing as other Comanche. He often wore whatever clothing he could steal from the white braves. His claim to be able to obtain their power in this manner was nothing new. Black Owl took a seat on one of the saddles to observe what he knew was coming next. Little White Man was nothing if not predictable.

Sure enough, after describing his extraordinary exploits, he resumed taunting the weakened captive. He snatched a limb from the fire that flickered red with heat. Dancing ever closer to the Texan so feeble he had to be secured to a tree with rope, he waved the scorching embers near his face. Irritated with the indifference, he pressed the stick to his cheek, and unable to refrain, his prisoner let out a shriek of agony. The sulfuric odor of burnt hair and flesh filled the cool air of camp. This only encouraged Little White Man to experiment with new parts to burn. Repeatedly he went back again and again to torment his enemy until he finally succumbed, unresponsive against the ropes.

Little White Man retreated to the fire and tossed the stick into the flames. He turned to face the incoherent Texan sagging against the rope binding him to the tree. It was getting late and Little White Man read the mood of his brothers. It was time to end the entertainment. He wished the longhair could keep his eyes open to see what was in store, but he had passed out, breathing, but barely clinging to life. Stepping behind the Texan, Little White Man brandished his knife high above him, beholding it like it was an object deserving worship. In a bloodlust trance, he returned his attention to his captive, and grabbed a wad of the Texan's long hair. Wrapping the hair around his hand, he snapped the head back exposing the soft flesh of the Texan's throat. He placed his blade against the windpipe, glancing at his brothers with a devilish grin on his face making sure they witnessed his control and amusement he derived from this sensational conclusion. In one swift slash, he severed the throat and the life giving blood drained into a pool under his prized hostage. The Texan slumped into a pile of useless flesh, liberated in death from his pain.

The culmination of the celebration ended when Little White Man cut a circular incision around the long hair of the dead Texan and jerked it free with a pop. Black Owl watched Little White Man lift the scalp triumphantly and carry on in his finale of dancing and whooping. They all joined in with shouts of congratulations at the climax of the night's entertainment. It had been a long show carried out with the expertise of an experienced performer.

As they bedded down for badly needed rest, Black Owl drifted to sleep with a reoccurring thought. The white man had been a valiant opponent. They caught him totally unaware in his bed, but he had reacted courageously. He had almost slain Black Owl out of the natural instinct of a true warrior. He had fought with determination and skill until his life's essence had bled into the dirt. It was the same fighting tenacity he would expect of his Comanche brothers if they had been shocked into action from their beds. A question burned in his mind as the cobwebs of fatigue cloaked him in sleep. Why hadn't he shot the Texan one more time to send him to his spirit world without the insults heaped upon him by Little White Man?

THIRTY

"It don't make sense to me," Nate repeated.

In the dark before sunup Matt couldn't read Nate's expression, but he knew the frown he frequently wore was on display from the tone in his voice. Nate never had a problem voicing his opinions.

Matt could hear the hoarse breathing of JB and Hunter sleeping at the edge of camp. Tom had sentry duty at the other side of camp and everybody else was still sleeping with Dawson bedded down outside the ring of Rangers near Tom's post. Dawson had informed Matt that he would maintain as low a profile as possible in order to avoid stepping on the toes of men that preferred he didn't join their ranks. It was a good idea and Matt would have suggested it if Dawson hadn't offered the proposal on the ride back to the Ranger camp. Dawson had supper by himself and avoided eye contact with the suspicious glances cast his way after Matt announced the addition of one more gun to the party.

Tom and Charles were the only men to offer their support for the extra firepower. Charles had witnessed the mutilation of Hobbs' men. He had an irrefutable understanding of the importance of what one more gun could do to help even the odds against a confident and formidable opponent they were likely to encounter. Tom had simply suggested Dawson looked like a scrapper to him and if that was what it took to get the job done; then so be it. In his view that was all that counted. Get the job done. Get it done fast and get all the men back home safe.

Nate had been in an uproar when the opinions supporting Matt's decision had driven him from the discreet conversation being held out of hearing range to the other men. He had nursed the sore subject all night long and couldn't wait to broach the matter again. Even if it meant giving up sack time while Matt was isolated performing his guard duties.

"I'm tellin' you, Matt. You cain't trust him. He'll kill you first chance he gits. Maybe me too."

Matt nodded his head. There was no reason to upset Nate any further. Besides, what Nate said was a distinct possibility.

"You'll have to be constantly lookin' over your shoulder," Nate added.

Matt plucked a stem of grass and stuck it between his lips. The conversation with Nate had morphed into a lecture. Nate meant well, but Matt felt his blood pressure rising and the sun still napped well below the horizon. The veins in his neck throbbed and the heat was climbing to his cheeks. The burn in his stomach was real. He was very aware of the fact that shooting a man you had a beef with had occurred all too often on both sides in the big war. It was too early for this.

Nate let his gaze sink. His lips puckered as if tasting something bitter. He raised his head and bored in on Matt with his typical bluntness. "It's what I'd do if I was him."

"You'd shoot a man in cold blood?"

Nate kicked at a rock.

"In the back?" Matt asked.

Peering into the black woods, Nate avoided the question.

"Is that what *you're* gonna do? Shoot him first chance you git?" Matt probed.

"Not what I meant."

"It's what you said. You don't ever mince words."

"If I was *him*," Nate paused to let Matt think on the perspective change, "that's what I'd do."

"It's not in him. He's not Kern."

"Sorry, Matt, but *that* opinion is in the minority."

"So that's what the men think?"

"Pretty much right down the line exceptin' Charles and Tom."

"Well, I guess that's no surprise considering his reputation."

"It don't change your mind none?'

Matt didn't hesitate. "Nope. It's a risk I'll take."

Nate shook his head in disbelief. He couldn't fathom how he had ended up on the same side as a man that worked for a snake like Ames. "It's your call." He glanced at the clouds, barely visible as they rolled across the night sky. "But let me ask you a question."

"Fire away."

"He looks like he's makin' a move on you. We eliminate him?"

Matt shifted the grass to the other side of his mouth. He chewed a little before he said, "I don't have to answer that. You know what to do."

Nate grinned. It was what he wanted to hear. If the bastard made one wrong move, he'd bust him. He'd put the word out to the men that didn't share Matt's assessment of Dawson.

Matt ordered, "Rouse the men. We leave at first light."

False dawn crawled over the horizon gray and dismal accompanied by a damp wind blowing north from the gulf. A drizzle started falling as soon as the Rangers mounted up for the ride. Reluctantly pulling their rain slickers out, the men bundled up for another long day on the trail.

Nate spurred ahead of the men to perform his scouting duties. He kept his concentration glued to the rocky terrain searching for fresh Indian sign and all the while keeping a wary eye out for ambush. It was a tedious procedure, but he wanted to make sure there wouldn't be a repeat of the Hobbs massacre on his watch. The miles clicked by with tracking conditions made a little easier by the damp conditions. Any passing of mounted Indians would be unmistakable, but there was nothing to see except for the tracks of deer, coyotes, and raccoons mixed in with an occasional cat print. He found his mind wandering to the Pedernales crossing and the unpleasant realities of taking up arms against the Comanche.

Within a couple of hours he topped out at the crest of a long spine bare of trees where rocky knolls faded into the hazy curtain of the persistent drizzle. Just visible beyond a pair of small undulating hills was the confluence of the Colorado and Pedernales. The dreary appearance of the landscape seemed appropriate to Nate. In his gut he felt the uneasy stirrings of apprehension. This mission had a sense of failure permeating the air around its objectives, and the miserable weather drowned any chance of optimism flaring up.

Their first objective was within sight in a vicinity he normally considered stunning and wild in natural beauty, just the way he liked it. No indication of settlement for miles around the junction of the rivers. Today was different though. Bodies of fellow Rangers waited to be buried. Matt was making questionable judgments. Things just didn't seem right. He couldn't shake the dread and chuckled, but not with pleasure. Dismayed by the prospects, he said, "Hell, I feel it in my bones. Somethin' bad's gonna happen."

Matt rode up to Nate and they both scoured the woods and grasslands spreading down to the bluffs above the crossing. Nate kept his distressing thoughts to himself. Matt wasn't in the mood to hear more of his opinions, and it was apparent he didn't look forward to the upcoming task either. A simple nod from Matt was all it took for him to proceed. He prodded his dun off the ridge.

After traversing the hills, Nate reined up to study the entrance to the narrow defile where Hobbs' men had been ambushed. He gladly accepted Charles beside him as he contemplated the gruesome chore waiting for their completion. They sat in the saddle quietly absorbed in their own sentiment. This was where it came to pass. Good men lost their lives. Right there in the gulch they were about to enter. It was a perfect spot for an ambush. It had been completely unnecessary.

Charles sucked up the grit to say, "Nate, it ain't gonna be pretty. How's about I lead the way?"

"Obliged to have your help."

Pivoting in the saddle, Charles found Matt pulled up twenty yards back on the trail. Using hand signs he indicated that they would clear the gully. Matt directed half the men to disperse in a semicircle to cover their rear and moved the rest closer to the ravine for support if it was required. He didn't expect an attack, but the proximity to death made all the men on edge, including him.

All of them did as they were commanded, except for Dawson. He stopped under a huge oak tree at the far right of the men guarding the rear. He reached into his saddlebag and tore off a plug of chew thinking it would be interesting to observe how the Southern boys reacted to Comanche depravity. He had an indifferent outlook concerning the loss of the men with Hobbs. He didn't know any of the dead Rangers, and didn't have any skin in the game. These men he rode with were neighbors, and had suffered the pang of loss from numerous Comanche raids. He had different goals than the Texans, but the memory of the treacherous Sioux helped him understand their attitude. Comanche blood or Sioux made no difference to him. He had a job to do and had been paid a handsome figure to perform. Unwillingly maybe, but there had been an exchange of money for a service to be rendered. Besides earning his pay, sending a few Comanche to their spirit world would help ease an old grudge he held against all redskins.

He caught Travis glancing back to check on his whereabouts, a slight uncertainty plainly visible on the lad's face. The youngster was about to receive an education on the brutality Indians were capable of committing. Hearing about it was one thing. Seeing the results first hand was another. He spat a brown stream of juice at the base of the oak and gave Travis a knowing nod. Travis barely dipped his head in recognition of the gesture before he turned away.

It only took Charles and Nate five minutes to verify the area was clear of any current danger. Matt heard the voice of Charles crack with anger when he gave the okay to bring the men through the cleft in the riverside bluffs. Motioning for the men to follow, he tapped Whiskey on the flanks to start down the trail threading between boulders that had tumbled from the ancient limestone walls in the distant past. He broke out of the constricted gully, and rode up beside Charles sitting listless in the saddle, his chestnut mare munching at a clump of grass. Nate was down the slope a short way dismounted and examining something white on the ground.

Looking the other direction, Matt could see the remains of at least three men. There wasn't much left. The varmints had been thorough. Bones lay in the grass dotted all the way up the slope to the rocks piled at the base of the cliff. He knew the number of men because he could see three different skulls stripped clean of flesh.

Despite his experience in such matters, he felt a sick bubbling in his gut. Analyzing the lay of the land he saw that the bluffs lined the river bottoms as far as the eye could see. The trail from the other side descended into the only suitable location for crossing in the immediate valley. He couldn't imagine riding headlong into such an obvious spot for an ambush. He mumbled to Charles,

"What the hell was Hobbs thinking?'

Charles looked over his shoulder to make sure nobody was listening. "He was a fool."

"Well, damn him for taking good men with him."

"I tried to advise him. He wouldn't listen."

The column of men began to arrive and spread out to the sides in dismay. A murmur of disgust rose amongst them as the hard reality sunk in. There was no way to ignore the grisly evidence. Travis took in the chilling scene wide-eyed and in awe of his first encounter with the casualties of a deadly Comanche attack. Nate took the reins from Travis and tied his palomino off without saying a word. He was too preoccupied to talk while he considered the possibility that his bones could soon be sprinkled about like trash bleaching under the hot Texas sun.

"We got work to do!" Matt bellowed. "Bust out the shovels."

The murmur ended. Each man dismounted and secured their ride unsure of what was next. Indecision didn't last long. Matt had already sized up the situation and Charles confirmed it when he glanced his way and shook his head. Identification would be impossible. Mistaken identification would be unforgiveable. Some of the bones had small bits of dried flesh still attached, but that was no help to recognize the remains. Clothes were torn loose from the cadavers with no apparent owner to the scattered apparel. It was a scene Matt had witnessed too many times in the past. He wanted to get the dirty work over as soon as possible. "Hunter!" he bawled, "You and JB git started on a hole. Make it big enough for all of 'em."

That's when he noticed the withered demeanor of Cliff. The man looked ill. The memory of losing Gary was still fresh in his mind. Feeling his pain, Matt grabbed a shovel and handed it to Cliff. "Here," he said, "take this and git to digging. It'll help."

The rest of the men fanned out and began collecting the bones while Matt moved to the trees and inspected the rope used to bind a deceased Ranger. He had never seen Indians do this to dead men. It didn't make sense to his way of thinking.

"What do you make of it?" he asked Charles.

"They see things different than you and me. Wanted to send a message. Put the spooks in anybody that found the men."

Matt saw the regret. He knew what Charles was experiencing.

"Wasn't nothin' you could do," he assured Charles.

"I watched long enough to see too much. Too many Comanch for me to tackle alone. Rodgers hurt and turned tail . . ." His voice tapered off. He couldn't finish his thought. Survivor's guilt was eating him alive.

"We'll hit 'em, Charles. We'll hit 'em hard."

Matt sliced the rope off the tree. He hurled it into some thick brush where it could rot and never remind travelers of the pointless loss of life. He said, "We'll mark the grave with some flat stones so kinfolk can visit if they've a mind to."

Dawson watched with interest as Matt tossed the rope away. He decided to be of help and located another tree where a Ranger had been bound and mutilated. He drew out his Bowie knife and put it to use. Then he walked the opposite direction of the other men. He followed the tree line until he found another rope. This one still secured the partial remains of a Ranger. He sliced the rope and pitched it behind a boulder. He gathered the remains and carried them to the growing stack of bones accumulating next to the dirt thrown out by JB and Hunter. He made it a point to avoid eye contact.

Travis caught sight of Dawson helping in his own way. His jaw hung loose at the lethal appearance of such a large knife. There wasn't anything about Dawson that wasn't intimidating. Rumors had him responsible for the deaths of ten men or more. That number hadn't seemed possible, but seeing the knife and confident movements of Dawson in the face of such tragedy made him start to believe. He now thought the number of dead men might be too low.

He ducked when Dawson unexpectedly whirled and caught him watching. The steely assessment of Dawson did nothing to make him feel comfortable. It only turned his insides to jelly. He was glad Dawson was on their side. Or was he? The tongues had been wagging out of Dawson's hearing. Tom assured him the Yankee didn't present a threat, but he did say it was best to keep him under a watchful eye. Travis wasn't sure what to think. He bent to wrestle with a large flat stone to mark the burial site, glad to be occupied with a chore that broke the connection with the brute of a man.

The burial finished, Matt called for Tom to break out his bible and give a reading over their fallen comrades. Tom thumbed through the pages of his tattered bible until he found one of his favorite passages and began to read, "To every thing there is a season, and a time to every purpose under the heaven—A time to love, and a time to hate; a time of war, and a time of peace."

Hearty expressions of amen followed Tom's heartfelt recital of the biblical passage the men became familiar with in their upbringings. Dawson stood outside the circle of men clutching his hat in his hands. He hadn't heard this sincere of an Ecclesiastes reading since his mother taught him the passage when he was a teenager. She had been a true believer that lived her convictions in her relationships with her fellow man until the day the Sioux bucks materialized intent on mayhem and death. And rape. She and his sister didn't stand a chance with all the men working the harvest at a neighbor's farm miles away. Snapped out of his memories, he heard Matt say, "If we want peace, we've got business to do first."

Dawson pulled his hat down snug and mumbled under his breath, "Amen to that."

THIRTY-ONE

Nate pushed his hat back on his head and wiped his sleeve across his brow. The sun beat down without mercy now that the cloud cover had cleared. Late winter in Texas could change within an hour and make a man wish for the cold to return. Matt's hard stare added to the warmth building under his hat. He yanked it off and fanned his sweat-stained brow.

"Hell, Nate, where's all the damn sign? We been on the hunt for days now."

"They're out there sure as hell's waiting on 'em." He squinted in the brightness of the day as he scanned the grass-covered fields and low rolling hillocks leading down to the Llano River shining like polished silver in the slanting rays of the sun. "Maybe we ought to cut over to Packsaddle Mountain. This side of the Llano certainly seems empty don't it?"

Matt stood in his stirrups to get a better view as if he could will the Comanche to emerge from their hiding. He knew they were somewhere in the hills nearby. But where? Seeing nothing but buzzards soaring over a vacant panorama he settled back in the saddle. He took a deep breath and made his decision. "Won't hurt nothin' to try. Wasted enough time on this side."

Dawson reclined in the shade of an elm watching Travis tend to the packhorses when he heard Matt give the order to mount up and ride. He observed that Travis hopped to it when Matt spoke. Every time. It was obvious the kid intended to please his uncle. It sickened him when he thought back to his young days and his futile exertions to satisfy his father. In the end none of his efforts meant a damn thing to the old man.

It wasn't until he was out on his own that he realized he had the abilities and right frame of mind to use his size and skills of intimidation to earn a living. He didn't need to hop to it for no man unless it fit his own desires. He stumbled into working for Ames and it had been mutually beneficial for a long time. The status and authority the Colonel wielded gave him a shield to operate behind. No lawman had ever challenged his aggressive behavior with Ames pulling their strings behind an impenetrable curtain of clout, bribes and coercion. It had always been a good setup during the war and even more so after the defeat of the South where the investment costs were low, opportunities abundant, and profits unbelievably high. He growled, "Hop to it, Travis."

Travis jumped at the sound of Dawson's brusque voice. He shot him a quick look of contempt over his shoulder. There was some quality about Dawson he couldn't put his finger on. He could seem friendly enough at times, while at others there was evidence of a storm brewing behind his eyes. He had tired of trying to figure out what motivated him.

Dawson nodded in approval at the spunk Travis finally showed. He knew the boy had it in him. It was a pity the kid still didn't know it himself. "You'll do well, boy. Keep it up."

Sparks flared in his eyes as Travis grabbed between his legs and retorted, "Feel again. Ain't no boy here!"

After mounting, Dawson leaned on his pommel giving Travis a critical onceover. He liked testing men and the age of Travis made him a prime candidate to challenge. Prodding a man to react gave him an idea of what to expect in future circumstances. Would he turn and run? Stand and fight? Or cower in fear and pee his pants? He just learned more about Travis than the boy probably knew about himself.

Tom rode between them trailing the other packhorses. He gave Dawson a nod to lead the way. He preferred to keep the Yankee in front of him whenever possible. He had to admit Dawson had been useful at times and didn't appear inclined to cause problems, but he still wasn't totally convinced that he was trustworthy. He had caught him giving Matt a peculiar look several times, like he was making some sort of calculations in his head. Not sure how to read Dawson's intentions, he planned to heed Matt's advice and keep an eye on him at all times.

Dawson nonchalantly clicked his tongue to ease his horse behind the departing column. He'd do what Tom said without a fuss. Get along to get along was his motto until the right time arrived. And he knew it would. All that was required was patience.

They trailed down a slope strewn with chunks of stove-sized boulders carpeted in prolific growths of orange and yellow lichen. Cacti and mesquite tore at their pants as the men cut trail through the inhospitable terrain. Rocks the size of a man's fist rolled under the horses as they descended gullies and then caused them to teeter on the brink of falling as they scrambled back out. It necessitated careful riding to avoid blown knees on their mounts as Nate led them deeper and deeper into the unforgiving hill country.

Slow but steady progress eventually delivered them without a serious incident to the broad floodplain of the Llano River where the water split into a meandering web of channels gushing over bottomless sand. Nate waited for Matt to catch up at a flat outcropping of granite protruding into the current above an emerald pool.

Sizing up the crossing, Matt didn't like the thick growth of brush and willow on the bank lining the wide-open bottoms. He could picture any number of scenarios that ended with his men caught in an ambush with no place to hide in the flood scoured riverbed. Charles pulled alongside Matt and said, "Looks like a good spot for 'em to waylay us."

"Scout it out," Matt said. "Careful as you go."

In tandem they splashed into the river where the flow lapped at the bellies of their horses. Splitting at the other side of the first pool they cautiously picked their way through the ribbons of water to the opposite bank where they reined up to inspect the options within sight of each other. Close to the brush on the bank they examined the lush growth before they committed to flushing out any Comanche, the fate of Hobbs foremost on their minds.

Matt felt a tinge of trepidation as he watched them tie off their horses and disappear into the jumble of thick vegetation afoot. A covey of quail burst into the air above Nate. A sudden flush of alarm throbbed through Matt's entire body. This is how he had watched on a past mission as scouts entered a tangle of brush only to be found later with their throats slashed and missing their hair.

He sat stoic in the saddle, knowing it was always a flip of the coin as to whether or not the extra effort was necessary. If it turned out Nate and Charles uncovered an ambush it would be considered a good decision to scout, but it would also be likely to produce a couple of dead or wounded Rangers. It was all about gambling and he'd learned the hard way it was better to wager two lives than the entire command.

Twenty long minutes crawled by, each longer than the preceding. Across the river several crows landed in the top of a cottonwood splintered from lightning and naked of leaves. They silently preened and fluffed their glossy black feathers seemingly unconcerned with events far below their safe perch. Matt kept a vigilant eye on the birds that more often than not took pleasure in broadcasting his presence in the woods regardless of his wish to be anonymous. For a few minutes they casually went about their business.

The first caw electrified Matt. Both birds then erupted in a symphony of raucous cawing as they turned their attention to the brush and hopped in irritation along the bare limbs. As usual the keen-eyed birds announced their discovery to the world with an agitation impossible to ignore. Conversation among the men ceased as they all fastened their concentration on the far bank. Matt expected to hear war whoops and the sound of gunfire at any time. His hand reached for the Henry in its scabbard out of reflex. Whiskey's ears went erect sensing Matt's tremor of apprehension. The crows lifted from the branches and soared upstream on the breeze, flapping hard to escape the cause of their fright.

Matt saw movement inside a heavy screen of willows upriver from Nate's horse. It wasn't much. Just a flash of brown seen through a small gap in the foliage. Could have been anything. Bird. Deer. *Indian.*

Whiskey stomped the sand ready to join the horses at the other side. Matt pulled up the slack in the reins to constrain his ride, but also to be ready to bolt across the river if need be.

"Steady, boy," he reassured Whiskey.

Cliff appeared at Matt's side. The other men spread out in order to have a direct line in front of them should the need to charge arise. Dawson dropped behind Travis and Tom to size up the situation to his advantage. He noticed Travis glance back several times to keep tabs on his whereabouts. Moments later Tom duplicated the check up under the guise of testing the lead rope on the packhorses.

"Indians?" Cliff asked Matt.

"Crows are always fussing. Hard to tell."

Cliff couldn't contain his eagerness. "Shouldn't we cross?"

"Give 'em time to do their job. You've seen what happens when you don't take care of business out here."

Too late. Matt saw the consequence of his words. Who was *he* telling about the business of fighting Indians? Cliff knew exactly what Comanche could do. Looking across the river Cliff's expression burned with hatred and the desire for revenge. He would toss caution to the wind if he smelled half a chance to spill Indian blood. Matt knew he should have chosen his words with better care.

This time the veiled movement busted out of the bankside brush. There was no doubt it was Nate. He raised his hand in a gesture that it was clear to advance. Matt waved back and pointed the direction Charles patrolled to indicate they would wait on his assessment. A few more minutes passed and Charles emerged with a go-ahead to cross.

Matt waded Whiskey into the water with Cliff riding close on his rear. Bringing up the back of the column, Tom waited for Dawson and Travis to cross before he took his turn trailing the packhorses. This was a good arrangement for the ride and so far Dawson had made no complaints about the obvious reasons for his place in the column. Which was a good thing in Tom's opinion. He really didn't relish the idea of tangling with a man the size and makeup of the formidable Yankee.

Midafternoon found the men riding deep into a rugged maze of shallow cut-up draws that Matt knew all too well. This was the area the Ranger expedition passed through on their way to the sacred rock used by the Comanche as a sanctuary to hide with the Havens girl. Nate was currently leading them through the territory for dual purposes. It was a route frequently used by parties of marauding Indians, and the likelihood of stumbling upon Comanche sign was good in this region. Secondly, Matt had made a promise to Cliff that they would stop by the site of his son's grave if at all possible. Considering the lack of Indian sign thus far, this was the perfect opportunity to kill two birds with one stone, and Nate followed Matt's instructions to the letter.

Up ahead of the column stood the bleached limbs of a dead sycamore reaching high in the sky as if beseeching heaven with a prayer. The memory of the ghostly tree marking the gravesite made Matt's blood run cold. It had been so unnecessary. Such a waste of a young life. A cold and lonesome setting to bury a father's pride and joy.

Matt halted the column and motioned for Cliff to pull up. Rocks clattered and rolled under Cliff's horse as he made his way to Matt. It was the only sound that could be heard as the men in the column held their chatter in what was to be a solemn moment. Cliff studied the sycamore. It was just like he had heard it described. He swallowed hard.

Matt cleared his throat to hide his sentiment. He said, "This is the place."

Cliff coughed into his hand. In his heart he had yearned to be here, and now that he was, it was overwhelming. Beneath that forlorn and solitary tree in the middle of a howling wilderness rested the remnants of his former life. A happier time he knew was destined to never return. Content memories of Gary snuggled in his arms as a two year old flashed through his mind. There had been such hope in the future and getting to watch him grow into a man. Now that dream was destroyed. Everything gone. He sucked in a deep breath like he was suffocating. And then he quit breathing. He forgot who he was. All he saw was the sycamore that marked the end of his life as a father. He wondered where do you go when you get to the end of your dreams? A whisper of sadness floated away on the wind when he finally let his breath out. Matt gave Cliff a pat on the shoulder as he nudged Whiskey forward.

Near the rear of the column, Dawson watched the drama unfold like an eagle, missing nothing, understanding it all. Memories of his mother dead and pallid on the black farmland came back in a flood. Yes, he knew what Cliff must have been feeling. There was no getting over that kind of loss.

A flush of excitement grew in his belly. He gazed at the hills. They were out there. Maybe right now. Maybe on the hummocks west of them watching. He could sense it in the air. He rubbed the cool metal of his Spencer. Retribution time was coming. It had been too long a wait. The predator in him was ready to taste blood.

Nate came galloping back to meet Matt waiting with Cliff at the head of the column, the somber mood evident. In a low voice respecting the moment, he reported, "All clear. Ain't no sign of Comanch nowhere."

"Thanks, Nate. We'll rest a spell at the grave. Put JB and Tully out as pickets."

As they neared the tree, the charred black trunk stood out as a distinctive marking. Cliff would have recognized the sycamore without any help. He had envisioned the tree in his mind enough that it seemed like he passed by here everyday, and in a way he did. In essence he perished under this lonely tree with a rock-covered grave of his son at its base. He tried not to think of the torture Gary endured. He tried not to dwell on his son murdered and then discarded as if he were nothing but a mongrel dog. But of course that had been impossible. There was nobody he could turn to at home for support, and his inability to prevent Gary's death ate at him constantly, relentlessly driving him crazy with grief.

The men dispersed in a semicircle and dismounted. There would be none of the usual joking. They stood silent in respect of Cliff dismounting to kneel in prayer at the mound of indistinct rocks.

Cliff murmured in a voice only heard by him and the spirit of his son, Gary. "I'm sorry I couldn't be there that day, son. It's my fault what happened. I should've been there to protect y'all." He broke down in a loss for words that would do any good. He wondered what kind of father allowed his children to be whisked away by bloodthirsty barbarians? The answer lay in the cold hard ground. A particularly bad father. A fact driven home by his estranged wife at every opportunity she could find. The fight was over. He had nothing left to offer in his defense. He was in agreement with her.

He rose above the grave and said a prayer asking for forgiveness while fully expecting none in return. A caldron of toxic hate burned in his chest. Nothing mattered except killing those responsible for the destruction of a faithful and loving family he had worked hard to build.

Matt came alongside, hat in his hand when Cliff motioned him over. Distraught, Cliff said, "You've been where I'm at."

Matt thought about Cora still at his side. Distant to him, but still alive and rearing the kids. Losing Josh had devastated him beyond description, but he still had the rest of his family. For what it was worth, Cora hadn't left him.

"It's tough," Matt said.

"How've you made it this far?"

"One day at a time. It's all a man can do."

"Not sure I can look at it that way."

"One day at a time. It's the only option we have."

"Options are an illusion to my way of thinking."

"May be. We're just human. Our choices are always limited. It's our plight."

Cliff's eyes glazed over examining the grave. It didn't make sense, but nobody could change the cruel facts of life on the frontier. He had known putting down roots within range of raiding Indians could be disastrous. Yet he did it anyway. He made the decisions that cost him his family.

Reading Cliff's thoughts, Matt said, "Don't be hard on yourself. It ain't your fault them Comanche are heartless murderers. Others in our group have suffered at the hands of Injuns."

"Hah. It's my duty to protect my family." He shook his head in disbelief. "Didn't do a very good job." Pointing at the rocks, he said, "There's the proof."

Hardened to the reality he couldn't escape, he glanced at Matt, eyes vacant. It was a look Matt had seen before when death stripped the meaning of life out of virtuous people trying to make an honest living.

"You know it, and I know it," Cliff reiterated.

Matt didn't reply. Cliff was right. Some facts couldn't be argued with no matter how much a man wanted things to be different. Things were what they were. They had both lost a son because they failed in their number one responsibility to keep the family safe.

"We share a connection," Cliff said.

Uncomfortable with the truth, Matt shifted his stance and said, "Yes, we do."

They stood shoulder to shoulder, heads bent downward, staring at the grave, thinking about lost opportunities.

"Now let me ask you," Cliff said. "You mentioned options. I've only got one that matters. When are we gonna find 'em?"

"Nate's been ridin' double our miles. I'm sure he'll cut sign soon unless they've lit out for the plains." He tilted his hat back on his head and gazed along the line of ridges to the west. "But I doubt that. They've had too much success to give it up yet."

"I hope you're right. I'd ride through hell and back to find 'em if need be."

Cliff then asked for time to fashion a cross to mark the grave. He searched until he found two limbs he tied together and wedged tight between rocks at the head of the grave. Stepping back to consider his improvement, a bit of the weight was lifted from his grief.

Nate gave Matt a sly inquisitive look unseen by the other men. Matt nodded back with an unspoken approval.

Cliff finally turned his back to the grave and that gave Matt the chance to line out the rest of the day. His voice was full of confidence when he said, "We'll trail over to Packsaddle Mountain for the night. Camp on top and scan the country in the mornin'. Can't nobody pass without us seeing 'em."

Nate knew the plan and was already well up the trail before Matt led the Rangers away from the depressing scene. They would have to put in some hard miles to reach the summit of the large prominence that passed for a mountain in the boundless hills of Texas. But their riding would not compare to Nate's additional chore for the afternoon. As soon as he could, he made a loop back to the gravesite. It was a rotten job, but it was a necessary evil.

He rode back to the sycamore undetected and slid out of the saddle to the hard rocky ground. In his opinion it was the most lonesome and sad grave he had ever seen. Out of the way of normal traveling routes, only feral creatures passed near the grave. And this included the red men that Nate considered the wildest of all the beasts he had ever encountered. There was little doubt they would pass this way again. It was one of their favorite trails to travel for hunting and pillaging. The next time they happened by there was also no doubt the cross would attract their attention. Being curious, they would question what valuables they could dig out of the rocks they had no reason to notice except for the dead giveaway of the cross. This was unacceptable. Matt knew it, and he knew it. Cliff didn't.

The cross was easy to pull free. He twisted it out of the rocks and flipped it behind the brush. In a hurry, he never looked back as he rode away to regain the lead on the column. Their luck had to change.

THIRTY-TWO

High atop Packsaddle Mountain the view of the lustrous night sky was unobstructed. The cloudless atmosphere above the mountain twinkled and pulsed with a profound energy that brought Matt a spiritual connection with the heavens much closer to any harmony he ever felt in a church. Comfortable on his bedroll softened by plush grass, he cradled his hands behind his head and enjoyed the peace of the night accented by a spectacular show of celestial beauty any author would struggle to describe.

He couldn't sleep. Too many difficulties existed in life and he often found himself seeking solutions in the depths of a long night. Tonight was no different than many a night spent in his cabin staring at the ceiling. Where were the Indians? Days on the hunt and nothing to show for all the effort had started to gnaw on him. Lying here under the tranquil sky he could imagine that he was pursuing a quarry that didn't exist. If only it were that simple.

Perhaps the Comanche had vacated the hills for their haunts on the high plains content with the results of their recently destructive raids. But he knew that was unlikely. Hell, they had already hit his ranch three times altogether. It all began with the heartbreaking loss of Josh. Nothing had been the same since the death of his youngest son. The timing of their incursions could not have come at a worse moment with the economy reeling from the post war conditions. It was everything he could do to scratch out a living with the severe shortage of opportunities to earn some legal tender.

His old Confederate graybacks had become worthless when he returned from the endless brawl against the Yankees. Nearly destitute, and always desperate for a means to secure a living, the loss of Josh had been traumatic at a time when he could least deal with the despair heaped upon his family, and in particular Cora.

Next came the daring attempt by the Comanche to steal from his food supply in the middle of the night. A wounded brave shot in the doorway and a hasty pursuit the next morning resulted in two dead Indians out of three. But of course the one that got away on a splendid appaloosa pony was the one he most remembered. The black painted face and lithe physique of the warrior was unforgettable. From all the available evidence he was sure this imposing buck went by the name of Black Owl. How he longed for the day to even the score with this vile Comanche brave.

The attempted theft of his horses and simultaneous abduction of Becky rounded out the three raids he and his family had personally experienced. He counted his blessings that the Comanche didn't press the attack on the last raid or he might have returned to a burned-out shell of a cabin with nobody left alive to tell the tale. It could happen. Plenty of families that risked settling in remote locations separated from the assistance of friendly neighbors met such a fate. He shuddered at the thought of the unthinkable.

Disturbing images of his family at the mercy of the Comanche became too much to bear. He threw his wool blanket to the side. Bolting upright, he strode to a nearby boulder squared off at the sides as if it had been milled. Taking a seat, he gazed at the black velvet sky along the eastern horizon where it fused with the terrain below. Hanging like a diamond glistening in the dark abyss, Venus, the morning star, shone brilliant. Too remarkably bright for his comfort. He shrunk inside. The splendor of the star actually hurt to witness. It was like the eye of God was judging him. He felt small and insignificant beneath the expansive mystery on display in the night sky.

Alone at the edge of a slumbering camp, awareness grew in Matt that they shared the vast and inhospitable landscape with predators. Somewhere below the mountain in the dark woodlands camped a band of roaming Comanche intent upon spreading death and destruction. It was in their nature. They couldn't help their intrinsic disposition. They lived their lives as part of the natural fabric where survival of the fittest was all that mattered in an unforgiving environment. They thrived off the honor earned in war against their foes, red or white. He felt their fearsome presence growing in his gut as sure as the coming sunrise.

A piercing scream ripped through the stillness of the night air. It sliced like a knife to the core of Matt's soul. He leapt from the boulder, turning mid-circle in the air to counter his exposure to an attack. His heart beat like a drum. A second hair-raising shriek of fury blasted across the camp. Feet spread wide, he assumed a defensive stance, but was unable to locate the threat in the shroud of darkness.

The big cat was near. Too damn near! There was no mistaking the unearthly scream of an adult mountain lion. His eyes scanned the pitch-black emptiness in vain. He couldn't see the cat, but he knew the cat saw him.

Backing up, his attention glued to the woods, he returned to his bedroll for his Henry under the blanket.

Travis was sitting up, eyes as white as an onion. "What the hell?" he wailed as he groped for his scattergun. "Did I dream that?"

Excitement erupted in the camp as the startled men came alive.

Quick to ascertain the situation, Travis answered his own question with an unequivocal, "Guess not."

Matt faced the direction the cry came from. Out of the side of his mouth he said, "It's what you thought."

"Too damn close," Travis said.

Matt relaxed a little after the initial jolt. "Yeah, he is."

"Think he'll make a play for the horses?"

That was also Matt's concern. Nate was on guard duty by the picket line. It was a reassuring to hear him shout, "Woohoo! That boy's close! Keep your eyes peeled 'less you want to be breakfast."

Matt chuckled at the wry comment. With the camp awake and stirring there was little chance the cat would try anything. He was probably halfway down the mountain as afraid of the commotion he caused as the men were of him.

Travis said, "Never heard one when I was sleepin' in the open. Makes a fellow feel naked."

"Got your attention, did it?" Matt asked.

"Yeah, it did," Travis said in a pensive tone.

It was early, but Matt could sense the premature start of the day added to the heavy load already shouldered by Travis. He waited for his nephew to speak, but nothing came of the opening, so Matt decided to probe on his own when he asked, "How's it going back there with Dawson?"

"Dawson?" Travis said as he warily glanced to the other side of camp where the Yankee had bedded down near the horses. The last thing he wanted was to be caught talking about the intimidating man. "I don't much care for him."

"Figured that. He's a hard man to git to know. What I'm askin' is there any trouble I need to know about?"

Travis massaged the rough stubble of beard on his chin. It was too early to think, but Matt wanted answers. "No. No problems. He's actually helped with the horses at times. Keeps to himself mostly." He wavered a moment and searched Matt's face for his reaction, but it was too dark to make out. "Don't change nothin' though. I still don't trust him."

Matt nodded in approval of the report. Dawson was a risk that worried him, but he still stuck by his decision to include him in the patrol. One more gun in competent hands could make a difference if they ever located the Comanche.

"Fair enough," Matt replied. "Keep an eye out. You're doing fine."

Travis gawked at the star filled sky. He too felt small, insignificant, and green in the company of hardened men under a vast universe he understood not at all. Hesitating before asking, he spoke in a timid voice he would only reveal in the presence of his uncle. "Is that what it's like?"

Puzzled, Matt asked, "What's that?"

"Facin' Comanche."

"Facin' Comanche?"

"Yeah, you know. Is it the same panic you feel when a panther screams from out of nowhere?"

So that was the concern chewing on Travis so early. He was untested in so many ways and the reality of being a greenhorn was weighing on him. There was no doubt in Matt's mind that making him a horse holder at the rear was where he belonged until he had been baptized under fire.

"Travis, that surge of fear is normal. A man has to decide real quick out here. Fight or flight."

"That's my worry. I'll be honest with you. If I hadn't been sleepin' . . . I wonder if I'd of run."

"We'll never know."

"You seen men run?"

Matt didn't want to undermine the boy's self-confidence, but he asked an honest question and deserved an honest answer.

"Yeah, I've seen plenty of men run."

Travis was astounded. He let the notion sink in, wondering how they lived with the knowledge they would be branded as cowards. He grew quiet contemplating his own store of courage.

Matt dug in his haversack and pulled out some pemmican sweetened with black dewberries. He broke it in half and offered a chunk to Travis. "Here you go. Have a little of Cora's specialty. It'll be daylight soon. Might as well stay awake."

"Cain't git back to sleep no how. I'd dream that cat had me by the throat."

Matt laughed and slapped Travis on the back. "He might at that. You can't trust them big cats. There sneaky as the devil."

"Bad as the Comanche?"

"One and the same."

The camp was roused and only a couple of the men returned to their bedrolls. Most gathered around the center of camp, and it wasn't long before the tall tales and lies commenced. The perilous nature of their assignment was on hold while they enjoyed the camaraderie and uniqueness of camping atop the highest mountain in the vicinity where they looked forward to a partial day's rest. The idea was to let the horses graze in a meadow where they would be hidden from the sight of any Indians that chanced to be passing below. While the men took a day of rest Matt wanted them to scatter and act as lookouts for movement through the extensive hills and prairies surrounding Packsaddle Mountain.

Matt finished the pemmican and climbed to the top of a knob in the darkness before the other men could finish their breakfast and wild yarns. He found a solid oak he located from the evening before and sat with his back resting against the rough bark of the trunk. Momentarily free of responsibility, his thoughts wandered over his plight with Cora that appeared to be at an impasse. He kept coming up with a blank to bridge the chasm isolating them from each other. It was up to her. She held the cards. The women always did.

He dozed a moment lost in dreams of how their relationship used to be with days that didn't seem to end lost in the bliss of new love. They had land that was theirs to do with as they saw fit. All of the potential was in front of them as if it were a gift from God. But He had different plans. Sometimes the clouds thickened overhead. The sun didn't shine. The birds didn't sing. He fell into a fretful bit of sleep wondering how his formerly happy marriage had slipped from his grasp leaving him with nothing but a pile of stale ashes.

A short while later, his eyes flew open at the sound of a horse snorting. He grimaced at the realization that his lower back muscles had tightened into a knot from sitting against the tree. Groaning, he slowly rose, his knees popping in protest from the annoying stiffness of too many hours in the saddle. Arching his back and clasping his hands behind his head, he felt the muscles pull in stubborn resistance to the stretching.

He froze in astonishment at what spread out before him.

The awakening of dawn was flooding the sky in a feeble pink illumination. Dumbfounded at the scene that had been indistinguishable in the blackness of night, his arms drooped to his sides. As far as he could see, the hills were blanketed under a dense bank of fog clinging to the edge of the bluff just below camp. Here and there a few of the higher peaks thrust above the fog like dark and secluded islands in the ocean. All the way to the faint horizon a cloud of fog hid everything from view. Turning northward more of the same greeted Matt's inspection. Packsaddle Mountain poked its head above a cloudy sea of obscurity.

Unseen, but clearly heard through the foggy conditions, a couple of turkeys began gobbling as they flew their roost and strutted like kings to gather their flock. Despite the gloomy weather the turkeys were going about their daily routine. Wildlife didn't have an option. They had to adapt to any conditions.

The reality hit Matt like the swinging of a club. So would the Comanche. Much like the turkey, they were creatures of the forest well adapted to any weather condition they encountered. The fog wouldn't keep them from conducting their incursions. In his gut he had a strong premonition that they were out there at this very moment.

He searched his memory of the topography surrounding Packsaddle Mountain. It was the most prominent feature in the region and he recalled a patrol from long ago following the trail of a renegade band of Apache. The wily Apache eluded them at the northwest base of peaks strung together in resemblance of a packsaddle. That was where there was an old trace used by generations of Indians that traversed a ridge dividing the drainages of several creeks. The largest of those branches went by the name of Honey Creek. That was it! He knew it as well as he knew anything. The Comanche would be prowling this old raiding trail that was a favorite of their tribe.

Reining in his excitement, he deliberated the options. The fog could last all day if the conditions were right, and he had no way of predicting when it would lift. It could take hours or it could hang around all day. The thought of sitting on his hands waiting for the fog to lift seemed a waste of time. Little to nothing was gained by delaying their reconnaissance. All things considered, it wasn't that hard to figure. He made the decision to move before the Comanche slithered by right under his nose. They couldn't be allowed to inflict pain and torment on some unsuspecting frontiersman and maybe an innocent family. Without any reservations he knew they needed to ride.

THIRTY-THREE

Matt rode behind the ghostly silhouette of Nate slowly leading the column down the fog-shrouded slopes of Packsaddle Mountain. They wanted to proceed quietly, but Matt could hear the hollow clunking of wet stones as they rolled down the hill, echoes drifting through the moisture-soaked thickets. One of the men tried unsuccessfully to suppress a cough. A horse snorted, impatient with the poor footing on the game trail. Matt cringed at their lack of stealth, but there was little that could be done about the noise of men and stock descending the rock-strewn skirt of the mountain.

Nate hunched over the flank of his dun engaged in the hunt for the slightest sign of evidence that Indians had recently passed. It was a known fact that they too liked to set up observation from the higher ridges of the mountain. There was no reason the Comanche weren't sharing the same ideas as the Rangers. He could turn a corner in the overgrown trail and suddenly be face to face with a dozen redskins ready to stick him with an arrow. Occasionally he made a stop to investigate a suspicious track or bent blade of grass. Knowing he would be the first casualty, he didn't cherish the prospect of a surprise confrontation at close range.

Another game trail intersected the path they were following and Nate paused to put his nose in the air. Matt saw Nate's hat tilt back as he worked the fog for scent. Nate claimed he could smell an Indian a hundred yards deep in a cedar break. He said the skill was nothing special. Anybody should be able to detect the distinct odor of the yarrow and bear grease they rubbed on their bodies to fend off mosquitos, not to mention the campfire smoke that saturated their skin like a side of pork in the smokehouse. His task was made challenging by the fog as he worked his nose like one of his prized hounds on the scent of a coon. He twisted in the saddle, looked back at Matt and shrugged his shoulders in frustration. Nothing there. Gently nudging the flanks of his mount, they eased down the slope.

After a tedious ride checking for sign, they approached the banks of clean running Honey Creek. The spring fed creek flowed over a bed of gravel interrupted by tranquil emerald pools collecting between a series of granite slabs spanning the width of the channel. The vegetation beside the bank was green and lush from sucking at the dependable supply of water in a drought prone section of the hills. Nate found an opening in the creekside brush large enough to accommodate the horses and rode through to let his dun slurp at the sweet water. The other men followed suit and lined out along the stream to take a short break. A couple of them took the opportunity to refill canteens upstream from the horses sullying the brook.

Men and stock content after the pause, Matt nodded at Nate to lead them up the opposite bank and under a sparse grove of live oaks on a gentle rise. Verdant stands of low growing sotol colonized the meadows surrounding the oaks. They carefully avoided the needles of the sotol until a profuse growth of bee brush obliged them to detour around the impenetrable barrier. A roadrunner carrying a writhing lizard in its beak burst out of the thicket when Nate stopped to scrutinize the open field ahead of him. He watched the bird scamper through the knee-high grass and disappear behind a patch of cactus.

Matt pulled alongside Nate and they studied the opening in silence, each absorbed in their individual thoughts. A faint bellowing of misery echoed across the grasses. They looked at each other inquisitively, unsure of what to make of the development. Another bellow sounded, a little louder with an edge of suffering.

Matt's concentration intensified when they heard it a third time.

"What's that?" Nate asked.

"Somethin' big," Matt ventured.

"Yes it is."

"Could be a buff."

Nate listened again as the bawling seemed to move their direction. The hair on the back of his neck stood on end. "I'd say it's a cow, but we're in the middle of nowhere."

Matt said, "They'll wander if let be." He passed instructions down the line to hold in place while they tried to get a handle on the situation. Turning back to Nate he said, "Ain't right. Whatever it is."

He nodded his head for Nate to ease out. Then he slipped his Henry from the scabbard expecting the worse.

The bellowing grew louder as they neared the center of the meadow. The blurry shadow of oaks hid the source of the bawling. Something was hurting bad. Matt became agitated at the sound of an animal in distress. He hated the idea of prolonged suffering by any of God's creatures. He rested his Henry against the backside of the pommel ready for action.

Nate reined up when he heard the unmistakable cracking of limbs. The beast was charging directly at them! Both of them shouldered their rifles at the sudden emergence of a large brown animal busting out of the tree cover.

Eyes rolling in terror, showing all white, a cow staggered across their front. An arrow was lodged behind her shoulder, blood streaming down her leg. The pain stricken bovine tumbled into a scrawny mesquite oblivious to any obstacles in her path. Knocked off balance by the collision, she stumbled to the side and collapsed to the damp soil with her legs flailing, too weak to regain her footing. The bawling continued, but with less and less intensity as the reserves of her will bled out and soaked into the porous sand where she lay.

Nate muttered, "They're damn near." His eyes flared in an attempt to penetrate the hazy motte of oaks. "They could be watchin' us right now."

Charles rode up and suggested, "Me and Nate can scout them woods."

Matt said, "It's gotta be done." He nodded toward the oaks in approval and secured their reins after they dismounted to scout on foot. JB came beside and took the reins from Matt leaving him free to use hand signals to position the men across the meadow. He motioned for them to remain mounted and wait for further developments. At the rear, Tom, Dawson, and Travis halted with the packhorses behind the screen of bee brush. Dawson casually stole ahead of them to the edge of the brush where he had an unobstructed view of Matt's back.

Twenty tense minutes passed before the two scouts reappeared with excitement gleaming in their eyes. Nate gushed with enthusiasm, "Found their tracks and you're right, Matt. They're on that old trail leading south."

Matt pinched his lips together, his expression hardening with resolve. He rose in his stirrups to stretch out the troublesome muscles in his back. Grimacing in pain, he choked down any thoughts of succumbing to the fire raging up his spinal nerves. Bending his back in an arc to seek relief, he stared at the woods, racking his brain for a tactic to employ. "How many?" he asked.

"Bunch," Nate said. He glanced over his shoulder where the potential conflict could spring up at anytime. "Trail is tore up bad. Could be twenty. Maybe thirty."

Charles added, "Fog's a problem. Be easy to ride into an ambush."

"We can't control the fog," Matt said.

The rest of the men observed the discussion mindful that the situation favored the Indians. Dawson took a cigar stub and shoved it in the corner of his mouth. When things got interesting he liked the calming distraction of something to gnaw on. He was finally going to see the famed Ranger in action, and now that he was here, a realization dawned on him. Critical questions about the strength of the Comanche were unanswered. The arrangement of the Rangers was tentative at best. He shifted the cigar stub nervously from one corner of his mouth to the other. His ass was on the line.

Easing into the saddle, Matt took a moment to reach a conclusion. In a matter-of-fact voice he said, "It's obvious we can't close on 'em playing it safe." He peered into the murky atmosphere. Shaking his head, he didn't like the decision, but stated it in no uncertain terms, "Me and Nate will take point. Charles, space the men out behind us so we can avoid full engagement if they ambush us. You partner up with Tully and Hunter for a flanking move from the back of the column if needed. Have Tom and Travis stay in front of you with the packhorses for now."

"What about Dawson?"

"Keep him between you and Tom."

Confident in the experience Charles possessed, Matt left him to arrange the men in trailing order as he led Nate into the woods. Water dripped from the overhead branches and plopped on his hat as soon as they entered the bleak timber. Visibility was restricted. A dull thud of hooves sinking into the soft turf and the occasional clink of iron shoes against rock could not be avoided. He scanned the thicket for Comanche like a hawk scouring the fields for a mouse. There was so much wrong about this maneuver. A feeling of dread rose in his gut. He let Nate pull alongside.

"How much further to the trail?" he whispered to Nate.

"Not much." Nate glanced at Matt. "You got the willies too?"

"Don't care for ridin' naked through their backyard, but it's what we're gonna do. You watch right. I'll cover left."

Riding point took a special kind of courage in the best conditions and both of them had done so without hesitation in former times. But in the poor visibility they took comfort in sharing the duty. Snaking through the tangled growth of tree and brush they knew an arrow from nowhere could stick them at any moment. They continued to ride cautiously and on edge anticipating the buzz of an arrow until the Comanche trail emerged at the base of a low cliff topped off with a growth of yucca. It presented an eerie sight with the stalks of the plant fading into the murkiness of fog above them.

Studying the jumble of pony tracks, Matt asked, "How long ago?"

"I'd say an hour at most."

"What about the cow? You reckon it took her an hour to bleed out?"

"She was a ways from the trail. Hard to figure what that means. She could've come from who knows where."

Matt looked over his shoulder as the rest of the men caught up and waited in silence. All of them were anxiously surveying the creepy terrain completely aware of their hazardous exposure below the bluff.

Matt said, "These tracks are headed south." Turning back to face Nate he noted, "We could also have 'em on our rear for all we know."

"Possible I suppose."

"So it gits interesting."

"Want to go it afoot?" Nate asked.

"Not yet." Matt nodded down the trail. "They're in front of us."

"You sure of that?"

"I'm willing to bet they're ahead of us on this trail. That's all I'm sure of. It's all I need to know for now. Ain't got time to fumble around on what else might be. We're not gonna let the cat git outta the bag."

Nate didn't like to state the obvious, but he liked living even more. "Matt, just because these tracks are an hour old don't mean they couldn't be suckin' us into a trap. That trail could stop just around the next bend."

His testiness growing, Matt spat back, "Hell, I know that! It could also mean they've got an hour head start that grows every second we sit here debatin'. Where would that leave us?"

"Don't mean no disrespect."

Having developed a surly mood, Matt didn't respond. He was too far into analysis to hear the apology of his good scout. It was his call and his alone. None of the men could tell him anything he didn't already know. He had to discern the intentions of the war party that left *these* tracks on *this* trail. It was a trail that led south to the outlying ranches and eventually Austin. It was true that a few trails branched off in other directions, and the Comanche didn't have to follow trails, but they had been particularly bold lately. There was every reason to believe they would continue their pattern of raiding. That meant one thing to him. His place could be in their plans again. Or Bull's. The Indians had already pushed Cliff and his family from their homestead. That was the goal of the Comanche, to drive back the line of settlement. Reclaim their former land. He wasn't left with a choice. The Indians had made his decision for him.

"Nate, I'll take point."

"Ain't no need in that."

"Anybody can follow a trail this obvious. Stay on my ass and we'll be fine."

Nate looked in the gray eyes as hard as steel. Matt had made his decision. There was no point in disagreeing and he nodded his head in understanding as Charles rode up to gather the latest information. Matt ordered, "Same as before. We're closing on 'em. Spread the word to be ready."

Without a backwards glance, confident in his men to obey orders, Matt spurred Whiskey down the trail. He was a bit fast in Nate's opinion, but that opinion had now been deemed secondary in importance. He had seen Matt like this before, and the futility of opposing him was pointless. That was one of the traits that made Matt the man he was. His intuition of what to do and when to do it was a well-known and respected talent that separated him from his peers. That was why men would follow him to the gates of hell if he asked.

Undeterred by the risks, Matt maintained a steady pace along the pony trail despite passing several points that provided ideal ambush opportunities. The soupy ambivalence of dense woods pressed in tight to the men. Nate kept within sight of Matt's back out of a sense of self-preservation and determination to be available if events cascaded out of control. Glancing back occasionally, he was always pleased to find the men close enough for mutual support and spaced out far enough to allow room for evasive maneuvers if necessary.

At the crossing of a steep wash Matt suddenly halted Whiskey and dropped out of the saddle. Bending down he plucked the broken shaft of an arrow off the ground where the pounding of hooves had trampled it into the mud. After examining the artifact he held it up for Nate to inspect.

"What do you make of that, Nate?"

"Gittin' a little careless it seems."

"Not like 'em to be that way." He pointed at the jumbled tracks and asked, "What do you think?"

Nate eased out of the saddle and knelt to analyze the chewed up mud and upended rocks. He felt along the edges of the prints for firmness and scanned the water in the impressions of the hooves. He said, "Water's still muddy. Soft edges." It was obvious in his mind. He said, "Less than thirty minutes out I'd reckon."

Matt said, "Gittin' close. Maybe too close."

"Their rear guard may have already seen us." Nate's tone was cautionary. "They could be just over the hill. Waitin' on us to make a mistake."

Matt knelt to have his own look at the evidence. He swirled the water with his finger to buy time to think. He watched the mud settle. Nate was right. It was no surprise to him. Nate knew his business. An ambush could be right over the hill.

In the distance the dull report of a large caliber rifle wafted through the baffles of fog. Matt glanced at the men sitting on horseback at the top of the wash. The first rider he saw wasn't a Ranger. It was Dawson. He was looking on with the casual observation of an uninvolved spectator.

Nate said, "That's a call to action."

"Yep, time to move," Matt replied while taking a read on Dawson. They locked eyes, but Matt didn't have time to dissect the significance. He spun to mount Whiskey. Resolute in the saddle, he held his finger to his lips when he faced the men.

"Keep it quiet. We'll close in. Rifles out and ready."

Easing to the lip of the gully, Matt peered over the edge. A field of grass faded into the fog. In his estimation the shot came from beyond his limited vision. He nudged Whiskey to ease forward on the trail. It was do or die time.

After fifteen minutes of cautious advancement Matt came to where the main trail split into several different lanes of depressed grass leading around large thickets of mesquite and scrub. Signaling Nate and JB to join him, Matt instructed the rest of the men to hold their positions while the three of them proceeded on foot. It wasn't long before Nate picked up the odor of smoke indicating activity of some sort. Using his acute sense of smell, Nate led them on a direct path to the source through a tangle of scrub brush adorned with needle-sharp thorns that tore at their shirts.

Carefully emerging out of the thorn patch, Matt and Nate saw it at the same time. The camp had been looted. Pots and pans were overturned and strewn about. The handle of a shovel smoldered in the dying embers of a campfire that had recently been a point of comfort. Under a lean-to of wrinkled tarps lay several pickaxes, rock hammers and shovels used for mineral probing. The occupants were missing along with any sign of Indians.

Nate slinked out of the concealment of brush while Matt and JB covered him with their rifles shouldered. The camp was a wreck. Items were thrown everywhere. Nate picked his way through the debris to the tarp and jerked it back expecting to find dead bodies.

Instead he found a couple of coffee stained pillows in what he guessed to be a bed for at least two or maybe three.

Matt stepped out of the brush reasoning that the camp was clear of threat. Noticing a splotch of red on a moisture soaked blanket he lifted it up to show JB. It was blood. And a lot of it. He tossed it to the side and said, "Prospectors."

JB said, "Dead prospectors I'd venture."

"What the hell are they out here for?" Nate asked.

Matt answered, "Some folks are still trying to find the abandoned Spanish mine up on Packsaddle Mountain. Or the one rumored to be on Red Ochre Hill."

"Damn fools." JB shook his head.

Matt said, "That ore never did amount to much, but people being people gotta dream." Thoroughly alert, he swept his gaze across the area searching for details that might help identify the missing men. Seeing nothing, he noted in a brusque manner, "Looks like somebody's dream ended bad. Question is, where are they now?"

Two more shots, fired in rapid succession sounded about as distant as the first. A faint cry floated through the desolate camp.

"That's a white man," Matt said.

A third report rang out. Then a deathly silence prevailed after the echo died.

Matt grabbed JB by the arm and said, "Go back and bring the men up to this point. Have 'em load up plenty of ammo and proceed on foot from here. Nate and I are gonna head out and see what we can do before it's too late for some poor soul. Depending on what we find, we'll wait on y'all if we can."

JB turned to leave, but Matt stopped him with one more order. "Make sure Travis and Tom stay with the horses right here in camp. Now go!"

Without another word needed Nate located the most obvious path away from the camp and headed toward the sound of shooting. Stopping to listen inside a copse of live oaks they heard nothing else to alarm them. Within fifty yards of leaving the oaks they discovered the scalped body of an older white man draped over the burnt fork of a cedar stump. His head drooped against the charred bark exposing the bare cranium where his thin white hair had been sliced away. One arrow protruded from his back buried half way up the shaft. A nasty exit wound from a slug had blown away the side of his neck and blood still dribbled from the gaping hole.

Repulsed, Matt said, "There's others we gotta worry about now."

Nate stood spellbound by the viciousness of the Comanche. He had seen similar scenes in previous times, but it always amazed him how brutal their methods were. Matt thumped him on the back to snap him out of the daze.

"We gotta go," Matt said.

Nate didn't say anything. He just turned to follow Matt's hasty departure. He snuck a look back at the unfortunate prospector with one thought on his mind; could that be him someday, and was today that day?

THIRTY-FOUR

They could hear the muffled whoops from excited Indians a short distance away. Unaware the Rangers had discovered them, their boisterous conduct provided an excellent beacon to guide them through the maze of brush without wasting valuable time. From the level of exhilaration he could hear, Matt knew it didn't bode well for any hapless white men in their clutches. He was painfully aware of the urgency to rescue whoever it was suffering the torment of the barbaric Comanche, but there was a difference between aggression and suicide on his part. Visibility was limited and there was no way to be certain what they were up against in numbers and type of arms. Nearing the source of the celebrating, Matt froze in place and motioned for Nate to spread farther apart in a clump of stunted cedar, but stay in sight. Impatient to proceed, Matt knew they had to gather more information before they engaged. He strained to peer through the dense haze of moisture.

His decision to hold up to ascertain their options was immediately rewarded when the thundering hooves of two Indian ponies warned him of their imminent arrival. First one brave appeared on horseback and then another riding on his tail. The second rider was holding onto his mount with clenched knees while he loosed an arrow at an object dragging behind the first pony. The leader of the two was dressed in a white man's hat with red streamers wrapped around the crown and fluttering in the breeze.

Nate and Matt ducked low to avoid detection. Through an opening in the cedar Matt caught a glimpse of a naked white man strung by rope behind the first rider. Several broken arrows protruded from his lacerated and bleeding torso. As they rode away Matt saw the body bounce off a large rock with a hollow thump that made him cringe in sympathy. The captive let out a pitiful cry. His shriek of pain enticed the trailing Comanche to release a hideous screech as he brought his bow up to deliver another arrow. Drawing back fully, he let it sail, and Matt heard the dull thud as the arrow found its mark. As suddenly as they appeared the two Comanche were swallowed up in the fog.

Matt and Nate were left with the troubling image of a situation beyond their control. Their anger and frustration was heightened by the ghoulish laughter wafting through the dreary woods. From the diversity of voices Matt determined they were up against a large party of Comanche, and apparently they had gone unnoticed by the riders. It was a small advantage, but it was all they had.

Nate duck-walked over and whispered, "What're we gonna do?"

"Wait 'til the others move up."

"There could be other Comanche around besides these."

"Could be, but I imagine they're all here in one place for the fun."

Nate glowered in the direction of the captives and reluctantly nodded in agreement.

The shouting of glee continued. At one point they heard a distressed "Nooo!" erupt from where the Comanche were assembled. The pathetic wailing of the captured prospector incited whistles and a roar of delight from his captors. It was all Matt could do to remain patient. Every cell in his body screamed for action.

Charles wasn't the kind of man to disappoint and today proved to be no exception. In what Matt deemed an extraordinarily swift response, he found Charles at his ear assuring him, "I've got the men ready to go."

"Mighty fine," Matt said. "Spread 'em out." He waved his arm where he wanted the men situated. "They're just across yonder." He pointed out where the Comanche were working their expertise at inflicting torture.

"I saw the dead prospector," Charles said.

"They've kilt two for sure, but I think there's at least one more alive."

Charles nodded in support of the urgency. He melted back to see to the proper dispersal of the men. JB grinned when he took up a spot next to Matt. Out of all the Rangers he took a remarkably fierce pleasure in killing Indians. Losing a younger brother to them made a man that way.

Unseen, and to their rear, Dawson took up a position behind JB. There was a decent sized tree to hide behind and he had a clear view of the action as directed by Matt. He settled in ready to seize opportunity when it presented itself. Slipping away from Tom was easy in the confusion and Charles was at the far right flank the last he saw of him. Things were developing to his favor.

Matt gave the men a few minutes to get prepared and oriented to their new surroundings. It wouldn't be hard for them to gauge where they were needed with the frequent whooping giving away the location of the Comanche, although their numbers remained an unknown variable. Another lengthy and tortured scream from the prospector sent chills down Matt's back. He knew that his men would be motivated to impose justice with the sounds of torment floating through their ranks. The blood in his veins pulsed in rushing torrents and left him unsure how much longer he could refrain from attacking.

As fate would have it the answer to his impatience broke at that exact moment. A stiff breeze stirred up by the rising sun parted the fog wide open. A white shaft of light illuminated the separation in the moisture, and for the first time that morning objects at a distance could be distinguished. Visibility was fleeting, but it was enough for the sharp-eyed denizens of the forest to establish their change in circumstance.

Their celebratory mood ended abruptly. It took only a glance for several of them to spot the hats of their hated adversaries protruding above the grass. They flushed like a covey of quail calling out a feral war cry. Instantly their rifles began to crack. A deluge of hot lead rained down on the outnumbered Rangers.

Matt, being in the center of the line and thus one of the easiest to identify, became the prime target. He dove to the ground when several rounds buzzed close to his head. The thin branches of cedar above him were ripped apart by the lead and pelted him with fragments. His senses on high alert, he inhaled the exceptionally resinous aroma of the severed boughs. The greens of the foliage appeared darker. His depth of field was acute. He recognized the onset of a greater awareness for his surroundings the commencement of hostilities always produced.

Hugging the dirt in a protective reflex, he cursed the bad timing of the atmospheric phenomenon that exposed their placement. Flustered cursing erupted along the Ranger line as the fracas opened prematurely. All he could do now was hope for the men to survive this initial onslaught.

Gazing to his right, he saw JB a short gap away through slender blades of tawny grass. JB was looking at him to determine if his captain had been hit. Matt could see his lips moving, but couldn't make out what he was saying in the tumult of gunfire. He waved at JB to take protection behind the dense cedar where he would be hidden.

Too late—the Comanche marksmen were accurate. Matt had a good view when the bullet struck JB's right ear with a sickening *thud*. His head snapped with the vicious explosion of the round exiting in a spray of brain tissue and small bits of bone. He was dead before he tumbled to the ground. Eyes open wide in shock, he stared at Matt as if he couldn't comprehend the abruptness of death.

Caught peering around JB at the time of the impact, Dawson received the full brunt of the gore splattered indiscriminately by the big bore projectile. Globs of brain matter lodged up his nose and shrouded his eyes. He was blinded by the combination of blood and tissue forced under his eyelids. Several chunks of bone fragment punctured the skin of his cheek. He gagged in revulsion. The obnoxious odor of body fluids and the sickening turn of events overwhelmed his ability to cope. Forgetting the immediate danger, he stumbled backwards wiping the gore from his eyes, dropping his carbine in a panic to clear the assault on his senses. Adding to his panic, he felt the blistering heat of a slug that grazed the flesh on his shoulder.

He could hear the crescendo of Rangers shooting up and down the line, but his only thought was to find his canteen to wash away the gore. Plunging to the base of the tree where he stashed his gear, he blindly groped for his canteen. He ran his hands through the leaves and twigs that littered the soil. In an escalating horror he wasn't sure he had the right tree. He tried to open his eyes to no avail. Covered in slime, everything was blurry. Throwing himself to the ground he broadened his search as he drug his arms through the detritus, frantic to make contact with the canteen.

Still pressed to the ground, Matt looked to his left for Nate and found him scrambling backwards like a crab with his belly dragging in the dirt. There were too many bullets buzzing in the air to risk standing, but Nate never took his eyes off the Comanche, wary of a charge. Grabbing his haversack full of ammo, Matt made his own awkward belly crawl to the rear. He *had* to find better protection than the scrawny cedar and waist high grasses. He remembered a large bur oak that would be perfect and detoured to the side where he expected to find refuge.

Instead he was surprised to meet Dawson hysterically thrashing his arms through the stubble while flopped behind the bur oak. He roared "Dawson!"

Dawson flipped to his side facing Matt in surprise, muck and loose grass glued to the sticky mess covering his face.

Matt said, "Here, let me help," as he snatched the canteen just out of Dawson's reach. Upending the canteen, Matt sloshed the water out while Dawson scrubbed the gooey slime away with both hands. Blinking to clear his vision, he began to regain his ability to function.

"Where's your rifle?" Matt asked.

Dawson sheepishly pointed to the other side of the tree. Matt shook his head no. It was too risky to make a try for the rifle with bullets ripping the brush apart. Scanning to the other side he found Nate had established a firing station behind a large cedar elm. Judging his cover adequate, Matt carefully eased into a kneeling stance beside the bur oak, and slipped his Henry around the edge for a couple of quick shots. He wasn't sure of an individual target, but the surprisingly effective Indian volley had to be suppressed. He heard the distinctive report of Nate's Spencer reply as several Comanche rounds splatted against the oak, forcing him to swing his Henry behind cover.

Dawson groaned when a slug ricocheted off a nearby cedar, nicking him in the shin. He sucked his legs up to his chest and angrily cussed, "I'll be damned! They got me again!"

"Gotta git your rifle back."

"Screw that!" Dawson drew out his Colt and began firing steadily around the base of the tree until he emptied all the chambers. The Comanche were out of range, but they were now aware they had stirred up a hornet's nest with the intensifying return fire.

As sudden as it started the hail of gunfire from the Comanche ended. An eerie calm settled across the battlefield as the Rangers responded in kind to the evaporation of suitable targets. The Comanche had withdrawn into a grove of live oaks and tall grass. Wisps of fog curled up, dispersing as the sun rose higher above the horizon. Matt lowered the brim of his hat to block the harsh sunlight while he attempted to understand the evolving situation.

Dawson slid to the ground beside him and pulled up his bloody pants leg to examine his wounded shin. "Son of a bitch! I think my bones cracked. Hurts like hell."

Matt tossed him a handkerchief. "Here, tie this around it to stop the bleeding. See if you can stand. That'll tell you if it's broke."

Dawson quickly applied the makeshift bandage and grimaced with pain when he tentatively put pressure on the leg. "It ain't broke, but I'm not gonna be able to run."

"Then take this." Matt handed him his Henry. "Cover me while I git your rifle back."

Dawson noticed Nate watching his every move while Matt scrambled to recover the rifle. He decided to do what Matt suggested and peeked around the tree searching for a buck to shoot. The woods where the Comanche had been firing from were silent as if nothing had ever transpired. The sight of JB's flaccid body destroyed that illusion as he watched Matt dash out to recover his Spencer carbine. He made it back to the tree breathing hard, but the Comanche did not respond to his open exposure. They exchanged rifles and Dawson voiced a question, "Think they've left?"

Matt gazed at the deceptively quiet Comanche position, his eyes as fierce as an eagle. "Injuns have some strange ways when it comes to makin' war. They're out there though. Doubt they've had enough."

"It's like we're shooting at ghosts. Don't think I saw a single buck. Just a bunch of bullets coming our way."

"We'll have to flush 'em out at some point."

Dawson jammed a cartridge through his carbine to verify all was in order. Satisfied the mechanism was functional he said, "I'm ready. When will that be?"

Matt pointed to their left flank and said, "Right now!"

Four Comanche mounted on brilliantly painted ponies busted out of the thicket hell bent for the far end of the Ranger's left flank. At the lead point rode a distinctly adorned warrior. Bold yellow stripes swept downward from his eyes and along his jaw he worked in a feverish warble. A broad brimmed hat with red ribbons fluttering in the breeze was pulled down snug on his forehead. His pony thundered across the rock-strewn terrain. Wild whoops spewed from the riders behind him as they urged their mounts to sweep by the far left side of the Ranger line.

"Let 'em have it!" Matt bellowed. He leveled his Henry in a vain effort to strike a target out of range for his sixteen shot repeater. He jacked the lever fast, but only managed a couple of rounds when a withering return fire opened up. The Comanche fired from cleverly secreted vantage points in the trees across from the Rangers. All along the line Matt and his men ducked for cover.

Hunkered against the same bur oak, Matt and Dawson had been rendered ineffective, and that left Matt perplexed. He didn't like this unusual technique employed by the Comanche. They were not breaking up in the face of stiff resistance. Instead they were engaged in a tactic used by trained soldiers, and held his main line in check while they sent riders around his flank. He took solace in the knowledge that the left end of the skirmish line was anchored by Tully. He was a competent hand who had overcome many a hard time in many a brawl over the years.

But Tully wasn't at the far end of the line. In the haste to form up a defense, Cliff had mistakenly secured a position beyond Tully. Isolated at the end he now faced the brunt of the Comanche swinging around their vulnerable flank. A warm rush of adrenaline resulted from the nightmarish spectacle of barbarians on horseback surging his way. Cliff let the first round from his rifle explode. It sailed harmlessly behind the Comanche, but produced a calming influence on him. His desire to even the score with the Comanche was coming true. It was up to him to get the job done.

Up the Ranger line Nate discharged several rounds from his Spencer rifle. One of the Comanche sweeping the left flank collapsed from his mount when the big bore slug tore a half-inch hole through his ribcage. The sight of the fallen Comanche encouraged Cliff. What had seemed inevitable didn't necessarily need to be. He settled the brass buttplate of his Sharps snug against his shoulder and peered down its sights. His aim centered on a warrior that altered direction when he saw his brother flop off his pony in a twisted heap. The ferocious looking brave was now charging directly at him, a savage want on his face as he spied his intended quarry. Cliff knew his marksmanship had to be precise. He had enough time for one shot and no time to reload.

It was impossible! He couldn't get a bead on the fast riding buck hunched in tight to the side of his pony, darting first one way and then unpredictably, another. He heard other rounds hissing past, but they were just wasted lead cutting holes in the air. The Comanche came on in a mad pounding rush. Cliff felt his lungs heaving. His heart throbbing. His hands turning clammy.

He had no way to know it, but it was the notorious Buffalo Hump that had selected Cliff for death. The ghastly image of his Comanche brother with a gaping hole in his ribs had modified Buffalo Hump's thinking. The sweep around the end of the Rangers to strike them from the rear now became secondary. Gone too was the plan to capture or scatter the mounts the Texans usually hid at their rear. Directly in front of him kneeled one of the hated Texans. The coward was petrified in the face of his Comanche daring and prowess. It didn't require analysis. This white man stood out. He would be an easy target and he would pummel him with his war club as he rode past. He longed to use his advanced skill he had perfected from endless practicing.

Discerning the intentions of the Comanche, Cliff steadied his aim, determined to make the bullet count. On the Comanche rode, handling his pony with expertise, ignoring the weapon pointed his direction. In a heated rush to smite his foe a shriek from hell rose from the warrior's gut.

Cliff tracked the progress of the buck unwilling to waste his one chance to counter the attack that had become personal. His peripheral vision narrowed. He didn't see Little White Man skirting the end of their line. The rattle of weapons on the battlefield faded in importance. He knew what he had to do. And when.

In order to make a poor target, the charging Comanche kept his body pressed to his pony's side and at the last possible moment straightened his course to strike his foe. Cliff leveled his rifle to center on the chest of the oncoming pony. He released the lethal bullet at pointblank range. As if hitting a wall, the pony buckled in a blur of disjointed body contortions, dead before his tumble brought him to a skidding halt in front of Cliff.

There was no time to relish the precision of his aim. The Comanche sprang from the ground with a knife replacing the war club he had lost in the collapse of his mount. In one fluid motion, the bronzed warrior knocked Cliff off balance before he could unholster his revolver. He smelled the sour odor of bear grease. Felt the muscles of the Indian rippling with strength as he seized the knife-wielding arm.

Using the momentum of the rush, he swung the brave to the side locked in an embrace to the death. As fluid as a snake, the Comanche slithered with ease. Teeth bit into his ear. Cliff felt the skin ripping as the warrior growled like a rabid wolf. In the desperate struggle he became vaguely aware that his ear had been stripped from his head. As they rolled and tumbled through the grass his grip on the greasy wrist of the Comanche failed. As quick as a lightning bolt he felt the blade of steel plunge deep into his stomach. An immediate shock of pain blinded his vision in a bright white light.

Collecting all his will to live, he summoned the energy to push Buffalo Hump off in one mighty shove. He had but one chance. He rolled to the side while reaching for his Colt. He was too slow. Buffalo Hump was on him like a cat, knife raised above his head. Screaming like a banshee, Buffalo Hump thrust the glistening blade toward Cliff's throat.

Colt in his hand, Cliff managed to strike the arm of Buffalo Hump and deflect the knife. It struck below his collarbone instead of his neck. Wedged in tight, Buffalo Hump was slowed in removing his blade to finish the job.

It was all the delay Cliff needed. He swung the Colt up and shot pointblank into the mouth that shrieked at him with a blind rage. Buffalo Hump's head snapped upward as it absorbed the entire force of the .44 caliber round. His dead weight crumpled onto Cliff pinning him to the ground.

THIRTY-FIVE

Matt noticed two Rangers stumbling from tree to tree and dodging bullets until they reached Nate's position. Gasping for breath they paused near him in an attempt to gather their composure. Nate's steadfast covering fire seemed to return their courage although they continued to hug the protection of the trees and rarely discharged their weapons. Hunter staggered in from the right fringe of the line badly shook up, pale and bloodied. Matt sat him down behind a thick clump of cedar, inspected his wounds and found them to be flesh deep; the type that he would get over once the shock wore off. Hunter could only shake his head in dismay when Matt inquired about the condition of the right flank.

Hunter's lack of a report didn't matter. Matt recognized the prognosis. It was a natural occurrence when demoralized men under duress sought the relative security of their fellow soldiers. The cohesiveness of their skirmish line could completely evaporate if he didn't reverse this obvious erosion of confidence. He had seen clusters of dead soldiers after a battle and knew it indicated a failure of the commanders to prevent the unraveling of stability among the troops.

This act of bunching into a circle for mutual defense would also be easily recognized by the Comanche as an opportunity to deliver the final blow. Matt knew he had a crisis developing. It required quick action or he would be facing a catastrophic defeat. Or perhaps annihilation.

The appearance of Charles creeping his way from the right confirmed his worst nightmare. They were in imminent danger of being overrun with his left flank disintegrated, Tully unaccounted for, and Indians lurking in his rear. Taking a chance and breaking from cover Matt rushed up to Charles and demanded an update.

Squatting on their haunches and out of view of the Comanche, Charles smacked his dry lips trying to form the words. "Can't seem to shut 'em down—it's tight. The men—they're inching this way."

Instinctively Matt knew the momentum of the engagement was turning against them. It was time for a bold action. He didn't hesitate forming an alternative to their predicament. "Go ahead and slide your men over to replace the men at my position. You'll direct covering fire from here while I take a few of us on a sweep around their left flank. You gotta keep 'em pinned down while we make the move."

Charles understood the plan before it was explained. It was a classic move and their best option in the deteriorating circumstance. In less than a minute Charles had the men spread out in new emplacements ready to suppress the demoralizing enfilade from the Comanche.

Dawson watched Matt round up Nate, Harper and Pipkin, and then fade to the rear out of sight. He cursed under his breath at the continuation of his bad luck. He needed to be included in the group, but Matt knew his bum leg would hold him back and had Charles direct him to remain at the center of the new line. The precarious circumstances and the stabbing ache of his wounds had narrowed his aspirations. Left behind and positioned alongside Charles he realized he faced the real possibility of missing the chance to accomplish anything of importance if another Comanche bullet found him. And just then he felt the concussion of a slug humming by within an inch of his head as if to emphasis his wisdom. He was now reduced to considering himself lucky if he could just live to see the sunset with his scalp intact.

Tully suddenly appeared from nowhere, rattled, hatless and scrambling low to acquire some kind of security. He crouched at the tree abandoned by Nate, and his movement caught the attention of several Comanche. Sensing opportunity, they exposed themselves to risk a shot at Tully. Their bullets whizzed by within a hair's width as he dove in a frantic attempt to disappear at the base of the tree.

Seizing the chance, Dawson hurried with a reply from his carbine that buzzed near the braves and forced them into an imitation of Tully.

Off to his right Dawson heard Charles order the men to initiate a steady volley of covering fire. The spasmodic cracking of Ranger rifles gradually escalated into a deafening roar as the rounds relentlessly peppered the Comanche. Branches shattered into shards above the heads of the warriors forcing them to hug the soil. One young Comanche succumbed to his fears and bolted to the rear out of harm's way. He ran stooped over, and in a zigzag fashion, thinking it would make him too difficult to hit. Charles waited until the fleeing brave passed a clearing in the brush and led him with an accuracy learned from years of frontier experience. The frightened brave piled up at the foot of a mesquite when a slug of hot lead disintegrated his heart.

<<<<< • >>>>>

Black Owl had thought the ride by Buffalo Hump and Little White Man leading the others around the Texans a brave, but risky thing to accomplish. It was disheartening to witness one of his favorite brothers tumble from his pony mortally wounded, and especially distressful to be unsure of the fate of Buffalo Hump. Ducking to avoid the accurate aim of the Texans he had missed the details of Buffalo Hump's ill advised and straight on charge against the Texan holding the end position. All he was left with was a fleeting glimpse of the pony hurtling to the ground when the bullet smashed into him pointblank. He couldn't be sure, but it appeared that Buffalo Hump had jumped free and unharmed to continue his attack. And that was the last he had seen of the brave Comanche warrior.

He was left to ponder their next move. The current situation was unacceptable. The worst thing a Comanche could do was be involved in a battle of attrition. He expected Little White Man to rout the Texans from their protected cover with a charge against their rear. Scattering their horses held in reserve and pressuring them into the open had been the goal. The expected panic of the hairy-faced men should have made them easy prey. As easy as clubbing pups. Something was wrong. It was taking too long for Little White Man to make a difference. They needed results and they needed them now before events took a disastrous turn against them.

With Buffalo Hump and Little White Man absent the decision on how to proceed fell on his shoulders. He gathered his confidant, Crow Feet, to speak in his ear above the roar of the engagement. Together they made plans to launch another group of four braves to locate Little White Man and attack the rear of the Texans. They both agreed that as little time as possible would be wasted on finding the whereabouts of Little White Man. It was more imperative to disrupt the white men with harassment that could rout them from their cover and make them much easier to cut down.

In the process of organizing for the attack, Black Owl heard the distinctive howl of wolves through a temporary lull in the firing. It wasn't their four legged companions of the prairies. No, they were not that blessed. Instead, their fortunes had been reversed! The wail he was hearing duplicated the same howl used by the white warriors that routed them at the Sandy Creek battle just as his Comanche brothers had total victory in their grasp.

Recognizing their vulnerability as the bullets began to tear into their exposed left wing, Black Owl shouted words of encouragement and implored his fellow Comanche to remain brave. Nearest to the danger, Red Feather stood to obtain a better point to meet the onslaught of howling palefaces. Before he could get a shot off a slug ripped into his chest. Unable to maintain his balance, he stumbled backwards from the violent impact. The trauma of a second round knocked him to his stomach where he dug his moccasins into the damp dirt, pushing it into a loose mound as he bled out.

Several braves witnessed the graphic and deadly casualty of Red Feather. Powerless to resist, they surrendered to their intrinsic desire to survive. Two Moons immediately ducked and ran behind a screen of low hanging oak limbs in a frenzied sprint to escape the wrath of the advancing wild men. Their roaring howls shook him to his core. It was as if demon spirits had been loosed on his tail. The consequence of his terror was contagious. His brother next to him, Lone Horse, was a little slower to recognize the change in circumstance. The moment's hesitation made all the difference for his individual fate. A slug caught him in the shoulder and rotated him just enough to meet another round blowing his lower jaw into fragments. His jawbone was left dangling by tattered strips of flesh. He slumped to the gravel, rendered useless as he writhed in agony.

Black Owl saw what was happening. He let go with a snap shot at the Texans as they continued to advance. Several rounds hummed past him from different locations. He knelt to acquire a shooting stance. A bullet slammed into the rifle of a brave several feet away. The stock fractured into separate pieces and embedded splinters of walnut across his face. Blinded, he strayed into an opening where a bullet from Matt struck home with a *whump* against his temple. He toppled to the soil absent his eyes blown from their sockets.

The grisly devastation so close to him couldn't help but unnerve Black Owl. Turning to face the original position of the Texans he saw things were going from bad to worse. All along the line he saw the determined faces of bearded white demons boldly standing with their rifles delivering a thunderous fusillade. To his left another Comanche snapped off a couple of rounds to stem the tide, but he was met with a barrage of bullets that lifted him off his feet. He landed in a tangled heap having seen his last sunrise.

There seemed to be no point left in continuing the fight. All around him the unity of purpose had been destroyed. Lifeless Comanche littered the ground like acorns in the moon of falling leaves. Black Owl scrambled back to the ponies, hollering for his brothers to mount up, save their lives, scatter and meet later at the spirit rock. They had to escape now or they would all be food for the vultures. It was a mad hysteria surrounding the ponies as bullets started to tear through the trees and strike them at random. Terrified, some of the warriors dropped their weapons in order to free their hands and mount the bucking ponies. Despairing to escape the pressure of an all-out slaughter, a snarled commotion of horse and rider fought with each other. Ponies whinnied and screeched as their eyes rolled and they pawed the air, struggling to break free of the rein holders. Another shot to the head ended another Comanche life. At that moment it had become complete pandemonium.

Black Owl had never been a part of such an outright loss of determination. Death's ugly influence had conquered the will of his brothers to fight. Several despondent braves gave up on securing a ride and staggered into the brush to disappear from the grinding teeth of an evil thing. Now mounted on his distinctive white appaloosa speckled with orange splotches, Black Owl shouldered his rifle and fired a parting shot at a Texan he saw sneaking through the trees. A wave of satisfaction swept over him watching his victim pitch backwards as the bullet struck home. He felt a tremendous pride to have the presence of mind and courage to display the bravery expected from a Comanche warrior.

A surge of anger and resentment possessed him. He brandished his rifle in defiance and shouted a promise to spill white blood wherever he could find it. Sure that he was the last to leave; he spun his appaloosa and ducked under the limbs as he joined in the retreat of the braves vanishing into the haunts of their former homeland.

<<<<< • >>>>>

Black Owl's parting shot struck Harper between the eyes. He never knew what hit him. He was slammed against an oak and collapsed across a rotting limb at its base.

Matt saw the Comanche responsible for the remarkable accuracy. He was mounted on a vividly marked appaloosa. Matt raised his Henry and squeezed off a couple of quick rounds that missed the last warrior to join the procession of escaping Indians. All he was left with was the image of the long black hair lifted by the breeze as Comanche and pony evaporated into the woods. It was a sight that brought on a strong wave of déjà vu he didn't have the time to contemplate.

It was useless, he knew that, but he had to check on Harper. Waving Nate and Pipkin on to join the other Rangers in pursuit of the routed Indians, he soon located where Harper lay sprawled out in death. He turned away, repulsed by the sickening aftermath of a bullet to the head. Harper's eyes were locked in a blank stare below a circular entry point in the center of his forehead. His mouth gaped open as if he were about to call out a warning. The spreading pool of blood under his head was evidence of the destruction. There was nothing left of the man. After all the death Matt had witnessed, it still caught him off-guard to behold the absolute emptiness of a body abandoned by the soul. During times like this he sensed a return of his personal doubt about the meaning of life that often plagued him. But he didn't have the time to indulge in self-pity. The bark of rifles receding into the thickets brought him back to consider the things that were within his control. Death was a shadow that fell where it may. He had to accept the definitive results of providence in this unjust life. And by necessity his concern had to be focused on the living.

Shouts of anger from Rangers dogging the Comanche were punctuated by the sharp crack of carbines. The action fading into the distance convinced Matt that he needed to turn his attention to surveying the battleground and assessing the condition of any men left behind. Hidden nearby, he heard the moaning of an injured Comanche engulfed in agony. Searching for the warrior in the scrub he noticed Dawson limping his way. The hulk of a man seemed to bristle with resentment, his progress slowed by the painful leg wound. Pausing in his search, Matt perceived more to Dawson's condition than frustration over the hindering consequences of his injury. Something else was eating at him.

They made eye contact. Matt identified a feral desire in Dawson's penetrating blue eyes. He was out for blood. It was a manifestation Matt had seen before that produced a crushing grip on a man. The only cure for the homicidal impulse was the exercise of dominance over the victim of choice. Only then would the delivery of a violent death sate the pent-up emotions that created the beast.

Dawson stopped behind a clump of brush beneath the swooping limbs of an oak. He held eye contact with Matt. Neither man spoke. Both unsure of the other's intentions.

Matt stepped out for a better view of Dawson. What he saw was disconcerting. Dawson had his hand rested on the grip of his Colt.

In the excitement Matt had lost count of the number of rounds fired from his Henry. There should be another round or two left. But there was always the possibility he was wrong. He had never been quick on the draw and the rifle occupied his right hand above his holstered Colt. Now wasn't the time to find out if Dawson was fast or not.

Sensing the time had arrived, Dawson eased closer, placing the scrub brush between him and Matt without breaking eye contact.

Matt couldn't get a good read. The man was obviously plotting a move. But what?

Dawson averted his eyes momentarily.

Seizing the opportunity, Matt dropped his Henry. His hand now freed, he drew his Colt. Mirroring the moves of Dawson he acquired a clear line of sight above the big man's waist.

The clatter of Matt's rifle dropping sharpened the killer instinct of Dawson. He glared at Matt as he growled, "It's something I've got to do."

Screwing his courage up a notch, Matt said, "Do what you have to."

"Prefer you didn't get in my way."

Confused, Matt held back on a reply.

In the brush, and to the side of Matt, Lone Horse summoned all the reserves he had left to make a break. With one shoulder and arm rendered useless from a Ranger bullet, he used the other hand to hold the dangling remnants of his destroyed jaw. He had only the swiftness of his feet to whisk him away from certain death. The white men were evil.

Dawson cleared his leather in a blur of motion the likes of which Matt had never witnessed before. The Comanche didn't take two steps before the Colt rang out with authority. His spine splintered, the brave fell to the ground convulsing in death spasms.

Admiring his work, Dawson turned to gauge the reaction of Matt. He was a little put off to see Matt with his revolver centered on his chest. Stoic and in total control, Matt resembled a cold-blooded killer. Lacking any viable options, Dawson holstered his Colt. A lopsided grin replaced the callous intensity on Dawson, but Matt didn't holster his piece.

"No need for that, Matt."

"I'll be the judge of what's needed."

Dawson shrugged. "Have it your way."

"Believe I will."

"I got what I come for."

Matt stepped forward to glance at the bloodstained Comanche.

"That's right," Dawson said. "A dead Indian to help settle an old grudge."

"Some would say you've got other intentions too."

Dawson nodded in understanding. Matt wasn't stupid. It served no purpose to insult his intelligence. "You done a good job today. I thought we were goners."

Matt didn't need or want the approval of Dawson. He waited while the silence settled between them.

"You won't like it none, but Colonel Ames plucked our ass out of a similar situation. He used the same tactic against the flank of you Rebs at Shiloh."

Spitting like he had swallowed a bug, Matt said, "You're right. I don't like it none."

"Colonel Ames wasn't always the man he is now."

"His past don't interest me none."

Dawson nodded again. He didn't hold Matt's opinion against him.

Matt lowered his Colt. In his gut he still harbored a suspicion that the right hand man of Ames had ulterior motives. But he had been right about needing every gun he could wrangle. Dawson had played an important role in a desperate mêlée. He had the blood running down his leg to prove his worth.

"How's the leg?" Matt asked.

"Bit banged up, but it'll heal."

"Well, come on, we gotta check on the wounded. Git you doctored up too."

A detail lost in the endless chaos of battle dawned on him. Several Comanche had skirted their left flank. Unaccounted for, he assumed the worst. Travis and Tom needed help.

THIRTY-SIX

Snagging his Henry, Matt slammed home fourteen fresh rounds into the magazine under the barrel. Barely able to squelch his anxiety, he spit out his instructions. "Check the left flank for Cliff. I lost track of him. I'll check on Hunter on my way back to the horses."

He didn't wait for a reply, but dashed across the field to where Hunter slumped against the cedar he had left him behind. After nursing the canteen and resting, Hunter had regained some of his color. He noted the agitation Matt was suffering from and gave him a thumbs up when Matt said he needed to take off and check on Tom, Travis, and the horses.

Not wasting time, Matt ran with abandon through the woods to the prospector's camp. An acute remorse flushed over him when he realized he had not taken the opportunity to check on the welfare of the prospectors sacrificed for Comanche entertainment. Rationalizing his failure to perform his duties, he reasoned they were beyond anybody's help. The Comanche would have finished them off as soon as the shooting started. It didn't matter which way things played out, he knew the sting of guilt was sure to flare up somewhere down the line when he least expected it.

Slowing as he neared the camp, he peered through the trees to verify the horses were still in the picket line. One of them whinnied, tossed her head and pawed at the dirt. Otherwise, things appeared calm, but that could be deceiving. He didn't see Travis or

Tom. Slipping behind the screen of a large hackberry he peeped around the trunk to make sure the campsite was secure. Nothing. There was no movement at all. It was eerie considering the dire possibilities.

Puzzled by the apparent desertion, he figured that if the Comanche had made an attack and overrun them, surely they would have made off with the stock. He wanted to hail the men, but thought better of it until he knew the particulars. He stole up to another tree for a closer view all the while suspicious of an ambush.

That's when he saw it. A dead body was partially concealed inside a thick cluster of grama grass. The fragment of clothing he could see was soaked red with blood, and the cadaver looked to be about the same size as Travis. His pulse racing, he eased forward for a closer assessment. It was no use. The corpse was too low in the grass for identification from his position. But he made another startling discovery. There was another body farther back in the woods. Was it Tom? Had they both been killed?

Certain that he was too late; he warily approached the horses. He had to know what he was getting into before he gave away his presence. That's when he heard the cough. Then an indistinct murmur of a man's voice came from the other side of the horses. It sounded like someone was whispering in order to avoid detection. He froze to listen.

Again. He heard a mumble. But was it Comanche?

He crept alongside the horses until he caught a glimpse of movement. Whoever it was stood. Unable to make out details, he threw his Henry to his shoulder for a spontaneous potshot.

His sights settled on the head.

But he held his fire.

It was Travis!

Relief flooded his voice, "Damn! I'm glad it's you!"

Travis was rendered speechless by the sudden arrival of his uncle. He held Matt's gaze, but refrained from returning the greeting. Intuitively, Matt knew something was wrong. He split through the line of horses and stopped short when he spotted Tom prostrate at the feet of Travis. His pants were blood soaked and sliced open on his left leg. Travis had applied a bandage, but Tom's color was pale.

Tom nodded at Matt and nonchalantly asked, "How're the men."

Kneeling to inspect the bandage, Matt thought it was like Tom to be anxious about the other men while he was the one hurting. Patting his friend on the arm, Matt said, "Took some hard licks. But gave more'n we took."

Grimacing, Tom bit on his upper lip as the burn in his leg intensified. Choking down the raw pain, he said, "We done the same here."

"I seen the bodies. What happened?"

Tom's eyes danced with admiration despite his injury. He said, "Tell him, Travis."

Travis hesitated. He had grown accustomed to hearing the exhilarating tales of Rangers and repeating his own exploits was a new experience. He wasn't sure he could spin a good story. Especially in front of two men he held up on a pedestal.

"Let's have it, Travis. What happened?" Matt snapped.

Matt wasn't known for his patience and there remained essential work to be completed. His command was dispersed in the hills chasing Comanche and men were left unaccounted for. His gruffness contributed to the awkwardness felt by his nephew.

Travis began with trepidation, "Well, sir. Them Comanche showed up unexpected like." He kicked at a stick buying time to gather his thoughts. It had all occurred so quickly. The fight took place without any time to think. He had reacted spontaneously and had to replay the chaotic episode in his mind to put things in order. The words began to flow like a river when he had his role composed in a storyline he could effectively communicate.

"They rushed in on Tom like a wolf pack on a lost fawn. Figured he would be easy pickin's. Started blastin' away 'fore we seen 'em. Caught us off-guard." He paused to relive the hectic moments of the attack while hunting for the right words to add emphasis and drama to his tale. "Had their ponies stashed back in the cedar. Came rushin' in on foot thinkin' Tom would be a pushover. He got a shot or two off. Slowed 'em a bit, but they came on strong and concentrated their aim on Tom 'til he took a round in his leg. They weren't gonna be denied them horses. It was just like you said it'd be. They wanted to put us afoot knowin' we'd be up a creek without our rides. They saw him fall and threw caution to the wind."

Warming to the interest Matt displayed, he continued, "Well, that was their big mistake. All they saw was Tom hittin' the dirt and them horses wide open for the takin'." He winked at Tom when he said, "It turned out just like we hoped. They never seen me squatted down low in the brush. Ran right past me to git to Tom, but he had gone to hidin' behind some logs he piled up for a fort."

Tom actually grinned as Travis unintentionally puffed out his chest. It was a moment in time Matt marked as one he would never forget.

"With them Indians distracted, I popped up at their rear. They didn't have a clue. I brung the scattergun down on 'em. Let a load of buckshot take the closest one right off his feet. That got the attention of the one wearin' a hat with red ribbons. I'll never forgit the look on his face when he turned and looked down the barrel." Once again he paused to recollect the most important moment in his life to date. He shook his head as if he couldn't believe his good fortune. "Yeah, he had a helluva look knowin' he was dead meat. I unloaded the other barrel on his sorry ass and that was that."

Matt beamed with pride. Travis had performed admirably. He patted him on the back and said, "You done real good. Damn proud of you."

"I bandaged Tom up best I could. Then I patrolled around to check for any other Injuns. Didn't find anythin' to worry about. I know where their ponies are tied up. We heard all the shootin' your way. Got mighty nervous. That's why we was layin' low."

"Mighty fine," Matt said. "Y'all done an outstanding job. Now we gotta git back to the other men. Got a chore for ya while I git this string ready to depart."

"What's that?" Travis was ready to skin a bear. He could do anything in the euphoria that lifted him a foot off the ground.

"Go on back to them ponies." Matt looked Travis square in the eyes. This one was going to hurt. He pitched the Henry to him and said, "Take this with you."

Travis accepted the Henry, confused, not sure why Matt would surrender his prized weapon.

"You're gonna need it. I want you to put the ponies down."

Speechless at the request, his puzzled expression begged for justification.

"It's a sorry job," Matt began, "but we got more than enough problems to be messin' with unruly animals. And I ain't leavin' them bucks a chance to have their rides back. Them ponies could be used to trail us back home if we leave 'em here."

Travis didn't like the repugnant assignment, but accepted it as his duty. Plus Matt had mentioned home. The idea of returning to a bed and a roof over his head had never sounded so appealing. And he could complete another task he had in mind on the way back from dispatching the ponies. It would all work out for the best. Over time he had recognized that things turned out better when Matt's instructions were followed to the letter.

Matt knelt next to Tom giving him a onceover. "You up to ridin'?"

"Reckon I'll have to be. Keep the tourniquet tight and it should stop the bleeding. Won't be no picnic, but I'll make do."

"A couple of shots of whiskey should dull the pain."

"Mama didn't raise no fool. I'll take a swig of whatever helps."

Matt went to work getting the horses strung together for the trip back to the main battleground. He arranged the gear for Tom's horse and had Travis fixed up when he heard the first gunshot immediately followed up by a second. Travis loved horses and Matt knew it had to hurt. Hurt bad. But that was the only solution he could think of when he took into account the ragged condition of his command. Loose ends left behind could prove calamitous. He had enough on his hands with dead Rangers and who knew how many wounded strewn across the field.

He had just mounted Whiskey when he caught sight of Travis hunched over the body of one of the dead Comanche. The boy was clutching something black in his hands as he started back to the horses, but Matt couldn't pick out what it was through the screen of limbs. When Travis busted out of the brush Matt almost didn't recognize his nephew. His face was taut. Hard. The day's events had transformed the youth into a man.

"What you got there, Travis?"

Travis handed the Henry back to Matt without an answer. He turned and made his way to his own horse where he draped two long black scalps across the pommel. Effortlessly, he swung up in the saddle. Settling in, he plucked a bloody scalp off the horn and held it up to admire. Deadpan, his cold assessment of the greasy hair spoke volumes. "Why these here are for Frank."

Matt had seen it happen before. The stress of combat altered a man's outlook. Nothing would ever be the same once a man had survived the intensity of a lethal engagement. Taking a life destroyed preconceived notions of right and wrong. It was an event that had to be experienced to be fully appreciated. That was why there was a breach in life perceptions between ordinary citizens and Matt's fellow Rangers. Matt understood the conversion well. There would be no turning back. Travis had been hardened under fire. On the frontier he would learn it was easy to be hard.

THIRTY-SEVEN

Dawson was kneeling at the outer end of what had been the left flank during the opening moments of the clash. His body language didn't bode good news. Something appeared to be dreadfully wrong by the looks of Dawson's drooping posture. He needed help. Matt kept an eye on the scene while he took care of helping Travis secure the horses and saw to it that Tom was eased out of his saddle and made comfortable next to Hunter. Across the field he saw Pipkin coming to join them.

Matt said to Travis, "Keep your guard up. You can never tell what them bucks will do. Some might return. Pipkin's on his way." Pointing at Dawson, he explained, "I'm going over there to check on the situation."

Watching Matt closing the gap to his position Dawson got up to walk out and meet him. It was an unexpected sight for Matt to see Dawson visibly disturbed. His brow wrinkled with the weight of what he had been dealing with alone. They stopped out of hearing range of the motionless Ranger that Dawson had been kneeling beside.

"It ain't good," were the first words out of his mouth.

"Cliff?" Matt asked.

Pinching his lips together Dawson simply nodded.

"How bad?"

He took a breath, waited a moment, and replied, "Bleeding bad. Knife wound to his stomach. His guts are . . . well, you get the picture."

"Damn."

"Took a nasty cut to his shoulder too."

"Son of a bitch."

"Matt, he ain't got long. I done what I could, but it wasn't much."

Mustering his resolve to contend with a heartrending prospect, Matt said, "Okay, let's go see him."

It took all of Cliff's willpower to acknowledge Matt when he knelt beside him. His hands clutched at the saddle blanket Dawson had removed from one of the dead Indian ponies and rested across his stomach. It had been a vain attempt to confine the protruding intestines. His color was ashen. Short of breath, he bordered on complete shock. Death was circling like a vulture. And Cliff knew full well his final destiny was near.

Matt couldn't find the right words to comfort. They didn't exist. The damage he saw was beyond anybody's abilities to correct. All he could do now was help ease the transition to the other side. There was nothing left to say. It would only increase the agony to encourage Cliff to engage in conversation. They both knew where this was leading.

Dawson stood off to the side feeling like an intruder in this moment between two men that knew each other. He was no stranger to death, but it was always an objectionable thing to witness the slow draining away of a man's life. And he felt no obligation to a man he didn't know. He had done his best for Cliff, and besides he needed to have a poultice applied to his own wounds that had already been neglected too long. The threat of infection worried him. He had seen too many amputations from poorly tended wounds rotting with gangrene. Matt gave him a nod of the head and he slowly melted away without Cliff noticing.

Cliff moaned softly and even that caused him immense distress. A shiver raced through his depleted body. The pool of blood beneath him grew larger. His heart beat uncontrollably and he shuddered with weakness as the state of shock deepened. Drenched in sweat, he gazed up at Matt who was lost to him in a fuzzy and indistinct haze.

"Water," he mumbled.

Matt opened his canteen and dribbled a small amount into his mouth. Cliff reminded him of a baby bird, his parched mouth open, desperate to receive life-sustaining nourishment. It was a sad sight to behold. The act of swallowing proved troublesome. He gagged and rolled his head to the side, letting the water pour over his lips and bleed into the soil.

Succumbing to his growing weakness, Cliff's grip on the saddle blanket loosened and his hand plopped to the dirt. Unbound from the restraining pressure, more of his intestines coiled to the ground like a snake wet with slime. For a moment Cliff found his focus. He stared into Matt's eyes as he gasped for breath. Expending the small amount of strength he retained, he muttered, "Bury me."

Matt waited. Cliff wanted to say more. He swallowed hard. His shoulders relaxed. His breathing flattened out. He whispered, "With my . . . son."

Matt placed his hand on Cliff's arm and said, "We will, Cliff. Whatever you want. We'll do it."

Cliff's eyes closed. He raised his hand ever so slightly, acknowledging he understood. Slipping away, his breathing became intermittent with ever-longer periods where he failed to inhale. His chest heaved with one last mighty effort to retain life.

And then he was still.

Matt bowed his head, and offered a brief prayer releasing Cliff's soul to the care of Almighty God above. Hunched over in grief, Matt felt no compunction in cursing the plight of mankind. There were times it all became too much. Cliff had been a good man. His life had become a never-ending procession of disaster. He had hoped Cliff could uncover an answer to his dilemma out here on the trail. But that wasn't meant to be. The hard hills had their own ways. While the hills stood mute and indifferent, Matt was left with the burning question of how much more death and suffering was a man supposed to endure?

It was something he often contemplated. A man was born into the world alone and that was the only way to leave it. Nobody escaped the final judgment. Was kneeling beside a dying man while he slipped away the best he could do? There was no alternative. He knew that, but whenever the ambiguity of life on the frontier reared its ugly head it became a devastating load to bear. He stood and ran his hands down his cheeks as if he could wipe away the pain of loss. The emotional sentiment he felt was useless. Words of condolence, tears, and mourning did nothing in the long run to overcome the incorrigible ache of living.

Taking a protracted look at Cliff, he said, "We'll git you taken care of, Cliff. It's all I can do."

He turned to see Charles marching his direction. They met halfway back to the tree where Tom rested and the other Rangers were now gathering. Covered with sweat and streaked with dirt, Charles offered his report, "We trailed 'em for a few miles. They've flown to the wind. Some on horseback and some on foot. Picked off a couple of stragglers along the way. Put the fear of God in 'em. Don't think they'll take a shine to returning for more."

"Good job, Charles." Matt glanced at his boots and asked, "What about the prospectors?"

Charles shook his head, "No luck. They're gone. You know how thorough them Comanche are."

"Yeah, unfortunately I do. How about our boys?"

Charles pulled his hat off and waved at a fly buzzing a bloody scratch across his neck. "Four dead. Grant took several rounds early on. You know about Harper and JB." He gazed toward Cliff, and said, "Cliff makes four."

"Wounded?"

"Cass and Hunter from the right flank. Tom and Dawson make four."

Matt ran the math and shook his head in disgust. His voice was heavy with regret. "Over fifty percent casualties."

"Bad as it is, we were damn near somethin' a lot worse. You turned 'em back in the nick of time."

Charles was right. Matt knew it to be true. But it was still a hell of a bitter pill to swallow. The only good news was that except for Cliff all the deceased men were single. Their families would be devastated at the loss, but no women and children were depending on them for support. He grimly snickered at the notion. There didn't exist a way for him to look at the losses with anything but a sad acceptance of the disastrous results. Fighting against what he saw as a barbaric culture was a hazardous occupation, but it had to be done if the frontier was to be a safe place for families to raise their children.

Sucking in a breath of fresh country air, Matt snapped out of his melancholy outlook. By necessity the time for mourning was short.

Just that quick he shifted into taking care of the wounded and living. Waving his hand to a grove of trees he said, "We'll bury the prospectors in the middle of those trees where the Comanche won't find 'em. Identify 'em if we can so I can notify their kin. Round up their gear and we'll take it back to Austin to be claimed. Can the wounded ride?"

Charles looked back at the tree, appraising the injuries of the men congregated at its base. He nodded his head, "I think so. Won't be easy on 'em, but they can make it."

There was no hesitation in Matt's commands when he made it back to the Rangers waiting on his instructions. "Charles will help you wounded men git bandaged for the trail. I know it's gonna be tough, but we aren't stayin' here to have them Comanche return. The rest of you can help me bury the prospectors. We're hittin' the trail home as soon as we're done."

Black Owl sat rigid on his appaloosa at the top of Red Ochre Hill. He watched the white men gather their dead and injured far below the ridge satisfied they were at a safe distance. He had nothing to worry about. They had their hands full licking their wounds while all his brothers had scattered in the storm of battle like leaves in a fall breeze. It was a humiliating setback. He was left alone, and would like one more chance at the Texans while they were distracted with their losses. But that was not to be. Too many Comanche warriors had departed this life today. Defeated in body count, and medicine turned sour, the most he could hope for was a reunited war party at the spirit rock by nightfall.

He thought back on what had been a woeful day for his brothers. The errors had continued to stack up soon after they awoke to a blanket of dismal gray fog. It had started with what was supposed to be a simple task when one of the braves located and arrowed the paleface buffalo. But the mundane chore became complicated when the animal ran into the fog and couldn't be found. The innocent error was a bad omen to start the day and his instincts had proven to be correct. He considered the failure and fog a sign of things to come.

When they stumbled upon the white men camping it had

seemed to be an unexpected bonus that might prove his suspicions wrong. The men were poorly prepared for the sudden appearance of Comanche braves and offered a chance for them to extract retribution. Unfortunately, what should have been a quickly executed and crushing blow turned into another chance for Little White Man to practice his morbid indulgence in torture. It had made little sense in his mind to waste time engaged in such diversions when more important matters required their undivided attention. But Little White Man held sway over the brothers always ready to enjoy a rare moment of opportunity against their despised enemies.

Buffalo Hump had watched impassive to the distraction orchestrated by Little White Man. And so it came to pass that valuable time was wasted on tormenting their hostages, and to compound his concerns, several guns had been discharged in the process. The sound would carry for miles and he knew it was a direct invitation to be discovered. They had failed to take advantage of the fog that would have concealed their movements to their main objective on the Colorado River. The thrill of a short-term pleasure had blinded them and weakened their medicine.

Now he was left alone on the hilltop to contemplate the future. There was no assurance that Buffalo Hump or Little White Man had survived to meet him at the rendezvous point they had agreed upon. This had been a particularly bloody encounter with the Texans. These white warriors fought with a ferocious tenacity that destroyed what was left of the potent magic conjured up for this raid. He detected a significant shift in power had occurred with this defeat. And he was sure that this setback was a defining moment in his life. Regardless of the opinions of Buffalo Hump or Little White Man or any of the other brothers that might disagree with his decision, he had made up his mind to permanently move north.

This would be his last battle to defend his homeland in the hills. The Texans were too strong and as numerous as ticks on a javelina. The land was forever ruined by their presence. His heart was broken with the futility of resisting the inevitable. He remained a proud Comanche, but a beaten warrior just the same. The bleeding off of Comanche lives could no longer be sustained. There was a better way of life available and it would be foolish not to seek a safe haven where he could raise children and increase the influence of his band. This new existence was obtainable on the vast grasslands and red rock canyons to the north where the Kwahadi band of Comanche lived in isolation seldom penetrated by the whites.

The sky above him had turned a startling blue now that the moisture had burned off. Glancing at the inspirational skies he spotted a pair of hawks soaring together in a circle high above the hill. They were slowly drifting north. He took their appearance as confirmation he was making a wise decision. It was a lesson he had learned from his grandfather a long time ago. Spirit birds would guide a warrior and provide direction if he was sincere in his quest.

In contrast to the beauty of the hawks, he saw one of the hated Texans below the hill glaring his way. Sitting on his appaloosa he was plainly visible against the horizon. But it was of no consequence. He had nothing to fear of these men while they reorganized. He wondered what drove them to be such mighty warriors? They had fought like a cornered bear. Their medicine and cunning was undeniable. It was a disgrace, but he knew they would come to dominate the land anywhere they wished to roam. This strange tribe of men could not be driven away like the Apache or the Tonkawa the People had forced out of the hills. Those victories against other red men had allowed the People to expand and control vast amounts of prime territory full of boundless herds of buffalo. During those times of plenty their future was secure and their babies fat and happy. Now there were fewer and fewer buffalo and white men on the land as thick as locust. Now the old ones sat around the campfires telling tales of their glorious deeds from the days of old when the Comanche had been considered the lords of the plains.

That was then and this was now. Below him watched a bearded white warrior leading men seemingly capable of the complete destruction of the People. They were an abhorrent race of men. Despised and hated. But they had to be respected for their terrifying skills in battle. Today was a great loss for his tribe. It was a miserable reversal he accepted with grief. But tomorrow he would take his first steps to improve his chances for a safe future and a growing family with his Kwahadi brothers on the high prairies. He was sure he could convince others in his southern tribe to follow his lead. He would make something positive grow and flourish from this defeat!

Grasping his bow, he thrust it high above his head and waved it in a circle. The paleface below the hill stood observing him separated from the other Texans. He had his attention. He locked eyes on the cold scowl of the white man. There was a link that connected them. They both fought vigorously for their families. They both fought for the right to pursue life as they saw fit.

Black Owl brought the bow down to his side. They continued to glare at one another. Overhead the shriek of the hawks was distinct in the moisture cleansed air. Their call was shrill and defiant. The spirit birds had served him notice it was time to depart. He gently kneed his appaloosa and they turned as one to leisurely descend the backside of the hill. He would never see this white man again and it was good. Enough blood had been shed between them to last a lifetime.

THIRTY-EIGHT

Matt watched as the Comanche swayed with the motion of his pony and vanished over the crest of Red Ochre Hill. The image sparked a memory. The strange sense of déjà vu from earlier in the day cleared up now that hostilities had ended and he had time to think. It was the unique markings of the appaloosa he remembered. The long flowing black hair of the Comanche as he faded from view was a sight he had seen before, and the lithe physique in harmony with his pony left him with no doubt. This was the same Indian that had escaped from him and Lee in the pecan bottoms after they killed his two brothers. That meant he had missed another chance at the infamous buck known as Black Owl.

Fleeting thoughts crossed his mind to mount Whiskey and pursue the Comanche to hell and back like Cliff had suggested he would do if necessary. But that notion was all fantasy with wounded men on his hands, and dead Rangers and prospectors to bury. They were also low on ammunition. Another drawn-out fracas could land them in a jam they couldn't escape. Like it or not, his hands were tied. He heard Charles crunching through the brush headed his direction.

He was all business when he reported, "Found a good place to bury the prospectors. Soil's loose. Be easy to dig. Easy to hide."

Matt nodded that he understood, but continued to stare at the hill where Black Owl had disappeared. He had to forget it. The opportunity was lost. Turning to face Charles he asked, "Room enough for our men too?"

Charles answered, "It'll do."

"Good then. Let's go ahead and bury our men here. Cliff wants to be buried next to Gary. So we'll grant him his last request."

They trudged off to attend to the vilest duty a Ranger had to face. It wasn't the first time they had buried Rangers in empty locations absent the care of their loved ones. The wild frontier was blemished with abandoned graves, but their current obligation wasn't made easier by the knowledge that others had shared the same fate. Matt stood next to the bodies arranged in a row under the canopy of live oaks. Charles waved his hat over the dead men asking, "Is it worth the cost?"

A grim composure overtook Matt. He took his time to form a response. "Land to call your own. Free to do as you like. Work hard and prosper. It's the only chance some folks have to escape the chains of slavery others keep 'em in." His anger flaring, he snarled, "Yeah, it's worth it."

He seized the extra shovel and plunged it deep into the soil. Digging with vigor he soon had a mound of dirt piled to the side while Nate dug a separate hole a few feet away. Charles drifted away to help Travis prepare the horses for the trail and make sure the wounded were ready for the ride. Nobody was in the mood to talk as they took turns digging seven graves.

Nate led the men away from the battlefield after a short ceremony bestowing honor and blessings over the ones left behind. He took them in a direct route that he calculated would deliver them to the site of Gary's grave by late afternoon. Sucking up their discomfort for the good of the command, the wounded men did little complaining while they bounced along on horseback. They understood the need to make good time was paramount to their survival. They were in no condition to wage another protracted battle and there was no guarantee other Comanche bands weren't shadowing them.

As the sun fell in flames of vermillion Matt saw the lonesome sycamore that marked the gravesite of Cliff's son come into view. Scanning the hills along the way he had not detected any Comanche tailing the column, but that did not assure him that camp under the tree would be safe. As soon as they dismounted he put Nate and Charles on a sweep of their perimeter to ensure no

Comanche were nearby. They returned from their patrol in the dark as satisfied as they could be. With Comanche the men knew there was never a sure bet.

Wary of discovery by unseen eyes Matt had instructed the preparation of a shallow grave for Cliff after the curtains of night had been drawn. When the grave was dug the men gathered around for a solemn prayer led by Tom. He had to lean on the shoulder of Matt for support while he delivered a short eulogy. Overhead a dazzling array of stars bathed the men in a faint blue luminance. Each man noted the unusual glow on their companions mourning the loss of a man they had grown to admire and like. They knew Cliff's unfortunate history and all of them had hoped he could find redemption on the mission.

As Cliff was lowered to his final place of rest a sense of camaraderie bonded the men together as if ordained from God above. Matt was overcome with an undeniable image of the men standing in a circle as if he were a bird looking down on the assembly. He thought it prophetic that without a cue, and as one, the men spontaneously recited the Lord's Prayer. At the conclusion of the invocation the saddened men split up and wandered to their respective bedrolls to collapse in total fatigue. Soon the sounds of snoring floated across the camp.

Matt and Nate took first sentry duty at opposite ends of the slumbering men. Matt found himself leaning against the sycamore as he searched for answers about the burial of Cliff. Upon reflection, he found it strange how the men broke into a unified prayer without any prompting. And the image of them in a circle with their heads bowed in prayer was imprinted on his mind as if he saw it all from above. It was a new experience for him. There was no doubt in his mind that the presence of the Lord was among the men and was the answer to the phenomenon. Never an overtly religious man, he had to admit a newfound spiritual belief had taken root here at the site of two forlorn graves destined to be forgotten.

Adrift in his thoughts, Matt was surprised to hear the clink of rocks behind him. He turned to see a large shadowy figure slinking through the dark toward him. A man that large had to be Dawson. Matt slid his hand down to his Colt.

A silhouette in the night, Dawson was a few yards short of the sycamore. He froze in place, staring at Matt. His personality cast an aura of domination. It was a trait he had no control over. He came by it naturally.

Matt eased the Colt out of his holster. The leather squeaked with his covert movement. Dawson shifted his stance.

They stood silent in the black of night. Each unable to see the eyes of the other. Dawson took a step forward.

"What do you want?" The tone in Matt's voice stopped Dawson in his tracks.

"No reason to be unfriendly."

"I'll be the judge of that."

"Fair enough."

"Go on. State your business."

"Can't sleep."

Matt had no response.

"Too big a day," Dawson explained. He waited, but Matt held his tongue.

"Wanted to clue you in."

"I'm listening." Matt seemed indifferent.

"I'll be taking my leave come sunup."

"That right?"

"I've taken care of most of my business out here."

"Killed you an Indian and you're good to go?"

Dawson chuckled. "That was only part of what I come for. Still a little unfinished chore I gotta take care of."

Matt raised the Colt, unsure of Dawson.

"You can lower the gun."

Matt ignored the comment.

"We're past that."

"So I *was* on the list of work to be done?"

"Ames has his own needs."

"Men like him usually do."

Dawson was still trying to understand how it was he had grown to like Matt. Working with men like Ames for years he had found it rare to like anybody. It didn't change his mind about his inherent dislike of men just because he had met one he could admire. He said, "I reckon we *all* do."

Matt sneered. "There's no need to cause harm to those that don't deserve it."

"The golden rule. Ma taught me that one. It's a rule nobody pays attention to these days."

"Depends on the class of men you associate with."

Dawson nodded his head in agreement while the memory of the money he took from Ames awakened a bit of guilt on his part. Technically it was money he didn't earn. But he wasn't changing his mind, and it was too late to reverse his course. Ames was a crook. Why should he care? He said, "I'm done with Ames."

"Congratulations."

Dawson let his thoughts drift to Fredericksburg where the widow waited on his return. He had the good fortune of meeting her while in town for the business Ames had sent him to complete before Kern was killed. Enjoying her companionship, he had extended his stay while they got to know each other, and he considered it time well spent. It was worth the ass chewing he got from Ames for being too late to help Kern with the problems Matt presented. What a difference those few days made. Matt had killed Kern and the dirty money paid to Kern was now in his own pocket instead of on its way to New Orleans where the mulatto would have wasted it on whores. The bastard had such a high opinion of himself.

Ames wouldn't miss the money. He had plenty to spare and an endless assortment of scams to extort even more. But the money meant everything to him. It was sufficient to transport him and the widow to San Francisco where they planned a new start. Her company had made him feel like a young man that still had hope for a normal life. She was special and unlike any woman he had ever met. They both hungered for a new beginning. The cash was their seed for a happy future together.

Snapping back to the present Dawson said, "Thanks, I guess."

"Ames is a no good sorry son of a bitch."

"No argument here."

Matt slid his Colt back in the holster. He asked, "So what's next?"

"Trying a new line of work. Something you'd call respectable."

"You'll sleep better."

Saying the word respectable brought up a passing thought that he wasn't holding up his end of the bargain with Ames. But it was fleeting and had no basis in fact. Matt was right about Ames. He didn't owe the filthy bastard anything.

"I'll sleep fine come tomorrow night. Things are gonna be different here on out."

Matt's suspicions grew the more Dawson talked. He had heard all he wanted for one day. The less he knew about the man the better off he would be.

"Take over here. You can't sleep and I need some shuteye."

Dawson pulled out a plug of tobacco and broke off a healthy sized wad. He crammed it between his cheek and gums and said, "I got it from here."

He gazed at the broad expanse of nighttime sky with the milky torrent of stars stretched across the canvas from horizon to horizon. It was a vista that could take a man's breath away when he contemplated how small and insignificant he was in the scheme of things. Far down the ravine a bobcat wailed in loneliness for a mate.

"Damn wild out here," Dawson observed. "This is a night I'll always remember."

Matt appraised Dawson with a new appreciation. It was hard to tell what lurked under a man's skin. People never quit amazing him. He nodded his head and said, "I've had a lot of 'em out here in the wilds. Being out here never gits old in my book."

"You southern boys got a special land here in Texas."

Matt said, "Yes it is." A shooting star streaked above the black outline of a jagged hill and burned out in a tail of glittering dust falling to the earth. "Yes it is," he repeated with conviction.

THIRTY-NINE

She closed her eyes and laid her head back to soak up the warm rays of the sun. A gentle breeze kissed her cheeks. The yard was quiet except for a squirrel fussing in the lower branches of the pecans lining the creek. Her laundry fluttered beside her on the clothesline while it dried. Becky had the kids inside the cabin studying their lessons for the day. It was a rare moment when she was caught up on the seemingly endless chores that dogged her every day. In no hurry, she ambled over to take a seat on a barrel sitting next to the corral fence.

The squirrel scampered down to the leaf-covered soil and scratched around in search of overlooked pecans. Behind her Lee's mare chomped on the feed she had put out before hanging up the freshly laundered garments of her children. There was a vibrant sky the color of topaz above her with just a hint of the warmth to come after winter eventually released its grip. One of those rare days when everything seemed to be in balance. The type of day she craved. For the moment her problems had faded.

She leaned back against the cedar rail of the fence, succumbing to the serenity of the afternoon. She started to drift into a peaceful nap. It felt too good to be real. Lee was at work in the shed next to the corral and she felt secure with him at her back. This would be a fleeting moment where she could relax in the belief that all was okay in the world. Sometimes folks had to fool themselves in order to maintain their sanity.

Time seemed to stand still. She dozed while lost in a trance of memories that were pleasing to recall.

Caught in a listless void, she floated in a detached state of wellbeing. The tether of responsibility was temporarily cast aside.

Much too soon, the shadow of a cloud passed over and aroused her from her daydreams. Opening her eyes, the world seemed fuzzy. She had lost track of time, but sensed she had napped far longer than it appeared. The sun had arced across the sky and hung just inside the crown of the trees. Glancing at the base of the pecans she spotted movement coming up the trail from the river. Easing off the barrel she massaged the sleep from her eyes, not sure she was seeing things correctly. Clearing her vision, she realized she wasn't imaging things. Two riders were approaching. Rapidly.

Turning to the shed, she shouted, "Lee!"

He burst into the yard with his Spencer in his hands ready to use. Uncertain who the riders might be, she backed up toward Lee. They wore hats, but were too far away to identify. They could be outlaws for all she knew.

Lee instructed Cora to warn Robert and the others in the cabin that they had company. She got everybody roused and stepped onto the porch not sure what to expect. A rifle was cradled in her arms, but she was relieved when the riders rode within range to make out their identities. One was Nate. She was sure of that, but the other rider she wasn't so positive about despite the fact that he was riding the palomino favored by Travis.

As Nate entered the yard she weakened at what she saw beside him. The other rider had hard set eyes sunk into a gaunt face. Dark stubble of a beard covered his chin beneath a grim turn of his lips. Bloodstains soaked the right leg of his pants, and a dried swath of blood smeared the front of his shirt. Worst of all, she saw the unmistakable greasy black hair of several Indian scalps tied across the pommel of his saddle.

Reality took her breath away. This was Travis. She hardly recognized him. He had changed into somebody else in the short time he had been on the trail with the Rangers. But he was home and that was what mattered. The question that threatened to break her heart was left unanswered. Where was Matt? He always rode at the front. And was that Matt's blood on Travis? She hugged the porch post for support as her angst took flight. Had her premonition of a catastrophe come to pass? Matt should be leading. Where was he?

Lee saw her wilted condition and walked over to steady her while Travis and Nate dismounted to tie up their mounts. Becky and the children followed Robert out to the porch fully aware of the apprehension drowning Cora. They gathered around her unsure of what lady fate held in her hand.

Nate tied his horse to the hitching rail and marched across the yard to the anxious family waiting for the news that could mark everlasting changes in their life. Cora focused on Travis and his bloodstained clothes, dubious about the outcome of the Ranger mission, and Matt in particular. It was highly unusual to have only two Rangers out of a party of fourteen show up by themselves. Considering the dire possibilities, the color drained from her face.

The gruff voice of Nate broke the impasse. "Where's Ma?"

Lee answered, "Down at the far end of the river pasture helpin' your brothers build the new cabin."

"We're gonna need her. Got a couple of men hurt bad."

Cora swooned, incapable of asking about Matt, fearing the implications of Nate's statement.

"Where are they?" Lee asked.

"Restin' on the trail 'bout three miles back. I come in to git things ready for 'em."

Cora's heart pounded as her anxiety crested. She fixed her gaze on Travis as he walked up. "Are you okay?" she probed.

He ran his hand across his chest mindful of the bad impression it had to have on her. "Ain't my blood."

His shortness riled her. "Who's?" she demanded.

He shrugged his shoulders and said, "Tom's mostly."

Nate interrupted, "We've had a helluva time." He held back on the details, unwilling to add to Cora's distress.

The fright in her eyes grew wild. Her tone harsh, she asked, "Matt?"

"Matt's fine," Nate said. He couldn't imagine it being any different. A brave and capable leader like Matt always came home. Why was she so high-strung?

Travis elbowed his way to the water barrel and scooped up a cupful of the sweetest liquid he had ever tasted. He intended to avoid conversation. His thoughts had turned to Sarah now that he was back and pay was owed him. He wanted the money. He wanted Sarah. That was all he could think about.

His aloof manner didn't go unnoticed by Cora, but she paid him no heed as the news that Matt was okay worked like an elixir on her nerves. The relief was temporary as Nate filled in the details of the battle as gently as possible. Horrified at the bad news, she instructed Lee to fetch Granny Johnston and her special medications while she and Becky prepared hot water and fresh bandages for the men when they arrived. She also threw together a chicken soup that would be easy on the stomach and revive the strength of men depleted by injuries and forced to endure a long hard ride.

Working efficiently with Becky's help, Cora had the necessary materials ready and Granny Johnston at her side when Matt led the Rangers into the yard. She met the gaze of Matt that gave away very little. He was obviously exhausted and she had nursing that took priority over talk. Efficient in their skills, the women had the wounded men cleaned and bandaged before Matt had the horses fed, watered, and provisions stored.

Talking beside the corral with Bull and his sons about the costly mission, Matt took little regard of Cora until he entered the cabin and found her carrying out the soiled water used to cleanse wounds. He didn't say anything. He already knew what she was thinking. They exchanged a glance and nothing more. It was an old routine they had perfected. Why waste words when they both knew what the other was thinking?

His stock and wounded men cared for; Matt greeted the kids and received his usual hero's welcome home. Peppered with questions, he answered them in a way that spared their young ears the painful truth about the tragic loss of four Rangers. The sight of the injured men tempered their curiosity about the Rangers that didn't return, and he ushered them outside to tend to their daily chores.

It was his bed that he sought. He just needed five minutes of rest. Plopping to the thin mattress he fluffed up his pillow and collapsed with it tucked under his head. That's when he saw the dress hanging on a peg in the corner of the room. The beautiful sky-blue cloth glowed like a light in the dimly lit interior of the cabin. She had done her finest sewing ever with the top-quality materials he had provided. Now he considered the cash he earned as a Ranger on his last mission to be money well spent. He stood and caressed the smooth texture of the cotton while admiring the feminine lace she had used to highlight the neckline and sleeves. In awe of her creation, he imagined the lightness of her touch he had long been denied. The dress reminded him of the young woman he had once wooed and married so many years ago. Lifting the dress off the hook, he held it to his nose. He could smell her favorite lavender perfume on the material.

Behind him he heard Cora clear her throat. He casually hung the dress back on the peg and turned to see her watching him with interest.

"Do you like it?"

"It's the best one you've ever made."

"Good material is easy to work with. You chose well."

With reverence he lifted the dress from the peg and held it against her.

"The color becomes you."

"You have a good eye."

"No, I had good advice from the clerk. It'll look good on you."

"Good enough to escort me in town?"

Surprised at the suggestion he said, "Dumb question."

"You won't be embarrassed to be seen with me?"

He wouldn't honor her lack of confidence with a response. Instead he stepped around her and glanced outside. The men were involved in getting ready to spend a couple of days at his place for recuperation while the wounded were in the expert care of Granny Johnston. He snatched Cora by the hand and guided her to the door. Waiting for the right moment he led her onto the porch when nobody was looking, and they disappeared down the river trail unobserved.

They walked in silence until they arrived at his favorite spot on the bank above the gurgling current of the Colorado. Cora took a seat on the downed log and watched Matt search for a flat rock. Finding a suitable stone, he grinned at her before he let it sail in a level flight across the pool. They watched it skip a dozen times to the other side where it stopped with a thud in the gooey black mud. He stood with his back to her long enough to observe the ripples expand on the water and fade into nothing.

Turning to peer into her eyes, he said, "It's damn good to be back."

She had learned about the high costs of the campaign from Nate. Knowing Matt, she thought it better not to speak of it this soon. He would unburden himself in due time, on his own accord, but it was too fresh for him at this time. He internalized his concerns and unloaded when the need became too much for him to bear alone. She patted the log beside her.

He sat next to her and she stretched her arm around his waist. They stared at the striated limestone bluff rising above the opposite bank. This was one of his meditating spots. He often came here to be alone and think things out. She placed her hand lightly against his arm. His muscles hardened at her touch. The tension in him was as taut as a wire fence. Her husband had flirted with death. Men he cared for didn't make it back. She knew Matt. The survivor's guilt would eat at him. He took the fate of those that depended on him personal. Like any man, the strains of responsibility exerted an enormous pressure on his capacity to cope. The man in him needed the feel of a woman. A woman she had refused to be.

For his part he savored the tenderness of her hand resting on his arm. It was caring and different in some way. Not like the Cora he had been dealing with for a long time. Curious, he asked her, "How have you been?"

"Worried as usual."

"Goes without saying."

"Won't ever change."

Matt nodded his head in resignation. She was female. She was born counting her worries on her fingers. Women came by it naturally. And his chosen line of work didn't help her condition at all. At times he wanted to throw his hands up and curse his luck. He had lost so much in the process of gaining all he had ever wanted.

She noticed his tendency to brood growing stronger. She was too happy that he returned home safe to let him go there. Distracting him, she asked, "So you like the dress?"

"Like I said, it's the finest you've made."

"Good. It's time to show it off."

There was a mischievous flirt in her tone. An old flame smoldered in her eyes. She was exhibiting a playfulness he hadn't seen since Josh died. Looking deep, he saw the old Cora. The frisky gal he fell in love with and willingly gave up his wildcatting habits to wed sat beside him again. The rosy glow of the sun reflecting on her face made her appear ten years younger. He recognized the intent of her mannerisms. She had regained her sense of living.

Despite his aversion to another journey to Austin, it was a necessity he couldn't avoid. An idea popped into his head that she could tag along on the ride. He knew she craved a break the outing would provide and her companionship would make it more enjoyable.

"Trip into town?" he asked.

Not sure, she shrugged her shoulders, pressing her breasts together in the movement.

Cocking an eyebrow, he asked, "You're wanting fresh sheets for a night?"

"We deserve it don't you think?"

Matt couldn't believe what he was hearing. She was providing a delightful surprise here on the banks of the river he loved.

Her voice danced with excitement when she asked, "You know what else?"

"What's that?"

"On the way back from town we can stay a night or two at our old campsite."

Matt chuckled. She meant what she said. Pleasantly surprised, he didn't know what to say for fear of breaking the spell.

"You remember the one?" she asked.

"How could I forget?"

"You can't. We had some good times in the back of the wagon. Didn't we?" She stroked his arm and slid her hand into his hair. "It's time we revisited our past. Put things back the way they should be."

Matt drew her tight against his chest. Smelled her sweet fragrance. Felt the softness of her body. In his strong embrace, she melted against him. It was nice to have Cora back.

EPILOGUE

Black Owl reunited with the defeated warriors at Enchanted Rock. From there he convinced them to follow him to the security of the grass-covered Llano Estacado where the buffalo were still plentiful. For a few years the remote canyons and grasslands proved to be a sanctuary where they could live in relative peace. He settled into a new routine with his family that grew to include a couple of children. For a short happy period he held on to the dream that the People could carry on in their old ways. His hopes eventually faded as the white men began to show up hungry for more and more land. They could never be satisfied. They had to own it all, and far too soon the men with beards started to harass and trail them from one secret refuge to another until the Comanche on the plains were left with no choice. It was a sad day when Black Owl had to accompany Quanah Parker to the reservation in Oklahoma. Quanah was the last war chief to surrender and a great man that learned to accept the white man's ways and became what they termed a success. As for Black Owl, he lived out the remainder of his life captured in a hollow shell of what a true Comanche warrior considered his birthright. His death was a merciful event that freed his dejected spirit to soar above the toils and tribulations of a fate no man should suffer, be he red or white.

Sheriff Cole retained his job until an early retirement was forced upon him by a narrow escape with death. He disregarded one of the most important lessons of being a lawman when he underestimated the capabilities of a drunk and took a bullet to the chest that ended his working days. After recovery he was reduced to spending his nights with a bottle of whiskey, reminiscing about whores he had known. And in particular he recalled a good-looking waitress he never had the pleasure to know named Carmin. She had disappeared into West Texas and was never heard from again. A destiny he often wished he could follow. He longed to be anybody but the forgotten man he had become.

The former Captain Harris was elected to the House of Representatives where he created a lucrative political alliance with Senator Archer. They collaborated on deals that lined their pockets with cash at the expense of the constituents they were elected to represent. Their political alliance evolved into an unbeatable combination able to pound out unsavory deals backed by plenty of brawn to impose their terms when needed. The partnership was the envy of other politicians in Austin up to the day Archer fell face first into his steak dinner at the café, a victim of a massive heart attack. Representative Harris seized the opportunity and was elected to the seat vacated by Archer where he increased his reputation as a shrewd and completely unethical politician. He served until the end of his life and his funeral attracted a large turnout. But he could not claim a true friend from the entire gathering of vultures scavenging over the scraps of a barren and narcissistic man whose life had been measured solely in the value of power and money. Not a single member of his alienated family was counted in attendance.

Harris was in the company of Senator Archer when they found Colonel Ames semiconscious and incoherent several hours after the beating administered by Dawson. Lost in a fog, all Ames could remember of the day was what he had eaten for breakfast that morning. He didn't have the slightest idea who put him in the dazed condition and never regained his memory of the beating or the possible whereabouts of the two thousand dollars that was missing. He kept the missing cash a safely guarded secret after the scrutiny heaped upon him by his superiors at the main office. With confidence in his abilities destroyed, he was recalled to work under close supervision due to his impaired cognitive functions. Performing low-level tasks, he was made the butt of jokes and was known among his colleagues as having a "loose" brain.

Dawson made good on his desire to start a respectable line of work. He married the widow from Fredericksburg and found a hilly tract of land in the foothills above San Francisco where they ran a small, but successful ranch and raised three girls. His children were the apple of his eye and his neighbors never suspected he had once been a man of violence.

As for Mary, moving to Galveston proved to be the best decision she could have made to improve the life of her children. She settled into an occupation that earned her an adequate income to support her family until she had the good fortune to meet a wealthy shipping magnate. Not only did he have the funds to pamper her, he was also the ultimate gentleman dedicated to her happiness. They lay side by side every night for the rest of her life and not once did he realize the time she spent in the hours of predawn darkness staring at the ceiling lost in thoughts of what could have been with Matt.

She received regular updates on the state of affairs in Matt's life through correspondence with her daughter, Sarah. Travis was faithful to his word and whisked Sarah back to the hills following a hasty marriage in Galveston one year after the Packsaddle Mountain battle. They built their own cabin on a high promontory above Matt's place with far-reaching views of the Colorado valley winding through the hill country. Sarah often penned letters back home while sitting on the porch enjoying the spectacular sunsets that lit the peaks in a fiery orange glow. She made repeated pleas for her mother to come visit once the Indian danger had abated, but it was a visit that never occurred. Mary saw no reason to stir up risky passions that had long since grown dormant.

Matt went on to serve with distinction in the Texas Rangers as they became better organized and funded by the Texas government. He received the laurels of high-ranking officials for his unwavering bravery and proficient ability to get the job done when it came to clearing the hills of the menacing threat of Indian raids. As the problem of Indian depredations lessened, he shifted his efforts to battling the lawless element preying on the hard working and honest citizens scratching out a living from demanding circumstances. He felt the utmost empathy with the men and women out to make the hardscrabble country a safe environment to raise a family and seek prosperity. Using his famous tenacity to his advantage, he was credited with breaking up several notorious outlaw gangs that roamed the hills and rivers the Comanche formerly called home.

His partnership with Bull and his family proved to be mutually prosperous. Lee developed a lucrative trade in horses that supplied the cattle drives and met the needs of military and government contracts. Combining the lush crops grown in the bottomlands along with the endless horse-trading, the partnership built up a cash flow sufficient to take care of their growing families. Becky overcame her fear of being alone and they built a comfortable cabin on a fertile five-acre bench above the creek a mile upstream from Matt's place. She thought it was a beautiful setting to raise their five children.

Bull and Granny lived for another decade and long enough to witness the success of the partnership. Bull often commented how surprised he was that his boys buckled down and worked hard when it was needed even if that meant sacrificing an all night coon hunt or an all night drunk, two of their favorite pastimes. Nate remained a bachelor to the end, never able to tame his desire to roam where his will took him, but he never let his father's famous moonshine run low on stock. Bull and Granny died with confidence that their grandchildren lived in a secure cabin tucked into the hills they loved to call home until their last days.

Matt retired in 1890 and spent the twilight years of his life sipping coffee and watching wildlife from his porch every morning with Cora. She preceded him in death by six months and he went to be with her in 1906. In honor of his service as a Ranger, Governor Lanham ordered the flag be flown at half-mast on the grounds of the state capitol. Cora and Matt are buried beside each other in the family cemetery under a secluded grove of live oaks. Listening close you can hear the soft gurgle of a waterfall casting a perpetual spell of peace over the land that shaped their love into an everlasting bond.

AUTHOR'S NOTE

This trilogy began life as a fictionalized short story about an actual incident that occurred on the homestead of my great-great grandfather on the Colorado River upstream from Austin. I was fortunate as a young man to roam and hunt the canyons and hills that once supported the ancestors on my mother's side of the family. Land rich and dollar poor was a fairly common problem in the hills and according to the stories I've been told the acreage was ultimately lost to back taxes. Our relatives no longer owned the land I came to know and love, but they did maintain a set of contacts that allowed us to enjoy exploring the old homestead.

Time spent on the property was always a special event that I have fond memories of, and I wanted to capture the feel of the land in words. Thus began a dramatized short story about the true-life Indian raid on a smokehouse in the middle of a dark night long ago. The slumbering guard was real. The wounded Indian was real. The hillside where his companions waited on his return with the stolen food was real. I can still visit the site of the original cabin and look up the hill and visualize three mounted Comanche gazing down with hatred for my ancestors. It was a tragic time in history. The pain and suffering on both sides was real.

The characters in the *Hard Land to Rule Trilogy* are figments of my imagination built upon what I thought men from that era would be like. They had to be a no-nonsense and hardy bunch of men. Life demanded no less if you wanted to have a full belly and survive. The one exception to the cast of fictional characters is

Governor Throckmorton. He served as governor in a time of upheaval after the Civil War. His problems in office proved to be insurmountable. Hamstrung by the competing political interests of the time, he struggled to deal with the mistrust of federal military officers. He was removed from office in the summer of 1867, later in the same year that Matt confronted the Comanche below Packsaddle Mountain.

The storyline of the trilogy is based upon actual events that happened often in the Texas Hill Country as intrepid Rangers and settlers tamed the wild land. Today we can travel in our cars insulated from the harsh weather and dangerous situations encountered by early pioneers. Only through studying and reading detailed accounts about that time period can the state of war that existed between the Texans and Native Americans be appreciated. Decades of conflict bloodied the land and numerous graves have been excavated, filled with companions and loved ones, and then forgotten, lost to time as those who witnessed the events passed away. The fictional graves dug by Matt and his men exist throughout the hills for real. The bones of settlers and Indians alike have turned to dust; yet their spirit lives on. We pass by these locations on every pleasure drive we take across the Hill Country in ignorance of the ultimate sacrifice brave men paid to control their destinies.

When he was a young man my grandfather discovered a burial site in a cave tucked into a rugged and remote canyon on the old homestead. The skull he located had a hole in it that provided evidence of a violent death. Personal effects of an Indian lay beside the bones indicating he had stumbled upon the resting place of a warrior. He left them where he found them and to the best of my knowledge never returned or divulged their exact location to anyone. There is a possibility the remains are still waiting to be rediscovered in that remote and hard to find cave.

His stories of the old days were a major influence that inspired me to create this tale about the early homesteaders overcoming the challenges of the wild Texas Hill Country. There are several books I would recommend to anyone wanting to learn the truth about the tragedy of that epoch. When these books were written there was no such thing as political correctness. These authors collected the real-life tales straight from the survivors, and what the reader is left with are the raw facts to interpret without any spin applied. These books are a great introduction to the frontier of Texas where war raged for decades and the bones of the participants are still buried in hidden locations. It was an inevitable clash between cultures as amenable to each other as oil is to water.

Indian Depredations in Texas by J. W. Wilbarger is an excellent book describing the reality of the pioneer times as the Comanche and other tribes resisted the tide of change upending their culture. It is a collection of stories straight from the participants illustrating the plight of the frontiersman settling Texas during a period of intense competition for the right to call the wilderness home. The harsh reality of the conditions faced by the settlers is a real eye opener. Recently, I've referenced *Texas Indian Fighters: Early Settlers and Indian Fighters of Southwest Texas* by A. J. Sowell for authentic tales of life mainly north and west of San Antonio. These stories also come straight from the memories of the original pioneers and help provide an understanding of the difficulties that existed on the Texas frontier.

To learn more about a variety of historical subjects you can follow my website blog at www.anthonywhitt.com. Or find me on your favorite social media site listed below. Thanks again for your support!

www.twitter.com/AnthonyWhitt_

www.facebook.com/AnthonyWhitt.Author

www.goodreads.com/author/show/7334347.Anthony_Whitt

www.pinterest.com/roost49